MURDER FOR CHRISTMAS

and other yuletide malfeasance
as perpetrated by

A.A. Milne

Woody Allen

Margery Allingham

Marjorie Bowen

G.K. Chesterton

Agatha Christie

John Collier

Lillian de la Torre

Carter Dickson

Charles Dickens

Arthur Conan Doyle

Stanley Ellin

Thomas Hardy

O. Henry

Edward Hoch

H.R.F. Keating

Baynard Kendrick

Ngaio Marsh

Baroness Orczy

Ellery Queen

Damon Runyon

Dorothy Sayers

Georges Simenon

Robert Louis Stevenson

Rex Stout

D.B. Wyndham Lewis

graphically illustrated by
GAHAN WILSON
edited by
THOMAS GODFREY

First Published in Great Britain by
Michael O'Mara Books Ltd
20 Queen Anne Street, London WlN 9FB, 1987
Reprinted 1987

ISBN 0 948397 90 X

Printed and bound by Redwood Burn Limited,
Trowbridge Wiltshire

Murder
for
Christmas

Edited by Thomas Godfrey

Illustrated by Gahan Wilson

MICHAEL O'MARA BOOKS LIMITED

★

CONTENTS

To

Kathy

The Best Thing that ever
Happened to me

Introduction

Here at last is the perfect Christmas present for the person who has everything and plans to leave it to you:

Twenty-six seasonal suggestions for the "difficult" person on your shopping list.

Assembled into one collection for the first time are twenty-five of the most inspired pieces of mayhem brimming with the true spirit of the holiday season by the great masters of mystery and suspense.

Read on, if you dare, as Agatha Christie, Arthur Conan Doyle and Margery Allingham serve up literary delicacies for the season that could make you the talk of your cellblock. Delight to the ingenuity of Ellery Queen and Ngaio Marsh as they spin tales of Christmas contrivances that could make you a legend in your own family for generations to follow. Why not let Stanley Ellin and Dorothy L. Sayers guide your gift-giving ideas this year? No more ties for Dad. No spirits for the boss. This year let it be ...

But let's not be too hasty for there will be some contributions from old masters of the trade like Robert Louis Stevenson, Charles Dickens and Baroness Orczy for your consideration. And some unlikely food for thought from unexpected contributors like Thomas Hardy, O. Henry and film director Woody Allen and some delights from new masters like Georges Simenon, H.R.F. Keating and a few other surprises.

So come to a most unique Christmas party. Join guests like Sherlock Holmes, Hercules Poirot, Lord Peter Wimsey and Father Brown. Rub elbows with Inspectors Ghote, Maigret, Ellery Queen and Nero Wolf, Roderick Alleyn and Albert Campion, Lady Molly of Scotland Yard and the fascinating Captain Duncan Maclain.

There now. Relax. Draw up a chair. Settle back and glance through a few pages. Forget the rigours of shopping and last minute wrapping, that's right. Read on.

Ignore that odd sound in your chimney, that peculiar after-taste to the brandy, that strange red liquid oozing from the stockings at the mantelpiece. Disregard that heavy breathing just behind you. Read and enjoy. And God help us every one.

Thomas F. Godfrey

THE MURDER FOR CHRISTMAS
GUIDE TO GIFT GIVING

Obviously there should be a standard value for a certain type of Christmas present. One may give what one will to one's own family or particular friends; that is all right. But in a Christmas house-party there is a pleasant interchange of parcels, of which the string and the brown paper and the kindly thought are the really important ingredients, and the gift inside is nothing more than an excuse for these things. It is embarrassing for you if Jones has apologised for his brown paper with a hundred cigars and you have only excused yourself with twenty-five cigarettes; perhaps still more embarrassing if it is you who have lost so heavily on the exchange. An understanding that the contents were to be worth five shillings exactly would avoid this embarrassment.

And now ... I am reminded of the ingenuity of a friend of mine, William by name, who arrived at a large country house for Christmas without any present in his bag. He had expected neither to give nor to receive anything, but to his horror he discovered on the 24th that everybody was preparing a Christmas present for him, and that it was taken for granted that he would require a little privacy and brown paper on Christmas Eve for the purpose of addressing his own offerings to others. He had wild thoughts of telegraphing to London for something to be sent down, and spoke to other members of the house-party in order to discover what sorts of presents would be suitable.

"What are you giving our host?" he asked one of them.

"Mary and I are giving him a book," said John, referring to his wife.

William then approached the youngest son of the house, and discovered that he and his next brother Dick were sharing in this, that, and the other. When he had heard this, William retired to his room and thought profoundly.

He was the first down to breakfast on Christmas morning. All the places at the table were piled high with presents. He looked at John's place. The top parcel said, "To John and Mary from Charles." William took out his fountain-pen and added a couple of words to the inscription. It then read, "To John and Mary from Charles and William," and in William's opinion looked just as effective as before. He moved on to the next place. "To Angela from Father," said the top parcel. "And William," wrote William. At his hostess' place he hesitated for a moment. The first present there was for "Darling Mother, from her loving children." It did not seem that an "and William" was quite suitable. But his hostess was not to be deprived of William's kindly thought; twenty seconds later the handkerchiefs "from John and Mary and William" expressed all the nice things which he was feeling for her. He passed on to the next place ...

[8]

It is of course impossible to thank every donor of a joint gift; one simply thanks the first person whose eye one happens to catch. Sometimes William's eye was caught, sometimes not. But he was spared all embarrassment; and I can recommend his solution of the problem with perfect confidence to those who may be in a similar predicament next Christmas.

A.A. Milne

Back for Christmas

by John Collier

"Doctor," said Major Sinclair, "we certainly must have you with us for Christmas." It was afternoon and the Carpenters' living room was filled with friends who had come to say last-minute farewells to the Doctor and his wife.

"He shall be back," said Mrs. Carpenter. "I promise you."

"It's hardly certain," said Dr. Carpenter. "I'd like nothing better, of course."

"After all," said Mr. Hewitt, "you've contracted to lecture only for three months."

"Anything may happen," said Dr. Carpenter.

"Whatever happens," said Mrs. Carpenter, beaming at them, "he shall be back in England for Christmas. You may all believe me."

They all believed her. The Doctor himself almost believed her. For ten years she had been promising him for dinner parties, garden parties, committees, heaven knows what, and the promises had always been kept.

The farewells began. There was a fluting of compliments on dear Hermione's marvellous arrangements. She and her husband would drive to Southampton that evening. They would embark the following day. No trains, no bustle, no last-minute worries. Certainly the Doctor was marvellously looked after. He would be a great success in America. Especially with Hermione to see to everything. She would have a wonderful time, too. She would see the skyscrapers. Nothing like that in Little Godwearing. But she must be very sure to bring him back. "Yes, I will bring him back. You may rely upon it." He mustn't be persuaded. No extensions. No wonderful post at some super-American hospital. Our infirmary needs him. And he must be back by Christmas. "Yes," Mrs. Carpenter called to the last departing guest, "I shall see to it. He shall be back by Christmas."

The final arrangements for closing the house were very well managed. The maids soon had the tea things washed up; they came in, said goodbye, and were in time to catch the afternoon bus to Devizes.

Nothing remained but odds and ends, locking doors, seeing that everything was tidy. "Go upstairs," said Hermione, "and change into

[11]

your brown tweeds. Empty the pockets of that suit before you put it in your bag. I'll see to everything else. All you have to do is not to get in the way.''

The Doctor went upstairs and took off the suit he was wearing, but instead of the brown tweeds, he put on an old, dirty bath gown, which he took from the back of his wardrobe. Then, after making one or two little arrangements, he leaned over the head of the stairs and called to his wife, ''Hermione! Have you a moment to spare?''

''Of course, dear. I'm just finished.''

''Just come up here for a moment. There's something rather extraordinary up here.''

Hermione immediately came up. ''Good heavens, my dear man!'' she said when she saw her husband. ''What are you lounging about in that filthy old thing for? I told you to have it burned long ago.''

''Who in the world,'' said the Doctor, ''has dropped a gold chain down the bathtub drain?''

''Nobody has, of course,'' said Hermione. ''Nobody wears such a thing.''

''Then what is it doing there?'' said the Doctor. ''Take this flashlight. If you lean right over, you can see it shining, deep down.''

''Some Woolworth's bangle off one of the maids,'' said Hermione. ''It can be nothing else.'' However, she took the flashlight and leaned over, squinting into the drain. The Doctor, raising a short length of lead pipe, struck two or three times with great force and precision, and tilting the body by the knees, tumbled it into the tub.

He then slipped off the bathrobe and, standing completely naked, unwrapped a towel full of implements and put them into the washbasin. He spread several sheets of newspaper on the floor and turned once more to his victim.

She was dead, of course—horribly doubled up, like a somersaulter, at one end of the tub. He stood looking at her for a very long time, thinking of absolutely nothing at all. Then he saw how much blood there was and his mind began to move again.

First he pushed and pulled until she lay straight in the bath, then he removed her clothing. In a narrow bathtub this was an extremely clumsy business, but he managed it at last and then turned on the taps. The water rushed into the tub, then dwindled, then died away, and the last of it gurgled down the drain.

''Good God!'' he said. ''She turned it off at the main.''

There was only one thing to do: the Doctor hastily wiped his hands on a towel, opened the bathroom door with a clean corner of the towel, threw it back onto the bath stool, and ran downstairs, barefoot, light as a cat. The cellar door was in a corner of the entrance hall, under the stairs. He knew just where the cut-off was. He had reason to: he had been pottering about down there for some time past—trying to scrape out a bin for wine, he had told Hermione. He pushed open the cellar door, went down the steep steps, and just before the closing door plunged the cellar into pitch darkness, he put his hand on the tap and turned it on. Then he felt his way back along the grimy wall till he came to the steps. He was about to ascend them when the bell rang.

The Doctor was scarcely aware of the ringing as a sound. It was like a spike of iron pushed slowly up through his stomach. It went on until it reached his brain. Then something broke. He threw himself down in the coal dust on the floor and said, "I'm through. I'm through."

"They've got no right to come. Fools!" he said. Then he heard himself panting. "None of this," he said to himself. "None of this."

He began to revive. He got to his feet, and when the bell rang again the sound passed through him almost painlessly. "Let them go away," he said. Then he heard the front door open. He said, "I don't care." His shoulder came up, like that of a boxer, to shield his face. "I give up," he said.

He heard people calling. "Herbert!" "Hermione!" It was the Wallingfords. "Damn them! They come butting in. People anxious to get off. All naked! And blood and coal dust! I'm done! I'm through! I can't do it."

"Herbert!"

"Hermione!"

"Where the dickens can they be?"

"The car's there."

"Maybe they've popped round to Mrs. Liddell's."

"We must see them."

"Or to the shops, maybe. Something at the last minute."

"Not Hermione. I say, listen! Isn't that someone having a bath? Shall I shout? What about whanging on the door?"

"Sh-h-h! Don't. It might not be tactful."

"No harm in a shout."

"Look, dear. Let's come in on our way back. Hermione said they wouldn't be leaving before seven. They're dining on the way, in Salisbury."

"Think so? All right. Only I want a last drink with old Herbert. He'd be hurt."

"Let's hurry. We can be back by half past six."

The Doctor heard them walk out and the front door close quietly behind them. He thought, "Half past six. I can do it."

He crossed the hall, sprang the latch of the front door, went upstairs, and taking his instruments from the washbasin, finished what he had to do. He came down again, clad in his bath gown, carrying parcel after parcel of

[13]

towelling or newspaper neatly secured with safety pins. These he packed carefully into the narrow, deep hole he had made in the corner of the cellar, shovelled in the soil, spread coal dust over all, satisfied himself that everything was in order, and went upstairs again. He then thoroughly cleansed the bath, and himself, and the bath again, dressed, and took his wife's clothing and his bath gown to the incinerator.

One or two more little touches and everything was in order. It was only quarter past six. The Wallingfords were always late; he had only to get into the car and drive off. It was a pity he couldn't wait till after dusk, but he could make a detour to avoid passing through the main street, and even if he was seen driving alone, people would only think Hermione had gone on ahead for some reason and they would forget about it.

Still, he was glad when he had finally got away, entirely unobserved, on the open road, driving into the gathering dusk. He had to drive very carefully; he found himself unable to judge distances, his reactions were abnormally delayed, but that was a detail. When it was quite dark he allowed himself to stop the car on the top of the downs, in order to think.

The stars were superb. He could see the lights of one or two little towns far away on the plain below him. He was exultant. Everything that was to follow was perfectly simple. Marion was waiting in Chicago. She already believed him to be a widower. The lecture people could be put off with a word. He had nothing to do but establish himself in some thriving out-of-the-way town in America and he was safe forever. There were Hermione's clothes, of course, in the suitcases: they could be disposed of through the porthole. Thank heaven she wrote her letters on the typewriter—a little thing like handwriting might have prevented everything. "But there you are," he said. "She was up-to-date, efficient all along the line. Managed everything. Managed herself to death, damn her!"

"There's no reason to get excited," he thought. "I'll write a few letters for her, then fewer and fewer. Write myself—always expecting to get back, never quite able to. Keep the house one year, then another, then another; they'll get used to it. Might even come back alone in a year or two and clear it up properly. Nothing easier. But not for Christmas!" He started up the engine and was off.

In New York he felt free at last, really free. He was safe. He could look back with pleasure—at least after a meal, lighting his cigarette, he could look back with a sort of pleasure—to the minute he had passed in the cellar listening to the bell, the door, and the voices. He could look forward to Marion.

As he strolled through the lobby of his hotel, the clerk, smiling, held up letters for him. It was the first batch from England. Well, what did that matter? It would be fun dashing off the typewritten sheets in Hermione's downright style, signing them with her squiggle, telling everyone what a success his first lecture had been, how thrilled he was with America but how certainly she'd bring him back for Christmas. Doubts could creep in later.

He glanced over the letters. Most were for Hermione. From the Sinclairs, the Wallingfords, the vicar, and a business letter from Holt & Sons, Builders and Decorators.

He stood in the lounge, people brushing by him. He opened the letters with his thumb, reading here and there, smiling. They all seemed very confident he would be back for Christmas. They relied on Hermione. "That's where they make their big mistake," said the Doctor, who had taken to American phrases. The builders' letter he kept to the last. Some bill, probably. It was:

DEAR MADAM,

We are in receipt of your kind acceptance of estimate as below and also of key.

We beg to repeat you may have every confidence in same being ready in ample time for Christmas present as stated. We are setting men to work this week.

We are, Madam,

Yours faithfully,
PAUL HOLT & SONS

To excavating, building up, suitably lining one sunken wine bin in cellar as indicated, using best materials, making good, etc.

.........£18/0/0

"Good Heavens — this must mean we've practically finished him off."

★

Mr. Big

by Woody Allen

I WAS SITTING in my office, cleaning the debris out of my thirty-eight and wondering where my next case was coming from. I like being a private eye, and even though once in a while I've had my gums massaged with an automobile jack, the sweet smell of greenbacks makes it all worth it. Not to mention the dames, which are a minor preoccupation of mine that I rank just ahead of breathing. That's why, when the door to my office swung open and a long-haired blonde named Heather Butkiss came striding in and told me she was a nudie model and needed my help, my salivary glands shifted into third. She wore a short skirt and a tight sweater and her figure described a set of parabolas that could cause cardiac arrest in a yak.

"What can I do for you, sugar?"

"I want you to find someone for me."

"Missing person? Have you tried the police?"

"Not exactly, Mr. Lupowitz."

"Call me Kaiser, sugar. All right, so what's the scam?"

"God."

"God?"

"That's right, God. The Creator, the Underlying Principle, the First Cause of Things, the All Encompassing. I want you to find Him for me."

I've had some fruit cakes up in the office before, but when they're built like she was, you listened.

"Why?"

"That's my business, Kaiser. You just find Him."

"I'm sorry, sugar. You got the wrong boy."

"But why?"

"Unless I know all the facts," I said, rising.

"O.K., O.K.," she said, biting her lower lip. She straightened the seam of her stocking, which was strictly for my benefit, but I wasn't buying any at the moment.

"Let's have it on the line, sugar."

"Well, the truth is—I'm not really a nudie model."

"No?"

[17]

"No. My name is not Heather Butkiss, either.. It's Claire Rosensweig and I'm a student at Vassar. Philosophy major. History of Western Thought and all that. I have a paper due January. On Western religion. All the other kids in the course will hand in speculative papers. But I want to *know*. Professor Grebanier said if anyone finds out for sure, they're a cinch to pass the course. And my dad's promised me a Mercedes if I get straight A's."

I opened a deck of Luckies and a pack of gum and had one of each. Her story was beginning to interest me. Spoiled coed. High IQ and a body I wanted to know better.

"What does God look like?"

"I've never seen him."

"Well, how do you know He exists?"

"That's for you to find out."

"Oh, great. Then you don't know what he looks like? Or where to begin looking?"

"No. Not really. Although I suspect he's everywhere. In the air, in every flower, in you and I—and in this chair."

"Uh huh." So she was a pantheist. I made a mental note of it and said I'd give her case a try—for a hundred bucks a day, expenses, and a dinner date. She smiled and okayed the deal. We rode down in the elevator together. Outside it was getting dark. Maybe God did exist and maybe He didn't, but somewhere in that city there were sure a lot of guys who were going to try and keep me from finding out.

My first lead was Rabbi Itzhak Wiseman, a local cleric who owed me a favor for finding out who was rubbing pork on his hat. I knew something was wrong when I spoke to him because he was scared. Real scared.

"Of course there's a you-know-what, but I'm not even allowed to say His name or He'll strike me dead, which I could never understand why someone is so touchy about having his name said."

"You ever see Him?"

"Me? Are you kidding? I'm lucky I get to see my grandchildren."

"Then how do you know He exists?"

"How do I know? What kind of question is that? Could I get a suit like this for fourteen dollars if there was no one up there? Here, feel a gabardine—how can you doubt?"

"You got nothing more to go on?"

"Hey—what's the Old Testament? Chopped liver? How do you think Moses got the Israelites out of Egypt? With a smile and a tap dance? Believe me, you don't part the Red Sea with some gismo from Korvette's. It takes power."

"So he's tough, eh?"

[18]

"Yes. Very tough. You'd think with all that success he'd be a lot sweeter."

"How come you know so much?"

"Because we're the chosen people. He takes best care of us of all His children, which I'd also like to someday discuss with Him."

"What do you pay Him for being chosen?"

"Don't ask."

So that's how it was. The Jews were into God for a lot. It was the old protection racket. Take care of them in return for a price. And from the way Rabbi Wiseman was talking, He soaked them plenty. I got into a cab and made it over to Danny's Billiards on Tenth Avenue. The manager was a slimy little guy I didn't like.

"Chicago Phil here?"

"Who wants to know?"

I grabbed him by the lapels and took some skin at the same time.

"What, punk?"

"In the back," he said, with a change of attitude.

Chicago Phil. Forger, bank robber, strong-arm man, and avowed atheist.

"The guy never existed, Kaiser. This is the straight dope. It's a big hype. There's no Mr. Big. It's a syndicate. Mostly Sicilian. It's international. But there is no actual head. Except maybe the Pope."

"I want to meet the Pope."

"It can be arranged," he said, winking.

"Does the name Claire Rosensweig mean anything to you?"

"No."

"Heather Butkiss?"

"Oh, wait a minute. Sure. She's that peroxide job with the bazooms from Radcliffe."

"Radcliffe? She told me Vassar."

"Well, she's lying. She's a teacher at Radcliffe. She was mixed up with a philosopher for a while."

"Pantheist?"

"No. Empiricist, as I remember. Bad guy. Completely rejected Hegel or any dialectical methodology."

"One of those."

"Yeah. He used to be a drummer with a jazz trio. Then he got hooked on Logical Positivism. When that didn't work, he tried Pragmatism. Last I heard he stole a lot of money to take a course in Schopenhauer at Columbia. The mob would like to find him—or get their hands on his textbooks so they can resell them."

"Thanks, Phil."

"Take it from me, Kaiser. There's no one out there. It's a void. I couldn't pass all those bad checks or screw society the way I do if for one second I was able to recognize any authentic sense of Being. The universe is strictly phenomenological. Nothing's eternal. It's all meaningless."

"Who won the fifth at Aqueduct?"

"Santa Baby."

I had a beer at O'Rourke's and tried to add it all up, but it made no sense at all. Socrates was a suicide—or so they said. Christ was murdered. Nietzsche went nuts. If there was someone out there, He sure as hell didn't want anybody to know it. And why was Claire Rosensweig lying about Vassar? Could Descartes have been right? Was the universe dualistic? Or did Kant hit it on the head when he postulated the existence of God on moral grounds?

That night I had dinner with Claire. Ten minutes after the check came, we were in the sack and, brother, you can have your Western thought. She went through the kind of gymnastics that would have won first prize in the Tia Juana Olympics. After, she lay on the pillow next to me, her long blond hair sprawling. Our naked bodies still intertwined. I was smoking and staring at the ceiling.

"Claire, what if Kierkegaard's right?"

"You mean?"

"If you can never really *know*. Only have faith."

"That's absurd."

"Don't be so rational."

"Nobody's being rational, Kaiser." She lit a cigarette. "Just don't get ontological. Not now. I couldn't bear it if you were ontological with me."

She was upset. I leaned over and kissed her, and the phone rang. She got it.

"It's for you."

The voice on the other end was Sergeant Reed of Homicide.

"You still looking for God?"

"Yeah."

"An all-powerful Being? Great Oneness, Creator of the Universe? First Cause of All Things?"

"That's right."

"Somebody with that description just showed up at the morgue. You better get down here right away."

It was Him all right, and from the looks of Him it was a professional job.

"He was dead when they brought Him in."

"Where'd you find Him?"

"A warehouse on Delancey Street."

"Any clues?"

"It's the work of an existentialist. We're sure of that."

[20]

"How can you tell?"

"Haphazard way how it was done. Doesn't seem to be any system followed. Impulse."

"A crime of passion?"

"You got it. Which means you're a suspect, Kaiser."

"Why me?"

"Everybody down at headquarters knows how you feel about Jaspers."

"That doesn't make me a killer."

"Not yet, but you're a suspect."

Outside on the street I sucked air into my lungs and tried to clear my head. I took a cab over to Newark and got out and walked a block to Giordino's Italian Restaurant. There, at a back table, was His Holiness. It was the Pope, all right. Sitting with two guys I had seen in half a dozen police line-ups.

"Sit down," he said, looking up from his fettucine. He held out a ring. I gave him my toothiest smile, but didn't kiss it. It bothered him and I was glad. Point for me.

"Would you like some fettucine?"

"No thanks, Holiness. But you go ahead."

"Nothing? Not even a salad?"

"I just ate."

"Suit yourself, but they make a great Roquefort dressing here. Not like at the Vatican, where you can't get a decent meal."

"I'll come right to the point, Pontiff. I'm looking for God."

"You came to the right person."

"Then He does exist?" They all found this very amusing and laughed. The hood next to me said, "Oh, that's funny. Bright boy wants to know if He exists."

I shifted my chair to get comfortable and brought the leg down on his little toe. "Sorry." But he was steaming.

"Sure He exists, Lupowitz, but I'm the only one that communicates with him. He speaks only through me."

"Why you, pal?"

"Because I got the red suit."

"This get-up?"

"Don't knock it. Every morning I rise, put on this red suit, and suddenly I'm a big cheese. It's all in the suit. I mean, face it, if I went around in slacks and a sports jacket, I couldn't get arrested religion-wise."

"Then it's a hype. There's no God."

"I don't know. But what's the difference? The money's good."

"You ever worry the laundry won't get your red suit back on time and you'll be like the rest of us?"

"I use the special one-day service. I figure it's worth the extra few cents to be safe."

"Name Claire Rosensweig mean anything to you?"

"Sure. She's in the science department at Bryn Mawr."

"Science, you say? Thanks."

"For what?"

"The answer, Pontiff." I grabbed a cab and shot over the George Washington Bridge. On the way I stopped at my office and did some fast checking. Driving to Claire's apartment, I put the pieces together, and for the first time they fit. When I got there she was in a diaphanous peignoir and something seemed to be troubling her.

"God is dead. The police were here. They're looking for you. They think an existentialist did it."

"No, sugar. It was you."

"What? Don't make jokes, Kaiser."

"It was you that did it."

"What are you saying?"

"You, baby. Not Heather Butkiss or Claire Rosensweig, but Doctor Ellen Shepherd."

"How did you know my name?"

"Professor of physics at Bryn Mawr. The youngest one ever to head a department there. At the midwinter Hop you get stuck on a jazz musician who's heavily into philosophy. He's married, but that doesn't stop you. A couple of nights in the hay and it feels like love. But it doesn't work out because something comes between you. God. Y'see, sugar, he believed, or wanted to, but you, with your pretty little scientific mind, had to have absolute certainty."

"No, Kaiser, I swear."

"So you pretend to study philosophy because that gives you a chance to eliminate certain obstacles. You get rid of Socrates easy enough, but Descartes takes over, so you use Spinoza to get rid of Descartes, but when Kant doesn't come through you have to get rid of him too."

"You don't know what you're saying."

"You made mincemeat out of Leibnitz, but that wasn't good enough for you because you knew if anybody believed Pascal you were dead, so he had to be gotten rid of too, but that's where you make your mistake because you trusted Martin Buber. Except, sugar, he was soft. He believed in God, so you had to get rid of God yourself."

"Kaiser, you're mad!"

"No, baby. You posed as a pantheist and that gave you access to Him—*if* He existed, which he did. He went with you to Shelby's party and when Jason wasn't looking, you killed Him."

[22]

"Who the hell are Shelby and Jason?"

"What's the difference? Life's absurd now anyway."

"Kaiser," she said, suddenly trembling. "You wouldn't turn me in?"

"Oh yes, baby. When the Supreme Being gets knocked off, *somebody's* got to take the rap."

"Oh, Kaiser, we could go away together. Just the two of us. We could forget about philosophy. Settle down and maybe get into semantics."

"Sorry, sugar. It's no dice."

She was all tears now as she started lowering the shoulder straps of her peignoir and I was standing there suddenly with a naked Venus whose whole body seemed to be saying, Take me—I'm yours. A Venus whose right hand tousled my hair while her left hand had picked up a forty-five and was holding it behind my back. I let go with a slug from my thirty-eight before she could pull the trigger, and she dropped her gun and doubled over in disbelief.

"How could you, Kaiser?"

She was fading fast, but I managed to get it in, in time.

"The manifestation of the universe as a complex idea unto itself as opposed to being in or outside the true Being of itself is inherently a conceptual nothingness or Nothingness in relation to any abstract form of existing or to exist or having existed in perpetuity and not subject to laws of physicality or motion or ideas relating to nonmatter or the lack of objective Being or subjective otherness."

It was a subtle concept but I think she understood before she died.

What! Not a Christmas story, you say? I refer you to the winner of the fifth race at Aqueduct.

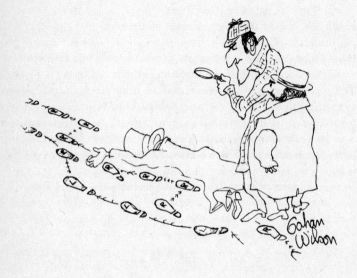

"What makes you think the murderer is a dance instructor?"

★

The Adventure of the Blue Carbuncle

by Sir Arthur Conan Doyle

I HAD CALLED UPON my friend Sherlock Holmes upon the second morning after Christmas, with the intention of wishing him the compliments of the season. He was lounging upon the sofa in a purple dressing-gown, a pipe-rack within his reach upon the right, and a pile of crumpled morning papers, evidently newly studied, near at hand. Beside the couch was a wooden chair, and on the angle of the back hung a very seedy and disreputable hard-felt hat, much the worse for wear, and cracked in several places. A lens and a forceps lying upon the seat of the chair suggested that the hat had been suspended in this manner for the purpose of examination.

"You are engaged," said I; "perhaps I interrupt you."

"Not at all. I am glad to have a friend with whom I can discuss my results. The matter is a perfectly trivial one"—he jerked his thumb in the direction of the old hat—"but there are points in connection with it which are not entirely devoid of interest and even of instruction."

I seated myself in his armchair and warmed my hands before his crackling fire, for a sharp frost had set in, and the windows were thick with the ice crystals. "I suppose," I remarked, "that, homely as it looks, this thing has some deadly story linked on to it—that it is the clue which will guide you in the solution of some mystery and the punishment of some crime."

"No, no. No crime," said Sherlock Holmes, laughing. "Only one of those whimsical little incidents which will happen when you have four million human beings all jostling each other within the space of a few square miles. Amid the action and reaction of so dense a swarm of humanity, every possible combination of events may be expected to take place, and many a little problem will be presented which may be striking and bizarre without being criminal. We have already had experience of such."

"So much so," I remarked, "that of the last six cases which I have added to my notes, three have been entirely free of any legal crime."

"Precisely. You allude to my attempt to recover the Irene Adler papers, to the singular case of Miss Mary Sutherland, and to the adventure of the man with the twisted lip. Well, I have no doubt that this small matter will fall into the same innocent category. You know Peterson, the commissionaire?''

''Yes.''

''It is to him that this trophy belongs.''

''It is his hat.''

''No, no; he found it. Its owner is unknown. I beg that you will look upon it not as a battered billycock but as an intellectual problem. And, first, as to how it came here. It arrived upon Christmas morning, in company with a good fat goose, which is, I have no doubt, roasting at this moment in front of Peterson's fire. The facts are these: about four o'clock on Christmas morning, Peterson, who, as you know, is a very honest fellow, was returning from some small jollification and was making his way homeward down Tottenham Court Road. In front of him he saw, in the gaslight, a tallish man, walking with a slight stagger, and carrying a white goose slung over his shoulder. As he reached the corner of Goodge Street, a row broke out between this stranger and a little knot of roughs. One of the latter knocked off the man's hat, on which he raised his stick to defend himself and, swinging it over his head, smashed the shop window behind him. Peterson had rushed forward to protect the stranger from his assailants; but the man, shocked at having broken the window, and seeing an official-looking person in uniform rushing towards him, dropped his goose, took to his heels, and vanished amid the labyrinth of small streets which lie at the back of Tottenham Court Road. The roughs had also fled at the appearance of Peterson, so that he was left in possession of the field of battle, and also of the spoils of victory in the shape of this battered hat and a most unimpeachable Christmas goose.''

''Which surely he restored to their owner?''

''My dear fellow, there lies the problem. It is true that 'For Mrs. Henry Baker' was printed upon a small card which was tied to the bird's left leg, and it is also true that the initials 'H.B.' are legible upon the lining of this hat; but as there are some thousands of Bakers, and some hundreds of Henry Bakers in this city of ours, it is not easy to restore lost property to any of them.''

''What, then, did Peterson do?''

''He brought round both hat and goose to me on Christmas morning, knowing that even the smallest problems are of interest to me. The goose we retained until this morning, when there were signs that, in spite of the slight frost, it would be well that it should be eaten without unnecessary delay. Its finder has carried it off, therefore, to fulfil the ultimate destiny of a goose, while I continue to retain the hat of the unknown gentleman who lost his Christmas dinner.''

[26]

"Did he not advertise?"

"No."

"Then, what clue could you have as to his identity?"

"Only as much as we can deduce."

"From his hat?"

"Precisely."

"But you are joking. What can you gather from this old battered felt?"

"Here is my lens. You know my methods. What can you gather yourself as to the individuality of the man who has worn this article?"

I took the tattered object in my hands and turned it over rather ruefully. It was a very ordinary black hat of the usual round shape, hard and much the worse for wear. The lining had been of red silk, but was a good deal discoloured. There was no maker's name; but, as Holmes had remarked, the initials "H.B." were scrawled upon one side. It was pierced in the brim for a hat-securer, but the elastic was missing. For the rest, it was cracked, exceedingly dusty, and spotted in several places, although there seemed to have been some attempt to hide the discolored patches by smearing them with ink.

"I can see nothing," said I, handing it back to my friend.

"On the contrary, Watson, you can see everything. You fail, however, to reason from what you see. You are too timid in drawing your inferences."

"Then, pray tell me what it is that you can infer from this hat?"

He picked it up and gazed at it in the peculiar introspective fashion which was characteristic of him. "It is perhaps less suggestive than it might have been," he remarked, "and yet there are a few inferences which are very distinct, and a few others which represent at least a strong balance of probability. That the man was highly intellectual is of course obvious upon the face of it, and also that he was fairly well-to-do within the last three years, although he has now fallen upon evil days. He had foresight, but has less now than formerly, pointing to a moral retrogression, which, when taken with the decline of his fortunes, seems to indicate some evil influence, probably drink, at work upon him. This may account also for the obvious fact that his wife has ceased to love him."

"My dear Holmes!"

"He has, however, retained some degree of self-respect," he continued, disregarding my remonstrance. "He is a man who leads a sendentary life, goes out little, is out of training entirely, is middle-aged, has grizzled hair which he has had cut within the last few days, and which he anoints with lime-cream. These are the more patent facts which are to be deduced from his hat. Also, by the way, that it is extremely improbable that he has gas laid on in his house."

"You are certainly joking, Holmes."

"Not in the least. Is it possible that even now, when I give you these results, you are unable to see how they are attained?"

"I have no doubt that I am very stupid, but I must confess that I am unable to follow you. For example, how did you deduce that this man was intellectual?"

For answer Holmes clapped the hat upon his head. It came right over the forehead and settled upon the bridge of his nose. "It is a question of cubic capacity," said he; "a man with so large a brain must have something in it."

"The decline of his fortunes, then?"

"This hat is three years old. These flat brims curled at the edge came in then. It is a hat of the very best quality. Look at the band of ribbed silk and the excellent lining. If this man could afford to buy so expensive a hat three years ago, and has had no hat since, then he has assuredly gone down in the world."

"Well, that is clear enough, certainly. But how about the foresight and the moral retrogression?"

Sherlock Holmes laughed. "Here is the foresight," said he, putting his finger upon the little disc and loop of the hat-securer. "They are never sold upon hats. If this man ordered one, it is a sign of a certain amount of foresight, since he went out of his way to take this precaution against the wind. But since we see that he has broken the elastic and has not troubled to replace it, it is obvious that he has less foresight now than formerly, which is a distinct proof of a weakening nature. On the other hand, he has endeavored to conceal some of these stains upon the felt by daubing them with ink, which is a sign that he has not entirely lost his self-respect."

"Your reasoning is certainly plausible."

"The further points, that he is middle-aged, that his hair is grizzled, that it has been recently cut, and that he uses lime-cream, are all to be gathered from a close examination of the lower part of the lining. The lens discloses a large number of hair-ends, clean cut by the scissors of the barber. They all appear to be adhesive, and there is a distinct odour of lime-cream. This dust, you will observe, is not the gritty, gray dust of the street but the fluffy brown dust of the house, showing that it has been hung up indoors most of the time; while the marks of moisture upon the inside are proof positive that the wearer perspired very freely, and could therefore, hardly be in the best of training."

"But his wife—you said that she had ceased to love him."

"This hat has not been brushed for weeks. When I see you, my dear Watson, with a week's accumulation of dust upon your hat, and when your wife allows you to go out in such a state, I shall fear that you also have been unfortunate enough to lose your wife's affection."

"But he might be a bachelor."

"Nay, he was bringing home the goose as a peace-offering to his wife. Remember the card upon the bird's leg."

"You have an answer to everything. But how on earth do you deduce that the gas is not laid on in his house?"

"One tallow stain, or even two, might come by chance; but when I see no less than five, I think that there can be little doubt that the individual must be brought into frequent contact with burning tallow—walks upstairs at night probably with his hat in one hand and a guttering candle in the other. Anyhow, he never got tallow-stains from a gas-jet. Are you satisfied?"

"Well, it is very ingenious," said I, laughing; "but since, as you said just now, there has been no crime committed, and no harm done save the loss of a goose, all this seems to be rather a waste of energy."

Sherlock Holmes had opened his mouth to reply, when the door flew open, and Peterson, the commissionaire, rushed into the apartment with flushed cheeks and the face of a man who is dazed with astonishment.

"The goose, Mr. Holmes! The goose, sir!" he gasped.

"Eh? What of it, then? Has it returned to life and flapped off through the kitchen window?" Holmes twisted himself round upon the sofa to get a fairer view of the man's excited face.

"See here, sir! See what my wife found in its crop!" He held out his hand and displayed upon the center of the palm a brilliantly scintillating blue stone, rather smaller than a bean in size, but of such purity and radiance that it twinkled like an electric point in the dark hollow of his hand.

Sherlock Holmes sat up with a whistle. "By Jove, Peterson!" said he, "this is treasure trove indeed. I suppose you know what you have got?"

"A diamond, sir? A precious stone. It cuts into glass as though it were putty."

"It's more than a precious stone. It is *the* precious stone."

"Not the Countess of Morcar's blue carbuncle!" I ejaculated.

"Precisely so. I ought to know its size and shape, seeing that I have read the advertisement about it in *The Times* every day lately. It is absolutely unique, and its value can only be conjectured, but the reward offered of £1000 is certainly not within a twentieth part of the market price."

"A thousand pounds! Great Lord of mercy!" The commissionaire plumped down into a chair and stared from one to the other of us.

"That is the reward, and I have reason to know that there are sentimental considerations in the background which would induce the Countess to part with half her fortune if she could but recover the gem."

"It was lost, if I remember aright, at the Hotel Cosmopolitan," I remarked.

"Precisely so, on December 22nd, just five days ago. John Horner, a plumber, was accused of having abstracted it from the lady's jewel-case. The evidence against him was so strong that the case has been referred to the Assizes. I have some account of the matter here, I believe." He rummaged amid his newspapers, glancing over the dates, until at last he smoothed one out, doubled it over, and read the following paragraph:

"Hotel Cosmopolitan Jewel Robbery. John Horner, 26, plumber, was brought up upon the charge of having upon the 22d inst., abstracted from the jewel-case of the Countess of Morcar the valuable gem known as the blue carbuncle. James Ryder, upper-attendant at the hotel, gave his evidence to the effect that he had shown Horner up to the dressing-room of the Countess of Morcar upon the day of the robbery in order that he might solder the second bar of the grate, which was loose. He had remained with Horner some little time, but had finally been called away. On returning, he found that Horner had disappeared, that the bureau had been forced open, and that the small morocco casket in which, as it afterwards transpired, the Countess was accustomed to keep her jewel, was lying empty upon the dressing-table. Ryder instantly gave the alarm, and Horner was arrested the same evening; but the stone could not be found either upon his person or in his rooms. Catherine Cusack, maid to the Countess, deposed to having heard Ryder's cry of dismay on discovering the robbery, and to having rushed into the room, where she found matters as described by the last witness. Inspector Bradstreet, B division, gave evidence as to the arrest of Horner, who struggled frantically, and protested his innocence in the strongest terms. Evidence of a previous conviction for robbery having been given against the prisoner, the magistrate refused to deal summarily with the offence, but referred it to the Assizes. Horner, who had shown signs of intense emotion during the proceedings, fainted away at the conclusion and was carried out of court.

"Hum! So much for the police-court," said Holmes thoughtfully, tossing aside the paper. "The question for us now to solve is the sequence of events leading from a rifled jewel-case at one end to the crop of a goose in Tottenham Court Road at the other. You see, Watson, our little deductions have suddenly assumed a much more important and less innocent aspect. Here is the stone; the stone came from the goose, and the goose came from Mr. Henry Baker, the gentleman with the bad hat and all the other characteristics with which I have bored you. So now we must set ourselves very seriously to finding this gentleman and ascertaining what part he has played in this little mystery. To do this, we must try the simplest means first, and these lie undoubtedly in an advertisement in all the evening papers. If this fail, I shall have recourse to other methods."

"What will you say?"

"Give me a pencil and that slip of paper. Now, then:

"Found at the corner of Goodge Street, a goose and a black felt hat. Mr. Henry Baker can have the same by applying at 6:30 this evening at 221B Baker Street.

That is clear and concise."

"Very. But will he see it?"

"Well, he is sure to keep an eye on the papers, since, to a poor man, the loss was a heavy one. He was clearly so scared by his mischance in breaking the window and by the approach of Peterson that he thought of nothing but flight, but since then he must have bitterly regretted the impulse which caused him to drop his bird. Then, again, the introduction of his name will cause him to see it, for everyone who knows him will direct his attention to it. Here you are, Peterson, run down to the advertising agency and have this put in the evening papers."

"In which, sir?"

"Oh, in the *Globe, Star, Pall Mall, St. James's, Evening News Standard, Echo,* and any others that occur to you."

"Very well, sir. And this stone?"

"Ah, yes, I shall keep the stone. Thank you. And, I say, Peterson, just buy a goose on your way back and leave it here with me, for we must have one to give to this gentleman in place of the one which your family is now devouring."

When the commissionaire had gone, Holmes took up the stone and held it against the light. "It's a bonny thing," said he. "Just see how it glints and sparkles. Of course it is a nucleus and focus of crime. Every good stone is. They are the devil's pet baits. In the larger and older jewels every facet may stand for a bloody deed. This stone is not yet twenty years old. It was found in the banks of the Amoy River in southern China and is remarkable in having every characteristic of the carbuncle, save that it is blue in shade instead of ruby red. In spite of its youth, it has already a sinister history. There have been two murders, a vitriol-throwing, a suicide, and several robberies brought about for the sake of this forty-grain weight of crystallized charcoal. Who would think that so pretty a toy would be a purveyor to the gallows and the prison? I'll lock it up in my strong box now and drop a line to the Countess to say that we have it."

"Do you think that this man Horner is innocent?"

"I cannot tell."

"Well, then, do you imagine that this other one, Henry Baker, had anything to do with the matter?"

"It is, I think, much more likely that Henry Baker is an absolutely innocent man, who had no idea that the bird which he was carrying was of considerably more value than if it were made of solid gold. That, however, I shall determine by a very simple test if we have an answer to our advertisement."

"And you can do nothing until then?"

"Nothing."

"In that case I shall continue my professional round. But I shall come back in the evening at the hour you have mentioned, for I should like to see the solution of so tangled a business."

"Very glad to see you. I dine at seven. There is a woodcock, I believe. By the way, in view of recent occurrences, perhaps I ought to ask Mrs. Hudson to examine its crop."

I had been delayed at a case, and it was a little after half-past six when I found myself in Baker Street once more. As I approached the house I saw a tall man in a Scotch bonnet with a coat which was buttoned up to his chin waiting outside in the bright semicircle which was thrown from the fanlight. Just as I arrived the door was opened, and we were shown up together to Holmes's room.

"Mr. Henry Baker, I believe," said he, rising from his armchair and greeting his visitor with the easy air of geniality which he could so readily assume. "Pray take this chair by the fire, Mr. Baker. It is a cold night, and I observe that your circulation is more adapted for summer than for winter. Ah, Watson, you have just come at the right time. Is that your hat, Mr. Baker?"

"Yes, sir, that is undoubtedly my hat."

He was a large man with rounded shoulders, a massive head, and a broad, intelligent face, sloping down to a pointed beard of grizzled brown. A touch of red in nose and cheeks, with a slight tremor of his extended hand, recalled Holmes's surmise as to his habits. His rusty black frock-coat was buttoned right up in front, with the collar turned up, and his lank wrists protruded from his sleeves without a sign of cuff or shirt. He spoke in a slow staccato fashion, choosing his words with care, and gave the impression generally of a man of learning and letters who had had ill-usage at the hands of fortune.

"We have retained these things for some days," said Holmes, "because we expected to see an advertisement from you giving your address. I am at a loss to know now why you did not advertise."

Our visitor gave a rather shamefaced laugh. "Shillings have not been so plentiful with me as they once were," he remarked. "I had no doubt that the gang of roughs who assaulted me had carried off both my hat and the bird. I did not care to spend more money in a hopeless attempt at recovering them."

"Very naturally. By the way, about the bird, we were compelled to eat it."

"To eat it!" Our visitor half rose from his chair in his excitement.

"Yes, it would have been of no use to anyone had we not done so. But I presume that this other goose upon the sideboard, which is about the same weight and perfectly fresh, will answer your purpose equally well?"

"Oh, certainly, certainly," answered Mr. Baker with a sigh of relief.

"Of course, we still have the feathers, legs, crop, and so on of your own bird, so if you wish—"

The man burst into a hearty laugh. "They might be useful to me as relics of my adventure," said he, "but beyond that I can hardly see what use the *disjecta membra* of my late acquaintance are going to be to me. No, sir, I think that, with your permission, I will confine my attentions to the excellent bird which I perceive upon the sideboard."

Sherlock Holmes glanced sharply across at me with a slight shrug of his shoulders.

"There is your hat, then, and there your bird," said he. "By the way, would it bore you to tell me where you got the other one from? I am somewhat of a fowl fancier, and I have seldom seen a better grown goose."

"Certainly, sir," said Baker, who had risen and tucked his newly gained property under his arm. "There are a few of us who frequent the Alpha Inn, near the Museum—we are to be found in the Museum itself during the day, you understand. This year our good host, Windigate by name, instituted a goose club, by which, on consideration of some few pence every week, we were each to receive a bird at Christmas. My pence were duly paid, and the rest is familiar to you. I am much indebted to you, sir, for a Scotch bonnet is fitted neither to my years nor my gravity." With a comical pomposity of manner he bowed solemnly to both of us and strode off upon his way.

"So much for Mr. Henry Baker," said Holmes when he had closed the door behind him. "It is quite certain that he knows nothing whatever about the matter. Are you hungry, Watson?"

"Not particularly."

"Then I suggest that we turn our dinner into a supper and follow up this clue while it is still hot."

"By all means."

It was a bitter night, so we drew on our ulsters and wrapped cravats about our throats. Outside, the stars were shining coldly in a cloudless sky, and the breath of the passers-by blew out into smoke like so many pistol shots. Our footfalls rang out crisply and loudly as we swung through the doctors' quarter, Wimpole Street, Harley Street, and so through Wigmore Street into Oxford Street. In a quarter of an hour we were in Bloomsbury at the Alpha Inn, which is a small public-house at the corner of one of the streets which runs down into Holborn. Holmes pushed open the door of the private bar and ordered two glasses of beer from the ruddy-faced, white-aproned landlord.

"Your beer should be excellent if it is as good as your geese," said he.

"My geese!" The man seemed surprised.

"Yes. I was speaking only half an hour ago to Mr. Henry Baker, who was a member of your goose club."

"Ah! yes, I see. But you see, sir, them's not *our* geese."

"Indeed! Whose, then?"

"Well, I got the two dozen from a salesman in Covent Garden."

"Indeed? I know some of them. Which was it?"

"Breckinridge is his name.."

"Ah! I don't know him. Well, here's your good health, landlord, and prosperity to your house. Good-night.

"Now for Mr. Breckinridge," he continued, buttoning up his coat as we came out into the frosty air. "Remember, Watson, that though we have so homely a thing as a goose at one end of this chain, we have at the other a man who will certainly get seven years' penal servitude unless we can establish his innocence. It is possible that our inquiry may but confirm his guilt; but, in any case, we have a line of investigation which has been missed by the police, and which a singular chance has placed in our hands. Let us follow it out to the bitter end. Faces to the south, then, and quick march!"

We passed across Holborn, down Endell Street, and so through a zigzag of slums to Covent Garden Market. One of the largest stalls bore the name of Breckinridge upon it, and the proprietor, a horsy-looking man, with a sharp face and trim side-whiskers, was helping a boy to put up the shutters.

"Good-evening. It's a cold night," said Holmes.

The salesman nodded and shot a questioning glance at my companion.

"Sold out of geese, I see," continued Holmes, pointing at the bare slabs of marble.

"Let you have five hundred to-morrow morning."

"That's no good."

"Well, there are some on the stall with the gas-flare."

"Ah, but I was recommended to you."

"Who by?"

"The landlord of the Alpha."

"Oh, yes; I sent him a couple of dozen."

"Fine birds they were, too. Now where did you get them from?"

To my surprise the question provoked a burst of anger from the salesman.

"Now, then, mister," said he, with his head cocked and his arms akimbo, "what are you driving at? Let's have it straight, now."

"It is straight enough. I should like to know who sold you the geese which you supplied to the Alpha."

"Well, then, I shan't tell you. So now!"

"Oh, it is a matter of no importance; but I don't know why you should be so warm over such a trifle."

"Warm! You'd be as warm, maybe, if you were as pestered as I am. When I pay good money for a good article there should be an end of the business; but it's 'Where are the geese?' and 'Who did you sell the geese to?' and 'What will you take for the geese?' One would think they were the only geese in the world, to hear the fuss that is made over them."

"Well, I have no connection with any other people who have been making inquiries," said Holmes carelessly. "If you won't tell us the bet is off, that is all. But I'm always ready to back my opinion on a matter of fowls, and I have a fiver on it that the bird I ate is country bred."

"Well, then, you've lost your fiver, for it's town bred," snapped the salesman.

"It's nothing of the kind."

"I say it is."

"I don't believe it."

"D'you think you know more about fowls than I, who have handled them ever since I was a nipper? I tell you, all those birds that went to the Alpha were town bred."

"You'll never persuade me to believe that."

"Will you bet, then?"

"It's merely taking your money, for I know that I am right. But I'll have a sovereign on with you, just to teach you not to be obstinate."

The salesman chuckled grimly. "Bring me the books, Bill," said he.

The small boy brought round a small thin volume and a great greasy-backed one, laying them out together beneath the hanging lamp.

"Now then, Mr. Cocksure," said the salesman, "I thought that I was out of geese, but before I finish you'll find that there is still one left in my shop. You see this little book?"

"Well?"

"That's the list of the folk from whom I buy. D'you see? Well, then, here on this page are the country folk, and the numbers after their names are where their accounts are in the big ledger. Now, then! You see this other page in red ink? Well, that is a list of my town suppliers. Now, look at that third name. Just read it out to me."

"Mrs. Oakshott, 117, Brixton Road—249," read Holmes.

"Quite so. Now turn that up in the ledger."

Holmes turned to the page indicated. "Here you are, 'Mrs. Oakshott, 117 Brixton Road, egg and poultry supplier.' "

"Now, then, what's the last entry?"

" 'December 22d. Twenty-four geese at 7s. 6d.' "

"Quite so. There you are. And underneath?"

" 'Sold to Mr. Windigate of the Alpha, at 12s.' "

"What have you to say now?"

Sherlock Holmes looked deeply chagrined. He drew a sovereign from his pocket and threw it down upon the slab, turning away with the air of a man whose disgust is too deep for words. A few yards off he stopped under a lamp-post and laughed in the hearty, noiseless fashion which was peculiar to him.

"When you see a man with whiskers of that cut and the 'Pink 'un' protruding out of his pocket, you can always draw him by a bet," said he. "I daresay that if I had put £100 down in front of him, that man would not have given me such complete information as was drawn from him by the idea that he was doing me on a wager. Well, Watson, we are, I fancy, nearing the end of our quest, and the only point which remains to be determined is whether we should go on to this Mrs. Oakshott to-night, or whether we should reserve it for to-morrow. It is clear from what that surly fellow said that there are others besides ourselves who are anxious about the matter, and I should—"

His remarks were suddenly cut short by a loud hubbub which broke out from the stall which we had just left. Turning round we saw a little rat-faced fellow standing in the centre of the circle of yellow light which was thrown by the swinging lamp, while Breckinridge, the salesman, framed in the door of his stall, was shaking his fists fiercely at the cringing figure.

"I've had enough of you and your geese," he shouted. "I wish you were all at the devil together. If you come pestering me any more with your silly talk I'll set the dog at you. You bring Mrs. Oakshott here and I'll answer her, but what have you to do with it? Did I buy the geese off you?"

"No; but one of them was mine all the same," whined the little man.

"Well, then, ask Mrs. Oakshott for it."

"She told me to ask you."

"Well, you can ask the King of Proosia, for all I care. I've had enough of it. Get out of this!" He rushed fiercely forward, and the inquirer flitted away into the darkness.

"Ha! this may save us a visit to Brixton Road," whispered Holmes. "Come with me, and we will see what is to be made of this fellow." Striding through the scattered knots of people who lounged round the flaring stalls, my companion speedily overtook the little man and touched him upon the shoulder. He sprang round, and I could see in the gas-light that every vestige of colour had been driven from his face.

"Who are you, then? What do you want?" he asked in a quavering voice.

"You will excuse me," said Holmes blandly, "but I could not help overhearing the questions which you put to the salesman just now. I think that I could be of assistance to you."

"You? Who are you? How could you know anything of the matter?"

"My name is Sherlock Holmes. It is my business to know what other people don't know."

"But you can know nothing of this?"

"Excuse me, I know everything of it. You are endeavoring to trace some geese which were sold by Mrs. Oakshott, of Brixton Road, to a salesman named Breckinridge, by him in turn to Mr. Windigate, of the Alpha, and by him to his club, of which Mr. Henry Baker is a member."

"Oh, sir, you are the very man whom I have longed to meet," cried the little fellow with outstretched hands and quivering fingers. "I can hardly explain to you how interested I am in this matter."

Sherlock Holmes hailed a four-wheeler which was passing. "In that case we had better discuss it in a cosy room rather than in this wind-swept market-place," said he. "But pray tell me, before we go farther, who it is that I have the pleasure of assisting."

The man hesitated for an instant. "My name is John Robinson," he answered with a sidelong glance.

"No, no; the real name," said Holmes sweetly. "It is always awkward doing business with an alias."

A flush sprang to the white cheeks of the stranger. "Well, then," said he, "my real name is James Ryder."

"Precisely so. Head attendant at the Hotel Cosmopolitan. Pray step into the cab, and I shall soon be able to tell you everything which you would wish to know."

The little man stood glancing from one to the other of us with half-frightened, half-hopeful eyes, as one who is not sure whether he is on the verge of a windfall or of a catastrophe. Then he stepped into the cab, and in half an hour we were back in the sitting-room at Baker Street. Nothing had been said during our drive, but the high, thin breathing of our new companion, and the claspings and unclaspings of his hands, spoke of the nervous tension within him.

"Here we are!" said Holmes cheerily as we filed into the room. "The fire looks very seasonable in this weather. You look cold, Mr. Ryder. Pray take the basket-chair. I will just put on my slippers before we settle this little matter of yours. Now, then! You want to know what became of those geese?"

"Yes, sir."

"Or rather, I fancy, of that goose. It was one bird, I imagine, in which you were interested—white, with a black bar across the tail."

Ryder quivered with emotion. "Oh, sir," he cried, "can you tell me where it went to?"

"It came here."

"Here?"

"Yes, and a most remarkable bird it proved. I don't wonder that you should take an interest in it. It laid an egg after it was dead—the bonniest, brightest little blue egg that ever was seen. I have it here in my museum."

Our visitor staggered to his feet and clutched the mantelpiece with his right hand. Holmes unlocked his strongbox and held up the blue carbuncle, which shone out like a star, with a cold, brilliant, many-pointed radiance. Ryder stood glaring with a drawn face, uncertain whether to claim or to disown it.

"The game's up, Ryder," said Holmes quietly. "Hold up, man, or you'll be into the fire! Give him an arm back into his chair, Watson. He's not got blood enough to go in for felony with impunity. Give him a dash of brandy. So! Now he looks a little more human. What a shrimp it is, to be sure!"

For a moment he had staggered and nearly fallen, but the brandy brought a tinge of colour into his cheeks, and he sat staring with frightened eyes at his accuser.

"I have almost every link in my hands, and all the proofs which I could possibly need, so there is little which you need tell me. Still, that little may as well be cleared up to make the case complete. You had heard, Ryder, of this blue stone of the Countess of Morcar's?"

"It was Catherine Cusack who told me of it," said he in a crackling voice.

"I see—her ladyship's waiting-maid. Well, the temptation of sudden wealth so easily acquired was too much for you, as it has been for better men before you; but you were not very scrupulous in the means you used. It seems to me, Ryder, that there is the making of a very pretty villain in you. You knew that this man Horner, the plumber, had been concerned in some such matter before, and that suspicion would rest the more readily upon him. What did you do, then? You made some small job in my lady's room—you and your confederate Cusack—and you managed that he should be the man sent for. Then, when he had left, you rifled the jewel-case, raised the alarm, and had this unfortunate man arrested. You then—"

Ryder threw himself down suddenly upon the rug and clutched at my companion's knees. "For God's sake, have mercy!" he shrieked. "Think

[38]

of my father! of my mother! It would break their hearts. I never went wrong before! I never will again. I swear it. I'll swear it on a Bible. Oh, don't bring it into court! For Christ's sake, don't!''

"Get back into your chair!" said Holmes sternly. "It is very well to cringe and crawl now, but you thought little enough of this poor Horner in the dock for a crime of which he knew nothing."

"I will fly, Mr. Holmes. I will leave the country, sir. Then the charge against him will break down."

"Hum! We will talk about that. And now let us hear a true account of the next act. How came the stone into the goose, and how came the goose into the open market? Tell us the truth, for there lies your only hope of safety."

Ryder passed his tongue over his parched lips. "I will tell you it just as it happened, sir," said he. "When Horner had been arrested, it seemed to me that it would be best for me to get away with the stone at once, for I did not know at what moment the police might not take it into their heads to search me and my room. There was no place about the hotel where it would be safe. I went out, as if on some commission, and I made for my sister's house. She had married a man named Oakshott, and lived in Brixton Road, where she fattened fowls for the market. All the way there every man I met seemed to me to be a policeman or a detective; and, for all that it was a cold night, the sweat was pouring down my face before I came to the Brixton Road. My sister asked me what was the matter, and why I was so pale; but I told her that I had been upset by the jewel robbery at the hotel. Then I went into the back yard and smoked a pipe, and wondered what it would be best to do.

"I had a friend once called Maudsley, who went to the bad, and has just been serving his time in Pentonville. One day he had met me, and fell into talk about the ways of thieves, and how they could get rid of what they stole. I knew that he would be true to me, for I knew one or two things about him; so I made up my mind to go right on to Kilburn, where he lived, and take him into my confidence. He would show me how to turn the stone into money. But how to get to him in safety? I thought of the agonies I had gone through in coming from the hotel. I might at any moment be seized and searched, and there would be the stone in my waistcoat pocket. I was leaning against the wall at the time and looking at the geese which were waddling about round my feet, and suddenly an idea came into my head which showed me how I could beat the best detective that ever lived.

"My sister had told me some weeks before that I might have the pick of her geese for a Christmas present, and I knew that she was always as good as her word. I would take my goose now, and in it I would carry my stone to Kilburn. There was a little shed in the yard, and behind this I drove one of the birds—a fine big one, white, with a barred tail. I caught it, and, prying its bill open, I thrust the stone down its throat as far as my finger could reach. The bird gave a gulp, and I felt the stone pass along its gullet and down into its crop. But the creature flapped and struggled, and out came my sister to know what was the matter. As I turned to speak to her the brute broke loose and fluttered off among the others.

"'Whatever were you doing with that bird, Jem?' says she.

"'Well,' said I, 'you said you'd give me one for Christmas, and I was feeling which was the fattest.'

"'Oh,' says she, 'we've set yours aside for you—Jem's bird, we call it. It's the big white one over yonder. There's twenty-six of them, which makes one for you, and one·for us, and two dozen for the market.'

"'Thank you, Maggie,' says I; 'but if it is all the same to you, I'd rather have that one I was handling just now.'

"'The other is a good three pound heavier,' said she, 'and we fattened it expressly for you.'

"'Never mind. I'll have the other, and I'll take it now,' said I.

"'Oh, just as you like,' said she, a little huffed. 'Which is it you want, then?'

"'That white one with the barred tail, right in the middle of the flock.'

"'Oh, very well. Kill it and take it with you.'

"Well, I did what she said, Mr. Holmes, and I carried the bird all the way to Kilburn. I told my pal what I had done, for he was a man that it was easy to tell a thing like that to. He laughed until he choked, and we got a knife and opened the goose. My heart turned to water, for there was no sign of the stone, and I knew that some terrible mistake had occurred. I left the bird, rushed back to my sister's, and hurried into the back yard. There was not a bird to be seen there.

"'Where are they all, Maggie?' I cried.

"'Gone to the dealer's, Jem.'

"'Which dealer's?'

"'Breckinridge, of Covent Garden.'

"'But was there another with a barred tail?' I asked, 'the same as the one I chose?'

"'Yes, Jem; there were two barred-tailed ones, and I could never tell them apart.'

"Well, then, of course I saw it all, and I ran off as hard as my feet would carry me to this man Breckinridge; but he had sold the lot at once, and not one word would he tell me as to where they had gone. You heard him your-selves to-night. Well, he has always answered me like that. My sister thinks that I am going mad. Sometimes I think that I am myself. And now—and

[40]

now I am myself a branded thief, without ever having touched the wealth for which I sold my character. God help me! God help me!'' He burst into convulsive sobbing, with his face buried in his hands.

There was a long silence, broken only by his heavy breathing, and by the measured tapping of Sherlock Holmes's finger-tips upon the edge of the table. Then my friend rose and threw open the door.

''Get out!'' said he.

''What, sir! Oh, Heaven bless you!''

''No more words. Get out!''

And no more words were needed. There was a rush, a clatter upon the stairs, the bang of a door, and the crisp rattle of running footfalls from the street.

''After all, Watson,'' said Holmes, reaching up his hand for his clay pipe, ''I am not retained by the police to supply their deficiencies. If Horner were in danger it would be another thing; but this fellow will not appear against him, and the case must collapse. I suppose that I am commuting a felony, but it is just possible that I am saving a soul. This fellow will not go wrong again; he is too terribly frightened. Send him to jail now, and you make him a jail-bird for life. Besides, it is the season of forgiveness. Chance has put in our way a most singular and whimsical problem, and its solution is its own reward. If you will have the goodness to touch the bell, Doctor, we will begin another investigation, in which, also, a bird will be the chief feature.''

"I've just told Fettle about the will."

★

The Adventure of the Christmas Pudding

by Agatha Christie

The Adventure of the Christmas Pudding is an indulgence of my own, since it recalls to me, very pleasurably, the Christmases of my youth. After my father's death, my mother and I always spent Christmas with my brother-in-law's family in the north of England — and what superb Christmases they were for a child to remember! Abney Hall had everything! The garden boasted a waterfall, a stream, and a tunnel under the drive! The Christmas fare was of gargantuan proportions. I was a skinny child, appearing delicate, but actually of robust health and perpetually hungry! The boys of the family and I used to vie with each other as to who could eat most on Christmas Day. Oyster Soup and Turbot went down without undue zest, but then came Roast Turkey, Boiled Turkey and an enormous Sirloin of Beef. The boys and I had two helpings of all three! We then had Plum Pudding, Mince-pies, Trifle and every kind of dessert. During the afternoon we ate chocolates solidly. We neither felt, nor were, sick! How lovely to be eleven years old and greedy!

What a day of delight from "Stockings" in bed in the morning, Church and all the Christmas hymns, Christmas dinner, Presents, and the final Lighting of the Christmas Tree!

And how deep my gratitude to the kind and hospitable hostess who must have worked so hard to make Christmas Day a wonderful memory to me still in my old age.

So let me dedicate this to the memory of Abney Hall — it's kindness and its hospitality.

And a happy Christmas to all who read (it).

Agatha Christie

[43]

I regret exceedingly—'' said M. Hercule Poirot.

He was interrupted. Not rudely interrupted. The interruption was suave, dexterous, persuasive rather than contradictory.

"Please don't refuse offhand, M. Poirot. There are grave issues of State. Your co-operation will be appreciated in the highest quarters."

"You are too kind," Hercule Poirot waved a hand, "but I really cannot undertake to do as you ask. At this season of the year—"

Again Mr. Jesmond interrupted. "Christmas time," he said, persuasively. "An old-fashioned Christmas in the English countryside."

Hercule Poirot shivered. The thought of the English countryside at this season of the year did not attract him.

"A good old-fashioned Christmas!" Mr. Jesmond stressed it.

"Me—I am not an Englishman," said Hercule Poirot. "In my country, Christmas, it is for the children. The New Year, that is what we celebrate."

"Ah," said Mr. Jesmond, "but Christmas in England is a great institution and I assure you at Kings Lacey you would see it at its best. It's a wonderful old house, you know. Why, one wing of it dates from the fourteenth century."

Again Poirot shivered. The thought of a fourteenth-century English manor house filled him with apprehension. He had suffered too often in the historic country houses of England. He looked round appreciatively at his comfortable modern flat with its radiators and the latest patent devices for excluding any kind of draught.

"In the winter," he said firmly, "I do not leave London."

"I don't think you quite appreciate, M. Poirot, what a very serious matter this is." Mr. Jesmond glanced at his companion and then back at Poirot.

Poirot's second visitor had up to now said nothing but a polite and formal "How do you do." He sat now, gazing down at his well-polished shoes, with an air of the utmost dejection on his coffee-coloured face. He was a young man, not more than twenty-three, and he was clearly in a state of complete misery.

"Yes, yes," said Hercule Poirot. "Of course the matter is serious. I do appreciate that. His Highness has my heartfelt sympathy."

"The position is one of the utmost delicacy," said Mr. Jesmond.

Poirot transferred his gaze from the young man to his older companion. If one wanted to sum up Mr. Jesmond in a word, the word would have been discretion. Everything about Mr. Jesmond was discreet. His well-cut but inconspicuous clothes, his pleasant, well-bred voice which rarely soared out of an agreeable monotone, his light-brown hair just thinning a little at the temples, his pale serious face. It seemed to Hercule Poirot that he had known not one Mr. Jesmond but a dozen Mr. Jesmonds in his time, all using sooner or later the same phrase—"A position of the utmost delicacy."

"The police," said Hercule Poirot, "can be very discreet, you know."

Mr. Jesmond shook his head firmly.

"Not the police," he said. "To recover the—er—what we want to recover will almost inevitably invoke taking proceedings in the law courts and we know so little. We *suspect,* but we do not *know.*"

"You have my sympathy," said Hercule Poirot again.

If he imagined that his sympathy was going to mean anything to his two visitors, he was wrong. They did not want sympathy, they wanted practical help. Mr. Jesmond began once more to talk about the delights of an English Christmas.

"It's dying out, you know," he said, "the real old-fashioned type of Christmas. People spend it at hotels nowadays. But an English Christmas with all the family gathered round, the children and their stockings, the Christmas tree, the turkey and plum pudding, the crackers. The snowman outside the window—"

In the interests of exactitude, Hercule Poirot intervened.

"To make a snow-man one has to have the snow," he remarked severely. "And one cannot have snow to order, even for an English Christmas."

"I was talking to a friend of mine in the meteorological office only to-day," said Mr. Jesmond, "and he tells me that it is highly probable there *will* be snow this Christmas."

It was the wrong thing to have said. Hercule Poirot shuddered more forcefully than ever.

"Snow in the country!" he said. "That would be still more abominable. A large, cold, stone manor house."

"Not at all," said Mr. Jesmond. "Things have changed very much in the last ten years or so. Oil-fired central heating."

"They have oil-fired central heating at Kings Lacey?" asked Poirot. For the first time he seemed to waver.

Mr. Jesmond seized his opportunity. "Yes, indeed," he said, "and a splendid hot water system. Radiators in every bedroom. I assure you, my dear M. Poirot, Kings Lacey is comfort itself in the winter time. You might even find the house *too* warm."

"That is most unlikely," said Hercule Poirot.

With practised dexterity Mr. Jesmond shifted his ground a little.

"You can appreciate the terrible dilemma we are in," he said, in a confidential manner.

Hercule Poirot nodded. The problem was, indeed, not a happy one. A young potentate-to-be, the only son of the ruler of a rich and important

[45]

native State had arrived in London a few weeks ago. His country had been passing through a period of restlessness and discontent. Though loyal to the father whose way of life had remained persistently Eastern, popular opinion was somewhat dubious of the younger generation. His follies had been Western ones and as such looked upon with disapproval.

Recently, however, his betrothal had been announced. He was to marry a cousin of the same blood, a young woman who, though educated at Cambridge, was careful to display no Western influence in her own country. The wedding day was announced and the young prince had made a journey to England, bringing with him some of the famous jewels of his house to be reset in appropriate modern settings by Cartier. These had included a very famous ruby which had been removed from its cumbersome old-fashioned necklace and had been given a new look by the famous jewellers. So far so good, but after this came the snag. It was not to be supposed that a young man possessed of much wealth and convivial tastes, should not commit a few follies of the pleasanter type. As to that there would have been no censure. Young princes were supposed to amuse themselves in this fashion. For the prince to take the girl friend of the moment for a walk down Bond Street and bestow upon her an emerald bracelet or a diamond clip as a reward for the pleasure she had afforded him would have been regarded as quite natural and suitable, corresponding in fact to the Cadillac cars which his father invariably presented to his favourite dancing girl of the moment.

But the prince had been far more indiscreet than that. Flattered by the lady's interest, he had displayed to her the famous ruby in its new setting, and had finally been so unwise as to accede to her request to be allowed to wear it—just for one evening!

The sequel was short and sad. The lady had retired from their supper table to powder her nose. Time passed. She did not return. She had left the establishment by another door and since then had disappeared into space. The important and distressing thing was that the ruby in its new setting had disappeared with her.

These were the facts that could not possibly be made public without the most dire consequences. The ruby was something more than a ruby, it was a historical possession of great significance, and the circumstances of its disappearance were such that any undue publicity about them might result in the most serious political consequences.

Mr. Jesmond was not the man to put these facts into simple language. He wrapped them up, as it were, in a great deal of verbiage. Who exactly Mr. Jesmond was, Hercule Poirot did not know. He had met other Mr. Jesmonds in the course of his career. Whether he was connected with the Home Office, the Foreign Secretary or some more discreet branch of public

[46]

service was not specified. He was acting in the interests of the Commonwealth. The ruby must be recovered.

M. Poirot, so Mr. Jesmond delicately insisted, was the man to recover it.

"Perhaps—yes," Hercule Poirot admitted, "but you can tell me so little. Suggestion—suspicion—all that is not very much to go upon."

"Come now, Monsieur Poirot, surely it is not beyond your powers. Ah, come now."

"I do not always succeed."

But this was mock modesty. It was clear enough from Poirot's tone that for him to undertake a mission was almost synonymous with succeeding in it.

"His Highness is very young," Mr. Jesmond said. "It will be sad if his whole life is to be blighted for a mere youthful indiscretion."

Poirot looked kindly at the downcast young man. "It is the time for follies, when one is young," he said encouragingly, "and for the ordinary young man it does not matter so much. The good papa, he pays up; the family lawyer, he helps to disentagle the inconvenience; the young man, he learns by experience and all ends for the best. In a position such as yours, it is hard indeed. Your approaching marriage—"

"That is it. That is it exactly." For the first time words poured from the young man. "You see she is very, very serious. She takes life very seriously. She has acquired at Cambridge many very serious ideas. There is to be education in my country. There are to be schools. There are to be many things. All in the name of progress, you understand, of democracy. It will not be, she says, like it was in my father's time. Naturally she knows that I will have diversions in London, but not the scandal. No! It is the scandal that matters. You see it is very, very famous, this ruby. There is a long trail behind it, a history. Much bloodshed—many deaths!"

"Deaths," said Hercule Poirot thoughtfully. He looked at Mr. Jesmond. "One hopes," he said, "it will not come to that?"

Mr. Jesmond made a peculiar noise rather like a hen who has decided to lay an egg and then thought better of it.

"No, no indeed," he said, sounding rather prim. "There is no question, I am sure, of anything of *that* kind."

"You cannot be sure," said Hercule Poirot. "Whoever has the ruby now, there may be others who want to gain possession of it, and who will not stick at a trifle, my friend."

"I really don't think," said Mr. Jesmond, sounding more prim than ever, "that we need enter into speculation of that kind. Quite unprofitable."

"Me," said Hercule Poirot, suddenly becoming very foreign, "me, I explore all the avenues, like the politicians."

Mr. Jesmond looked at him doubtfully. Pulling himself together, he said, "Well, I can take it that is settled, M. Poirot? You will go to Kings Lacey?"

"And how do I explain myself there?" asked Hercule Poirot.

Mr. Jesmond smiled with confidence.

"That, I think, can be arranged very easily," he said. "I can assure you that it will all seem quite natural. You will find the Laceys most charming. Delightful people."

"And you do not deceive me about the oil-fired central heating?"

"No, no, indeed." Mr. Jesmond sounded quite pained. "I assure you you will find every comfort."

"*Tout confort moderne,*" murmured Poirot to himself, reminiscently. "*Eh bien,*" he said, "I accept."

II

The temperature in the long drawing-room at Kings Lacey was a comfortable sixty-eight as Hercule Poirot sat talking to Mrs. Lacey by one of the big mullioned windows. Mrs. Lacey was engaged in needlework. She was not doing *petit point* or embroidered flowers upon silk. Instead, she appeared to be engaged in the prosaic task of hemming dishcloths. As she sewed she talked in a soft reflective voice that Poirot found very charming.

"I hope you will enjoy our Christmas party here, M. Poirot. It's only the family, you know. My granddaughter and a grandson and a friend of his and Bridget who's my great niece, and Diana who's a cousin and David Welwyn who is a very old friend. Just a family party. But Edwina Morecombe said that that's what you really wanted to see. An old-fashioned Christmas. Nothing could be more old-fashioned than we are! My husband you know, absolutely lives in the past. He likes everything to be just as it was when he was a boy of twelve years old, and used to come here for his holidays." She smiled to herself. "All the same old things, the Christmas tree and the stockings hung up and the oyster soup and the turkey—two turkeys, one boiled and one roast—and the plum pudding with the ring and the bachelor's button and all the rest of it in it. We can't have sixpences nowadays because they're not pure silver any more. But all the old desserts, the Elvas plums and Carlsbad plums and almonds and raisins, and crystallised fruit and ginger. Dear me, I sound like a catalogue from Fortnum and Mason!"

"You arouse my gastronomic juices, Madame."

"I expect we'll all have frightful indigestion by to-morrow evening," said Mrs. Lacey. "One isn't used to eating so much nowadays, is one?"

She was interrupted by some loud shouts and whoops of laughter outside the window. She glanced out.

"I don't know what they're doing out there. Playing some game or other, I suppose. I've always been so afraid, you know, that these young people would be bored by our Christmas here. But not at all, it's just the opposite. Now my own son and daughter and their friends, they used to be rather sophisticated about Christmas. Say it was all nonsense and too much fuss and it would be far better to go out to a hotel somewhere and dance. But the younger generation seems to find all this terribly attractive. Besides," added Mrs. Lacey practically, "schoolboys and schoolgirls are always hungry, aren't they? I thing they must starve them at these schools. After all, one does know children of that age each eat about as much as three strong men."

Poirot laughed and said, "It is most kind of you and your husband, Madame, to include me in this way in your family party."

"Oh, we're both delighted, I'm sure," said Mrs. Lacey. "And if you find Horace a little gruff," she continued, "pay no attention. It's just his manner, you know."

What her husband, Colonel Lacey, had actually said was: "Can't think why you want one of these damned foreigners here cluttering up Christmas? Why can't we have him some other time? Can't stick foreigners! All right, all right, so Edwina Morecombe wished him on us. What's it got to do with *her*. I should like to know? Why doesn't *she* have him for Christmas?"

"Because you know very well," Mrs. Lacey had said, "that Edwina always goes to Claridge's."

Her husband had looked at her piercingly and said, "Not up to something, are you, Em?"

"Up to something?" said Em, opening very blue eyes. "Of course not. Why should I be?"

Old Colonel Lacey laughed, a deep, rumbling laugh. "I wouldn't put it past you, Em," he said. "When you look your most innocent is when you *are* up to something."

Revolving these things in her mind, Mrs. Lacey went on: "Edwina said she thought perhaps you might help us....I'm sure I don't know quite how, but she said that friends of yours had once found you very helpful in—in a case something like ours. I—well, perhaps you don't know what I'm talking about?"

Poirot looked at her encouragingly. Mrs. Lacey was close on seventy, as upright as a ramrod, with snow-white hair, pink cheeks, blue eyes, a ridiculous nose and a determined chin.

[49]

"If there is anything I can do I shall only be too happy to do it," said Poirot. "It is, I understand, a rather unfortunate matter of a young girl's infatuation."

Mrs. Lacey nodded. "Yes. It seems extraordinary that I should—well, want to talk to you about it. After all, you *are* a perfect stranger. . ."

"*And* a foreigner," said Poirot, in an understanding manner.

"Yes," said Mrs. Lacey, "but perhaps that makes it easier, in a way. Anyhow, Edwina seemed to think that you might perhaps know something—how shall I put it—something useful about this young Desmond Lee-Wortley."

Poirot paused a moment to admire the ingenuity of Mr. Jesmond and the ease with which he had made use of Lady Morecombe to further his own purposes.

"He has not, I understand, a very good reputation, this young man?" he began delicately.

"No, indeed, he hasn't! A very bad reputation! But that's no help so far as Sarah is concerned. It's never any good, is it, telling young girls that men have a bad reputation? It—it just spurs them on!"

"You are so very right," said Poirot.

"In my young day," went on Mrs. Lacey. "(Oh dear, that's a very long time ago!) We used to be warned, you know, against certain young men, and of course it *did* heighten one's interest in them, and if one could possibly manage to dance with them, or to be alone with them in a dark conservatory—" she laughed. "That's why I wouldn't let Horace do any of the things he wanted to do."

"Tell me," said Poirot, "exactly what it is that troubles you?"

"Our son was killed in the war," said Mrs. Lacey. "My daughter-in-law died when Sarah was born so that she has always been with us, and we've brought her up. Perhaps we've brought her up unwisely—I don't know. But we thought we ought always to leave her as free as possible."

"That is desirable, I think," said Poirot. "One cannot go against the spirit of the times."

"No," said Mrs. Lacey, "that's just what I felt about it. And, of course, girls nowadays do do these sort of things."

Poirot looked at her inquiringly.

"I think the way one expresses it," said Mrs. Lacey, "is that Sarah has got in with what they call the coffee-bar set. She won't go to dances or come out properly or be a deb or anything of that kind. Instead she has two rather unpleasant rooms in Chelsea down by the river and wears these funny clothes that they like to wear, and black stockings or bright green ones. Very thick stockings. (So prickly, I always think!) And she goes about without washing or combing her hair."

[50]

"*Ca, c'est tout à fait naturelle,*" said Poirot. "It is the fashion of the moment. They grow out of it."

"Yes, I know," said Mrs. Lacey. "I wouldn't worry about *that* sort of thing. But you see she's taken up with this Desmond Lee-Wortley and he really has a *very* unsavoury reputation. He lives more or less on well-to-do girls. They seem to go quite mad about him. He very nearly married the Hope girl, but her people got her made a ward in court or something. And of course that's what Horace wants to do. He says he must do it for her protection. But I don't think it's really a good idea, M. Poirot. I mean, they'll just run away together and go to Scotland or Ireland or the Argentine or somewhere and either get married or else live together without getting married. And although it may be contempt of court and all that—well, it isn't really an answer, is it, in the end? Especially if a baby's coming. One has to give in then, and let them get married. And then, nearly always, it seems to me, after a year or two there's a divorce. And then the girl comes home and usually after a year or two she marries someone so nice he's almost dull and settles down. But it's particularly sad, it seems to me, if there is a child, because it's not the same thing, being brought up by a stepfather, however nice. No, I think it's much better if we did as we did in my young days. I mean the first young man one fell in love with was *always* someone undesirable. I remember I had a horrible passion for a young man called—now what was his name now?—how strange it is, I can't remember his Christian name at all! Tibbitt, that was his surname. Young Tibbitt. Of course, my father more or less forbade him the house, but he used to get asked to the same dances, and we used to dance together. And sometimes we'd escape and sit out together and occasionally friends would arrange picnics to which we both went. Of course, it was all very exciting and forbidden and one enjoyed it enormously. But one didn't go to the — well, to the *lengths* that girls go nowadays. And so, after a while, the Mr. Tibbitts faded out. And do you know, when I saw him four years later I was surprised what I could *ever* have seen in him! He seemed to be such a *dull* young man. Flashy, you know. No interesting conversation.

"One always thinks the days of one's own youth are best," said Poirot, somewhat sententiously.

"I know," said Mrs. Lacey. "It's tiresome, isn't it? I mustn't be tiresome. But all the same I *don't* want Sarah, who's a dear girl really, to marry Desmond Lee-Wortley. She and David Welwyn, who is staying here, were always such friends and so fond of each other, and we did hope, Horace and I, that they would grow up and marry. But of course she just finds him dull now, and she's absolutely infatuated with Desmond."

"I do not quite understand, Madame," said Poirot. "You have him here now, staying in the house, this Desmond Lee-Wortley?"

[51]

"That's *my* doing," said Mrs. Lacey. "Horace was all for forbidding her to see him and all that. Of course, in Horace's day, the father or guardian would have called round at the young man's lodgings with a horse whip! Horace was all for forbidding the fellow the house, and forbidding the girl to see him. I told him that was quite the wrong attitude to take. 'No,' I said. 'Ask him down here. We'll have him down for Christmas with the family party.' Of course, my husband said I was mad! But I said, 'At any rate, dear, let's *try* it. Let her see him in *our* atmosphere and *our* house and we'll be very nice to him and very polite, and perhaps then he'll seem less interesting to her'!'"

"I think, as they say, you *have* something there, Madame," said Poirot. "I think your point of view is very wise. Wiser than your husband's."

"Well, I hope it is," said Mrs. Lacey doubtfully. "It doesn't seem to be working much yet. But of course he's only been here a couple of days." A sudden dimple showed in her wrinkled cheek. "I'll confess something to you, M. Poirot. I myself can't help liking him. I don't mean I *really* like him, with my *mind,* but I can feel the charm all right. Oh yes, I can see what Sarah sees in him. But I'm an old enough woman and have enough experience to know that he's absolutely no good. Even if I *do* enjoy his company. Though I do think," added Mrs. Lacey, rather wistfully, "he has *some* good points. He asked if he might bring his sister here, you know. She's had an operation and was in hospital. He said it was so sad for her being in a nursing home over Christmas and he wondered if it would be too much trouble if he could bring her with him. He said he'd take all her meals up to her and all that. Well now, I do think that *was* rather nice of him, don't you, M. Poirot?"

"It shows a consideration," said Poirot, thoughtfully, "which seems almost out of character."

"Oh, I don't know. You can have family affections at the same time as wishing to prey on a rich young girl. Sarah will be *very* rich, you know, not only with what we leave her—and of course that won't be very much because most of the money goes with the place to Colin, my grandson. But her mother was a very rich woman and Sarah will inherit all her money when she's twenty-one. She's only twenty now. No, I do think it was nice of Desmond to mind about his sister. And he didn't pretend she was anything very wonderful or that. She's a shorthand typist, I gather—does secretarial work in London. And he's been as good as his word and does carry up trays to her. Not all the time, of course, but quite often. So I think he has some nice points. But all the same," said Mrs. Lacey with great decision, "I don't want Sarah to marry him."

"From all I have heard and been told," said Poirot, "that would indeed be a disaster."

[52]

"Do you think it would be possible for you to help us in any way?" asked Mrs. Lacey.

"I think it is possible, yes," said Hercule Poirot, "but I do not wish to promise too much. For the Mr. Desmond Lee-Wortleys of this world are clever, Madame. But do not despair. One can, perhaps, do a little something. I shall at any rate, put forth my best endeavours, if only in gratitude for your kindness in asking me here for this Christmas festivity." He looked round him. "And it cannot be so easy these days to have Christmas festivities."

"No, indeed," Mrs. Lacey sighed. She leaned forward. "Do you know, M. Poirot, what I really dream of—what I would love to have?"

"But tell me, Madame."

"I simply long to have a small, modern bungalow. No, perhaps not a bungalow exactly, but a small, modern, easy to run house built somewhere in the park here, and live in it with an absolutely up-to-date kitchen and no long passages. Everything easy and simple."

"It is a very practical idea, Madame."

"It's not practical for me," said Mrs. Lacey. "My husband *adores* this place. He *loves* living here. He doesn't mind being slightly uncomfortable, he doesn't mind the inconveniences and he would hate, simply *hate,* to live in a small modern house in the park!"

"So you sacrifice yourself to his wishes?"

Mrs. Lacey drew herself up. "I do not consider it a sacrifice, M. Poirot," she said. "I married my husband with the wish to make him happy. He has been a good husband to me and made me very happy all these years, and I wish to give happiness to him."

"So you will continue to live here," said Poirot.

"It's not really too uncomfortable," said Mrs. Lacey.

"No, no," said Poirot, hastily. "On the contrary, it is most comfortable. Your central heating and your bath water are perfection."

"We spent a lot of money in making the house comfortable to live in," said Mrs. Lacey. "We were able to sell some land. Ripe for development, I think they call it. Fortunately right out of sight of the house on the other side of the park. Really rather an ugly bit of ground with no nice view, but we got a very good price for it. So that we have been able to have as many improvements as possible."

"But the service, Madame?"

"Oh, well, that presents less difficulty than you might think. Of course, one cannot expect to be looked after and waited upon as one used to be. Different people come in from the village. Two women in the morning, another two to cook lunch and wash it up, and different ones again in the evening. There are plenty of people who want to come and work for a few

[53]

hours a day. Of course for Christmas we are very lucky. My dear Mrs. Ross always comes in every Christmas. She is a wonderful cook, really first-class. She retired about ten years ago, but she comes in to help us in any emergency. Then there is dear Peverell.''

''Your butler?''

''Yes. He is pensioned off and lives in the little house near the lodge, but he is so devoted, and he insists on coming to wait on us at Christmas. Really, I'm terrified, M. Poirot, because he's so old and shaky that I feel certain that if he carries anything heavy he will drop it. It's really an agony to watch him. And his heart is not good and I'm afraid of his doing too much. But it would hurt his feelings dreadfully if I did not let him come. He hems and hahs and makes disapproving noises when he sees the state our silver is in and within three days of being here, it is all wonderful again. Yes. He is a dear faithful friend.'' She smiled at Poirot. ''So you see, we are all set for a happy Christmas. A white Christmas, too,'' she added as she looked out of the window. ''See? It is beginning to snow. Ah, the children are coming in. You must meet them, M. Poirot.''

Poirot was introduced with due ceremony. First, to Colin and Michael, the schoolboy grandson and his friend, nice polite lads of fifteen, one dark, one fair. Then to their cousin, Bridget, a black-haired girl of about the same age with enormous vitality.

''And this is my granddaughter, Sarah,'' said Mrs. Lacey.

Poirot looked with some interest at Sarah, an attractive girl with a mop of red hair; her manner seemed to him nervy and a trifle defiant, but she showed real affection for her grandmother.

''And this is Mr. Lee-Wortley.''

Mr. Lee-Wortley wore a fisherman's jersey and tight black jeans; his hair was rather long and it seemed doubtful whether he had shaved that morning. In contrast to him was a young man introduced as David Welwyn, who was solid and quiet, with a pleasant smile, and rather obviously addicted to soap and water. There was one other member of the party, a handsome, rather intense-looking girl who was introduced as Diana Middleton.

Tea was brought in. A hearty meal of scones, crumpets, sandwiches and three kinds of cake. The younger members of the party appreciated the tea. Colonel Lacey came in last, remarking in a non-committal voice:

''Hey, tea? Oh yes, tea.''

He received his cup of tea from his wife's hand, helped himself to two scones, cast a look of aversion at Desmond Lee-Wortley and sat down as far away from him as he could. He was a big man with bushy eyebrows and a red, weather-beaten face. He might have been taken for a farmer rather than the lord of the manor.

"Started to snow," he said. "It's going to be a white Christmas all right."

After tea the party dispersed.

"I expect they'll go and play with their tape recorders now," said Mrs. Lacey to Poirot. She looked indulgently after her grandson as he left the room. Her tone was that of one who says "The children are going to play with their toy soldiers."

"They're frightfully technical, of course," she said, "and very grand about it all."

The boys and Bridget, however, decided to go along to the lake and see if the ice on it was likely to make skating possible.

"*I* thought we could have skated on it this morning," said Colin. "But old Hodgkins said no. He's always so terribly careful."

"Come for a walk, David," said Diana Middleton, softly.

David hesitated for half a moment, his eyes on Sarah's red head. She was standing by Desmond Lee-Wortley, her hand on his arm, looking up into his face.

"All right," said David Welwyn, "yes, let's."

Diana slipped a quick hand through his arm and they turned towards the door into the garden. Sarah said:

"Shall we go, too, Desmond? It's fearfully stuffy in the house."

"Who wants to walk?" said Desmond. "I'll get my car out. We'll go along to the Speckled Boar and have a drink."

Sarah hesitated for a moment before saying:

"Let's go to Market Ledbury to the White Hart. It's much more fun."

Though for all the world she would not have put it into words, Sarah had an instinctive revulsion from going down to the local pub with Desmond. It was, somehow, not in the tradition of Kings Lacey. The women of Kings Lacey had never frequented the bar of the Speckled Boar. She had an obscure feeling that to go there would be to let old Colonel Lacey and his wife down. And why not? Desmond Lee-Wortley would have said. For a moment of exasperation Sarah felt that he ought to know why not! One didn't upset such old darlings as Grandfather and dear old Em unless it was necessary. They'd been very sweet, really, letting her lead her own life, not understanding in the least why she wanted to live in Chelsea in the way she did, but accepting it. That was due to Em of course. Grandfather would have kicked up no end of a row.

Sarah had no illusions about her grandfather's attitude. It was not his doing that Desmond had been asked to stay at Kings Lacey. That was Em, and Em was a darling and always had been.

When Desmond had gone to fetch his car, Sarah popped her head into the drawing-room again.

"We're going over to Market Ledbury," she said. "We thought we'd have a drink there at the White Hart."

There was a slight amount of defiance in her voice, but Mrs. Lacey did not seem to notice it.

"Well, dear," she said. "I'm sure that will be very nice. David and Diana have gone for a walk, I see. I'm so glad. I really think it was a brain-wave on my part to ask Diana here. So sad being left a widow so young—only twenty-two—I do hope she marries again *soon.*"

Sarah looked at her sharply. "What are you up to, Em?"

"It's my little plan," said Mrs. Lacey gleefully. "I think she's just right for David. Of course I know he was terribly in love with *you,* Sarah dear, but you'd no use for him and I realise that he isn't your type. But I don't want him to go on being unhappy, and I think Diana will really suit him."

"What a matchmaker you are, Em," said Sarah.

"I know," said Mrs. Lacey. "Old women always are. Diana's quite keen on him already, I think. Don't you think she'd be just right for him?"

"I shouldn't say so," said Sarah. "I think Diana's far too—well, too in-tense, too serious. I should think David would find it terribly boring being married to her."

"Well, we'll see," said Mrs. Lacey. "Anyway, *you* don't want him, do you, dear?"

"No, indeed," said Sarah, very quickly. She added, in a sudden rush, "You *do* like Desmond, don't you, Em?"

"I'm sure he's very nice indeed," said Mrs. Lacey.

"Grandfather doesn't like him," said Sarah.

"Well, you could hardly expect him to, could you?" said Mrs. Lacey reasonably, "but I dare say he'll come round when he gets used to the idea. You mustn't rush him, Sarah dear. Old people are very slow to change their minds and your grandfather *is* rather obstinate."

"I don't care what Grandfather thinks or says," said Sarah. "I shall get married to Desmond whenever I like!"

"I know, dear, I know. But do try and be realistic about it. Your grand-father could cause a lot of trouble, you know. You're not of age yet. In another year you can do as you please. I expect Horace will have come round long before that."

"You're on my side aren't you, darling?" said Sarah. She flung her arms round her grandmother's neck and gave her an affectionate kiss.

"I want you to be happy," said Mrs. Lacey. "Ah! there's your young man bringing his car round. You know, I like these very tight trousers these young men wear nowadays. They look so smart—only, of course, it does accentuate knock knees."

Yes, Sarah thought, Desmond *had* got knock knees, she had never noticed it before. . . .

"Go on, dear, enjoy yourself," said Mrs. Lacey.

She watched her go out to the car, then, remembering her foreign guest, she went along to the library. Looking in, however, she saw that Hercule Poirot was taking a pleasant little nap, and smiling to herself, she went across the hall and out into the kitchen to have a conference with Mrs. Ross.

"Come on, beautiful," said Desmond. "Your family cutting up rough because you're coming out to a pub? Years behind the times here, aren't they?"

"Of course they're not making a fuss," said Sarah, sharply as she got into the car.

"What's the idea of having that foreign fellow down? He's a detective, isn't he? What needs detecting here?"

"Oh, he's not here professionally," said Sarah. "Edwina Morecombe, my grandmother, asked us to have him. I think he's retired from professional work long ago."

"Sounds like a broken-down old cab horse," said Desmond.

"He wanted to see an old-fashioned English Christmas, I believe," said Sarah vaguely.

Desmond laughed scornfully. "Such a lot of tripe, that sort of thing," he said. "How you can stand it I don't know."

Sarah's red hair was tossed back and her aggressive chin shot up.

"I enjoy it!" she said defiantly.

"You can't, baby. Let's cut the whole thing to-morrow. Go over to Scarborough or somewhere."

"I couldn't possibly do that."

"Why not?"

"Oh, it would hurt their feelings."

"Oh, bilge! You know you don't enjoy this childish sentimental bosh."

"Well, not really perhaps, but—" Sarah broke off. She realised with a feeling of guilt that she was looking forward a good deal to the Christmas celebration. She enjoyed the whole thing, but she was ashamed to admit that to Desmond. It was not the thing to enjoy Christmas and family life. Just for a moment she wished that Desmond had not come down here at Christmas time. In fact, she almost wished that Desmond had not come down here at all. It was much more fun seeing Desmond in London than here at home.

In the meantime the boys and Bridget were walking back from the lake, still discussing earnestly the problems of skating. Flecks of snow had been falling, and looking up at the sky it could be prophesied that before long there was going to be a heavy snowfall.

"It's going to snow all night," said Colin. "Bet you by Christmas morning we have a couple of feet of snow."

The prospect was a pleasurable one.

"Let's make a snow-man," said Michael.

"Good lord," said Colin, "I haven't made a snow-man since—well, since I was about four years old."

"I don't believe it's a bit easy to do," said Bridget. "I mean, you have to know how."

"We might make an effigy of M. Poirot," said Colin. "Give it a big black moustache. There is one in the dressing-up box."

"I don't see, you know," said Michael thoughtfully, "how M. Poirot could ever have been a detective. I don't see how he'd ever be able to disguise himself."

"I know," said Bridget, "and one can't imagine him running about with a microscope and looking for clues or measuring footprints."

"I've got an idea," said Colin. "Let's put on a show for him!"

"What do you mean, a show?" asked Bridget.

"Well, arrange a murder for him."

"What a gorgeous idea," said Bridget. "Do you mean a body in the snow—that sort of thing?"

"Yes. It would make him feel at home, wouldn't it?"

Bridget giggled.

"I don't know that I'd go as far as that."

"If it snows," said Colin, "we'll have the perfect setting. A body and footprints—we'll have to think that out rather carefully and pinch one of Grandfather's daggers and make some blood."

They came to a halt and oblivious to the rapidly falling snow, entered into an excited discussion.

"There's a paintbox in the old schoolroom. We could mix up some blood—crimson-lake, I should think."

"Crimson-lake's a bit too pink, *I* think," said Bridget. "It ought to be a bit browner."

"Who's going to be the body?" asked Michael.

"I'll be the body," said Bridget quickly.

"Oh, look here," said Colin, "*I* thought of it."

"Oh, no, no," said Bridget, "it must be me. It's got to be a girl. It's more exciting. Beautiful girl lying lifeless in the snow."

"Beautiful girl! Ah-ha," said Michael in derision.

"I've got black hair, too," said Bridget.

"What's that got to do with it?"

"Well, it'll show up so well on the snow and I shall wear my red pyjamas."

"If you wear red pyjamas, they won't show the blood-stains," said Michael in a practical manner.

[58]

"But they'd look so effective against the snow," said Bridget, "and they've got white facings, you know, so the blood could be on that. Oh, won't it be gorgeous? Do you think he will really be taken in?"

"He will if we do it well enough," said Michael. "We'll have just your footprints in the snow and one other person's going to the body and coming away from it—a man's, of course. He won't want to disturb them, so he won't know that you're not really dead. You don't think," Michael stopped, struck by a sudden idea. The others looked at him. "You don't think he'll be *annoyed* about it?"

"Oh, I shouldn't think so," said Bridget, with facile optimism. "I'm sure he'll understand that we've just done it to entertain him. A sort of Christmas treat."

"I don't think we ought to do it on Christmas Day," said Colin reflectively. "I don't think Grandfather would like that very much."

"Boxing Day then," said Bridget.

"Boxing Day would be just right," said Michael.

"And it'll give us more time, too," pursued Bridget. "After all, there are a lot of things to arrange. Let's go and have a look at all the props."

They hurried into the house.

III

The evening was a busy one. Holly and mistletoe had been brought in in large quantities and a Christmas tree had been set up at one end of the dining-room. Everyone helped to decorate it, to put up the branches of holly behind pictures and to hang mistletoe in a convenient position in the hall.

"I had no idea anything so archaic still went on," murmured Desmond to Sarah with a sneer.

"We've always done it," said Sarah, defensively.

"What a reason!"

"Oh, don't be tiresome, Desmond. *I* think it's fun."

"Sarah my sweet, you *can't!*"

"Well, not—not really perhaps but—I do in a way."

"Who's going to brave the snow and go to midnight mass?" asked Mrs. Lacey at twenty minutes to twelve.

"Not me," said Desmond. "Come on, Sarah."

With a hand on her arm he guided her into the library and went over to the record case.

"There are limits, darling," said Desmond. "Midnight mass!"

"Yes," said Sarah. "Oh yes."

With a good deal of laughter, donning of coats and stamping of feet, most of the others got off. The two boys, Bridget, David and Diana set out for the ten minutes' walk to the church through the falling snow. Their laughter died away in the distance.

"Midnight mass!" said Colonel Lacey, snorting. "Never went to midnight mass in my young days. *Mass,* indeed! Popish, that is! Oh, I beg your pardon, Mr. Poirot."

Poirot waved a hand. "It is quite all right. Do not mind me."

"Matins is good enough for anybody, I should say," said the colonel. "Proper Sunday morning service. 'Hark the herald angels sing', and all the good old Christmas hymns. And then back to Christmas dinner. That's right, isn't it, Em?"

"Yes, dear," said Mrs. Lacey. "That's what *we* do. But the young ones enjoy the midnight service. And it's nice, really, that they *want* to go."

"Sarah and that fellow don't want to go."

"Well, there dear, I think you're wrong," said Mrs. Lacey. "Sarah, you know, *did* want to go, but she didn't like to say so."

"Beats me why she cares what that fellow's opinion is."

"She's very young, really," said Mrs. Lacey placidly. "Are you going to bed, M. Poirot? Good night. I hope you'll sleep well."

"And you, Madame? Are you not going to bed yet?"

"Not just yet," said Mrs. Lacey. "I've got the stockings to fill, you see. Oh, I know they're all practically grown up, but they do *like* their stockings. One puts jokes in them! Silly little things. But it all makes for a lot of fun."

"You work very hard to make this is a happy house at Christmas time," said Poirot. "I honour you."

He raised her hand to his lips in a courtly fashion.

"Hm," grunted Colonel Lacey, as Poirot departed. "Flowery sort of fellow. Still—he appreciates you."

Mrs. Lacey dimpled up at him. "Have you noticed, Horace, that I'm standing under the mistletoe?" she asked with the demureness of a girl of nineteen.

Hercule Poirot entered his bedroom. It was a large room well provided with radiators. As he went over towards the big four-poster bed he noticed an envelope lying on his pillow. He opened it and drew out a piece of paper. On it was a shakily printed message in capital letters.

DON'T EAT NONE OF THE PLUM PUDDING. ONE AS WISHES YOU WELL.

Hercule Poirot stared at it. His eyebrows rose. "Cryptic," he murmured, "and most unexpected."

IV

Christmas dinner took place at 2 p.m. and was a feast indeed. Enormous logs crackled merrily in the wide fireplace and above their crackling rose the babel of many tongues talking together. Oyster soup had been consumed, two enormous turkeys had come and gone, mere carcasses of their former selves. Now, the supreme moment, the Christmas pudding was brought in, in state! Old Peverell, his hands and his knees shaking with the weakness of his eighty years, permitted no one but himself to bear it in. Mrs. Lacey sat, her hands pressed together in nervous apprehension. One Christmas, she felt sure, Peverell would fall down dead. Having either to take the risk of letting him fall down dead or of hurting his feelings to such an extent that he would probably prefer to be dead than alive, she had so far chosen the former alternative. On a silver dish the Christmas pudding reposed in its glory. A large football of a pudding, a piece of holly stuck in it like a triumphant flag and glorious flames of blue and red rising round it. There was a cheer and cries of "Ooh-ah."

One thing Mrs. Lacey had done: prevailed upon Peverell to place the pudding in front of her so that she could help it rather than hand it in turn round the table. She breathed a sigh of relief as it was deposited safely in front of her. Rapidly the plates were passed round, flames still licking the portions.

"Wish, M. Poirot," cried Bridget. "Wish before the flame goes. Quick, Gran darling, quick."

Mrs. Lacey leant back with a sigh of satisfaction. Operation Pudding had been a success. In front of everyone was a helping with flames still licking it. There was a momentary silence all round the table as everyone wished hard.

There was nobody to notice the rather curious expression on the face of M. Poirot as he surveyed the portion of pudding on his plate. *"Don't eat none of the plum pudding."* What on earth did that sinister warning mean? There could be nothing different about his portion of plum pudding from that of everyone else! Sighing as he admitted himself baffled—and Hercule Poirot never liked to admit himself baffled—he picked up his spoon and fork.

"Hard sauce, M. Poirot?"

Poirot helped himself appreciatively to hard sauce.

"Swiped my best brandy again, eh Em?" said the colonel good-humouredly from the other end of the table. Mrs. Lacey twinkled at him.

"Mrs. Ross insists on having the best brandy, dear," she said. "She says it makes all the difference."

[61]

"Well, well," said Colonel Lacey, "Christmas comes but once a year and Mrs. Ross is a great woman. A great woman and a great cook."

"She is indeed," said Colin. "Smashing plum pudding, this. Mmmm." He filled an appreciative mouth.

Gently, almost gingerly, Hercule Poirot attacked his portion of pudding. He ate a mouthful. It was delicious! He ate another. Something tinkled on his place. He investigated with a fork. Bridget, on his left, came to his aid.

"You've got something, M. Poirot," she said. "I wonder what it is."

Poirot detached a little silver object from the surrounding raisins that clung to it.

"Oooh," said Bridget, "it's the bachelor's button! M. Poirot's got the bachelor's button!"

Hercule Poirot dipped the small silver button into the finger-glass of water that stood by his plate, and washed it clear of pudding crumbs.

"It is very pretty," he observed.

"That means you're going to be a bachelor, M. Poirot," explained Colin helpfully.

"That is to be expected," said Poirot gravely. "I have been a bachelor for many long years and it is unlikely that I shall change that status now."

"Oh, never say die," said Michael. "I saw in the paper that someone of ninety-five married a girl of twenty-two the other day."

"You encourage me," said Hercule Poirot.

Colonel Lacey uttered a sudden exclamation. His face became purple and his hand went to his mouth.

"Confound it, Emmeline," he roared, "why on earth do you let the cook put glass in the pudding?"

"Glass!" cried Mrs. Lacey, astonished.

Colonel Lacey withdrew the offending substance from his mouth. "Might have broken a tooth," he grumbled. "Or swallowed the damn' thing and had appendicitis."

He dropped the piece of glass into the finger-bowl, rinsed it, and held it up.

"God bless my soul," he ejaculated. "It's a red stone out of one of the cracker brooches." He held it aloft.

"You permit?"

Very deftly M. Poirot stretched across his neighbour, took it from Colonel Lacey's fingers and examined it attentively. As the squire had said, it was an enormous red stone the colour of a ruby. The light gleamed from its facets as he turned it about. Somewhere around the table a chair was pushed sharply back and then drawn in again.

"Phew!" cried Michael. "How wizard it would be if it was *real.*"

"Perhaps it is real," said Bridget hopefully.

"Oh, don't be an ass, Bridget. Why a ruby of that size would be worth thousands and thousands and thousands of pounds. Wouldn't it, M. Poirot?"

"It would indeed," said Poirot.

"But what *I* can't understand," said Mrs. Lacey, "is how it got into the pudding."

"Oooh," said Colin, diverted by his last mouthful, "I've got the pig. It isn't fair."

Bridget chanted immediately, "Colin's got the pig! Colin's got the pig! Colin is the greedy guzzling *pig!*"

"I've got the ring," said Diana in a clear, high voice.

"Good for you, Diana. You'll be married first, of us all."

"I've got the thimble," wailed Bridget.

"Bridget's going to be an old maid," chanted the two boys. "Yah, Bridget's going to be an old maid."

"Who's got the money?" demanded David. "There's a real ten shilling piece, gold, in this pudding. I know. Mrs. Ross told me so."

"I think I'm the lucky one," said Desmond Lee-Wortley.

Colonel Lacey's two next door neighbours heard him mutter, "Yes, you would be."

"*I've* got a ring, too," said David. He looked across at Diana. "Quite a coincidence, isn't it?"

The laughter went on. Nobody noticed that M. Poirot carelessly, as though thinking of something else, had dropped the red stone into his pocket.

Mince-pies and Christmas dessert followed the pudding. The older members of the party then retired for a welcome siesta before the tea-time ceremony of the lighting of the Christmas tree. Hercule Poirot, however, did not take a siesta. Instead, he made his way to the enormous old-fashioned kitchen.

"It is permitted," he asked, looking round and beaming, "that I congratulate the cook on this marvellous meal that I have just eaten?"

There was a moment's pause and then Mrs. Ross came forward in a stately manner to meet him. She was a large woman, nobly built with all the dignity of a stage duchess. Two lean grey-haired women were beyond in the scullery washing up and a tow-haired girl was moving to and fro between the scullery and the kitchen. But these were obviously mere myrmidons. Mrs. Ross was the queen of the kitchen quarters.

"I am glad to hear you enjoyed it, sir," she said graciously.

"Enjoyed it!" cried Hercule Poirot. With an extravagant foreign gesture he raised his hand to his lips, kissed it, and wafted the kiss to the ceiling.

[63]

"But you are a genius, Mrs. Ross! A genius! *Never* have I tasted such a wonderful meal. The oyster soup—" he made an expressive noise with his lips. "—and the stuffing. The chestnut stuffing in the turkey, that was quite unique in my experience."

"Well, it's funny that you should say that, sir," said Mrs. Ross graciously. "It's a very special recipe, that stuffing. It was given me by an Austrian chef that I worked with many years ago. But all the rest," she added, "is just good, plain English cooking."

"And is there anything better?" demanded Hercule Poirot.

"Well, it's nice of you to say so, sir. Of course, you being a foreign gentleman might have preferred the continental style. Not but what I can't manage continental dishes too."

"I am sure, Mrs. Ross, you could manage anything! But you must know that English cooking—*good* English cooking, not the cooking one gets in the second-class hotels or the restaurants—is much appreciated by *gourmets* on the continent, and I believe I am correct in saying that a special expedition was made to London in the early eighteen hundreds, and a report sent back to France of the wonders of the English puddings. 'We have nothing like that in France,' they wrote. 'It is worth making a journey to London just to taste the varieties and excellencies of the English puddings. And above all puddings," continued Poirot, well launched now on a kind of rhapsody, "is the Christmas plum pudding, such as we have eaten to-day. That was a home-made pudding, was it not? Not a bought one?"

"Yes, indeed, sir. Of my own making and my own recipe such as I've made for many years. When I came here Mrs. Lacey said that she'd ordered a pudding from a London store to save me the trouble. But no, Madam, I said, that may be kind of you but no bought pudding from a store can equal a home-made Christmas one. Mind you," said Mrs. Ross, warming to her subject like the artist she was, "it was made too soon before the day. A good Christmas pudding should be made some weeks before and allowed to wait. The longer they're kept, within reason, the better they are. I mind now that when I was a child and we went to church every Sunday, we'd start listening for the collect that begins 'Stir up O Lord we beseech thee' because that collect was the signal, as it were, that the puddings should be made that week. And so they always were. We had the collect on the Sunday, and that week sure enough my mother would make the Christmas puddings. And so it should have been here this year. As it was, that pudding was only made three days ago, the day before you arrived, sir. However, I kept to the old custom. Everyone in the house had to come out into the kitchen and have a stir and make a wish. That's an old custom, sir, and I've always held to it."

"Most interesting," said Hercule Poirot. "Most interesting. And so everyone came out into the kitchen?"

"Yes, sir. The young gentlemen, Miss Bridget and the London gentleman who's staying here, and his sister and Mr. David and Miss Diana—Mrs. Middleton, I should say—All had a stir, they did."

"How many puddings did you make? Is this the only one?"

"No, sir, I made four. Two large ones and two smaller ones. The other large one I planned to serve on New Year's Day and the smaller ones were for Colonel and Mrs. Lacey when they're alone like and not so many in the family."

"I see, I see," said Poirot.

"As a matter of fact, sir," said Mrs. Ross, "it was the wrong pudding you had for lunch to-day."

"The wrong pudding?" Poirot frowned. "How is that?"

"Well, sir, we have a big Christmas mould. A china mould with a pattern of holly and mistletoe on top and we always have the Christmas Day pudding boiled in that. But there was a most unfortunate accident. This morning, when Annie was getting it down from the shelf in the larder, she slipped and dropped it and it broke. Well, sir, naturally I couldn't serve that, could I? There might have been splinters in it. So we had to use the other one—the New Year's Day one, which was in a plain bowl. It makes a nice round but it's not so decorative as the Christmas mould. Really, where we'll get another mould like that I don't know. They don't make things in that size nowadays. All tiddly bits of things. Why, you can't even buy a breakfast dish that'll take a proper eight to ten eggs and bacon. Ah, things aren't what they were."

"No, indeed," said Poirot. "But to-day that is not so. This Christmas Day has been like the Christmas Days of old, is that not true?"

Mrs. Ross sighed. "Well, I'm glad you say so, sir, but of course I haven't the *help* now that I used to have. Not skilled help, that is. The girls nowadays—" she lowered her voice slightly, "—they mean very well and they're very willing but they've not been *trained,* sir, if you understand what I mean."

"Times change, yes," said Hercule Poirot. "I too find it sad sometimes."

"This house, sir," said Mrs. Ross, "it's too large, you know, for the mistress and the colonel. The mistress, she knows that. Living in a corner of it as they do, it's not the same thing at all. It only comes alive, as you might say, at Christmas time when all the family come."

"It is the first time, I think, that Mr. Lee-Wortley and his sister have been here?"

"Yes, sir." A note of slight reserve crept into Mrs. Ross's voice. "A very nice gentleman he is but, well—it seems a funny friend for Miss Sarah to have, according to our ideas. But there—London ways are different! It's sad that his sister's so poorly. Had an operation, she had. She seemed all

[65]

right the first day she was here, but that very day, after we'd been stirring the puddings, she was took bad again and she's been in bed ever since. Got up too soon after her operation, I expect. Ah, doctors nowadays, they have you out of hospital before you can hardly stand on your feet. Why, my very own nephew's wife . . . ." And Mrs. Ross went into a long and spirited tale of hospital treatment as accorded to her relations, comparing it unfavourably with the consideration that had been lavished upon them in older times.

Poirot duly commiserated with her. "It remains," he said, "to thank you for this exquisite and sumptuous meal. You permit a little acknowledgment of my appreciation?" A crisp five pound note passed from his hand into that of Mrs. Ross who said perfunctorily:

"You really shouldn't do *that,* sir."

"I insist. I insist."

"Well, it's very kind of you indeed, sir." Mrs. Ross accepted the tribute as no more than her due. "And I wish you, sir, a very happy Christmas and a prosperous New Year."

V

The end of Christmas Day was like the end of most Christmas Days. The tree was lighted, a splendid Christmas cake came in for tea, was greeted with approval but was partaken of only moderately. There was cold supper.

Both Poirot and his host and hostess went to bed early.

"Good night, M. Poirot," said Mrs. Lacey. "I hope you've enjoyed yourself."

"It has been a wonderful day, Madame, wonderful."

"You're looking very thoughtful," said Mrs. Lacey.

"It is the English pudding that I consider."

"You found it a little heavy, perhaps?" asked Mrs. Lacey delicately.

"No, no, I do not speak gastronomically. I consider its significance."

"It's traditional of course," said Mrs. Lacey. "Well, good night, M. Poirot, and don't dream too much of Christmas puddings and mince-pies."

"Yes," murmured Poirot to himself as he undressed. "It is a problem certainly, that Christmas plum pudding. There is here something that I do not understand at all." He shook his head in a vexed manner. "Well—we shall see."

After making certain preparations, Poirot went to bed, but not to sleep.

It was some two hours later that his patience was rewarded. The door of his bedroom opened very gently. He smiled to himself. It was as he had thought it would be. His mind went back fleetingly to the cup of coffee so politely handed him by Desmond Lee-Wortley. A little later, when Desmond's back was turned, he had laid the cup down for a few moments on a table. He had then apparently picked it up again and Desmond had had the satisfaction, if satisfaction it was, of seeing him drink the coffee to the last drop. But a little smile lifted Poirot's moustache as he reflected that it was not he but someone else who was sleeping a good sound sleep tonight. "That pleasant young David," said Poirot to himself, "he is worried, unhappy. It will do him no harm to have a night's really sound sleep. And now, let us see what will happen?"

He lay quite still breathing in an even manner with occasionally a suggestion, but the faintest suggestion, of a snore.

Someone came up to the bed and bent over him. Then, satisfied, that someone turned away and went to the dressing-table. By the light of a tiny torch the visitor was examining Poirot's belongings neatly arranged on top of the dressing-table. Fingers explored the wallet, gently pulled open the drawers of the dressing-table, then extended the search to the pockets of Poirot's clothes. Finally the visitor approached the bed and with great caution slid his hand under the pillow. Withdrawing his hand, he stood for a moment or two as though uncertain what to do next. He walked round the room looking inside ornaments, went into the adjoining bathroom from whence he presently returned. Then, with a faint exclamation of disgust, he went out of the room.

"Ah," said Poirot, under his breath. "You have a disappointment. Yes, yes, a serious disappointment. Bah! To imagine, even, that Hercule Poirot would hide something where you could find it!" Then, turning over on his other side, he went peacefully to sleep.

He was aroused next morning by an urgent soft tapping on his door.

"Qui est là? Come in, come in."

"Monsieur Poirot, Monsieur Poirot."

"But yes?" Poirot sat up in bed. "It is the early tea? But no. It is you, Colin. What has occurred?"

Colin was, for a moment, speechless. He seemed to be under the grip of some strong emotion. In actual fact it was the sight of the nightcap that Hercule Poirot wore that affected for the moment his organs of speech. Presently he controlled himself and spoke.

"I think—M. Poirot, could you help us? Something rather awful has happened."

"Something has happened? But what?"

"It's—it's Bridget. She's out there in the snow. I think—she doesn't move or speak and—oh, you'd better come and look for yourself. I'm terribly afraid—she may be *dead.*"

"What?" Poirot cast aside his bed covers. "Mademoiselle Bridget—dead!"

"I think—I think somebody's killed her. There's—there's blood and—oh do come!"

"But certainly. But certainly. I come on the instant."

With great practicality Poirot inserted his feet into his outdoor shoes and pulled a fur-lined overcoat over his pyjamas.

"I come," he said. "I come on the moment. You have aroused the house?"

"No. No, so far I haven't told anyone but you. I thought it would be better. Grandfather and Gran aren't up yet. They're laying breakfast downstairs, but I didn't say anything to Peverell. She—Bridget—she's round the other side of the house, near the terrace and the library window."

"I see. Lead the way. I will follow."

Turning away to hide his delighted grin, Colin led the way downstairs. They went out through the side door. It was a clear morning with the sun not yet high over the horizon. It was not snowing now, but it had snowed heavily during the night and everywhere around was an unbroken carpet of thick snow. The world looked very pure and white and beautiful.

"There!" said Colin breathlessly. "I—it's—*there!*" He pointed dramatically.

The scene was indeed dramatic enough. A few yards away Bridget lay in the snow. She was wearing scarlet pyjamas and a white wool wrap thrown round her shoulders. The white wool wrap was stained with crimson. Her head was turned aside and hidden by the mass of her outspead black hair. One arm was under her body, the other lay flung out, the fingers clenched, and standing up in the centre of the crimson stain was the hilt of a large curved Kurdish knife which Colonel Lacey had shown to his guests only the evening before.

"*Mon Dieu!*" ejaculated M. Poirot. "It is like something on the stage!"

There was a faint choking noise from Michael. Colin thrust himself quickly into the breach.

"I know," he said. "It—it doesn't seem *real* somehow, does it? Do you see those footprints—I suppose we mustn't disturb them?"

"Ah yes, the footprints. No, we must be careful not to disturb those footprints."

"That's what I thought," said Colin. "That's why I wouldn't let anyone go near her until we got you. I thought you'd know what to do."

"All the same," said Hercule Poirot briskly, "first, we must see if she is still alive? Is not that so?"

"Well—yes—of course," said Michael, a little doubtfully, "but you see, we thought—I mean, we didn't like—"

"Ah, you have the prudence! You have read the detective stories. It is most important that nothing should be touched and that the body should be left as it is. But we cannot be sure as yet if it *is* a body, can we? After all, though prudence is admirable, common humanity comes first. We must think of the doctor, must we not, before we think of the police?''

"Oh yes. Of course," said Colin, still a little taken aback.

"We only thought—I mean—we thought we'd better get you before we did anything," said Michael hastily.

"Then you will both remain here," said Poirot. "I will approach from the other side so as not to disturb these footprints. Such excellent footprints, are they not—so very clear? The footprints of a man and a girl going out together to the place where she lies. And then the man's footsteps come back but the girl's—do not."

"They must be the footprints of the murderer," said Colin, with bated breath.

"Exactly," said Poirot. "The footprints of the murderer. A long narrow foot with rather a peculiar type of shoe. Very interesting. Easy, I think, to recognise. Yes, those footprints will be very important."

At that moment Desmond Lee-Wortley came out of the house with Sarah and joined them.

"What on earth are you all doing here?" he demanded in a somewhat theatrical manner. "I saw you from my bedroom window. What's up? Good lord, what's this? It—it looks like—"

"Exactly," said Hercule Poirot. "It looks like murder, does it not?"

Sarah gave a gasp, then shot a quick suspicious glance at the two boys.

"You mean someone's killed the girl—what's-her-name—Bridget?" demanded Desmond. "Who on earth would want to kill her? It's unbelievable!"

"There are many things that are unbelievable," said Poirot. "Especially before breakfast, is it not? That is what one of your classics says. Six impossible things before breakfast." He added: "Please wait here, all of you."

Carefully making a circuit, he approached Bridget and bent for a moment down over the body. Colin and Michael were now both shaking with suppressed laughter. Sarah joined them, murmuring, "What have you two been up to?"

"Good old Bridget," whispered Colin. "Isn't she wonderful? Not a twitch!"

"I've never seen anything look so dead as Bridget does," whispered Michael.

Hercule Poirot straightened up again.

"This is a terrible thing," he said. His voice held an emotion it had not held before.

Overcome by mirth, Michael and Colin both turned away. In a choked voice Michael said:

"What—what must we do?"

[69]

"Bridget?" Diana stared at him. "But surely—isn't it a joke of some kind? I heard something—something last night. I thought that they were going to play a joke on you, M. Poirot?"

"Yes," said Poirot, "that was the idea—to play a joke on me. But now come into the house, all of you. We shall catch our deaths of cold here and there is nothing to be done until Mr. Lee-Wortley returns with the police."

"But look here," said Colin, "we can't—we can't leave Bridget here alone."

"You can do her no good by remaining," said Poirot gently. "Come, it is a sad, a very sad tragedy, but there is nothing we can do any more to help Mademoiselle Bridget. So let us come in and get warm and have perhaps a cup of tea or of coffee."

They followed him obediently into the house. Peverell was just about to strike the gong. If he thought it extraordinary for most of the household to be outside and for Poirot to make an appearance in pyjamas and an over-coat, he displayed no sign of it. Peverell in his old age was still the perfect butler. He noticed nothing that he was not asked to notice. They went into the dining-room and sat down. When they all had a cup of coffee in front of them and were sipping it, Poirot spoke.

"I have to recount to you," he said, "a little history. I cannot tell you all the details, no. But I can give you the main outline. It concerns a young princeling who came to this county. He brought with him a famous jewel which he was to have reset for the lady he was going to marry, but unfortunately before that he made friends with a very pretty young lady. This pretty young lady did not care very much for the man, but she did care for his jewel—so much so that one day she disappeared with the historic possession which had belonged to his house for generations. So the poor young man, he is in a quandary, you see. Above all he cannot have a scandal. Impossible to go to the police. Therefore he comes to me, to Hercule Poirot. 'Recover for me,' he says, 'my historic ruby.' *Eh bien,* this young lady, she has a friend and the friend, he has put through several questionable transactions. He has been concerned with blackmail and he has been concerned with the sale of jewellery abroad. Always he has been very clever. He is suspected, yes, but nothing can be proved. It comes to my knowledge that this very clever gentleman, he is spending Christmas here in this house. It is important that the pretty young lady, once she has ac-quired the jewel, should disappear for a while from circulation, so that no pressure can be put upon her, no questions can be asked her. It is arranged, therefore, that she comes here to Kings Lacey, ostensibly as the sister of the clever gentleman—"

Sarah drew a sharp breath.

[70]

"Oh, no. Oh, no, not *here!* Not with me here!"

"But so it is," said Poirot. "And by a little manipulation I, too, become a guest here for Christmas. This young lady, she is supposed to have just come out of hospital. She is much better when she arrives here. But then comes the news that I, too, arrive, a detective—a well-known detective. At once she has what you call the wind up. She hides the ruby in the first place she can think of, and then very quickly she has a relapse and takes to her bed again. She does not want that I should see her, for doubtless I have a photograph and I shall recognise her. It is very boring for her, yes, but she has to stay in her room and her brother, he brings her up the trays."

"And the ruby?" demanded Michael.

"I think," said Poirot, "that at the moment it is mentioned I arrive, the young lady was in the kitchen with the rest of you, all laughing and talking and stirring the Christmas puddings. The Christmas puddings are put into bowls and the young lady she hides the ruby, pressing it down into one of the pudding bowls. Not the one that we are going to have on Christmas Day. Oh no, that one she knows is in a special mould. She put it in the other one, the one that is destined to be eaten on New Year's Day. Before then she will be ready to leave, and when she leaves no doubt that Christmas pudding will go with her. But see how fate takes a hand. On the very morning of Christmas Day there is an accident. The Christmas pudding in its fancy mould is dropped on the stone floor and the mould is shattered to pieces. So what can be done? The good Mrs. Ross, she takes the other pudding and sends it in."

"Good lord," said Colin, "do you mean that on Christmas Day when Grandfather was eating his pudding that that was a *real* ruby he'd got in his mouth?"

"Precisely," said Poirot, "and you can imagine the emotions of Mr. Desmond Lee-Wortley when he saw that. *Eh bien,* what happens next? The ruby is passed round. I examine it and I manage unobtrusively to slip it in my pocket. In a careless way as though I were not interested. But one person at least observes what I have done. When I lie in bed that person searches my room. He searches me. He does not find the ruby. Why?"

"Because," said Michael breathlessly, "you had given it to Bridget. That's what you mean. And so that's why—but I don't understand quite— I mean—Look here, what *did* happen?"

Poirot smiled at him.

"Come now into the library," he said, "and look out of the window and I will show you something that may explain the mystery."

He led the way and they followed him.

"Consider once again," said Poirot, "the scene of the crime."

[71]

"There is only one thing to do," said Poirot. "We must send for the police. Will one of you telephone or would you prefer me to do it?"

"I think," said Colin, "I think—what about it, Michael?"

"Yes," said Michael, "I think the jig's up now." He stepped forward. For the first time he seemed a little unsure of himself. "I'm awfully sorry," he said, "I hope you won't mind too much. It—er—it was a sort of joke for Christmas and all that, you know. We thought we'd—well, lay on a murder for you."

"You thought you would lay on a murder for me? Then this—then this—"

"It's just a show we put on," explained Colin, "to—to make you feel at home, you know."

"Aha," said Hercule Poirot. "I understand. You make of me the April fool, is that it? But to-day is not April the first, it is December the twenty-sixth."

"I suppose we oughtn't to have done it really," said Colin, "but—but— you don't mind very much, do you, M. Poirot? Come on, Bridget," he called, "get up. You must be half-frozen to death already."

The figure in the snow, however, did not stir.

"It is odd," said Hercule Poirot, "she does not seem to hear you." He looked thoughtfully at them. "It is a joke, you say? You are sure this is a joke?"

"Why yes." Colin spoke uncomfortably. "We—we didn't mean any harm."

"But why then does Mademoiselle Bridget not get up?"

"I can't imagine," said Colin.

"Come on, Bridget," said Sarah impatiently. "Don't go on lying there playing the fool."

"We really are very sorry, M. Poirot," said Colin apprehensively. "We do really apologise."

"You need not apologise," said Poirot, in a peculiar tone.

"What do you mean?" Colin stared at him. He turned again. "Bridget! Bridget! What's the matter? Why doesn't she get up? Why does she go on lying there?"

Poirot beckoned to Desmond. "*You*, Mr. Lee-Wortley. Come here—"

Desmond joined him.

"Feel her pulse," said Poirot.

Desmond Lee-Wortley bent down. He touched the arm—the wrist.

"There's no pulse . . . ." he stared at Poirot. "Her arm's stiff. Good God, she really *is* dead!"

Poirot nodded. "Yes, she is dead," he said. "Someone has turned the comedy into a tragedy."

"Someone—who?"

[72]

"There is a set of footprints going and returning. A set of footprints that bears a strong resemblance to the footprints *you* have just made, Mr. Lee-Wortley, coming from the path to this spot."

Desmond Lee-Wortley wheeled round.

"What on earth—Are you accusing me? *ME?* You're crazy! Why on earth should I want to kill the girl?"

"Ah—why? I wonder . . . Let us see. . . ."

He bent down and very gently prised open the stiff fingers of the girl's clenched hand.

Desmond drew a sharp breath. He gazed down unbelievingly. In the palm of the dead girl's hand was what appeared to be a large ruby.

"It's that damn' thing out of the pudding!" he cried.

"Is it?" said Poirot. "Are you sure?"

"Of course it is."

With a swift movement Desmond bent down and plucked the red stone out of Bridget's hand.

"You should not do that," said Poirot reproachfully. "Nothing should have been disturbed."

"I haven't disturbed the body, have I? But this thing might—might get lost and it's evidence. The great thing is to get the police here as soon as possible. I'll go at once and telephone."

He wheeled round and ran sharply towards the house. Sarah came swiftly to Poirot's side.

"I don't understand," she whispered. Her face was dead white. "I don't *understand.*" She caught at Poirot's arm. "What did you mean about—about the footprints?"

"Look for yourself, Mademoiselle."

The footprints that led to the body and back again were the same as the ones just made accompanying Poirot to the girl's body and back.

"You mean—that it was Desmond? Nonsense!"

Suddenly the noise of a car came through the clear air. They wheeled round. They saw the car clearly enough driving at a furious pace down the drive and Sarah recognised what car it was.

"It's Desmond," she said. "It's Desmond's car. He—he must have gone to fetch the police instead of telephoning."

Diana Middleton came running out of the house to join them.

"What's happened?" she cried in a breathless voice. "Desmond just came rushing into the house. He said something about Bridget being killed and then he rattled the telephone but it was dead. He couldn't get an answer. He said the wires must have been cut. He said the only thing was to take a car and go for the police. Why the police? . . ."

Poirot made a gesture.

[73]

He pointed out of the window. A simultaneous gasp broke from the lips of all of them. There was no body lying on the snow, no trace of the tragedy seemed to remain except a mass of scuffled snow.

"It wasn't all a dream, was it?" said Colin faintly. "I—has someone taken the body away?"

"Ah," said Poirot. "You see? The Mystery of the Disappearing Body." He nodded his head and his eyes twinkled gently.

"Good lord," cried Michael. "M. Poirot, you are—you haven't—oh, look here, he's been having us on all this time!"

Poirot twinkled more than ever.

"It is true, my children, I also have had my little joke. I knew about your little plot, you see, and so I arranged a counter-plot of my own. Ah, *voilà* Mademoiselle Bridget. None the worse, I hope, for your exposure in the snow? Never should I forgive myself if you attrapped *une fluxion de poitrine.*"

Bridget had just come into the room. She wearing a thick skirt and a woolen sweater. She was laughing.

"I sent a *tisane* to your room," said Poirot severely. "You have drunk it?"

"One sip was enough!" said Bridget. "*I*'m all right. Did I do it well, M. Poirot? Goodness, my arm hurts still after that tourniquet you made me put on it."

"You were splendid, my child," said Poirot. "Splendid. But see, the others are still in the fog. Last night I went to Mademoiselle Bridget. I told her that I knew about your little *complot* and I asked her if she would act a part for me. She did it very cleverly. She made the footprints with a pair of Mr. Lee-Wortley's shoes."

Sarah said in a harsh voice:

"But what's the point of it all, M. Poirot? What's the point of sending Desmond off to fetch the police? They'll be very angry when they find out it's nothing but a hoax."

Poirot shook his head gently.

"But I do not think for one moment, Mademoiselle, that Mr. Lee-Wortley went to fetch the police," he said. "Murder is a thing in which Mr. Lee-Wortley does not want to be mixed up. He lost his nerve badly. All he could see was his chance to get the ruby. He snatched that, he pretended the telephone was out of order and he rushed off in a car on the pretence of fetching the police. I think myself it is the last you will see of him for some time. He has, I understand, his own ways of getting out of England. He has his own plane, has he not, Mademoiselle?"

Sarah nodded. "Yes," she said. "We were thinking of—" She stopped.

"He wanted you to elope with him that way, did he not? *Eh bien*, that is a very good way of smuggling a jewel out of the country. When you are

[74]

eloping with a girl, and that fact is publicised, then you will not be suspected of also smuggling a historic jewel out of the country. Oh yes, that would have made a very good camouflage.''

"I don't believe it," said Sarah. "I don't believe a word of it!"

"Then ask his sister," said Poirot, gently nodding his head over her shoulder. Sarah turned her head sharply.

A platinum blonde stood in the doorway. She wore a fur coat and was scowling. She was clearly in a furious temper.

"Sister my foot!" she said, with a short unpleasant laugh. "That swine's no brother of mine! So he's beaten it, has he, and left me to carry the can? The whole thing was *his* idea! *He* put me up to it! Said it was money for jam. They'd never prosecute because of the scandal. I could always threaten to say that Ali had *given* me his historic jewel. Des and I were to have shared the swag in Paris—and now the swine runs out on me! I'd like to murder him!" She switched abruptly. "The sooner I get out of here—Can someone telephone for a taxi?"

"A car is waiting at the front door to take you to the station, Mademoiselle," said Poirot.

"Think of everything, don't you?"

"Most things," said Poirot complacently.

But Poirot was not to get off so easily. When he returned to the dining-room after assisting the spurious Miss Lee-Wortley into the waiting car, Colin was waiting for him.

There was a frown on his boyish face.

"But look here, M. Poirot. *What about the ruby?* Do you mean to say you've let him get away with it?"

Poirot's face fell. He twirled his moustaches. He seemed ill at ease.

"I shall recover it yet," he said weakly. "There are other ways. I shall still—"

"Well, I do think!" said Michael. "To let that swine get away with the ruby!"

Bridget was sharper.

"He's having us on again," she cried. "You are, aren't you, M. Poirot!"

"Shall we do a final conjuring trick, Mademoiselle? Feel in my left-hand pocket."

Bridget thrust her hand in. She drew it out again with a scream of triumph and held aloft a large ruby blinking in crimson splendour.

"You comprehend," explained Poirot, "the one that was clasped in your hand was a paste replica. I brought it from London in case it was possible to make a substitute. You understand? We do not want the scandal. Monsieur Desmond will try and dispose of that ruby in Paris or in Belgium or wherever it is that he has his contacts, and then it will be discovered that the stone is not real! What could be more excellent? All finishes happily. The scandal is avoided, my princeling receives his ruby back again, he returns to his country and makes a sober and we hope a happy marriage. All ends well.''

"Except for me," murmured Sarah under her breath.

She spoke so low that no one heard her but Poirot. He shook his head gently.

"You are in error, Mademoiselle Sarah, in what you say there. You have gained experience. All experience is valuable. Ahead of you I prophesy there lies happiness."

"That's what *you* say," said Sarah.

"But look here, M. Poirot," Colin was frowning. "How did you know about the show we were going to put on for you?"

"It is my business to know things," said Hercule Poirot. He twirled his moustache.

"Yes, but I don't see how you could have managed it. Did someone split—did someone come and tell you?"

"No, no, not that."

"Then how? Tell us how?"

They all chorused, "Yes, tell us how."

"But no," Poirot protested. "But no. If I tell you how I deduced that, you will think nothing of it. It is like the conjurer who shows how his tricks are done!"

"Tell us, M. Poirot! Go on. Tell us, tell us!"

"You really wish that I should solve for you this last mystery?"

"Yes, go on. Tell us."

"Ah, I do not think I can. You will be so disappointed."

"Now, come on, M. Poirot, tell us. *How did you know?*"

"Well, you see, I was sitting in the library by the window in a chair after tea the other day and I was reposing myself. I had been asleep and when I awoke you were discussing your plans just outside the window close to me, and the window was open at the top."

"Is that all?" cried Colin, disgusted. "How simple!"

"Is it not?" said Hercule Poirot, smiling. "You see? You *are* disappointed!"

"Oh well," said Michael, "at any rate we know everything now."

"Do we?" murmured Hercule Poirot to himself. "*I* do not. *I,* whose business it is to know things."

He walked out into the hall, shaking his head a little. For perhaps the twentieth time he drew from his pocket a rather dirty piece of paper. "DON'T EAT NONE OF THE PLUM PUDDING. ONE AS WISHES YOU WELL."

Hercule Poirot shook his head reflectively. He who could explain everything could not explain this! Humiliating. Who had written it? *Why* had it been written? Until he found that out he would never know a moment's peace. Suddenly he came out of his reverie to be aware of a peculiar gasping noise. He looked sharply down. On the floor, busy with a dustpan and brush was a tow-headed creature in a flowered overall. She was staring at the paper in his hand with large round eyes.

"Oh sir," said this apparition. "Oh, *sir. Please,* sir."

"And who may you be, *mon enfant?*" inquired M. Poirot genially.

"Annie Bates, sir, please sir. I come here to help Mrs. Ross. I didn't mean, sir, I didn't mean to—to do anything what I shouldn't do. I did mean it well, sir. For your good, I mean."

Enlightenment came to Poirot. He held out the dirty piece of paper.

"Did you write that, Annie?"

"I didn't mean any harm, sir. Really I didn't."

"Of course you didn't, Annie." He smiled at her. "But tell me about it. Why did you write this?"

"Well, it was them two, sir. Mr. Lee-Wortley and his sister. Not that she *was* his sister, I'm sure. None of us thought so! And she wasn't ill a bit. We could all tell *that*. We thought—we all thought—something queer was going on. I'll tell you straight, sir. I was in her bathroom taking in the clean towels, and I listened at the door. *He* was in her room and they were talking together. I heard what they said plain as plain. 'This detective,' he was saying. 'This fellow Poirot who's coming here. We've got to do something about it. We've got to get him out of the way as soon as possible.' And then he says to her in a nasty, sinister sort of way, lowering his voice, 'Where did you put it?' And she answered him *'In the pudding.'* Oh sir, my heart gave such a leap I thought it would stop beating. I thought they meant to poison you in the Christmas pudding. I didn't know *what* to do! Mrs. Ross, she wouldn't listen to the likes of me. Then the idea came to me as I'd write you a warning. And I did and I put it on your pillow where you'd find it when you went to bed." Annie paused breathlessly.

Poirot surveyed her gravely for some minutes.

"You see too many sensational films, I think, Annie," he said at last, "or perhaps it is the television that affects you? But the important thing is that you have the good heart and a certain amount of ingenuity. When I return to London I will send you a present."

"Oh thank you, sir. Thank you very much, sir."

"What would you like, Annie, as a present?"

"Anything I like, sir? Could I have anything I like?"

"Within reason," said Hercule Poirot prudently, "yes."

"Oh sir, could I have vanity box? A real posh slap-up vanity box like the one Mr. Lee-Wortley's sister, wot wasn't his sister, had?"

"Yes," said Poirot, "yes, I think that could be managed.

[77]

"It is interesting," he mused. "I was in a museum the other day observing some antiquities from Babylon or one of those places, thousands of years old—and among them were cosmetic boxes. The heart of woman does not change."

"Beg pardon, sir?" said Annie.

"It is nothing," said Poirot, "I reflect. You shall have your vanity box, child."

"Oh thank you, sir. Oh thank you very much indeed, sir."

Annie departed ecstatically. Poirot looked after her, nodding his head in satisfaction.

"Ah," he said to himself. "And now—I do. There is nothing more to be done here."

A pair of arms slipped round his shoulders unexpectedly.

"If you *will* stand just under the mistletoe—" said Bridget.

Hercule Poirot enjoyed it. He enjoyed it very much. He said to himself that he had had a very good Christmas.

Dancing Dan's Christmas
by Damon Runyon

N OW one time it comes on Christmas, and in fact it is the evening before Christmas, and I am in Good Time Charley Bernstein's little
speakeasy in West Forty-seventh Street, wishing Charley a Merry
Christmas and having a few hot Tom and Jerrys with him.

This hot Tom and Jerry is an old time drink that is once used by one and
all in this country to celebrate Christmas with, and in fact it is once so
popular that many people think Christmas is invented only to furnish an
excuse for hot Tom and Jerry, although of course this is by no means true.

But anybody will tell you that there is nothing that brings out the true
holiday spirit like hot Tom and Jerry, and I hear that since Tom and Jerry
goes out of style in the United States, the holiday spirit is never quite the
same.

Well, as Good Time Charley and I are expressing our holiday sentiments
to each other over our hot Tom and Jerry, and I am trying to think up the
poem about the night before Christmas and all through the house, which I
know will interest Charley no little, all of a sudden there is a big knock at
the front door, and when Charley opens the door, who comes in carrying a
large package under one arm but a guy by the name of Dancing Dan.

This Dancing Dan is a good-looking young guy, who always seems well-
dressed, and he is called by the name of Dancing Dan because he is a great
hand for dancing around and about with dolls in night clubs, and other
spots where there is any dancing. In fact, Dan never seems to be doing anything else, although I hear rumors that when he is not dancing he is carrying on in a most illegal manner at one thing and another. But of course you
can always hear rumors in this town about anybody, and personally I am
rather fond of Dancing Dan as he always seems to be getting a great belt out
of life.

Anybody in town will tell you that Dancing Dan is a guy with no Barna-
by whatever in him, and in fact he has about as much gizzard as anybody
around, although I wish to say I always question his judgment in dancing
so much with Miss Muriel O'Neill, who works in the Half Moon night
club. And the reason I question his judgment in this respect is because
everybody knows that Miss Muriel O'Neill is a doll who is very well

thought of by Heine Schmitz, and Heine Schmitz is not such a guy as will take kindly to anybody dancing more than once and a half with a doll that he thinks well of.

Well, anyway, as Dancing Dan comes in, he weighs up the joint in one quick peek, and then he tosses the package he is carrying into a corner where it goes plunk, as if there is something very heavy in it, and then he steps up to the bar alongside of Charley and me and wishes to know what we are drinking.

Naturally we start boosting hot Tom and Jerry to Dancing Dan, and he says he will take a crack at it with us, and after one crack, Dancing Dan says he will have another crack, and Merry Christmas to us with it, and the first thing anybody knows it is a couple of hours later and we still are still having cracks at the hot Tom and Jerry with Dancing Dan, and Dan says he never drinks anything so soothing in his life. In fact, Dancing Dan says he will recommend Tom and Jerry to everybody he knows, only he does not know anybody good enough for Tom and Jerry, except maybe Miss Muriel O'Neill, and she does not drink anything with drugstore rye in it.

Well, several times while we are drinking this Tom and Jerry, customers come to the door of Good Time Charley's little speakeasy and knock, but by now Charley is commencing to be afraid they will wish Tom and Jerry, too, and he does not feel we will have enough for ourselves, so he hangs out a sign which says "Closed on Account of Christmas," and the only one he will let in is a guy by the name of Ooky, who is nothing but an old rum-dum, and who is going around all week dressed like Santa Claus and carry-ing a sign advertising Moe Lewinsky's clothing joint around in Sixth Avenue.

This Ooky is still wearing his Santa Claus outfit when Charley lets him in, and the reason Charley permits such a character as Ooky in his joint is because Ooky does the porter work for Charley when he is not Santa Claus for Moe Lewinsky, such as sweeping out, and washing the glasses, and one thing and another.

Well, it is about nine-thirty when Ooky comes in, and his puppies are aching, and he is all petered out generally from walking up and down and here and there with his sign, for any time a guy is Santa Claus for Moe Lewinsky he must earn his dough. In fact, Ooky is so fatigued, and his puppies hurt him so much that Dancing Dan and Good Time Charley and I all feel very sorry for him, and invite him to have a few mugs of hot Tom and Jerry with us, and wish him plenty of Merry Christmas.

But old Ooky is not accustomed to Tom and Jerry and after about the fifth mug he folds up in a chair, and goes right to sleep on us. He is wearing a pretty good Santa Claus make-up, what with a nice red suit trimmed with white cotton, and a wig, and false nose, and long white whiskers, and a big sack stuffed with excelsior on his back, and if I do not know Santa Claus is not apt to be such a guy as will snore loud enough to rattle the windows, I will think Ooky is Santa Claus sure enough.

Well, we forget Ooky and let him sleep, and go on with our hot Tom and Jerry, and in the meantime we try to think up a few songs appropriate to Christmas, and Dancing Dan finally renders My Dad's Dinner Pail in a nice baritone and very loud, while I do first rate with Will You Love Me in December As You Do in May?

About midnight Dancing Dan wishes to see how he looks as Santa Claus.

So Good Time Charley and I help Dancing Dan pull off Ooky's outfit and put it on Dan, and this is easy as Ooky only has this Santa Claus outfit on over his ordinary clothes, and he does not even wake up when we are undressing him of the Santa Claus uniform.

Well, I wish to say I see many a Santa Claus in my time, but I never see a better looking Santa Claus than Dancing Dan, especially after he gets the wig and white whiskers fixed just right, and we put a sofa pillow that Good Time Charley happens to have around the joint for the cat to sleep on down his pants to give Dancing Dan a nice fat stomach such as Santa Claus is bound to have.

"Well," Charley finally says, "it is a great pity we do not know where there are some stockings hung up somewhere, because then," he says, "you can go around and stuff things in these stockings, as I always hear this is the main idea of a Santa Claus. But," Charley says, "I do not suppose anybody in this section has any stockings hung up, or if they have," he says, "the chances are they are so full of holes they will not hold anything. Anyway," Charley says, "even if there are any stockings hung up we do not have anything to stuff in them, although personally," he says, "I will gladly donate a few pints of Scotch."

Well, I am pointing out that we have no reindeer and that a Santa Claus is bound to look like a terrible sap if he goes around without any reindeer, but Charley's remarks seem to give Dancing Dan an idea, for all of a sudden he speaks as follows:

"Why," Dancing Dan says, "I know where a stocking is hung up. It is hung up at Miss Muriel O'Neill's flat over here in West Forty-ninth Street. This stocking is hung up by nobody but a party by the name of Gammer O'Neill, who is Miss Muriel O'Neill's grandmamma," Dancing Dan says. "Gammer O'Neill is going on ninety-odd," he says, "and Miss Muriel O'Neill tells me she cannot hold out much longer, what with one thing and another, including being a little childish in spots.

"Now," Dancing Dan says, "I remember Miss Muriel O'Neill is telling me just the other night how Gammer O'Neill hangs up her stocking on Christmas Eve all her life, and," he says, "I judge from what Miss Muriel

[81]

O'Neill says that the old doll always believes Santa Claus will come along some Christmas and fill the stocking full of beautiful gifts. But,'' Dancing Dan says, ''Miss Muriel O'Neill tells me Santa Claus never does this, although Miss Muriel O'Neill personally always takes a few gifts home and pops them into the stocking to make Gammer O'Neill feel better.

"But, of course," Dancing Dan says, "these gifts are nothing much because Miss Muriel O'Neill is very poor, and proud, and also good, and will not take a dime off of anybody and I can lick the guy who says she will.

"Now," Dancing Dan goes on, "it seems that while Gammer O'Neill is very happy to get whatever she finds in her stocking on Christmas morning, she does not understand why Santa Claus is not more liberal, and," he says, "Miss Muriel O'Neill is saying to me that she only wishes she can give Gammer O'Neill one real big Christmas before the old doll puts her checks back in the rack.

"So," Dancing Dan states, "here is a job for us. Miss Muriel O'Neill and her grandmamma live all alone in this flat over in West Forty-ninth Street, and," he says, "at such an hour as this Miss Muriel O'Neill is bound to be working, and the chances are Gammer O'Neill is sound a-sleep, and we will just hop over there and Santa Claus will fill up her stocking with beautiful gifts.''

Well, I say, I do not see where we are going to get any beautiful gifts at this time of night, what with all the stores being closed, unless we dash into an all-night drug store and buy a few bottles of perfume and a bum toilet set as guys always do when they forget about their ever-loving wives until after store hours on Christmas Eve, but Dancing Dan says never mind about this, but let us have a few more Tom and Jerrys first.

So we have a few more Tom and Jerrys and then Dancing Dan picks up the package he heaves into the corner, and dumps most of the excelsior out of Ooky's Santa Claus sack, and puts the bundle in, and Good Time Charley turns out all the lights, but one, and leaves a bottle of Scotch on the table in front of Ooky for a Christmas gift, and away we go.

Personally, I regret very much leaving the hot Tom and Jerry, but then I am also very enthusiastic about going along to help Dancing Dan play Santa Claus, while Good Time Charley is practically overjoyed, as it is the first time in his life Charley is ever mixed up in so much holiday spirit.

As we go up Broadway, headed for Forty-ninth Street, Charley and I see many citizens we know and give them a large hello, and wish them Merry Christmas, and some of these citizens shake hands with Santa Claus, not knowing he is nobody but Dancing Dan, although later I understand there is some gossip among these citizens because they claim a Santa Claus with such a breath on him as our Santa Claus has is a little out of line.

And once we are somewhat embarrassed when a lot of little kids going home with their parents from a late Christmas party somewhere gather about Santa Claus with shouts of childish glee, and some of them wish to climb up Santa Claus' legs. Naturally, Santa Claus gets a little peevish, and calls them a few names, and one of the parents comes up and wishes to know what is the idea of Santa Claus using such language, and Santa Claus takes a punch at the parent, all of which is no doubt astonishing to the little kids who have an idea of Santa Claus as a very kindly old guy.

Well, finally we arrive in front of the place where Dancing Dan says Miss Muriel O'Neill and her grandmamma live, and it is nothing but a tenement house not far back of Madison Square Garden, and furthermore it is a walk-up, and at this time there are no lights burning in the joint except a gas jet in the main hall, and by the light of this jet we look at the names on the letter boxes, such as you always find in the hall of these joints, and we see that Miss Muriel O'Neill and her grandmamma live on the fifth floor.

This is the top floor, and personally I do not like the idea of walking up five flights of stairs, and I am willing to let Dancing Dan and Good Time Charley go, but Dancing Dan insists we must all go, and finally I agree with him because Charley is commencing to argue that the right way for us to do is to get on the roof and let Santa Claus go down a chimney, and is making so much noise I am afraid he will wake somebody up.

So up the stairs we climb and finally we come to a door on the top floor that has a little card in a slot that says O'Neill, so we know we reach our destination. Dancing Dan first tries the knob, and right away the door opens, and we are in a little two- or three-room flat, with not much furniture in it, and what furniture there is, is very poor. One single gas jet is burning near a bed in a room just off the one the door opens into, and by this light we see a very old doll is sleeping on the bed, so we judge this is nobody but Gammer O'Neill.

On her face is a large smile, as if she is dreaming of something very pleasant. On a chair at the head of the bed is hung a long black stocking, and it seems to be such a stocking as is often patched and mended, so I can see that what Miss Muriel O'Neill tells Dancing Dan about her grandmamma hanging up her stocking is really true, although up to this time I have my doubts.

Finally Dancing Dan unslings the sack on his back, and takes out his package, and unties this package, and all of a sudden out pops a raft of big diamond bracelets, and diamond rings, and diamond brooches, and diamond necklaces, and I do not know what else in the way of diamonds, and Dancing Dan and I begin stuffing these diamonds into the stocking and Good Time Charley pitches in and helps us.

There are enough diamonds to fill the stocking to the muzzle, and it is no small stocking, at that, and I judge that Gammer O'Neill has a pretty fair

[83]

set of bunting sticks when she is young. In fact, there are so many diamonds that we have enough left over to make a nice little pile on the chair
after we fill the stocking plumb up, leaving a nice diamond-studded vanity
case sticking out the top where we figure it will hit Gammer O'Neill's eye
when she wakes up.

And it is not until I get out in the fresh air again that all of a sudden I
remember seeing large headlines in the afternoon papers about a five-
hundred-G's stickup in the afternoon of one of the biggest diamond mer-
chants in Maiden Lane while he is sitting in his office, and I also recall once
hearing rumors that Dancing Dan is one of the best lone-hand git-'em-up
guys in the world.

Naturally, I commence to wonder if I am in the proper company when I
am with Dancing Dan, even if he is Santa Claus. So I leave him on the next
corner arguing with Good Time Charley about whether they ought to go
and find some more presents somewhere, and look for other stockings to
stuff, and I hasten on home and go to bed.

The next day I find I have such a noggin that I do not care to stir around,
and in fact I do not stir around much for a couple of weeks.

Then one night I drop around to Good Time Charley's little speakeasy,
and ask Charley what is doing.

"Well," Charley says, "many things are doing, and personally," he
says, "I'm greatly surprised I do not see you at Gammer O'Neill's wake.
You know Gammer O'Neill leaves this wicked old world a couple of days
after Christmas," Good Time Charley says, "and," he says, "Miss
Muriel O'Neill states that Doc Moggs claims it is at least a day after she is
entitled to go, but she is sustained," Charley says, "by great happiness in
finding her stocking filled with beautiful gifts on Christmas morning.

"According to Miss Muriel O'Neill," Charley says, "Gammer O'Neill
dies practically convinced that there is a Santa Claus, although of course,"
he says, "Miss Muriel O'Neill does not tell her the real owner of the gifts,
an all-right guy by the name of Shapiro leaves the gifts with her after Miss
Muriel O'Neill notifies him of finding of same.

"It seems," Charley says, "this Shapiro is a tender-hearted guy, who is
willing to help keep Gammer O'Neill with us a little longer when Doc
Moggs says leaving the gifts with her will do it.

"So," Charley says, "everything is quite all right, as the coppers cannot
figure anything except that maybe the rascal who takes the gifts from
Shapiro gets conscience-stricken, and leaves them the first place he can,
and Miss Muriel O'Neill receives a ten-G's reward for finding the gifts and
returning them. And," Charley says, "I hear Dancing Dan is in San Fran-
cisco and is figuring on reforming and becoming a dancing teacher, so he

can marry Miss Muriel O'Neill, and of course,'' he says, ''we all hope and trust she never learns any details of Dancing Dan's career.''

Well, it is Christmas Eve a year later that I run into a guy by the name of Shotgun Sam, who is mobbed up with Heine Schmitz in Harlem, and who is a very, very obnoxious character indeed.

''Well, well, well,'' Shotgun says, ''the last time I see you is another Christmas Eve like this, and you are coming out of Good Time Charley's joint, and,'' he says, ''you certainly have your pots on.''

''Well, Shotgun,'' I says, ''I am sorry you get such a wrong impression of me, but the truth is,'' I say, ''on the occasion you speak of, I am suffering from a dizzy feeling in my head.''

''It is all right with me,'' Shotgun says. ''I have a tip this guy Dancing Dan is in Good Time Charley's the night I see you, and Mockie Morgan, and Gunner Jack and me are casing the joint, because,'' he says, ''Heine Schmitz is all sored up at Dan over some doll, although of course,'' Shotgun says, ''it is all right now, as Heine has another doll.

''Anyway,'' he says, ''we never get to see Dancing Dan. We watch the joint from six-thirty in the evening until daylight Christmas morning, and nobody goes in all night but old Ooky the Santa Claus guy in his Santa Claus makeup, and,'' Shotgun says, ''nobody comes out except you and Good Time Charley and Ooky.

''Well,'' Shotgun says, ''it is a great break for Dancing Dan he never goes in or comes out of Good Time Charley's, at that, because,'' he says, ''we are waiting for him on the second-floor front of the building across the way with some nice little sawed-offs, and are under orders from Heine not to miss.''

''Well, Shotgun,'' I say, ''Merry Christmas.''

''Well, all right,'' Shotgun says, ''Merry Christmas.''

"It's here, again, Henri!"

Cambric Tea
by Marjorie Bowen

THE SITUATION was bizarre; the accurately trained mind of Bevis Holroyd was impressed foremost by this; that the opening of a door would turn it into tragedy.

"I am afraid I can't stay," he had said pleasantly, humouring a sick man; he was too young and had not been long enough completely successful to have a professional manner but a certain balanced tolerance just showed in his attitude to this prostrate creature.

"I've got a good many claims on my time," he added, "and I'm afraid it would be impossible. And it isn't the least necessary, you know. You're quite all right. I'll come back after Christmas if you really think it worth while."

The patient opened one eye; he was lying flat on his back in a deep, wide-fashioned bed hung with a thick dark, silk lined tapestry; the room was dark for there were thick curtains of the same material drawn half across the windows, rigidly excluding all save a moiety of the pallid winter light; to make his examination Dr. Holroyd had had to snap on the electric light that stood on the bedside table; he thought it a dreary unhealthy room, but had hardly found it worth while to say as much.

The patient opened one eye; the other lid remained fluttering feebly over an immobile orb.

He said in a voice both hoarse and feeble:

"But, doctor, I'm being poisoned."

Professional curiosity and interest masked by genial incredulity instantly quickened the doctor's attention.

"My dear sir," he smiled, "poisoned by this nasty bout of 'flu you mean, I suppose—"

"No," said the patient, faintly and wearily dropping both lids over his blank eyes, "by my wife."

"That's an ugly sort of fancy for you to get hold of," replied the doctor instantly. "Acute depression—we must see what we can do for you—"

The sick man opened both eyes now; he even slightly raised his head as he replied, not without dignity:

"I fetched you from London, Dr. Holroyd, that you might deal with my

[87]

case impartially—from the local man there is no hope of that, he is entirely impressed by my wife.''

Dr. Holroyd made a movement as if to protest but a trembling sign from the patient made him quickly subsist.

''Please let me speak. *She* will come in soon and I shall have no chance. I sent for you secretly, she knows nothing about that. I had heard you very well spoken of—as an authority on this sort of thing. You made a name over the Pluntre murder case as witness for the Crown.''

''I don't specialize in murder,'' said Dr. Holroyd, but his keen hand-some face was alight with interest. ''And I don't care much for this kind of case—Sir Harry.''

''But you've taken it on,'' murmured the sick man. ''You couldn't abandon me now.''

''I'll get you into a nursing home,'' said the doctor cheerfully, ''and there you'll dispel all these ideas.''

''And when the nursing home has cured me I'm to come back to my wife for her to begin again?''

Dr. Holroyd bent suddenly and sharply over the sombre bed. With his right hand he deftly turned on the electric lamp and tipped back the coral silk shade so that the bleached acid light fell full over the patient lying on his back on the big fat pillows.

''Look here,'' said the doctor, ''what you say is pretty serious.''

And the two men stared at each other, the patient examining his physician as acutely as his physician examined him.

Bevis Holroyd was still a young man with a look of peculiar energy and austere intelligence that heightened by contrast purely physical dark good looks that many men would have found sufficient passport to success; reso-lution, dignity and a certain masculine sweetness, serene and strong, dif-ferent from feminine sweetness, marked his demeanour which was further softened by a quick humour and a sensitive judgment.

The patient, on the other hand, was a man of well past middle age, light, flabby and obese with a flaccid, fallen look about his large face which was blurred and dimmed by the colours of ill health, being one pasty livid hue that threw into unpleasant relief the grey speckled red of his scant hair.

Altogether an unpleasing man, but of a certain fame and importance that had induced the rising young doctor to come at once when hastily sum-moned to Strangeways Manor House; a man of a fine, renowned family, a man of repute as a scholar, an essayist who had once been a politician who was rather above politics; a man whom Dr. Holroyd only knew vaguely by reputation, but who seemed to him symbolical of all that was staid, re-spectable and stolid.

And this man blinked up at him and whimpered:

"My wife is poisoning me."

Dr. Holroyd sat back and snapped off the electric light.

"What makes you think so?" he asked sharply.

"To tell you that," came the laboured voice of the sick man. "I should have to tell you my story."

"Well, if you want me to take this up—"

"I sent for you to do that, doctor."

"Well, how do you think you are being poisoned?"

"Arsenic, of course."

"Oh? And how administered?"

Again the patient looked up with one eye, seeming too fatigued to open the other.

"Cambric tea," he replied.

And Dr. Holroyd echoed:

"Cambric tea!" with a soft amazement and interest.

Cambric tea had been used as the medium for arsenic in the Pluntre case and the expression had become famous; it was Bevis Holroyd who had discovered the doses in the cambric tea and who had put his finger on this pale beverage as the means of murder.

"Very possibly," continued Sir Harry, "the Pluntre case made her think of it."

"For God's sake, don't," said Dr. Holroyd; for in that hideous affair the murderer had been a woman; and to see a woman on trial for her life, to see a woman sentenced to death, was not an experience he wished to repeat.

"Lady Strangeways," continued the sick man, "is much younger than I—I over persuaded her to marry me, she was at that time very much attracted by a man of her own age, but he was in a poor position and she was ambitious."

He paused, wiped his quivering lips on a silk handkerchief, and added faintly:

"Lately our marriage has been extremely unhappy. The man she preferred is now prosperous, successful and unmarried—she wishes to dispose of me that she may marry her first choice."

"Have you proof of any of this?"

"Yes. I know she buys arsenic. I know she reads books on poisons. I know she is eating her heart out for this other man."

"Forgive me, Sir Harry," replied the doctor, "but have you no near friend nor relation to whom you can confide your—suspicions?"

"No one," said the sick man impatiently. "I have lately come from the East and am out of touch with people. Besides I want a doctor, a doctor with skill in this sort of thing. I thought from the first of the Pluntre case and of you.''

Bevis Holroyd sat back quietly; it was then that he thought of the situation as bizarre; the queerness of the whole thing was vividly before him, like a twisted figure on a gem—a carving at once writhing and immobile.

''Perhaps,'' continued Sir Harry wearily, ''you are married, doctor?''

''No.'' Dr. Holroyd slightly smiled; his story was something like the sick man's story but taken from another angle; when he was very poor and unknown he had loved a girl who had preferred a wealthy man; she had gone out to India, ten years ago, and he had never seen her since; he remembered this, with sharp distinctness, and in the same breath he remembered that he still loved this girl; it was, after all, a common-place story.

Then his mind swung to the severe professional aspect of the case; he had thought that his patient, an unhealthy type of man, was struggling with a bad attack of influenza and the resultant depression and weakness, but then he had never thought, of course, of poison, nor looked nor tested for poison.

The man might be lunatic, he might be deceived, he might be speaking the truth; the fact that he was a mean, unpleasant beast ought not to weigh in the matter; Dr. Holroyd had some enjoyable Christmas holidays in prospect and now he was beginning to feel that he ought to give these up to stay and investigate this case; for he could readily see that it was one in which the local doctor would be quite useless.

''You must have a nurse,'' he said, rising.

But the sick man shook his head.

''I don't wish to expose my wife more than need be,'' he grumbled. ''Can't you manage the affair yourself?''

As this was the first hint of decent feeling he had shown, Bevis Holroyd forgave him his brusque rudeness.

''Well, I'll stay the night anyhow,'' he conceded.

And then the situation changed, with the opening of a door, from the bizarre to the tragic.

This door opened in the far end of the room and admitted a bloom of bluish winter light from some uncurtained, high windowed corridor; the chill impression was as if invisible snow had entered the shaded, dun, close apartment.

And against this background appeared a woman in a smoke coloured dress with some long lace about the shoulders and a high comb; she held a little tray carrying jugs and a glass of crystal in which the cold light splintered.

Dr. Holroyd stood in his usual attitude of attentive courtesy, and then, as the patient, feebly twisting his gross head from the fat pillow, said:

[90]

"My wife—doctor—" he recognized in Lady Strangeways the girl to whom he had once been engaged in marriage, the woman he still loved.

"This is Doctor Holroyd," added Sir Harry. "Is that cambric tea you have there?"

She inclined her head to the stranger by her husband's bed as if she had never seen him before, and he, taking his cue, and for many other reasons, was silent.

"Yes, this is your cambric tea," she said to her husband. "You like it just now, don't you? How do you find Sir Harry, Dr. Holroyd?"

There were two jugs on the tray; one of crystal half full of cold milk, and one of white porcelain full of hot water; Lady Strangeways proceeded to mix these fluids in equal proportions and gave the resultant drink to her husband, helping him first to sit up in bed.

"I think that Sir Harry has a nasty turn of influenza," answered the doctor mechanically. "He wants me to stay. I've promised till the morning, anyhow."

"That will be a pleasure and a relief," said Lady Strangeways gravely. "My husband has been ill some time and seems so much worse than he need—for influenza."

The patient, feebly sipping his cambric tea, grinned queerly at the doctor.

"So much worse—you see, doctor!" he muttered.

"It is good of you to stay," continued Lady Strangeways equally. "I will see about your room, you must be as comfortable as possible."

She left as she had come, a shadow-coloured figure retreating to a chill light.

The sick man held up his glass as if he gave a toast.

"You see! Cambric tea!"

And Bevis Holroyd was thinking: does she not want to know me? Does he know what we once were to each other? How comes she to be married to this man—her husband's name was Custiss—and the horror of the situation shook the calm that was his both from character and training; he went to the window and looked out on the bleached park; light, slow snow was falling, a dreary dance over the frozen grass and before the grey corpses that paled, one behind the other, to the distance shrouded in colourless mist.

The thin voice of Harry Strangeways recalled him to the bed.

"Would you like to take a look at this, doctor?" He held out the half drunk glass of milk and water.

"I've no means of making a test here," said Dr. Holroyd, troubled. "I brought a few things, nothing like that."

"You are not so far from Harley Street," said Sir Harry. "My car can

[91]

fetch everything you want by this afternoon—or perhaps you would like to go yourself?''

''Yes,'' replied Bevis Holroyd sternly. ''I would rather go myself.''

His trained mind had been rapidly covering the main aspects of his problem and he had instantly seen that it was better for Lady Strangeways to have this case in his hands. He was sure there was some hideous, fantastic hallucination on the part of Sir Harry, but it was better for Lady Strangeways to leave the matter in the hands of one who was friendly towards her. He rapidly found and washed a medicine bottle from among the sick room paraphernalia and poured it full of the cambric tea, casting away the remainder.

''Why did you drink any?'' he asked sharply.

''I don't want her to think that I guess,'' whispered Sir Harry. ''Do you know, doctor, I have a lot of her love letters—written by—''

Dr. Holroyd cut him short.

''I couldn't listen to this sort of thing behind Lady Strangeways's back,'' he said quickly. ''That is between you and her. My job is to get you well. I'll try and do that.''

And he considered, with a faint disgust, how repulsive this man looked sitting up with pendant jowl and drooping cheeks and discoloured, pouchy eyes sunk in pads of unhealthy flesh and above the spiky crown of Judas-coloured hair.

Perhaps a woman, chained to this man, living with him, blocked and thwarted by him, might be wrought upon to—

Dr. Holroyd shuddered inwardly and refused to continue his reflection.

As he was leaving the gaunt sombre house about which there was something definitely blank and unfriendly, a shrine in which the sacred flames had flickered out so long ago that the lamps were blank and cold, he met Lady Strangeways.

She was in the wide entrance hall standing by the wood fire that but faintly dispersed the gloom of the winter morning and left untouched the shadows in the rafters of the open roof.

Now he would not, whether she wished or no, deny her; he stopped before her, blocking out her poor remnant of light.

''Mollie,'' he said gently, ''I don't quite understand—you married a man named Custiss in India.''

''Yes. Harry had to take this name when he inherited this place. We've been home three years from the East, but lived so quietly here that I don't suppose anyone has heard of us.''

She stood between him and the firelight, a shadow among the shadows; she was much changed; in her thinness and pallor, in her restless eyes and nervous mouth he could read signs of discontent, even of unhappiness.

"I never heard of you," said Dr. Holroyd truthfully. "I didn't want to. I liked to keep my dreams."

Her hair was yet the lovely cedar wood hue, silver, soft and gracious; her figure had those fluid lines of grace that he believed he had never seen equalled.

"Tell me," she added abruptly, "what is the matter with my husband? He has been ailing like this for a year or so."

With a horrid lurch of his heart that was usually so steady, Dr. Holroyd remembered the bottle of milk and water in his pocket.

"Why do you give him that cambric tea?" he counter questioned.

"He will have it—he insists that I make it for him—"

"Mollie," said Dr. Holroyd quickly, "you decided against me, ten years ago, but that is no reason why we should not be friends now—tell me, frankly, are you happy with this man?"

"You have seen him," she replied slowly. "He seemed different ten years ago. I honestly was attracted by his scholarship and his learning as well as—other things."

Bevis Holroyd needed to ask no more; she was wretched, imprisoned in a mistake as a fly in amber; and those love letters? Was there another man?

As he stood silent, with a dark reflective look on her weary brooding face, she spoke again:

"You are staying?"

"Oh yes," he said, he was staying, there was nothing else for him to do.

"It is Christmas week," she reminded him wistfully. "It will be very dull, perhaps painful, for you."

"I think I ought to stay."

Sir Harry's car was announced; Bevis Holroyd, gliding over frozen roads to London, was absorbed with this sudden problem that, like a mountain out of a plain, had suddenly risen to confront him out of his level life.

The sight of Mollie (he could not think of her by that sick man's name) had roused in him tender memories and poignant emotions and the position in which he found her and his own juxtaposition to her and her husband had the same devastating effect on him as a mine sprung beneath the feet of an unwary traveller.

London was deep in the whirl of a snow storm and the light that penetrated over the grey roof tops to the ugly slip of a laboratory at the back of his consulting rooms was chill and forbidding.

Bevis Holroyd put the bottle of milk on a marble slab and sat back in the easy chair watching that dreary chase of snow flakes across the dingy London pane.

He was thinking of past springs, of violets long dead, of roses long since dust, of hours that had slipped away like lengths of golden silk rolled up, of

[93]

the long ago when he had loved Mollie and Mollie had seemed to love him; then he thought of that man in the big bed who had said:

"My wife is poisoning me."

Late that afternoon Dr. Holroyd, with his suit case and a professional bag, returned to Strangeways Manor House in Sir Harry's car; the bottle of cambric tea had gone to a friend, a noted analyst; somehow Doctor Holroyd had not felt able to do this task himself; he was very fortunate, he felt, in securing this old solitary and his promise to do the work before Christmas.

As he arrived at Strangeways Manor House which stood isolated and well away from a public high road where a lonely spur of the weald of Kent drove into the Sussex marshes, it was in a blizzard of snow that effaced the landscape and gave the murky outlines of the house an air of unreality, and Bevis Holroyd experienced that sensation he had so often heard of and read about, but which so far his cool mind had dismissed as a fiction.

He did really feel as if he was in an evil dream; as the snow changed the values of the scene, altering distances and shapes, so this meeting with Mollie, under these circumstances, had suddenly changed the life of Bevis Holroyd.

He had so resolutely and so definitely put this woman out of his life and mind, deliberately refusing to make enquiries about her, letting all knowledge of her cease with the letter in which she had written from India and announced her marriage.

And now, after ten years, she had crossed his path in this ghastly manner, as a woman her husband accused of attempted murder.

The sick man's words of a former lover disturbed him profoundly; was it himself who was referred to? Yet the love letters must be from another man for he had not corresponded with Mollie since her marriage, not for ten years.

He had never felt any bitterness towards Mollie for her desertion of a poor, struggling doctor, and he had always believed in the integral nobility of her character under the timidity of conventionality; but the fact remained that she had played him false—what if that *had* been "the little rift within the lute" that had now indeed silenced the music!

With a sense of bitter depression he entered the gloomy old house; how different was this from the pleasant ordinary Christmas he had been rather looking forward to, the jolly homely atmosphere of good fare, dancing, and friends!

When he had telephoned to these friends excusing himself his regret had been genuine and the cordial "bad luck!" had had a poignant echo in his own heart; bad luck indeed, bad luck—

She was waiting for him in the hall that a pale young man was decorating

[94]

with boughs of prickly stiff holly that stuck stiffly behind the dark heavy pictures.

He was introduced as the secretary and said gloomily:

"Sir Harry wished everything to go on as usual, though I am afraid he is very ill indeed."

Yes, the patient had been seized by another violent attack of illness during Dr. Holroyd's absence; the young man went at once upstairs and found Sir Harry in a deep sleep and a rather nervous local doctor in attendance.

An exhaustive discussion of the case with this doctor threw no light on anything, and Dr. Holroyd, leaving in charge an extremely sensible looking housekeeper who was Sir Harry's preferred nurse, returned, worried and irritated, to the hall where Lady Strangeways now sat alone before the big fire.

She offered him a belated but fresh cup of tea.

"Why did you come?" she asked as if she roused herself from deep reverie.

"Why? Because your husband sent for me."

"He says you offered to come; he has told everyone in the house that."

"But I never heard of the man before to-day."

"You had heard of me. He seems to think that you came here to help me."

"He cannot be saying that," returned Dr. Holroyd sternly, and he wondered desperately if Mollie was lying, if she had invented this to drive him out of the house.

"Do you want me here?" he demanded.

"I don't know," she replied dully and confirmed his suspicions; probably there was another man and she wished him out of the way; but he could not go, out of pity towards her he could not go.

"Does he know we once knew each other?" he asked.

"No," she replied faintly, "therefore it seems such a curious chance that he should have sent for you, of all men!"

"It would have been more curious," he responded grimly, "if I had heard that you were here with a sick husband and had thrust myself in to doctor him! Strangeways must be crazy to spread such a tale and if he doesn't know we are old friends it becomes nonsense!"

"I often think that Harry is crazy," said Lady Strangeways wearily; she took a rose silk lined work basket, full of pretty trifles, on her knee, and began winding a skein of rose coloured silk; she looked so frail, so sad, so lifeless that the heart of Bevis Holroyd was torn with bitter pity.

"Now I am here I want to help you," he said earnestly. "I am staying for that, to help you—"

[95]

She looked up at him with a wistful appeal in her fair face.

"I'm worried," she said simply. "I've lost some letters I valued very much—I think they have been stolen."

Dr. Holroyd drew back; the love letters; the letters the husband had found, that were causing all his ugly suspicions.

"My poor Mollie!" he exclaimed impulsively. "What sort of a coil have you got yourself into!"

As if this note of pity was unendurable, she rose impulsively, scattering the contents of her work basket, dropping the skein of silk, and hastened away down the dark hall.

Bevis Holroyd stooped mechanically to pick up the hurled objects and saw among them a small white packet, folded, but opened at one end; this packet seemed to have fallen out of a needle case of gold silk.

Bevis Holroyd had pounced on it and thrust it in his pocket just as the pale secretary returned with his thin arms most incongruously full of mistletoe.

"This will be a dreary Christmas for you, Dr. Holroyd," he said with the air of one who forces himself to make conversation. "No doubt you had some pleasant plans in view—we are all so pleased that Lady Strangeways had a friend to come and look after Sir Harry during the holidays."

"Who told you I was a friend?" asked Dr. Holroyd brusquely. "I certainly knew Lady Strangeways before she was married—"

The pale young man cut in crisply:

"Oh, Lady Strangeways told me so herself."

Bevis Holroyd was bewildered; why did she tell the secretary what she did not tell her husband?—both the indiscretion and the reserve seemed equally foolish.

Languidly hanging up his sprays and bunches of mistletoe the pallid young man, whose name was Garth Deane, continued his aimless remarks.

"This is really not a very cheerful house, Dr. Holroyd—I'm interested in Sir Harry's oriental work or I should not remain. Such a very unhappy marriage! I often think," he added regardless of Bevis Holroyd's darkling glance, "that it would be very unpleasant indeed for Lady Strangeways if anything happened to Sir Harry."

"Whatever do you mean, sir?" asked the doctor angrily.

The secretary was not at all discomposed.

"Well, one lives in the house, one has nothing much to do—and one notices."

Perhaps, thought the young man in anguish, the sick husband had been talking to this creature, perhaps the creature *had* really noticed something.

"I'll go up to my patient," said Bevis Holroyd briefly, not daring to

[96]

anger one who might be an important witness in this mystery that was at present so unfathomable.

Mr. Deane gave a sickly grin over the lovely pale leaves and berries he was holding.

"I'm afraid he is very bad, doctor."

As Bevis Holroyd left the room he passed Lady Strangeways; she looked blurred, like a pastel drawing that has been shaken; the fingers she kept locked on her bosom; she had flung a silver fur over her shoulders that accentuated her ethereal look of blonde, pearl and amber hues.

"I've come back for my work basket," she said. "Will you go up to my husband? He is ill again—"

"Have you been giving him anything?" asked Dr. Holroyd as quietly as he could.

"Only some cambric tea, he insisted on that."

"Don't give him anything—leave him alone. He is in my charge now, do you understand?"

She gazed up at him with frightened eyes that had been newly washed by tears.

"Why are you so unkind to me?" she quivered.

She looked so ready to fall that he could not resist the temptation to put his hand protectingly on her arm, so that, as she stood in the low doorway leading to the stairs, he appeared to be supporting her drooping weight.

"Have I not said that I am here to help you, Mollie?"

The secretary slipped out from the shadows behind them, his arms still full of winter evergreens.

"There is too much foliage," he smiled, and the smile told that he had seen and heard.

Bevis Holroyd went angrily upstairs; he felt as if an invisible net was being dragged closely round him, something which, from being a cobweb, would become a cable; this air of mystery, of horror in the big house, this sly secretary, these watchful-looking servants, the nervous village doctor ready to credit anything, the lovely agitated woman who was the woman he had long so romantically loved, and the sinister sick man with his diabolic accusations, a man Bevis Holroyd had, from the first moment, hated—all these people in these dark surroundings affected the young man with a miasma of apprehension, gloom and dread.

After a few hours of it he was nearer to losing his nerve than he had ever been; that must be because of Mollie, poor darling Mollie caught into all this nightmare.

And outside the bells were ringing across the snow, practising for Christ-

[97]

mas Day; the sound of them was to Bevis Holroyd what the sounds of the real world are when breaking into a sleeper's thick dreams.

The patient sat up in bed, fondling the glass of odious cambric tea.

"Why do you take the stuff?" demanded the doctor angrily.

"She won't let me off, she thrusts it on me," whispered Sir Harry.

Bevis Holroyd noticed, not for the first time since he had come into the fell atmosphere of this dark house that enclosed the piteous figure of the woman he loved, that husband and wife were telling different tales; on one side lay a burden of careful lying.

"Did she—" continued the sick man, "speak to you of her lost letters?"

The young doctor looked at him sternly.

"Why should Lady Strangeways make a confidante of me?" he asked. "Do you know that she was a friend of mine ten years ago before she married you?"

"Was she? How curious! But you met like strangers."

"The light in this room is very dim—"

"Well, never mind about that, whether you knew her or not—" Sir Harry gasped out in a sudden snarl. "The woman is a murderess, and you'll have to bear witness to it—I've got her letters, here under my pillow, and Garth Deane is watching her—"

"Ah, a spy! I'll have no part in this, Sir Harry. You'll call another doctor—"

"No, it's your case, you'll make the best of it—My God, I'm dying, I think—"

He fell back in such a convulsion of pain that Bevis Holroyd forgot everything in administering to him. The rest of that day and all that night the young doctor was shut up with his patient, assisted by the secretary and the housekeeper.

And when, in the pallid light of Christmas Eve morning, he went downstairs to find Lady Strangeways, he knew that the sick man was suffering from arsenic poison, that the packet taken from Mollie's work box was arsenic, and it was only an added horror when he was called to the telephone to learn that a stiff dose of the poison had been found in the specimen of cambric tea.

He believed that he could save the husband and thereby the wife also, but he did not think he could close the sick man's mouth; the deadly hatred of Sir Harry was leading up to an accusation of attempted murder; of that he was sure, and there was the man Deane to back him up.

He sent for Mollie, who had not been near her husband all night, and when she came, pale, distracted, huddled in her white fur, he said grimly:

"Look here, Mollie, I promised that I'd help you and I mean to, though

[98]

it isn't going to be as easy as I thought, but you have got to be frank with me.''

"But I have nothing to conceal—"

"The name of the other man—"

"The other man?"

"The man who wrote those letters your husband has under his pillow."

"Oh, Harry has them!" she cried in pain. "That man Deane stole them then! Bevis, they are your letters of the olden days that I have always cherished."

"*My* letters!"

"Yes, do you think that there has ever been anyone else?"

"But he says—Mollie, there is a trap or trick here, some one is lying furiously. Your husband is being poisoned."

"Poisoned?"

"By arsenic given in that cambric tea. And he knows it. And he accuses you."

She stared at him in blank incredulity, then she slipped forward in her chair and clutched the big arm.

"Oh, God," she muttered in panic terror. "He always swore that he'd be revenged on me—because he knew that I never cared for him—"

But Bevis Holroyd recoiled; he did not dare listen, he did not dare believe.

"I've warned you," he said, "for the sake of the old days, Mollie—"

A light step behind them and they were aware of the secretary creeping out of the embrowning shadows.

"A cold Christmas," he said, rubbing his hands together. "A really cold, seasonable Christmas. We are almost snowed in—and Sir Harry would like to see you, Dr. Holroyd."

"I have only just left him—"

Bevis Holroyd looked at the despairing figure of the woman, crouching in her chair; he was distracted, overwrought, near to losing his nerve.

"He wants particularly to see you," cringed the secretary.

Mollie looked back at Bevis Holroyd, her lips moved twice in vain before she could say: "Go to him."

The doctor went slowly upstairs and the secretary followed.

Sir Harry was now flat on his back, staring at the dark tapestry curtains of his bed.

"I'm dying," he announced as the doctor bent over him.

"Nonsense. I am not going to allow you to die."

"You won't be able to help yourself. I've brought you here to see me die."

"What do you mean?"

"I've a surprise for you too, a Christmas present. These letters now, these love letters of my wife's—what name do you think is on them?"

"Your mind is giving way, Sir Harry."

"Not at all—come nearer, Deane—the name is Bevis Holroyd."

"Then they are letters ten years old. Letters written before your wife met you."

The sick man grinned with infinite malice.

"Maybe. But there are no dates on them and the envelopes are all destroyed. And I, as a dying man, shall swear to their recent date—I, as a foully murdered man."

"You are wandering in your mind," said Bevis Holroyd quietly. "I refuse to listen to you any further."

"You shall listen to me. I brought you here to listen to me. I've got you. Here's my will, Deane's got that, in which I denounced you both, there are your letters, every one thinks that *she* put you in charge of the case, every one knows that you know all about arsenic in cambric tea through the Pluntre case, and every one will know that I died of arsenic poisoning."

The doctor allowed him to talk himself out; indeed it would have been difficult to check the ferocity of his malicious energy.

The plot was ingenious, the invention of a slightly insane, jealous recluse who hated his wife and hated the man she had never ceased to love; Bevis Holroyd could see the nets very skilfully drawn round him; but the main issue of the mystery remained untouched; who *was* administering the arsenic?

The young man glanced across the sombre bed to the dark figure of the secretary.

"What is your place in all this farrago, Mr. Deane?" he asked sternly.

"I'm Sir Harry's friend," answered the other stubbornly, "and I'll bring witness any time against Lady Strangeways. I've tried to circumvent her—"

"Stop," cried the doctor. "You think that Lady Strangeways is poisoning her husband and that I am her accomplice?"

The sick man, who had been looking with bitter malice from one to another, whispered hoarsely:

"That is what you think, isn't it, Deane?"

"I'll say what I think at the proper time," said the secretary obstinately.

"No doubt you are being well paid for your share in this."

"I've remembered his services in my will," smiled Sir Harry grimly. "You can adjust your differences then, Dr. Holroyd, when I'm dead, *poisoned, murdered*. It will be a pretty story, a nice scandal, you and she in the house together, the letters, the cambric tea!"

An expression of ferocity dominated him, then he made an effort to dominate this and to speak in his usual suave stilted manner.

"You must admit that we shall all have a very Happy Christmas, doctor."

Bevis Holroyd was looking at the secretary, who stood at the other side of the bed, cringing, yet somehow in the attitude of a man ready to pounce; Dr. Holroyd wondered if this was the murderer.

"Why," he asked quietly to gain time, "did you hatch this plan to ruin a man you had never seen before?"

"I always hated you," replied the sick man faintly. "Mollie never forgot you, you see, and she never allowed *me* to forget that she never forgot you. And then I found those letters she had cherished."

"You are a very wicked man," said the doctor dryly, "but it will all come to nothing, for I am not going to allow you to die."

"You won't be able to help yourself," replied the patient. "I'm dying, I tell you. I shall die on Christmas Day."

He turned his head towards the secretary and added:

"Send my wife up to me."

"No," interrupted Dr. Holroyd strongly. "She shall not come near you again."

Sir Harry Strangeways ignored this.

"Send her up," he repeated.

"I will bring her, sir."

The secretary left, with a movement suggestive of flight, and Bevis Holroyd stood rigid, waiting, thinking, looking at the ugly man who now had closed his eyes and lay as if insensible. He was certainly very ill, dying perhaps, and he certainly had been poisoned by arsenic given in cambric tea, and, as certainly, a terrible scandal and a terrible danger would threaten with his death; the letters were *not* dated, the marriage was notoriously unhappy, and he, Bevis Holroyd, was associated in every one's mind with a murder case in which this form of poison, given in this manner, had been used.

Drops of moisture stood out on the doctor's forehead; sure that if he could clear himself it would be very difficult for Mollie to do so; how could even he himself in his soul swear to her innocence!

Of course he must get the woman out of the house at once, he must have another doctor from town, nurses—but could this be done in time; if the patient died on his hands would he not be only bringing witnesses to his own discomfiture? And the right people, his own friends, were difficult to get hold of now, at Christmas time.

He longed to go in search of Mollie—she must at least be got away, but how, without a scandal, without a suspicion?

[101]

He longed to have the matter out with this odious secretary, but he dared not leave his patient.

Lady Strangeways returned with Garth Deane and seated herself, mute, shadowy, with eyes full of panic, on the other side of the sombre bed.

"Is he going to live?" she presently whispered as she watched Bevis Holroyd ministering to her unconscious husband.

"We must see that he does," he answered grimly.

All through that Christmas Eve and the bitter night to the stark dawn when the church bells broke ghastly on their wan senses did they tend the sick man who only came to his senses to grin at them in malice.

Once Bevis Holroyd asked the pallid woman:

"What was that white packet you had in your work box?"

And she replied:

"I never had such a packet."

And he:

"I must believe you."

But he did not send for the other doctors and nurses, he did not dare.

The Christmas bells seemed to rouse the sick man from his deadly swoon.

"You can't save me," he said with indescribable malice. "I shall die and put you both in the dock—"

Mollie Strangeways sank down beside the bed and began to cry, and Garth Deane, who by his master's express desire had been in and out of the room all night, stopped and looked at her with a peculiar expression. Sir Harry looked at her also.

"Don't cry," he gasped, "this is Christmas Day. We ought all to be happy—bring me my cambric tea—do you hear?"

She rose mechanically and left the room to take in the tray with the fresh milk and water that the housekeeper had placed softly on the table outside the door; for all through the nightmare vigil, the sick man's cry had been for "cambric tea."

As he sat up in bed feebly sipping the vapid and odious drink the tortured woman's nerves slipped her control.

"I can't endure those bells, I wish they would stop those bells!" she cried and ran out of the room.

Bevis Holroyd instantly followed her; and now as suddenly as it had sprung on him, the fell little drama disappeared, fled like a poison cloud out of the compass of his life.

Mollie was leaning against the closed window, her sick head resting against the mullions; through the casement showed, surprisingly, sunlight on the pure snow and blue sky behind the withered trees.

"Listen, Mollie," said the young man resolutely." I'm sure he'll live if you are careful—you mustn't lose heart—"

[102]

The sick room door opened and the secretary slipped out.

He nervously approached the two in the window place.

"I can't stand this any longer," he said through dry lips. "I didn't know he meant to go so far, he is doing it himself, you know; he's got the stuff hidden in his bed, he puts it into the cambric tea, he's willing to die to spite you two, but I can't stand it any longer."

"You've been abetting this!" cried the doctor.

"Not abetting," smiled the secretary wanly. "Just standing by. I found out by chance—and then he forced me to be silent—I had his will, you know, and I've destroyed it."

With this the strange creature glided downstairs.

The doctor sprang at once to Sir Harry's room; the sick man was sitting up in the sombre bed and with a last effort was scattering a grain of powder into the glass of cambric tea.

With a look of baffled horror he saw Bevis Holroyd but the drink had already slipped down his throat; he fell back and hid his face, baulked at the last of his diabolic revenge.

When Bevis Holroyd left the dead man's chamber he found Mollie still leaning in the window; she was free, the sun was shining, it was Christmas Day.

★

Death on Christmas Eve
by Stanley Ellin

A S A CHILD I had been vastly impressed by the Boerum house. It was fairly new then, and glossy; a gigantic pile of Victorian rickrack, fretwork, and stained glass, flung together in such chaotic profusion that it was hard to encompass in one glance. Standing before it this early Christmas Eve, however, I could find no echo of that youthful impression. The gloss was long since gone; woodwork, glass, metal, all were merged to a dreary gray, and the shades behind the windows were drawn completely so that the house seemed to present a dozen blindly staring eyes to the passerby.

When I rapped my stick sharply on the door, Celia opened it.

"There is a doorbell right at hand," she said. She was still wearing the long outmoded and badly wrinkled black dress she must have dragged from her mother's trunk, and she looked, more than ever, the image of old Katrin in her later years: the scrawny body, the tightly compressed lips, the colorless hair drawn back hard enough to pull every wrinkle out of her forehead. She reminded me of a steel trap ready to snap down on anyone who touched her incautiously.

I said, "I am aware that the doorbell has been disconnected, Celia," and walked past her into the hallway. Without turning my head, I knew that she was glaring at me; then she sniffed once, hard and dry, and flung the door shut. Instantly we were in a murky dimness that made the smell of dry rot about me stick in my throat. I fumbled for the wall switch, but Celia said sharply, "No! This is not the time for lights."

I turned to the white blur of her face, which was all I could see of her. "Celia," I said, "spare me the dramatics."

"There has been a death in this house. You know that."

"I have good reason to," I said, "but your performance now does not impress me."

"She was my own brother's wife. She was very dear to me."

I took a step toward her in the murk and rested my stick on her shoulder. "Celia," I said, "as your family's lawyer, let me give you a word of advice. The inquest is over and done with, and you've been cleared. But nobody believed a word of your precious sentiments then, and nobody ever will. Keep that in mind, Celia."

[105]

She jerked away so sharply that the stick almost fell from my hand. "Is that what you have come to tell me?" she said.

I said, "I came because I knew your brother would want to see me today. And if you don't mind my saying so, I suggest that you keep to yourself while I talk to him. I don't want any scenes."

"Then keep away from him yourself!" she cried. "He was at the inquest. He saw them clear my name. In a little while he will forget the evil he thinks of me. Keep away from him so that he can forget."

She was at her infuriating worst, and to break the spell I started up the dark stairway, one hand warily on the balustrade. But I heard her follow eagerly behind, and in some eerie way it seemed as if she were not addressing me, but answering the groaning of the stairs under our feet.

"When he comes to me," she said, "I will forgive him. At first I was not sure, but now I know. I prayed for guidance, and I was told that life is too short for hatred. So when he comes to me I will forgive him."

I reached the head of the stairway and almost went sprawling. I swore in annoyance as I righted myself. "If you're not going to use lights, Celia, you should, at least, keep the way clear. Why don't you get that stuff out of here?"

"Ah," she said, "those are all poor Jessie's belongings. It hurts Charlie to see anything of hers, I knew this would be the best thing to do—to throw all her things out."

Then a note of alarm entered her voice. "But you won't tell Charlie, will you? You won't tell him?" she said, and kept repeating it on a higher and higher note as I moved away from her, so that when I entered Charlie's room and closed the door behind me it almost sounded as if I had left a bat chittering behind me.

As in the rest of the house, the shades in Charlie's room were drawn to their full length. But a single bulb in the chandelier overhead dazzled me momentarily, and I had to look twice before I saw Charlie sprawled out on his bed with an arm flung over his eyes. Then he slowly came to his feet and peered at me.

"Well," he said at last, nodding toward the door, "she didn't give you any light to come up, did she?"

"No," I said, "but I know the way."

"She's like a mole," he said. "Gets around better in the dark than I do in the light. She'd rather have it that way too. Otherwise she might look into a mirror and be scared of what she sees there."

"Yes," I said, "she seems to be taking it very hard."

He laughed short and sharp as a sea-lion barking. "That's because she's still got the fear in her. All you get out of her now is how she loved Jessie,

[106]

and how sorry she is. Maybe she figures if she says it enough, people might get to believe it. But give her a little time and she'll be the same old Celia again.''

I dropped my hat and stick on the bed and laid my overcoat beside them. Then I drew out a cigar and waited until he fumbled for a match and helped me to a light. His hand shook so violently that he had hard going for a moment and muttered angrily at himself. Then I slowly exhaled a cloud of smoke toward the ceiling, and waited.

Charlie was Celia's junior by five years, but seeing him then it struck me that he looked a dozen years older. His hair was the same pale blond, almost colorless so that it was hard to tell if it was graying or not. But his cheeks wore a fine, silvery stubble, and there were huge blue-black pouches under his eyes. And where Celia was braced against a rigid and uncompromising backbone, Charlie sagged, standing or sitting, as if he were on the verge of falling forward. He stared at me and tugged uncertainly at the limp mustache that dropped past the corners of his mouth.

"You know what I wanted to see you about, don't you?" he said.

"I can imagine," I said, "but I'd rather have you tell me."

"I'll put it to you straight," he said. "It's Celia. I want to see her get what's coming to her. Not jail. I want the law to take her and kill her, and I want to be there to watch it."

A large ash dropped to the floor, and I ground it carefully into the rug with my foot. I said, "You were at the inquest, Charlie; you saw what happened. Celia's cleared, and unless additional evidence can be produced, she stays cleared."

"Evidence! My God, what more evidence does anyone need! They were arguing hammer and tongs at the top of the stairs. Celia just grabbed Jessie and threw her down to the bottom and killed her. That's murder, isn't it? Just the same as if she used a gun or poison or whatever she would have used if the stairs weren't handy?"

I sat down wearily in the old leather-bound armchair there and studied the new ash that was forming on my cigar. "Let me show it to you from the legal angle," I said, and the monotone of my voice must have made it sound like a well-memorized formula. "First, there were no witnesses."

"I heard Jessie scream and I heard her fall," he said doggedly, "and when I ran out and found her there, I heard Celia slam her door shut right then. She pushed Jessie and then scuttered like a rat to be out of the way."

"But you didn't *see* anything. And since Celia claims that she wasn't on the scene, there were no witnesses. In other words, Celia's story cancels out your story, and since you weren't an eyewitness you can't very well make a murder out of what might have been an accident."

[107]

He slowly shook his head.

"You don't believe that," he said. "You don't really believe that. Because if you do, you can get out now and never come near me again."

"It doesn't matter what I believe; I'm showing you the legal aspects of the case. What about motivation? What did Celia have to gain from Jessie's death? Certainly there's no money or property involved; she's as financially independent as you are."

Charlie sat down on the edge of his bed and leaned toward me with his hands resting on his knees. "No," he whispered, "there's no money or property in it."

I spread my arms helplessly. "You see?"

"But you know what it is," he said. "It's me. First, it was the old lady with her heart trouble any time I tried to call my soul my own. Then when she died and I thought I was free, it was Celia. From the time I got up in the morning until I went to bed at night, it was Celia every step of the way. She never had a husband or a baby—but she had me!"

I said quietly, "She's your sister, Charlie. She loves you," and he laughed that same unpleasant, short laugh.

"She loves me like ivy loves a tree. When I think back now, I still can't see how she did it, but she would just look at me a certain way and all the strength would go out of me. And it was like that until I met Jessie . . . I remember the day I brought Jessie home, and told Celia we were married. She swallowed it, but that look was in her eyes the same as it must have been when she pushed Jessie down those stairs."

I said, "But you admitted at the inquest that you never saw her threaten Jessie or do anything to hurt her."

"Of course I never *saw!* But when Jessie would go around sick to her heart every day and not say a word, or cry in bed every night and not tell me why, I knew damn well what was going on. You know what Jessie was like. She wasn't so smart or pretty, but she was good-hearted as the day was long, and she was crazy about me. And when she started losing all that sparkle in her after only a month, I knew why. I talked to her and I talked to Celia, and both of them just shook their heads. All I could do was go around in circles, but when it happened, when I saw Jessie lying there, it didn't surprise me. Maybe that sounds queer, but it didn't surprise me at all."

"I don't think it surprised anyone who knows Celia," I said, "but you can't make a case out of that."

He beat his fist against his knee and rocked from side to side. "What can I do?" he said. "That's what I need you for—to tell me what to do. All my life I never got around to doing anything because of her. That's what she's banking on now—that I won't do anything, and that she'll get away with it.

[108]

Then after a while, things'll settle down, and we'll be right back where we started from.''

I said, "Charlie, you're getting yourself all worked up to no end."

He stood up and stared at the door, and then at me. "But I can do something," he whispered. "Do you know what?"

He waited with bright expectancy of one who has asked a clever riddle that he knows will stump the listener. I stood up facing him, and shook my head slowly. "No," I said. "Whatever you're thinking, put it out of your mind."

"Don't mix me up," he said. "You know you can get away with murder if you're as smart as Celia. Don't you think I'm as smart as Celia?"

I caught his shoulders tightly. "For God's sake, Charlie," I said, "don't start talking like that."

He pulled out of my hands and went staggering back against the wall. His eyes were bright, and his teeth showed behind his drawn lips. "What should I do?" he cried. "Forget everything now that Jessie is dead and buried? Sit here until Celia gets tired of being afraid of me and kills me too?"

My years and girth had betrayed me in that little tussle with him, and I found myself short of dignity and breath. "I'll tell you one thing," I said. "You haven't been out of this house since the inquest. It's about time you got out, if only to walk the streets and look around you."

"And have everybody laugh at me as I go!"

"Try it," I said, "and see. Al Sharp said that some of your friends would be at his bar and grill tonight, and he'd like to see you there. That's my advice—for whatever it's worth."

"It's not worth anything," said Celia. The door had been opened, and she stood there rigid, her eyes narrowed against the light in the room. Charlie turned toward her, the muscles of his jaw knotting and unknotting.

"Celia," he said, "I told you never to come into this room!"

Her face remained impassive. "I'm not *in* it. I came to tell you that your dinner is ready."

He took a menacing step toward her. "Did you have your ear at that door long enough to hear everything I said? Or should I repeat it for you?"

"I heard an ungodly and filthy thing," she said quietly, "an invitation to drink and roister while this house is in mourning. I think I have every right to object to that."

He looked at her incredulously and had to struggle for words. "Celia," he said, "tell me you don't mean that! Only the blackest hypocrite alive or someone insane could say what you've just said, and mean it."

That struck a spark in her. "Insane!" she cried. "*You* dare use that word? Locked in your room, talking to yourself, thinking heaven knows

[109]

what!'' She turned to me suddenly. "You've talked to him. You ought to know. Is it possible that—''

"He is as sane as you, Celia," I said heavily.

"Then he should know that one doesn't drink in saloons at a time like this. How could you ask him to do it?"

She flung the question at me with such an air of malicious triumph that I completely forgot myself. "If you weren't preparing to throw out Jessie's belongings, Celia, I would take that question seriously!"

It was a reckless thing to say, and I had instant cause to regret it. Before I could move, Charlie was past me and had Celia's arms pinned in a paralyzing grip.

"Did you dare go into her room?" he raged, shaking her savagely. "Tell me!" And then, getting an immediate answer from the panic in her face, he dropped her arms as if they were red hot, and stood there sagging with his head bowed.

Celia reached out a placating hand toward him. "Charlie," she whimpered, "don't you see? Having her things around bothers you. I only wanted to help you."

"Where are her things?"

"By the stairs, Charlie. Everything is there."

He started down the hallway, and with the sound of his uncertain footsteps moving away I could feel my heartbeat slowing down to its normal tempo. Celia turned to look at me, and there was such a raging hatred in her face that I knew only a desperate need to get out of that house at once. I took my things from the bed and started past her, but she barred the door.

"Do you see what you've done?" she whispered hoarsely. "Now I will have to pack them all over again. It tires me, but I will have to pack them all over again—just because of you."

"That is entirely up to you, Celia," I said coldly.

"You," she said. "You old fool. It should have been you along with her when I—"

I dropped my stick sharply on her shoulder and could feel her wince under it. "As your lawyer, Celia," I said, "I advise you to exercise your tongue only during your sleep, when you can't be held accountable for what you say."

She said no more, but I made sure she stayed safely in front of me until I was out in the street again.

From the Boerum house to Al Sharp's Bar and Grill was only a few minutes' walk, and I made it in good time, grateful for the sting of the clear winter air in my face. Al was alone behind the bar, busily polishing glasses, and when he saw me enter he greeted me cheerfully. "Merry Christmas,

[110]

counsellor,'' he said.

"Same to you,'' I said, and watched him place a comfortable-looking bottle and a pair of glasses on the bar.

"You're regular as the seasons, counsellor,'' said Al, pouring out two stiff ones. "I was expecting you along right about now.''

We drank to each other and Al leaned confidingly on the bar. "Just come from there?''

"Yes,'' I said.

"See Charlie?''

"And Celia,'' I said.

"Well,'' said Al, "that's nothing exceptional. I've seen her too when she comes by to do some shopping. Runs along with her head down and that black shawl over it like she was being chased by something. I guess she is at that.''

"I guess she is,'' I said.

"But Charlie, he's the one. Never see him around at all. Did you tell him I'd like to see him some time?''

"Yes,'' I said. "I told him.''

"What did he say?''

"Nothing. Celia said it was wrong for him to come here while he was in mourning.''

Al whistled softly and expressively, and twirled a forefinger at his forehead. "Tell me,'' he said, "do you think it's safe for them to be alone together like they are? I mean, the way things stand, and the way Charlie feels, there could be another case of trouble there.''

"It looked like it for a while tonight,'' I said. "But it blew over.''

"Until next time,'' said Al.

"I'll be there,'' I said.

Al looked at me and shook his head. "Nothing changes in that house,'' he said. "Nothing at all. That's why you can figure out all the answers in advance. That's how I knew you'd be standing here right about now talking to me about it.''

I could still smell the dry rot of the house in my nostrils, and I knew it would take days before I could get it out of my clothes.

"This is one day I'd like to cut out of the calendar permanently,'' I said.

"And leave them alone to their troubles. It would serve them right.''

"They're not alone,'' I said. "Jessie is with them. Jessie will always be with them until that house and everything in it is gone.''

Al frowned. "It's the queerest thing that ever happened in this town, all right. The house all black, her running through the streets like something hunted, him lying there in that room with only the walls to look at, for—

[111]

when was it Jessie took that fall, counsellor?''

By shifting my eyes a little I could see in the mirror behind Al the reflection of my own face: ruddy, deep jowled, a little incredulous.

''Twenty years ago,'' I heard myself saying. ''Just twenty years ago tonight.''

A Christmas Tragedy
by Baroness Orczy

IT WAS a fairly merry Christmas party, although the surliness of our host somewhat marred the festivities. But imagine two such beautiful young women as my own dear lady and Margaret Ceely, and a Christmas Eve Cinderella in the beautiful ball-room at Clevere Hall, and you will understand that even Major Ceely's well-known cantankerous temper could not altogether spoil the merriment of a good, old-fashioned, festive gathering.

It is a far cry from a Christmas Eve party to a series of cattle-maiming outrages, yet I am forced to mention these now, for although they were ultimately proved to have no connection with the murder of the unfortunate Major, yet they were undoubtedly the means whereby the miscreant was enabled to accomplish the horrible deed with surety, swiftness, and as it turned out afterwards—a very grave chance of immunity.

Everyone in the neighbourhood had been taking the keenest possible interest in those dastardly outrages against innocent animals. They were either the work of desperate ruffians who stick at nothing in order to obtain a few shillings, or else of madmen with weird propensities for purposeless crimes.

Once or twice suspicious characters had been seen lurking about in the fields, and on more than one occasion a cart was heard in the middle of the night driving away at furious speed. Whenever this occurred the discovery of a fresh outrage was sure to follow, but, so far, the miscreants had succeeded in baffling not only the police, but also the many farm hands who had formed themselves into a band of volunteer watchmen, determined to bring the cattle maimers to justice.

We had all been talking about these mysterious events during the dinner which preceded the dance at Clevere Hall; but later on, when the young people had assembled, and when the first strains of "The Merry Widow" waltz had set us aglow with prospective enjoyment, the unpleasant topic was wholly forgotten.

The guests went away early, Major Ceely, as usual, doing nothing to detain them; and by midnight all of us who were staying in the house had gone up to bed.

[113]

My dear lady and I shared a bedroom and dressing-room together, our windows giving on the front. Clevere Hall is, as you know, not very far from York, on the other side of Bishopthorpe, and is one of the finest old mansions in the neighbourhood, its only disadvantage being that, in spite of the gardens being very extensive in the rear, the front of the house lies very near the road.

It was about two hours after I had switched off the electric light and called out "Good-night" to my dear lady, that something roused me out of my first sleep. Suddenly I felt very wide-awake, and sat up in bed. Most unmistakably—though still from some considerable distance along the road—came the sound of a cart being driven at unusual speed.

Evidently my dear lady was also awake. She jumped out of bed and, drawing aside the curtains, looked out of the window. The same idea had, of course, flashed upon us both, at the very moment of waking: all the conversations anent the cattle-maimers and their cart, which we had heard since our arrival at Clevere, recurring to our minds simultaneously.

I had joined Lady Molly beside the window, and I don't know how many minutes we remained there in observations, not more than two probably, for anon the sound of the cart died away in the distance along a side road. Suddenly we were startled with a terrible cry of "Murder! Help! Help!" issuing from the other side of the house, followed by an awful, deadly silence. I stood there near the window shivering with terror, while my dear lady, having already turned on the light, was hastily slipping into some clothes.

The cry had, of course, aroused the entire household, but my dear lady was even then the first to get downstairs, and to reach the garden door at the back of the house, whence the weird and despairing cry had undoubtedly proceeded.

That door was wide open. Two steps lead from it to the terraced walk which borders the house on that side, and along these steps Major Ceely was lying, face downwards, with arms outstretched, and a terrible wound between his shoulder-blades.

A gun was lying close by—his own. It was easy to conjecture that he, too, hearing the rumble of the wheels, had run out, gun in hand, meaning, no doubt, to effect, or at least to help, in the capture of the escaping criminals. Someone had been lying in wait for him; that was obvious—someone who had perhaps waited and watched for this special opportunity for days, or even weeks, in order to catch the unfortunate man unawares.

Well, it were useless to recapitulate all the various little incidents which occurred from the moment when Lady Molly and the butler first lifted the Major's lifeless body from the terrace steps until that instant when Miss Ceely, with remarkable coolness and presence of mind, gave what details

[114]

she could of the terrible event to the local police inspector and to the doctor, both hastily summoned.

These little incidents, with but slight variations, occur in every instance when a crime has been committed. The broad facts alone are of weird and paramount interest.

Major Ceely was dead. He had been stabbed with amazing sureness and terrible violence in the back. The weapon used must have been some sort of heavy, clasp knife. The murdered man was now lying in his own bedroom upstairs, even as the Christmas bells on that cold, crisp morning sent cheering echoes through the stillness of the air.

We had, of course, left the house, as had all the other guests. Everyone felt the deepest possible sympathy for the beautiful young girl who had been so full of the joy of living but a few hours ago, and was now the pivot round which revolved the weird shadow of tragedy, of curious suspicions and of an ever-growing mystery. But at such times all strangers, acquaintances, and even friends in a house, are only an additional burden to an already overwhelming load of sorrow and of trouble.

We took up our quarters at the "Black Swan," in York. The local superintendent, hearing that Lady Molly had been actually a guest at Clevere on the night of the murder, had asked her to remain in the neighbourhood.

There was no doubt that she could easily obtain the chief's consent to assist the local police in the elucidation of this extraordinary crime. At this time both her reputation and her remarkable powers were at their zenith, and there was not a single member of the entire police force in the kingdom who would not have availed himself gladly of her help when confronted with a seemingly impenetrable mystery.

That the murder of Major Ceely threatened to become such no one could deny. In cases of this sort, when no robbery of any kind has accompanied the graver crime, it is the duty of the police and also of the coroner to try to find out, first and foremost, what possible motive there could be behind so cowardly an assault; and among motives, of course, deadly hatred, revenge, and animosity stand paramount.

But here the police were at once confronted with the terrible difficulty, not of discovering whether Major Ceely had an enemy at all, but rather which, of all those people who owed him a grudge, hated him sufficiently to risk hanging for the sake of getting him out of the way.

As a matter of fact, the unfortunate Major was one of those miserable people who seem to live in a state of perpetual enmity with everything and everybody. Morning, noon and night he grumbled, and when he did not grumble he quarrelled either with his own daughter or with the people of his household, or with his neighbours.

I had often heard about him and his eccentric, disagreeable ways from

[115]

Lady Molly, who had known him for many years. She—like everybody in the county who otherwise would have shunned the old man—kept up a semblance of friendship with him for the sake of the daughter.

Margaret Ceely was a singularly beautiful girl, and as the Major was reputed to be very wealthy, these two facts perhaps combined to prevent the irascible gentleman from living in quite so complete an isolation as he would have wished.

Mammas of marriageable young men vied with one another in their welcome to Miss Ceely at garden parties, dances and bazaars. Indeed, Margaret had been surrounded with admirers ever since she had come out of the schoolroom. Needless to say, the cantankerous Major received these pretenders to his daughter's hand not only with insolent disdain, but at times even with violent opposition.

In spite of this the moths fluttered round the candle, and amongst this venturesome tribe none stood out more prominently than Mr. Laurence Smethick, son of the M.P. for the Pakethorpe division. Some folk there were who vowed that the young people were secretly engaged, in spite of the fact that Margaret was an outrageous flirt and openly encouraged more than one of her crowd of adorers.

Be that as it may, one thing was very certain—namely, that Major Ceely did not approve of Mr. Smethick any more than he did of the others, and there had been more than one quarrel between the young man and his prospective father-in-law.

On that memorable Christmas Eve at Clevere none of us could fail to notice his absence; whilst Margaret, on the other hand, had shown marked predilection for the society of Captain Glynne, who, since the sudden death of his cousin, Viscount Heslington, Lord Ullesthorpe's only son (who was killed in the hunting field last October, if you remember), had become heir to the earldom and its £40,000 a year.

Personally, I strongly disapproved of Margaret's behaviour the night of the dance; her attitude with regard to Mr. Smethick—whose constant attendance on her had justified the rumour that they were engaged—being more than callous.

On that morning of December 24th—Christmas Eve, in fact—the young man had called at Clevere. I remember seeing him just as he was being shown into the boudoir downstairs. A few moments later the sound of angry voices rose with appalling distinctness from that room. We all tried not to listen, yet could not fail to hear Major Ceely's overbearing words of rudeness to the visitor, who, it seems, had merely asked to see Miss Ceely, and had been most unexpectedly confronted by the irascible and extremely disagreeable Major. Of course, the young man speedily lost his temper,

[116]

too, and the whole incident ended with a very unpleasant quarrel between the two men in the hall, and with the Major peremptorily forbidding Mr. Smethick ever to darken his doors again.

On that night Major Ceely was murdered.

2

Of course, at first, no one attached any importance to this weird coincidence. The very thought of connecting the idea of murder with that of the personality of a bright, good-looking young Yorkshireman like Mr. Smethick seemed, indeed, preposterous, and with one accord all of us who were practically witnesses to the quarrel between the two men, tacitly agreed to say nothing at all about it at the inquest, unless we were absolutely obliged to do so on oath.

In view of the Major's terrible temper, this quarrel, mind you, had not the importance which it otherwise would have had; and we all flattered ourselves that we had well succeeded in parrying the coroner's questions.

The verdict at the inquest was against some person or persons unknown; and I, for one, was very glad that young Smethick's name had not been mentioned in connection with this terrible crime.

Two days later the superintendent at Bishopthorpe sent an urgent telephonic message to Lady Molly, begging her to come to the police-station immediately. We had the use of a motor all the while that we stayed at the "Black Swan," and in less than ten minutes we were bowling along at express speed towards Bishopthorpe.

On arrival we were immediately shown into Superintendent Etty's private room behind the office. He was there talking with Danvers—who had recently come down from London. In a corner of the room, sitting very straight on a high-backed chair, was a youngish woman of the servant class, who, as we entered, cast a quick, and I thought suspicious, glance at us both.

She was dressed in a coat and skirt of shabby looking black, and although her face might have been called good-looking—for she had fine, dark eyes —her entire appearance was distinctly repellent. It suggested slatternliness in an unusual degree; there were holes in her shoes and in her stockings, the sleeve of her coat was half unsewn, and the braid on her skirt hung in loops all round the bottom. She had very red and coarse-looking hands, and undoubtedly there was a furtive expression in her eyes, which, when she began speaking, changed to one of defiance.

Etty came forward with great alacrity when my dear lady entered. He looked perturbed, and seemed greatly relieved at sight of her.

"She is the wife of one of the outdoor men at Clevere," he explained rapidly to Lady Molly, nodding in the direction of the young woman, "and she has come here with such a queer tale that I thought you would like to hear it."

"She knows something about the murder?" asked Lady Molly.

"Noa! I didn't say that!" here interposed the woman, roughly, "doan't you go and tell no lies, Master Inspector. I thought as how you might wish to know what my husband saw on the night when the Major was murdered, that's all; and I've come to tell you."

"Why didn't your husband come himself?" asked Lady Molly.

"Oh, Haggett ain't well enough—he—" she began explaining, with a careless shrug of the shoulders, "so to speak—"

"The fact of the matter is, my lady," interposed Etty, "this woman's husband is half-witted. I believe he is only kept on in the garden because he is very strong and can help with the digging. It is because his testimony is so little to be relied on that I wished to consult you as to how we should act in the matter."

"What is his testimony, then?"

"Tell this lady what you have just told us, Mrs. Haggett, will you?" said Etty, curtly.

Again that quick, suspicious glance shot into the woman's eyes. Lady Molly took the chair which Danvers had brought forward for her, and sat down opposite Mrs. Haggett, fixing her earnest, calm gaze upon her.

"There's not much to tell," said the woman, sullenly. "Haggett is certainly queer in his head sometimes—and when he is queer he goes wandering about the place of nights."

"Yes?" said my lady, for Mrs. Haggett had paused awhile and now seemed unwilling to proceed.

"Well!" she resumed with sudden determination, "he had got one of his queer fits on on Christmas Eve, and didn't come in till long after midnight. He told me as how he'd seen a young gentleman prowling about the garden on the terrace side. He heard the cry of 'Murder' and 'Help' soon after that, and ran in home because he was frightened."

"Home?" asked Lady Molly, quietly, "where is home?"

"The cottage where we live. Just back of the kitchen garden."

"Why didn't you tell all this to the superintendent before?"

"Because Haggett only told me last night, when he seemed less queer-like. He is mighty silent when the fits are on him."

"Did he know who the gentleman was whom he saw?"

"No, ma'am—I don't suppose he did—leastways he wouldn't say— but—"

"Yes? But?"

"He found this in the garden yesterday," said the woman, holding out a

[118]

screw of paper which apparently she had held tightly clutched up to now, "and maybe that's what brought Christmas Eve and the murder back to his mind."

Lady Molly took the thing from her, and undid the soiled bit of paper with her dainty fingers. The next moment she held up for Etty's inspection a beautiful ring composed of an exquisitely carved moonstone surrounded with diamonds of unusual brilliance.

At the moment the setting and the stones themselves were marred by scraps of sticky mud which clung to them; the ring obviously having lain on the ground, and perhaps been trampled on for some days, and then been only very partially washed.

"At any rate you can find out the ownership of the ring," commented my dear lady after awhile, in answer to Etty's silent attitude of expectancy. "There would be no harm in that."

Then she turned once more to the woman.

"I'll walk with you to your cottage, if I may," she said decisively, "and have a chat with your husband. Is he at home?"

I thought Mrs. Haggett took this suggestion with marked reluctance. I could well imagine, from her own personal appearance, that her home was most unlikely to be in a fit state for a lady's visit. However, she could, of course, do nothing but obey, and, after a few muttered words of grudging acquiescence, she rose from her chair and stalked towards the door, leaving my lady to follow as she chose.

Before going, however, she turned and shot an angry glance at Etty.

"You'll give me back the ring, Master Inspector," she said with her usual tone of sullen defiance. "'Findings is keepings' you know."

"I am afraid not," replied Etty, curtly; "but there's always the reward offered by Miss Ceely for information which would lead to the apprehension of her father's murderer. You may get that, you know. It is a hundred pounds."

"Yes! I knew that," she remarked dryly, as, without further comment, she finally went out of the room.

3

My dear lady came back very disappointed from her interview with Haggett.

It seems that he was indeed half-witted—almost an imbecile, in fact, with but a few lucid intervals of which this present day was one. But, of course, his testimony was practically valueless.

He reiterated the story already told by his wife, adding no details. He had seen a young gentleman roaming on the terraced walk on the night of the murder. He did not know who the young gentleman was. He was going

homewards when he heard the cry of "Murder," and ran to his cottage because he was frightened. He picked up the ring yesterday in the perennial
border below the terrace and gave it to his wife.

Two of these brief statements made by the imbecile were easily proved to
be true, and my dear lady had ascertained this before she returned to me.
One of the Clevere under-gardeners said he had seen Haggett running
home in the small hours of that fateful Christmas morning. He himself had
been on the watch for the cattle-maimers that night, and remembered
the little circumstance quite plainly. He added that Haggett certainly looked to be in a panic.

Then Newby, another outdoor man at the Hall, saw Haggett pick up the
ring in the perennial border and advised him to take it to the police.

Somehow, all of us who were so interested in that terrible Christmas tragedy felt strangely perturbed at all this. No names had been mentioned as
yet, but whenever my dear lady and I looked at one another, or whenever
we talked to Etty or Danvers, we all felt that a certain name, one particular
personality, was lurking at the back of all our minds.

The two men, of course, had no sentimental scruples to worry them.
Taking the Haggett story merely as a clue, they worked diligently on that,
with the result that twenty-four hours later Etty appeared in our private
room at the "Black Swan" and calmly informed us that he had just got a
warrant out against Mr. Laurence Smethick on a charge of murder, and
was on his way even now to effect the arrest.

"Mr. Smethick did *not* murder Major Ceely," was Lady Molly's firm
and only comment when she heard the news.

"Well, my lady, that's as it may be!" rejoined Etty, speaking with that
deference with which the entire force invariably addressed my dear lady;
"but we have collected a sufficiency of evidence, at any rate, to justify the
arrest and, in my opinion, enough of it to hang any man. Mr. Smethick
purchased the moonstone and diamond ring at Nicholson's in Coney Street
about a week ago. He was seen abroad on Christmas Eve by several persons, loitering round the gates at Clevere Hall, somewhere about the time
when the guests were leaving after the dance, and, again, some few moments after the first cry of 'Murder' had been heard. His own valet admits
that his master did not get home that night until long after 2:00 am., whilst
even Miss Granard here won't deny that there was a terrible quarrel between Mr. Smethick and Major Ceely less than twenty-four hours before
the latter was murdered."

Lady Molly offered no remark to this array of facts which Etty thus piti-
lessly marshalled before us, but I could not refrain from exclaiming:

"Mr. Smethick is innocent, I am sure."

"I hope, for his sake, he may be," retorted Etty, gravely, "but somehow 'tis a pity that he don't seem able to give a good account of himself between midnight and two o'clock that Christmas morning.''

"Oh!" I ejaculated, "what does he say about that?"

"Nothing," replied the man, dryly; "that's just the trouble."

Well, of course, as you who read the papers will doubtless remember, Mr. Laurence Smethick, son of Colonel Smethick, M.P., of Pakethorpe Hall, Yorks, was arrested on the charge of having murdered Major Ceely on the night of December 24th-25th, and, after the usual magisterial inquiry, was duly committed to stand his trial at the next York assizes.

I remember well that, throughout his preliminary ordeal, young Smethick bore himself like one who had given up all hope of refuting the terrible charges brought against him, and, I must say, the formidable number of witnesses which the police brought up against him more than explained that attitude.

Of course, Haggett was not called, but, as it happened, there were plenty of people to swear that Mr. Laurence Smethick was seen loitering round the gates of Clevere Hall after the guests had departed on Christmas Eve. The head gardener, who lives at the lodge, actually spoke to him, and Captain Glynne, leaning out of his brougham window, was heard to exclaim:

"Hello, Smethick, what are you doing here at this time of night?"

And there were others, too.

To Captain Glynne's credit, be it here recorded, he tried his best to deny having recognised his unfortunate friend in the dark. Pressed by the magistrate, he said obstinately:

"I thought at the time that it was Mr. Smethick standing by the lodge gates, but on thinking the matter over I feel sure that I was mistaken."

On the other hand, what stood dead against young Smethick was, firstly, the question of the ring, and then the fact that he was seen in the immediate neighbourhood of Clevere, both at midnight and again at about two, when some men, who had been on the watch for the cattle-maimers, saw him walking away rapidly in the direction of Pakethorpe.

What was, of course, unexplainable and very terrible to witness was Mr. Smethick's obstinate silence with regard to his own movements during those fatal hours on that night. He did not contradict those who said that they had seen him at about midnight near the gates of Clevere, nor his own valet's statements as to the hour when he returned home. All he said was that he could not account for what he did between the time when the guests left the Hall and he himself went back to Pakethorpe. He realised the danger in which he stood, and what caused him to be silent about a matter which might mean life or death to him could not easily be conjectured.

The ownership of the ring he could not and did not dispute. He had lost it in the grounds of Clevere, he said. But the jeweller in Coney Street swore that he had sold the ring to Mr. Smethick on the 18th of December, whilst it was a well-known and an admitted fact that the young man had not openly been inside the gates of Clevere for over a fortnight before that.

On this evidence Laurence Smethick was committed for trial. Though the actual weapon with which the unfortunate Major had been stabbed had not been found, nor its ownership traced, there was such a vast array of circumstantial evidence against the young man that bail was refused.

He had, on the advice of his solicitor, Mr. Grayson—one of the ablest lawyers in York—reserved his defence, and on that miserable afternoon at the close of the year, we all filed out of the crowded court feeling terribly depressed and anxious.

4

My dear lady and I walked back to our hotel in silence. Our hearts seemed to weigh heavily within us. We felt mortally sorry for that good-looking young Yorkshireman, who, we were convinced, was innocent, yet at the same time seemed involved in a tangled web of deadly circumstances from which he seemed quite unable to extricate himself.

We did not feel like discussing the matter in the open streets, neither did we make any comment when presently, in a block in the traffic in Coney Street, we saw Margaret Ceely driving her smart dog-cart, whilst sitting beside her, and talking with great earnestness close to her ear, sat Captain Glynne.

She was in deep mourning, and had obviously been doing some shopping, for she was surrounded with parcels; so perhaps it was hypercritical to blame her. Yet somehow it struck me that just at the moment when there hung in the balance the life and honour of a man with whose name her own had oft been linked by popular rumour, it showed more than callous contempt for his welfare to be seen driving about with another man who, since his sudden access to fortune, had undoubtedly become a rival in her favours.

When we arrived at the "Black Swan," we were surprised to hear that Mr. Grayson had called to see my dear lady, and was upstairs waiting.

Lady Molly ran up to our sitting-room and greeted him with marked cordiality. Mr. Grayson is an elderly, dry-looking man, but he looked visibly affected, and it was some time before he seemed able to plunge into the subject which had brought him hither. He fidgeted in his chair, and started talking about the weather.

"I am not here in a strictly professional capacity, you know," said Lady Molly presently, with a kindly smile and with a view to helping him out of his embarrassment. "Our police, I fear me, have an exaggerated view of my capacities, and the men here asked me unofficially to remain in the

[122]

neighbourhood and to give them my advice if they should require it. Our chief is very lenient to me, and has allowed me to stay. Therefore, if there is anything I can do—''

''Indeed, indeed there is!'' ejaculated Mr. Grayson with sudden energy. ''From all I hear, there is not another soul in the kingdom but you who can save this innocent man from the gallows.''

My dear lady heaved a little sigh of satisfaction. She had all along wanted to have a more important finger in that Yorkshire pie.

''Mr. Smethick?'' she said.

''Yes; my unfortuante young client,'' replied the lawyer. ''I may as well tell you,'' he resumed after a slight pause, during which he seemed to pull himself together, ''as briefly as possible what occurred on December 24th last and on the following Christmas morning. You will then understand the terrible plight in which my client finds himself, and how impossible it is for him to explain his actions on that eventful night. You will understand, also, why I have come to ask your help and your advice. Mr. Smethick considered himself engaged to Miss Ceely. The engagement had not been made public because of Major Ceely's anticipated opposition, but the young people had been very intimate, and many letters had passed between them. On the morning of the 24th Mr. Smethick called at the Hall, his intention then being merely to present his *fiancée* with the ring you know of. You remember the unfortunate *contretemps* that occurred: I mean the unprovoked quarrel sought by Major Ceely with my poor client, ending with the irascible old man forbidding Mr. Smethick the house.

''My client walked out of Clevere feeling, as you may well imagine, very wrathful; on the doorstep, just as he was leaving, he met Miss Margaret, and told her very briefly what had occurred. She took the matter very lightly at first, but finally became more serious, and ended the brief interview with the request that, since he could not come to the dance after what had occurred, he should come and see her afterwards, meeting her in the gardens soon after midnight. She would not take the ring from him then, but talked a good deal of sentiment about Christmas morning, asking him to bring the ring to her at night, and also the letters which she had written him. Well—you can guess the rest.''

Lady Molly nodded thoughtfully.

''Miss Ceely was playing a double game,'' continued Mr. Grayson, earnestly. ''She was determined to break off all relationship with Mr. Smethick, for she had transferred her volatile affections to Captain Glynne, who had lately become heir to an earldom and £40,000 a year. Under the guise of sentimental twaddle she got my unfortunate client to meet her at night in the grounds of Clevere and to give up to her the letters which might have compromised her in the eyes of her new lover. At two o'clock a.m. Major Ceely was murdered by one of his numerous enemies; as to which I do not know, nor does Mr. Smethick. He had just parted from Miss Ceely at the very moment when the first cry of 'Murder' roused Clevere from its slumbers. This she could confirm if she only would, for the two were still in sight of each other, she inside the gates, he just a little way down the road. Mr. Smethick saw Margaret Ceely run rapidly back towards the house. He waited about a little while, half hesitating what to do; then he reflected that his presence might be embarrassing, or even compromising to her whom, in spite of all, he still loved dearly; and knowing that there were plenty of men in and about the house to render what assistance was necessary, he finally turned his steps and went home a broken-hearted man, since she had given him the go-by, taken her letters away, and flung contemptuously into the mud the ring he had bought for her.''

The lawyer paused, mopping his forehead and gazing with whole-souled earnestness at my lady's beautiful, thoughtful face.

"Has Mr. Smethick spoken to Miss Ceely since?'' asked Lady Molly, after a while.

"No; but I did,'' replied the lawyer.

"What was her attitude?''

"One of bitter and callous contempt. She denies my unfortunate client's story from beginning to end; declares that she never saw him after she bade him 'good morning' on the doorstep of Clevere Hall, when she heard of his unfortunate quarrel with her father. Nay, more; she scornfully calls the whole tale a cowardly attempt to shield a dastardly crime behind a still more dastardly libel on a defenceless girl.''

We were all silent now, buried in thought which none of us would have cared to translate into words. That the *impasse* seemed indeed hopeless no one could deny.

The tower of damning evidence against the unfortunate young man had indeed been built by remorseless circumstances with no faltering hand.

Margaret Ceely alone could have saved him, but with brutal indifference she preferred the sacrifice of an innocent man's life and honour to that of her own chances of a brilliant marriage. There are such women in the world; thank God I have never met any but that one!

Yet am I wrong when I say that she alone could save the unfortunate young man, who throughout was behaving with such consummate gallantry, refusing to give his own explanation of the events that occurred on that Christmas morning, unless she chose first to tell the tale. There was one present now in the dingy little room at the "Black Swan" who could disentangle that weird skein of coincidences, if any human being not gifted with miraculous powers could indeed do it at this eleventh hour.

She now said, gently:

"What would you like me to do in this matter, Mr. Grayson? And why have you come to me rather than to the police?"

"How can I go with this tale to the police?" he ejaculated in obvious despair. "Would they not also look upon it as a dastardly libel on a woman's reputation? We have no proofs, remember, and Miss Ceely denies the whole story from first to last. No, no!" he exclaimed with wonderful fervour. "I came to you because I have heard of your marvellous gifts, your extraordinary intuition. Someone murdered Major Ceely! It was not my old friend Colonel Smethick's son. Find out who it was, then! I beg of you, find out who it was!"

He fell back in his chair, broken down with grief. With inexpressible gentleness Lady Molly went up to him and placed her beautiful white hand on his shoulder.

"I will do my best, Mr. Grayson," she said simply.

5

We remained alone and singularly quiet the whole of that evening. That my dear lady's active brain was hard at work I could guess by the brilliance of her eyes, and that sort of absolute stillness in her person through which one could almost feel the delicate nerves vibrating.

The story told her by the lawyer had moved her singularly. Mind you, she had always been morally convinced of young Smethick's innocence, but in her the professional woman always fought hard battles against the sentimentalist, and in this instance the overwhelming circumstantial evidence and the conviction of her superiors had forced her to accept the young man's guilt as something out of her ken.

By his silence, too, the young man had tacitly confessed; and if a man is perceived on the very scene of a crime, both before it has been committed and directly afterwards; if something admittedly belonging to him is found within three yards of where the murderer must have stood; if, added to this, he has had a bitter quarrel with the victim, and can give no account of his actions or whereabouts during the fatal time, it were vain to cling to optimistic beliefs in that same man's innocence.

But now matters had assumed an altogether different aspect. The story told by Mr. Smethick's lawyer had all the appearance of truth. Margaret Ceely's character, her callousness on the very day when her late *fiancé* stood in the dock, her quick transference of her affections to the richer man, all made the account of the events on Christmas night as told my Mr. Grayson extremely plausible.

No wonder my dear lady was buried in thought.

"I shall have to take the threads up from the beginning, Mary," she said to me the following morning, when after breakfast she appeared in her neat coat and skirt, with hat and gloves, ready to go out, "so, on the whole, I think I will begin with a visit to the Haggetts."

"I may come with you, I suppose?" I suggested meekly.

"Oh, yes!" she rejoined carelessly.

Somehow I had an inkling that the carelessness of her mood was only on the surface. It was not likely that she—my sweet, womanly, ultra-feminine, beautiful lady—should feel callously on this absorbing subject.

We motored down to Bishopthorpe. It was bitterly cold, raw, damp, and foggy. The chauffeur had some difficulty in finding the cottage, the "home" of the imbecile gardener and his wife.

There was certainly not much look of home about the place. When, after much knocking at the door, Mrs. Haggett finally opened it, we saw before us one of the most miserable, slatternly places I think I ever saw.

In reply to Lady Molly's somewhat curt inquiry, the woman said that Haggett was in bed, suffering from one of his "fits."

"That is a great pity," said my dear lady, rather unsympathetically, I thought, "for I must speak with him at once."

"What is it about?" asked the woman, sullenly. "I can take a message."

"I am afraid not," rejoined my lady. "I was asked to see Haggett personally."

"By whom, I'd like to know," she retorted, now almost insolently.

"I dare say you would. But you are wasting precious time. Hadn't you better help your husband on with his clothes? This lady and I will wait in the parlour."

After some hesitation the woman finally complied, looking very sulky the while.

We went into the miserable little room wherein not only grinding poverty but also untidiness and dirt were visible all round. We sat down on two of the cleanest-looking chairs, and waited whilst a colloquy in subdued voices went on in the room over our heads.

The colloquy, I may say, seemed to consist of agitated whispers on one part, and wailing complaints on the other. This was followed presently by some thuds and much shuffling, and presently Haggett, looking uncared-for, dirty, and unkempt, entered the parlour, followed by his wife.

He came forward, dragging his ill-shod feet and pulling nervously at his forelock.

"Ah!" said my lady, kindly; "I am glad to see you down, Haggett, though I am afraid I haven't very good news for you."

"Yes, miss!" murmured the man, obviously not quite comprehending what was said to him.

"I represent the workhouse authorities," continued Lady Molly, "and I thought we could arrange for you and your wife to come into the Union to-night, perhaps."

"The Union?" here interposed the woman, roughly. "What do you mean? We ain't going to the Union?"

"Well! but since you are not staying here," rejoined my lady, blandly, "you will find it impossible to get another situation for your husband in his present mental condition."

"Miss Ceely won't give us the go-by," she retorted defiantly.

"She might wish to carry out her late father's intentions," said Lady Molly with seeming carelessness.

"The Major was a cruel, cantankerous brute," shouted the woman with unpremeditated violence. "Haggett had served him faithfully for twelve years, and—"

She checked herself abruptly, and cast one of her quick, furtive glances at Lady Molly.

Her silence now had become as significant as her outburst of rage, and it was Lady Molly who concluded the phrase for her.

"And yet he dismissed him without warning," she said calmly.

"Who told you that?" retorted the woman.

"The same people, no doubt, who declare that you and Haggett had a grudge against the Major for this dismissal."

"That's a lie," asserted Mrs. Haggett, doggedly; "we gave information about Mr. Smethick having killed the Major because—"

"Ah," interrupted Lady Molly, quickly, "but then Mr. Smethick did not murder Major Ceely, and your information therefore was useless!"

"Then who killed the Major, I should like to know?"

Her manner was arrogant, coarse, and extremely unpleasant. I marvelled why my dear lady put up with it, and what was going on in that busy brain of hers. She looked quite urbane and smiling, whilst I wondered what in the world she meant by this story of the workhouse and the dismissal of Haggett.

"Ah, that's what none of us know!" she now said lightly; "some folks say it was your husband."

"They lie!" she retorted quickly, whilst the imbecile, evidently not understanding the drift of the conversation, was mechanically stroking his red mop of hair and looking helplessly all round him.

"He was home before the cries of 'Murder' were heard in the house," continued Mrs. Haggett.

"How do you know?" asked Lady Molly, quickly.

"How do I know?"

"Yes; you couldn't have heard the cries all the way to this cottage—why, it's over half a mile from the Hall!"

"He was home, I say," she repeated with dogged obstinacy.

[127]

"You sent him?"

"He didn't do it—"

"No one will believe you, especially when the knife is found."

"What knife?"

"His clasp knife, with which he killed Major Ceely," said Lady Molly, quietly; "see, he has it in his hand now."

And with a sudden, wholly unexpected gesture she pointed to the imbecile, who in an aimless way had prowled round the room whilst this rapid colloquy was going on.

The purport of it all must in some sort of way have found an echo in his enfeebled brain. He wandered up to the dresser whereon lay the remnants of that morning's breakfast, together with some crockery and utensils.

In that same half-witted and irresponsible way he had picked up one of the knives and now was holding it out towards his wife, whilst a look of fear spread over his countenance.

"I can't do it, Annie, I can't—you'd better do it," he said.

There was dead silence in the little room. The woman Haggett stood as if turned to stone. Ignorant and supersitious as she was, I suppose that the situation had laid hold of her nerves, and that she felt that the finger of a relentless Fate was even now being pointed at her.

The imbecile was shuffling forward, closer and closer to his wife, still holding out the knife towards her and murmuring brokenly:

"I can't do it. You'd better, Annie—you'd better—"

He was close to her now, and all at once her rigidity and nerve-strain gave way; she gave a hoarse cry, and snatching the knife from the poor wretch, she rushed at him ready to strike.

Lady Molly and I were both young, active and strong; and there was nothing of the squeamish *grande dame* about my dear lady when quick action was needed. But even then we had some difficulty in dragging Annie Hagget away from her miserable husband. Blinded with fury, she was ready to kill the man who had betrayed her. Finally, we succeeded in wresting the knife from her.

You may be sure that it required some pluck after that to sit down again quietly and to remain in the same room with this woman, who already had one crime upon her conscience, and with this weird, half-witted creature who kept on murmuring pitiably:

"You'd better do it, Annie—"

Well, you've read the account of the case, so you know what followed. Lady Molly did not move from that room until she had obtained the woman's full confession. All she did for her own protection was to order me to open the window and to blow the police whistle which she handed to me.

The police-station fortunately was not very far, and sound carried in the frosty air.

She admitted to me afterwards that it had been foolish, perhaps, not to have brought Etty or Danvers with her, but she was supremely anxious not to put the woman on the alert from the very start, hence her circumlocutory speeches anent the workhouse, and Haggett's probable dismissal.

That the woman had had some connection with the crime, Lady Molly, with her keen intuition, had always felt; but as there was no witness to the murder itself, and all circumstantial evidence was dead against young Smethick, there was only one chance of successful discovery, and that was the murderer's own confession.

If you think over the interview between my dear lady and the Haggetts on that memorable morning, you will realise how admirably Lady Molly had led up to the weird finish. She would not speak to the woman unless Haggett was present, and she felt sure that as soon as the subject of the murder cropped up, the imbecile would either do or say something that would reveal the truth.

Mechanically, when Major Ceely's name was mentioned, he had taken up the knife. The whole scene recurred to his tottering mind. That the Major had summarily dismissed him recently was one of those bold guesses which Lady Molly was wont to make.

That Haggett had been merely egged on by his wife, and had been too terrified at the last to do the deed himself was no surprise to her, and hardly one to me, whilst the fact that the woman ultimately wreaked her own passionate revenge upon the unfortunate Major was hardly to be wondered at, in the face of her own coarse and elemental personality.

Cowed by the quickness of events, and by the appearance of Danvers and Etty on the scene, she finally made full confession.

She was maddened by the Major's brutality, when with rough, cruel words he suddenly turned her husband adrift, refusing to give him further employment. She herself had great ascendency over the imbecile, and had drilled him into a part of hate and of revenge. At first he had seemed ready and willing to obey. It was arranged that he was to watch on the terrace every night until such time as an alarm of the recurrence of the cattle-maiming outrages should lure the Major out alone.

This effectually occured on Christmas morning, but not before Haggett, frightened and pusillanimous, was ready to flee rather than to accomplish the villainous deed. But Annie Haggett, guessing perhaps that he would shrink from the crime at the last, had also kept watch every night. Picture the prospective murderer watching and being watched!

When Haggett came across his wife he deputed her to do the deed herself.

[129]

I suppose that either terror of discovery or merely desire for the promised reward had caused the woman to fasten the crime on another.

The finding of the ring by Haggett was the beginning of that cruel thought which, but for my dear lady's marvellous powers, would indeed have sent a brave young man to the gallows.

Ah, you wish to know if Margaret Ceely is married? No! Captain Glynne cried off. What suspicions crossed his mind I cannot say; but he never proposed to Margaret, and now she is in Australia—staying with an aunt, I think—and she has sold Clevere Hall.

★

Silent Night
by Baynard Kendrick

O N FRIDAY. Dec. 20th, a week to the day since six year old Ronnie Connatser had been kidnapped from Miss Murray's School, Arnold Cameron, Special Agent in Charge of the New York F.B.I., telephoned early in the morning to make an appointment with Capt. Duncan Maclain. It was arranged for 10:00 A.M. in Maclain's penthouse office twenty-six stories above 72nd Street and Riverside Drive. Cameron arrived promptly, bringing with him Special Agent Hank Weeks and Alan Connatser, Ronnie's father. The men were silent, grim.

Capt. Maclain, an ex-Intelligence Officer blinded in World War I, had carried on the work of a Private Investigator with the aid of his partner, Spud Savage, for nearly forty years. To him being a Licensed P.I. was a dedicated profession. He hoped by developing his remaining four senses, hearing, feeling, taste, and smell to the highest point of proficiency to prove to the world before he died that a blind man with sufficient intelligence could be just as good, if not a little bit better, than millions of people who had eyes with which to see.

Waiting for Cameron, the Captain had a gratified feeling that maybe after all these years he had at last succeeded. Duncan Maclain was no superman. He had certain peculiar talents that had proved most useful through the years to various law-enforcement agencies, among them the New York Police Department, and on several occasions the F.B.I.

He had known Arnold Cameron for a long time, and worked with him before Cameron became S.A.C. of the New York office. The Captain was the first to admit that neither he, nor any private operator, no matter where he worked, could get to first base without the co-operation of the local police or the F.B.I.

Cameron hadn't said what this case was about, except that it concerned the kidnapping of Connatser's six year old son. The Captain had heard about Alan Connatser, President and Treasurer of Connatser Products, Inc., the big plant that sprawled over acres on the edge of Long Island City. It was one of those industrial mushrooms that had grown in importance since World War II, mainly through Connatser's personality and engineering genius. The company did a lot of top security defense work, but the

F.B.I. was quite capable of handling any violations of security on their own. Kidnapping, too, for that matter.

Why go on guessing? Speculation was always fruitless and a waste of time. He'd know the details soon enough. Whatever they were he hoped he could help. It was flattering that Arnold Cameron had dealt him in.

At 9:55 Rena, the Captain's secretary showed the three men in. Maclain shook hands around. Cameron's grip was friendly as usual. Special Agent Hank Weeks was properly official, neither cold nor warm, with an element of doubt in it as though he didn't intend to commit himself even on the say-so of the S.A.C. unless he was shown. Maclain supressed a grin. He was skeptical himself about people who claimed they saw everything—even when they had 20-20 vision.

Alan Connatser wrung the Captain's hand with a grip that was full of despairing appeal. "Mr. Cameron thinks that you can help us, Captain Maclain. My son's been gone for a week now—more like a lifetime to Evelyn, my wife, and me. She has collapsed and is under a doctor's care. It isn't a question of money—I can pay a million and not be hurt. It's the life of my boy—our only child and we can never have another."

A very strong man, Alan Connatser, the Captain judged. Six foot, slow spoken, powerful as flexible steel, and younger than one would imagine. From his voice—not yet forty. And right now he was on the verge of flying into little pieces.

Maclain released himself wordlessly from the clinging grip and went to the bar set in the paneled wall near the diamond-paned doors to the terrace. He sloshed a liberal portion of cognac into a bell goblet and took it to the red leather divan where Connatser had slumped down.

"Slug it!" His face was grave with deep concern. "Your hand is as cold as a frozen fish. It won't help your boy if you crack up now and have a chill."

"Thanks. I guess you're right." Connatser downed the burning brandy in a gulp. "I'm afraid we're saddling you with a hopeless task."

"The world considers blindness hopeless. I haven't found it so." The Captain walked to his broad flat-top desk and sat down. "You say your son has been missing for a week?"

"He was kidnapped last Friday, Dec. 13th at ten past three," Arnold Cameron said. "He'd been to a Christmas party at his school. Miss Murray's at 66th Street and Fifth Avenue. The Connatsers live in a duplex at 82nd and Fifth—sixteen blocks away. Miss Murray saw Ronnie get into his father's Chrysler Imperial in front of the school at three-ten. The car was driven by a substitute chauffeur, who called himself Jules Rosine.

"Rosine stuck up Leon Gerard, who has driven for the family for years, in Gerard's apartment on East 82nd Street—right across the street from the garage where the Chrysler is kept. That was about eleven the night before. Rosine wore a stocking mask. He forced Leon to telephone at gun-point. Leon talked to Mrs. Murchison, the Connatser's housekeeper, said he was ill, and would send a reliable man to take his place the next day. Nobody thought it suspicious since it had happened a few times before. Leon is getting along in years and his health isn't too good."

Cameron paused. The Captain said, "If you fellows believe his story then I do, too."

"We don't believe anything until we've convinced ourselves that it's true," Cameron went on. "Weeks released Leon in his apartment after the kidnapping was reported to us on the evening of the thirteenth. The poor old guy was trussed up like a turkey with adhesive. Anyhow, nothing has been seen of Ronnie, or this Jules Rosine since ten past three in the afternoon a week ago."

A hopeless task, Connatser had said! The Captain ran a hand through his dark graying hair. The details of Charles A. Lindbergh, Jr., Bobby Greenlease, Jr., and the tiny month old Peter Weinberger, all coolly murdered by their kidnappers, were much too vivid in his mind not to realize that Connatser's fears were far from being groundless.

He kept his repellent thoughts to himself and tried to speak reassuringly: "I've known Arnold Cameron for many years, Mr. Connatser. Neither he nor the F.B.I. consider this hopeless or he wouldn't have brought you here to talk with me." His dark sightless eyes, so perfect that many people thought he could see, turned from Connatser to fix themselves on the S.A.C. "You must have some very good reason for thinking Ronnie is still alive, Arnold."

"We happen, in this case, to know he was alive on Tuesday or Wednesday, and probably yesterday."

"What proof?"

"The sound of his voice, Captain, plus an answer to a couple of questions asked by Ronnie's mother—answers that only Ronnie would know."

"Then you must have made contact by phone." The Captain's expressive eyebrows went up a fraction.

"No. They're the ones who have been in touch," Cameron said. "One-way touch, by Audograph records. Three of them. You've told me often that you live in a world of sound. I also know that you're the best man living on identification of voices. Furthermore, you work with an Audograph all the time and are familiar with its sounds and foibles. Isn't that true?"

Maclain nodded. "I have one right here in my desk drawer." He referred to a compact efficient dictating machine used in thousands of business offices. Not more than nine inches square and five inches high, it records dictation on a flexible blue disc, and the dictation can be played back through its built in loud-speaker, or through plugged-in headphones at the flip of a lever.

"Here's the first of the three. The first word from Ronnie's captors, for that matter, from Friday to Monday. Let the family suffer. Die a thousand deaths. It softens them up. I could—"

He broke off abruptly, leaned forward and put a brown manila envelope on the Captain's blotter. It was a standard mailing envelope for the feather light discs. Seven inches square. Printed on the front was: GRAY AUDO-GRAM FOR—a space for the address—and below that the words PLEASE DO NOT FOLD. The envelopes, like the discs, could be obtained from any Audograph dealer in cities throughout the country.

For an instant the Captain stared at the envelope as though by sheer intentness, he might develop some superhuman power to penetrate its secret.

"That was mailed to Mrs. Connatser at her home," Cameron explained. "Air mail. It's postmarked: Miami, Florida, Dec. 15th. That was last Sunday."

Maclain touched it gingerly with his forefinger. "I know what a working over you must have given these things. I was wondering about handwriting, or typing, on the address."

"Not this bird, Captain! He hasn't forgotten that we went through two million specimens of handwriting before we nailed LaMarca as kidnapper of the Weinberger baby. There's not even typewriting. No return address, of course. Mrs. Connatser's name and address has been stamped on with one of those kid's rubber stamps that has separate removable rubber letters. You can buy them in any store or Five-and-ten."

The Captain took his Audograph machine from the deep bottom left-hand desk drawer. He put it on the desk, then brought up a hand microphone which he plugged into a six-slotted receptacle on the left hand side of the machine. A switch in the handle of the mike controlled the playing of the record, turning it on when pressed in. For continuous playing, a flick of the thumb could lock the switch.

He took the record from the envelope, felt for the grooved side with his finger-nail, and turning it upward put the record on the machine. Unlike a regular phonograph record, the Audograph recorded from the center to the edge.

The Captain slid it into place, turned on the machine, and pushed a lever over to LISTEN. A red indicator light glowed. When recording, the light showed green. He locked the switch on the hand mike and laid the mike gently on the blotter beside the machine.

Out of nowhere the boyish treble of Ronnie Connatser's voice began to speak. Maclain reached out and turned the volume higher, as though that might help to bring the six-year-old closer to his home.

"Mommy, Mommy, can you hear me? The man says to tell you that I'm all right and that if I talk in here you can hear me. He says that Daddy can hear me, too, and that if you do what the man says he'll bring me home. Mommy, please tell Daddy to do what the man says. I'm all right, but I'm scared, Mommy. I don't want to spend Christmas here. I'm doing just what the man tells me to. Please hurry and do what the man says. I don't want to spend Christmas here. I don't like it and the man says he'll bring me home. So, please hurry."

Ronnie's voice quit abruptly. For an endless length of time—actually a few short seconds—the record revolved in mechanical silence. Cameron lit a cigarette. Smoke reached the Captain's nostrils. Leather squeaked as Connatser moved uneasily on the red divan. A man's voice took up where the child's voice had stopped:

"Your son's been kidnapped, but he hasn't been harmed. It's to prove that that I'm letting him talk to you. You'll be better off if you keep the police out of this as well as the F.B.I. Press me too hard and you'll never hear his voice again, let alone see him. If you follow out instructions to the letter you'll have him back very shortly. In case you don't think that's your son who was speaking, I'm going to offer you further proof. Ask him any two questions you want—questions that only he can answer. Put it in a Personal in the New York Times of Tuesday December the seventeenth. Sign it 'E.C.' You'll be answered by Ronnie on the next record we send to you. That's all for now. You'll never see me. Just call me: Junior."

"Is that all?" The Captain sat up straight in his chair, his face grim.

"End of Record One," Cameron told him.

Maclain swiftly adjusted the disc to play the last few lines a second time.

Faintly, but clearly, through the man's last few words had come the sound of chimes pealing the opening bars of "Silent Night." Then a singer had begun:

"Silent Night,
Holy Night,
All is—"

The song had ended with the click of the mike as the man said "Junior."

"The musical interlude," Cameron said glumly, "is the first song on Side One of Bing Crosby's Decca Recording DL-8128, entitled 'Merry Christmas.' Sales to date about two million. On the last report from our bunion-ridden Agents in Miami, they have found some two hundred radio, record, and music shops, super-markets, drive-ins, and various other publicity-minded places of business, including second-hand-car lots that have

[135]

P.A. systems working overtime. They have been deafening the public for a week or more to let them know the time of year. No. 1 on the Hit Parade is Bing's little dose of Christmas Cheer." He viciously snubbed out his cigarette.

"We don't think Ronnie's in Miami, anyhow. This Jules Rosine—who is trying hard to make us believe that that's his name by calling himself Junior from the initials J.R.—just doesn't strike me as the type, Captain, who would mail a letter or anything from a city where he has that boy. As a matter of fact, he jumps around the country like a twelve legged flea. The second record is from Kansas City and the third one is from Cleveland."

The Captain sat pinching his upper lip and saying nothing.

Cameron put the second envelope on his desk. "Here's the one where Ronnie answers his mother's questions. Mailed Wednesday, December the eighteenth. Air mail from K.C."

There was a tremor in the Captain's sensitive fingers as he removed the first record and put the second on.

"Mommy the man says that you and Daddy can hear me if I talk in here, but I don't see how you can hear me if I can't see you. He said I was to tell you what picture Ted Schuyler and I were going to see with Mrs. Murchison, and what I call my electric engine that pulls the train, and if I didn't tell you I wouldn't get back home. I thought you knew that Ted and I were going to see 'Snow White and the Seven Dwarfs'—except Daddy wanted me to come to the plant to meet him and I drank the Pepsi-Cola the chauffeur got me and got so sleepy. And you know my engine is called the Camel because it has a hump-back in its middle. I know you told me not to repeat things, but the man said unless I told you that and unless Daddy did just what he says, I won't get home for Christmas. I don't want to stay here. There's nobody to play with and I want to come home."

The man's voice took it up from there:

"That answers the questions you had in the Times and proves beyond doubt that your son's alive. Nobody is trying to torture you. You'll see when we write again that we're not after money. It's possible that we have even more of that than you. The next will tell you what we want. We know what you want, but don't think we're fooling. Stay away from the police and the F.B.I. and do exactly what I tell you or your precious son is going to die. Cheerio! Junior."

"Junior seems to have split himself in two," the Captain said as he took off the record. "The *man* has become *we*. Do you think it's merely a cover-up, Arnold, or is there really someone else involved beside the man?"

"Anywhere from two to two million. They're after something more precious than money." He put the third record on the desk. "Listen to this one and you'll see."

Agent Hank Weeks said, "I'm betting there's a woman. Purely because they've kept Ronnie harping on *the man.*"

The Captain nursed his chin for a moment. "I'm inclined to agree." He put the final record on.

"Do you mind if I have another brandy?" Alan Connatser's voice was tight and dry.

"Drink it all," the Captain said. "Ronnie isn't my son, but nevertheless these records are really getting me."

Connatser poured his drink and returned to his seat. "They're somehow worse than ransom notes to Evelyn and me. They're sadistic. Mean. I find myself wanting to answer Ronnie. Scream at him: 'Tell me where you are!' —as though he were hiding away in some ghostly world of his own. It's unbearable."

"I'd merely sound inane if I tried to express my sympathy." A sharp cold fury was setting the Captain's skin to tingling, turning him into a ruthless inhuman machine. His mind was being honed to a razor edge on a whetstone of revenge and implacability. "This is the one from Cleveland?"

"Mailed air mail yesterday. Thursday the nineteenth. It arrived in New York this morning at seven. We have a tag out for them at the Post Office. They notified us right away."

The Captain flipped the lever to LISTEN and started the disc to play.

"Mommy did you hear what I told you about the picture show? The Seven Dwarfs? And my engine, the Camel, on the electric train? I wish that you and Daddy would come for me, or answer me if you heard me, like the man said. He says he's telling Daddy exactly what to do right now, and if Daddy does it I'll come back home. Mommy tell him to hurry, please. Hurry and do it because I miss you so much and I want to see the Macy's parade and get my presents."

More unbearable silence then until the man cut in:

"At six-o'-clock, P.M.—eighteen hours Service Time—you and your pilot, Steven Donegan, will take off from the air strip at your plant on Long Island, flying your Cessna Twin. You will file no flight plan with anyone. At your regular cruising speed of two-hundred-and-ten miles per hour, flying at eight thousand feet, you will follow the regular plane route from New York to Philadelphia. From Philadelphia to Baltimore. From Baltimore to Washington. From Washington to Richmond. From Richmond to Wilmington, North Carolina. From Wilmington to Charleston, South Carolina. From Charleston to Savannah, Georgia. From Savannah to Jacksonville, Florida. From Jacksonville to Daytona. From Daytona to Vero Beach, and from Vero Beach to Miami.

Be on the alert. Somewhere between two of the places named you will be contacted by radio. When contact is made, if you broadcast an alarm your son will be killed.

[137]

Remember we'll be tuned in on you, too. We want the complete plans of the SF-800T Missile. Those plans consist of forty-four sheets of blueprints that were delivered to you by the Navy a month ago. You are the only one living who has immediate access to them all. Those forty-four blueprints are the price of your son. Particularly the details of the cone.

Once they are received they will be checked immediately by engineers just as competent as you. If they are not approved, or any attempt at trickery is discovered, your boy will die. The clearer those specifications are, the quicker you get your son. Remember, it's his life that's at stake.

Put the plans in a large pormanteau—not a dispatch-case—and weight the portmanteau with a couple of sash-weights. Paint the portmanteau with phosphorescent paint and be ready to drop it on a moment's notice. You will be contacted by the words: 'Cessna come down!' and will immediately start descending to a thousand feet still holding your course. Watch the ground. One minute before the drop you will be contacted again. Answer: Roger, Junior! and look for a red flasher that will turn on on top of a car. When you spot it say: Condition red! and drop portmanteau as close as possible to the flasher. You will be directed if you have to make a second try. Follow the straightest compass course between points and there will be no trouble. Another record will tell you where to pick up your boy. If weather reports are generally bad don't attempt to start. That's your hard luck and you'll have to make another try. Happy landings! Junior.''

"Sounds like something from out of the wild blue yonder," Maclain said as he stopped the record. "A modern Chekov nightmare manufactured in Moscow. What are the chances of pulling off such a scheme?"

"My pilot, Steve, says there's a damn good chance," Connatser told him. "I'm a pilot, myself, with some missions behind me, and I'm afraid I agree. Junior knows that we'll break our necks to drop that luminous suitcase on his head, if possible. He also knows that the SF-800T is an ace we have in the hole. So I'm supposed to stake the life of my son against the safety of my country."

The Captain gnawed at his clipped mustache. "At least the Soviets have one weakness that will never change: We know that it's impossible to fathom their way of thinking—but they fully believe that they know the thinking of every other country in the world. Now, it's the life of a child against the lives of untold millions. Tomorrow night! That's not much time to make up forty-four sheets of phony blue-prints. What does the F.B.I. think, Arnold? What are you going to do?"

"Mr. Connatser is going to drop the plans as ordered," Cameron said promptly. "You're right about Soviet thinking. We've learned a lot since the days of Klaus Fuchs and Harry Gold. Naval Intelligence draws up two sets of plans, today—when the design is for anything as vital as the SF-

[138]

800T. The second set is slightly different. To discover the bugs in it might take a corps of scientists a half a year. That's the set we're feeding to Junior tomorrow night.''

"Leaving three people only on the hot seat: Ronnie, my wife, and me!" Connatser's voice was low and deadly. "They're not going to keep Ronnie alive for six months. So they may find some bugs in a couple of days, and kill him then. Then there's always the chance when they get the plans that they'll consider it safer to murder him anyhow."

"So we better get busy with what we have, Mr. Connatser: Three records, the sound of a kidnapper's voice, and a snatch of song from a P.A. speaker." Maclain shook his head. "It's not very much, but somehow among us we've got to put it together. Before those plans are examined at all, we've got to find your boy. There is no other alternative."

"Knowing you as well as I do," Arnold Cameron said, "I have a vague uneasy feeling that you may be on to something that we've managed to overlook. God only knows, I hope so."

"I have some questions." There were lines creased on Maclain's forehead and his mobile face was set in a look of concentration as though his mind were far away. "Why did this man pick Audograph records?"

"We have fifteen Audographs in our office at the plant," Connatser explained. "I also have one for dictation at home."

"Do you think he was an ex-employee, Arnold?"

"That's a possibility that we're checking. We're getting a rundown on everyone who has worked at Connatser Products since the war. It's a big job, but it's a top-security plant so it shouldn't be impossible. But it is going to take plenty of time."

"Of which we have none," Connatser grunted. "Personally, I think it more likely that Junior called in as a salesman and saw the machines. Employees in our place are too closely checked for comfort."

"How would he know you had one home?"

"Maybe he didn't, but he knew I could always get one and take it home, since he's addressing his records to Evelyn there."

"Okay," Maclain said shortly. "I'm going to start just as though I knew what I was talking about: the same voices made all those records—Ronnie's and Junior's. Let's take it for granted that it's the same man who picked up Ronnie, and drove you to work under the name of Jules Rosine. Would you know him again, Mr. Connatser, if you saw him?"

Connatser gave it a little thought. "I doubt it. He wore a chauffeur's livery. He was dark, I believe, seemed personable enough, slightly built— that is, he didn't impress me as being particularly big and strong. I didn't see him standing up. From the few words he spoke, I'd say he had a French accent. On the drive to Long Island, after dropping Ronnie at school in the

[139]

morning, I was reading the paper and busy with some figures in the back seat of the car. Since I was occupied, I didn't give him too much thought really.''

"He is French, according to Leon Gerard,'' Hank Weeks stated positively. "He spoke fluent French to Leon when he held him up in his room and forced him to phone the housekeeper.''

"So his speech on the records, while marking him an educated man, has words in it that are British as a dish of bubble-and-squeak,'' Maclain declared. '"Phosphorescent paint'—'portmanteau'—'dispatch case.' We'd say briefcase, or luminous suitcase. But his accent isn't really British—just the words he uses. Let's mark him as a French Canadian—Quebec, or Montreal. Do you agree?''

"I think I'll buy that Canadian angle right now,'' Weeks said. "Since Igor Gouzenko skipped the Russian Embassy in Ottawa, in 1946, and turned up Klaus Fuchs, they've had troubles aplenty with certain Reds in Canada.''

"What would you guess his age to be?'' the Captain asked.

"Between thirty and forty at a guess.'' Connatser sounded a little unsure.

"Well, later if nothing happens, it might pay you to run back through the Year Books of Graduates in Engineering at McGill—University of Toronto, too. A picture just might jog your memory enough to spot him. There's another point I'd like to get clear: Ronnie certainly wasn't kidnapped in your own car—that is I don't think they'd chance driving him very far.''

"Just across the Queensboro Bridge,'' Cameron said. "The police found Mr. Connatser's Imperial parked under the approach to the bridge on the Long Island side at 6:20. Ronnie was going to a picture show with another boy, Ted Schuyler, at four. You heard that.''

Maclain nodded. "I'm interested as to how this Rosine got him to come along without a fuss, and then transferred him to another car. That's not easy in New York City between three and four in the afternoon.''

"You know as much as we do, Captain. From what Ronnie says on the records, the kidnapper gave him a line that Mr. Connatser wanted Ronnie to meet him at the plant. He bought Ronnie a bottle of Pepsi-Cola on the way. The police found the bottle still in the car and analyzed what was left. It showed Ronnie must have drunk three or four grains of Seconal. That would have put him out cold in fifteen minutes to half-an-hour, and he would have stayed out for eight to ten hours, maybe longer, according to the Medical Examiner. Of course they could have given him more on the trip if they were driving far.''

Maclain took a box of paper-clips from the middle desk drawer and slowly began to chain them together.

"That's what I was trying to figure—how long would they drive Ronnie and how far. Let's say four hundred miles—ten hours driving. That would put them where they were going about four in the early morning. I think Junior lives there and owns a house most likely. It's not easy to rent a place to hide a child. It must be fairly large—the town, I mean, or the city. Far too dangerous to take him to a small town—"

"What about an isolated farm?" Agent Weeks broke in on the Captain's audible reverie.

"Not close enough to a Post Office and an airport." The Captain put his clips back in the drawer and closed it with a snap of certainty. "Let's consider these records: It's obvious that nobody is flying around the country with a kidnapped boy. So the boy's in one place—probably guarded by Junior's wife or paramour. Women are better with children, anyhow. Now, listen to this." He found the Miami record and put it on, keeping his hand held up for silence until it was through.

"That record was made by Ronnie and the man on the machine, and at the same time. The machine may be old, or defective, for there's a murmuring drone in the background that records itself all the way through. Junior didn't notice it, so it must be a noise that he's used to. He noticed the start of 'Silent Night' quick enough and shut off the machine."

"The record was mailed from Miami, Captain," Cameron reminded him.

"That's my point, Arnold—nearness to an airport. The woman's mailing records to him. I believe that record was made Saturday evening, giving Ronnie time to come around and get instructions as to what he should say. Then Junior took it with him as soon as it was finished and caught a flight to Miami. In his suitcase he was carrying another Audograph machine. He mailed the record from Miami on Sunday. That would check as to time—ample time for him to stop off and make arrangements for the pick-up with some Deputy Sheriff, or town constable confederate, at any point along the way."

"You're right there," Cameron said glumly. "Deputy Sheriffs and Constables are a dime a dozen, and a police car is made to order—two way telephone, flasher and all. We can't police every point between here and Miami."

"So again the best bet is to find the woman and the boy," Maclain said. "She'll talk, I believe, if Junior has told her anything. We can be sure if he'd made arrangements in Miami the record wouldn't have been mailed from there, any more than if Ronnie was there. Anyhow, we know that

[141]

after the record was mailed, he hopped the first flight for Kansas City.''

"Typical Commie technique, that hopping about," Hank Weeks remarked. "The Boss, in his book 'Masters of Deceit' says they call it 'dry cleaning'—driving three hundred miles to cover thirty so no one will know where you've been or where you are."

"Go on, Captain!" Cameron sounded impatient. "You've got this Commie Canuck with his Audograph in K.C. now. Where do we go from there—outside of Cleveland?"

Without replying, Maclain put on the second record and played it to the end. "I know that Ronnie made this record on the same machine that recorded record No. 1. All the time that Ronnie is speaking you can hear that noise that runs through the first one. As soon as Junior starts to speak, the noise is gone. We must assume that the woman mailed this record to Junior in K.C., and he filled his part in on the Audograph he has with him. The New York Times is available in most cities the same, or the following day. The woman could have seen the personal and told Ronnie what to say, or Junior could have seen it and could have called her long-distance."

"Still more dry cleaning," Cameron said, "to help us Special Agents earn our pay, and put us through a wringer like we're going through today. Let's hear No. 3."

The Cleveland record just served to clinch the Captain's beliefs more firmly. A background noise when Ronnie was speaking, while Junior's words were clear.

"Could that noise come from a car or a plane?" Connatser asked. "I've used an Audograph in both, but I haven't been conscious of anything like that in the playbacks. Still, I might have overlooked it just like Junior has."

"It just won't hold water." The Captain's agile fingers beat a tattoo on the desk top. "I don't believe that Ronnie and his captor made that first record while driving in a car. There's that 'Silent Night' music, for one thing. Can you picture a man with a kidnapped boy in his car dictating a record and telling the boy what to say? Then a stop in front of a music store where there's a blaring P.A.?"

Hank Weeks said, "Hell no! Nor can I picture the kid being flown around to make records in a plane."

Maclain stood up abruptly. "Let's get what we can from the horse's mouth—the Sound Engineer at Gray Audograph. Let him hear these and see what he has to say."

In less than an hour they were in the Gray Audograph offices at 521 Fifth Ave., talking to Carl Schantz, the company's Chief Sound Engineer. Schantz, a stocky, phlegmatic, brilliant German, listened to Cameron, then played the three records through without comment.

Finished, he sat down in his desk chair and stared from one to another of his visitors through his gold-rimmed glasses. "The boy's voice and the man's—all of record one—was dictated to the same machine. The man's voice on records two and three was dictated to another machine. I'd say that both machines were old. Probably our Model Three, but there's nothing the matter with either of them. I'm certain of that."

"How do you know that?" Cameron asked. "The differences in the machines, I mean."

Schantz gave a slow smile. "You know from your work in the F.B.I. that there's a difference in every typewriter. Well, there's a difference in the needles of every dictating machine. They cut grooves of different depths on the records. The difference in those grooves is infinitesimal, but it shows up on a tape made by the electric-micrometer on our testing machine—the one I just played those on." He handed the S.A.C. a wide piece of ruled paper marked in purple ink with three wavy parallel lines. "Look for yourself."

All of the line made by record one, and the two lines made by Ronnie's voice on two and three were noticeably similar. There was a difference when Junior started to speak on the Kansas City and Cleveland records, but it still could be seen with the naked eye that those two lines were similar to each other.

"Does this mean that if we find those two machines and bring them in you can identify them for us?" Cameron's voice was eager.

"You bring them in. We'll give it a try!"

"What about that noise in the background?"

Schantz shrugged his heavy shoulders. "I'm afraid I can't help you there. Frankly, I don't know."

"Could it come from a nearby power plant or high-tension lines, something like that?" the Captain asked him.

Schantz shook his head. "We have Audographs running in offices with air-conditioners, calculators, and IBM sorting machines, sometimes right in the same room, and there's nothing but voice on the dictated record. Now and then, if you're not careful, you can get a loose connection in the six-hole receptacle where the mike plugs in. That will cause a nasty roar— but you can't dictate to the machine." He thought a moment. "The nearest thing to that noise I've heard was on a record dictated in an auto running at high speed with the windows open. The machine didn't pick up the motor, but it picked up the sound of the wind rushing by. That sound you have is steady like that, but deeper. It's almost like the lad was speaking through some distant hurricane." He sighed. "I'm really sorry I can't help you more."

"About those few lines of 'Silent Night'—have you any ideas there?" the Captain asked as Schantz was showing them out.

"I thought of a radio in another room, but it's too muffled. It's probably

[143]

from outside the house from a juiced-up P.A. system. If that's it, the place is right next door, or at the most right across the street. Anyhow, it must be very near.''

All afternoon, the Captain sat in his penthouse office listening to the records that Cameron had left with him. He had played them back through the Audograph speaker; listened to them with headphones on and finally using a jackplug, hopped them up to deafening volume on his hi-fi machine.

That background sound was all enveloping. The longer he listed to it, the more it took possession of him, until he almost believed what Schantz had said about a distant hurricane.

He thought of the ocean. It could keep people awake the first night, and in a day or two the noise would be gone. But the ocean wouldn't record like that unless it might be a wind-lashed sea.

Could they have the boy on a ship at sea? In a seven day storm? And mailing records air-mail to Junior in Kansas City? It showed how feeble the mind could get if you worked it on and on!

He kept coming back to that power plant. Why, when Schantz had said it wouldn't record? Could Schantz be wrong? Or could he, Maclain, whose ears had replaced his eyes, be clutching at straws and building into roaring volume some tiny wisp of sound? Was that noise, that should be a thousand jet planes busy ripping the skies, merely the hum of a washing machine, or an electric dryer? It had to be more.

Power! Overwhelming power! It had to be. With the life of a six year old boy at stake, he didn't dare to be wrong.

He'd stick to his own obsessions, too: They'd taken the boy, maybe dressed as a girl, on a single trip of ten hours. Four hundred miles at least. Then why not into Canada? If Junior was a Canadian, his car could have Canadian tags. It would be easy to cross the International Bridge in the middle of the night with a sleeping little girl accompanied by her father and mother . . .

The Captain jumped from the red divan, shut off the Audograph, and took his Braille map of New York State from a flat cabinet drawer. Moving faster than the eye could follow, he traced a line from New York City to Buffalo. Just three hundred and seventy-five miles!

Five minutes later he had Arnold Cameron on the phone. "I've got a fix, Arnold. Two points of sound, like when you're hunting down a hidden radio. Crosby singing 'Silent Night'—and the noise of the biggest power plant in the whole wide world. Now it's up to you to go get that boy!'' For a minute more he stammered on.

"Don't tell us how to run our business," Cameron cut in. "Get off the line so I can phone the Border Patrol of the Royal Canadian Mounted Police. It should be twice as easy to get a boy, since they're the chaps who always get their man!''

Just outside of the city limits, running at right angles to the river between Stanley Ave. and the Parkway, is a short street with eight neat houses on it. Five on one side and three on the other. On the side with the three houses and not quite forming a corner with the Parkway stands the Maple Leaf Tavern, boasting ten spotless bedrooms on the second floor, and downstairs a very good restaurant and a bar.

At seven o'clock, on Friday, Dec. 20th, Mr. Burns, who had owned and run the Maple Leaf for forty years, left his wife to superintend the cooking of dinner in the kitchen. He came into the bar to start his pick-up with Bing Crosby's ''Merry Christmas'' record. The first few chimes introducing ''Silent Night'' had scarcely pealed forth from the loud speaker over the Maple Leaf's front door, when Det. Sgt. McMurtrie, of the Ontario Provincial Police walked into the bar.

He and Burns were old friends. McMurtrie, tall and cadaverous with sad black eyes, was a startling contrast to the sandy-haired Burns, a Scot grown fat with good living through the years.

They shook hands. McMurtrie ordered an ale and sat down at a table in the empty bar. Burns joined him a moment later carrying two bottles and glasses.

''I'll have an ale wi' ye, Mac.''

''On me, if ye like. Looks to me, Matey, like you've driven all your trade away wi' that racket over the front door.''

''A racket ye call it! Don't be blasphemous, Mac. 'Tis one of God's songs, and there's others to come. I've been playing it every night now, except Sundays, for the past ten nights. 'Tis weather that's driven the trade away and not my offering passers-by a bit of warmth and Christmas cheer.''

''Hmph!'' McMurtrie swallowed some ale, his Adam's apple moving up and down. ''And would ye have a permit, Burns, to play that thing? Seems to me the good folks on this street would be kicking with you disturbing their TV and their sleep.''

''''Tis you who know perfectly well I have a permit, McMurtrie. Even though I'm outside of the city line, who but you has poked his long nose in here every chance he gets, checking every license and permit. And as for the folks on this street kicking, they're all good customers and friends of mine and glad of a little music.''

''All?'' Det. McMurtrie narrowed his bushy brows. ''Now there was one I recalled that you turned in for making subversive talk here during the war. What was his name?''

''Zwicker,'' Burns said. ''Francois Zwicker.'' Burns held up his glass of sparkling ale and looked at the bubbles against the light. "He owns the house right across the street. Number 3. God be praised, a year ago he lost his job at the Electric, where he was engineer, and moved away. The house stood vacant for a spell; then was rented for three months in the summer, to be vacant again until just this last Saturday."

"Rented?"

"No, he and his missus are back, but it won't be long, mark me. He'll hold a job nowhere with his anarchistic tongue. I've forbid him my place. His missus is no prize, either. Louise is her name, a Frenchie like him. Quebec or Three Rivers. She's there by herself right now. He's off again, hunting another job, I'll say. Not that he'll keep it long."

A party of four came in. Burns finished his ale and got up to greet them. "The ale's on me, Mac. Drop in again, and a Merry Christmas to ye!"

Outside, the detective got in a big black car where four men were waiting for him. "Let's go and get the search warrant," he said. "Zwicker's the name. The house is No. 3." The car moved off.

An hour later to the accompaniment of Bing's voice singing. "I'll Be Home for Christmas," McMurtrie rang the doorbell of No. 3. The door was opened finally by a white-faced woman with burning black eyes and raven hair.

"Provincial Police, Mrs. Zwicker," McMurtrie said. "There are four men posted about the house, and we have a search warrant. Let me in, please. We've come to get the boy."

At 6:00 P.M., on Saturday, Dec. 21st, Alan Connatser's Cessna Twin took off from the air strip at Connatser Products, on Long Island. With Steven Donegan, and Connatser, at the twin controls, it headed south as ordered. Instead of a phosphorescent-painted portmanteau, it was carrying Special Agent Hank Weeks, member of the F.B.I.

Ronnie, safely home with his mother, had made it in time for Macy's Christmas Parade.

Contact by radio was made at 8:20, and almost instantly a red flasher was turned-on on the ground in a large open area some twenty miles north of New Bern, North Carolina. As the Cessna headed for a point directly over the flasher, Hank Weeks spoke into the microphone:

"Zwicker, hear this now! This is a Special Agent of the F.B.I. speaking to you from the Cessna. Your wife has been arrested and we have the boy. She gave us the name of Walter Vollmer, the County Official who is with you now in that Patrol Car. You were followed and we know exactly where you are—in between Vanceboro and Blount Creek. You are hopelessly trapped, for cars are posted all along U.S. 17 and along State Road 33, as well as the country road you came in on. They have heard this and are closing in right now. That's all! There's no use your trying to escape."

[146]

Silent Night

The Cessna began to climb. "There's just one thing that gripes me, Hank," Connatser said disgruntedly. "Think of all the trouble you'd have saved if you'd done what Steve and I wanted to—loaded that portmanteau with just one little ol' bomb!"

Way up north in the Maple Leaf Tavern, Mr. Burns turned over the "Merry Christmas" record for the third time and started "Silent Night" again. On guard in the empty house across the street, in the event that the plans went wrong and Zwicker returned to his home, two members of the Ontario Provincial Police were engaged in a game of Rummy.

"It would be a silent night if Burns would shut that blasted thing off," one said to the other, slapping a card on the table.

"Aye," said the other, "still as the dead, if you're asking me!"

They went on playing unaware of the noise that filled every room, every cranny and every house and every street for miles around. They had lived in the midst of its deep reverberation far too long to hear it—the stunning boom of the Horseshoe Falls of Niagara, dumping its endless deafening millions of gallons down a drop of a hundred and fifty-eight feet just a half block away.

The Stolen Christmas Box
by Lillian de la Torre

THE DISAPPEARANCE of little Fanny Plumbe's Christmas box was but a prelude to a greater and more daring theft; and was itself heralded by certain uneasy signs and tokens. Of these was the strange cypher message which Mrs. Thrale intercepted; while I myself was never easy in my mind after seeing the old sailorman with the very particular wooden leg.

Dr. Sam: Johnson and I passed him on Streatham common as we approached the estate of the Thrales, there to spend our Christmas. He sat on a stone hard by the gates in the unseasonable sunshine, and whittled. He wore the neckerchief and loose pantaloons of a sea-faring man. He had a wind-beaten, heavy, lowering face, and a burly, stooped frame. His stump stuck out straight before him, the pantaloon drooping from it. That on which he whittled was his own wooden leg.

'Twas a very particular wooden leg. The cradle that accommodated his stump was high-pooped and arabesqued about like a man-of-war's bow with carvings, upon the embellishment of which he was at the moment engaged. Into the butt was screwed a cylindrical post of about half the bigness of my wrist, turned in a lathe and wickedly shod with iron.

As the carriage passed him at an easy pace, I stared down upon him. He extended his greasy flapped hat, and my venerable companion dropped into it a gratuity.

We found the Thrale household pernitious dumpish, for all it was nigh onto Christmas. The tall, silent brew-master Thrale greeted us with his usual cold courtesy, his diminutive rattle of a wife with her usual peacock screeches of delight. Of the party also were Thrale's grenadier of a sister, a strapping virago born to support the robes of a Lady Mayoress, and well on her way to that honour on the coat-tails of her husband, Alderman Plumbe. Plumbe topped his brother-in-law in height and doubled him in girth. His features were knobby and his temper cholerick. He scowled upon his children, Master Ralph, a lubber of fourteen, and Miss Fanny, a year older.

Master Ralph was rapidly shooting to his parents' height, but unable to keep pace in solidity. He continually closed his short upper lip over his long upper teeth, which as continually protruded again. He bowed and grinned and twisted his wrists in our honour.

Miss Fanny executed her duty curtsey with downcast eyes. Her person was tall and agreeably rounded, and sensibility played in red and white upon her cheek, playing the while, I own it, on the sensitive strings of my heart. Indeed, I could have been a knight-errant for Miss Fanny, had not I found below-stairs the veriest little witch of a serving-wench, pretty Sally, she who . . . but I digress.

Among the company circulated learned Dr. Thomas, the schoolmaster, assiduously pouring oil, as became a clergyman, on waters that were soon revealed to be troubled. Miss Fanny was in a fit of the sullens ('twas of a lover dismissed, I gathered so much), and Mrs. Plumbe was clean out of humour, and the Alderman alternately coaxing and shouting.

In an ill moment the latter conceived the idea of bribing Miss out of her pouts, and accordingly he fetches out the young lady's Christmas box, four days too soon, and bestows it upon her then and there; a step which he was bitterly to regret before the week was out.

"O Lud!" screamed Mrs. Thrale. "O Lud, 'tis a very Canopus!"

"'Tis indeed," said Dr. Sam: Johnson, "a star of the first magnitude."

'Twas a handsome jewel, though to my eyes scarce suitable for so young a lady—an intaglio artfully cut, and set with a diamond needlessly great, whether for the brooch or for the childish bosom 'twas designed to adorn.

"Sure," screeched Mrs. Thrale in her usual reckless taste, "such a size it is, it cannot be the right gem. Say, is't not paste?"

"Paste!" cried the Alderman, purpling to his wattles. "I assure you, ma'am, 'tis a gem of the first water, such that any goldsmith in the city will give you £200 for."

Ralph Plumbe sucked a front tooth; his prominent eyes goggled. Pretty Sally, the serving-maid, passing with the tea tray, stared with open mouth. Little Dr. Thomas joined his fingertips, and seemed to ejaculate a pious word to himself. The Alderman pinned the gem in his daughter's bosom, a task in which I longed to assist him. She bestowed upon him a radiant smile, like sun through clouds.

Her fickle heart was bought. She yielded to him with a pretty grace, those love-letters for which she had previously contested, and the footman carried them over the way that very afternoon to poor jilted Jack Rice, while Miss Fanny preened it with her jewel like a peacock.

'Twas a day or two later that I made one in a stroll about the Streatham grounds. Dr. Johnson and Mrs. Thrale beguiled our perambulation in discourse with learned Dr. Thomas about Welsh antiquities. Master Ralph Plumbe, ennuied by the disquisition, threw stones alternately at rocks and at Belle, the black-and-tawny spaniel bitch.

[150]

Coming by the kitchen garden, we marked curvesome Sally, in her blue gown and trim apron, skimming along under the wall. She passed us under full sail, with the slightest of running curtseys. Mrs. Thrale caught her sleeve.

"Pray, whither away so fast?"

"Only to the kitchen, ma'am."

Our sharp little hostess pounced.

"What have you in your hand?"

"Nothing, ma'am."

Mrs. Thrale, for all she is small, has a strong man's hand. She forced open the girl's plump fingers and extracted a folded billet.

"So, miss. You carry *billets doux.*"

"No, ma'am. I found it, if you please, ma'am," cried the girl earnestly.

"Ho ho," cried hobbledehoy Master Ralph, "'tis one of Fan's, I'll wager."

"We shall see," said Mrs. Thrale curtly, and unfolded the billet.

I craned my neck. 'Twas the oddest missive (save one) that I have ever seen. 'Twas all writ in an alphabet of but two letters:

```
aabababbabbaaaabaaba  ababbabbabbaaaabaaba
abbaa'abbabbaabaaabaabaaab  baabaaabaa
aabbbaaaaaababaabababaaabaa  ababa'aabaaaaaaabaabb
abbabbaabbabaaa  ababa'aaaaabaabbabbaaaabaa
abaaabaaaaaabaa  baabaaabaa
aabbaaaaaabaaaaaaabbaabaa  aabbbaaaaaabaaaabbaaaabaa
aaaaaabaaaababaabababaaabaa  aababababaaabaaaaaabaaabbaabaaba
```

Learned Dr. Thomas scanned the strange lines.

"'Tis some unknown, primordial tongue, I make no doubt."

"'Tis the talk of sheep! I cried. "Baabaaabaa!"

"No, sir; 'tis cypher," said Dr. Sam: Johnson.

"Good lack," screeched Mrs. Thrale, "'tis a French plot, I'll be bound, against our peace."

"No, ma'am," I hazarded, half in earnest, "'tis some imprisoned damsel, takes this means to beg release."

"Pfoh," said Mrs. Thrale, "ever the ruling passion, eh, Mr. Boswell?"

"To what end," demanded Dr. Johnson, "do we stand disputing here, when we might be reading the straight of the message?"

"My husband has the new book of cyphers," cried Mrs. Thrale, "I will fetch it at once."

She sailed off, pretty Sally forgotten; who put her finger to her eye and stood stock-still in the path, until, perceiving how eagerly I followed where Dr. Johnson and the cypher led, she flounced off with dry eyes.

Dr. Johnson made for the drawing-room, and we streamed after him.

Seating himself by the window, he peered at the strange paper. Dr. Thomas, Ralph Plumbe, and I peered with him, and Fanny came from the mirror, where we had surprized her preening, to peer too.

As Dr. Johnson smoothed the billet, I threw up my hands.

"What can be done with this!" I exclaimed. "We are to find out the 24 letters of the alphabet, and in this whole message we find but two symbols."

"What man can encypher, man can decypher," replied Dr. Johnson sententiously, "more especially when the encypherer is one of the inmates of Streatham, and the decypherer is Sam: Johnson. But see where our hostess comes."

She came empty-handed. The new book of cyphers was not to be found.

"Then," said Dr. Johnson, "we must make do with what we have in our heads. Let us examine this billet and see what it has to say to us."

We hung over his shoulder, Mrs. Thrale, Dr. Thomas, the Plumbe children, and I. Ralph sucked air through his teeth in excitement, little Fanny's pretty bosom lifted fast.

"Now, ma'am," began Dr. Johnson, addressing Mrs. Thrale, not ill-pleased to display his learning, "you must know, that cyphers have engaged the attention of the learned since the remotest antiquity. I need but name Polybius, Julius Africanus, Philo Mechanicus, Theodorus Bibliander, Johannes Walchius, and our own English Aristotle, Francis Bacon—"

"Oh, good lack, sir," cried little Fanny with a wriggle, "what does the paper say?"

"In good time, miss," replied the philosopher with a frown. "We have here 330 characters, all either *a* or *b;* writ in 16 groups on a page from a pocket book, with a fair-mended quill. 'Tis notable, that the writer wrote his letters in clusters of five, never more, never less; you may see between every group the little nodule of ink where the pen rested. Let us mark the divisions."

With his pen he did so. I watched the lines march:

    aabab/abbab/baaaa/baaba   ababb/abbab baaaa baaba
    abbaa'/abbab/baaba/aabaa/baaab   baaba   aabaa
    aabbb/aaaaa/ababa/ababa/aabaa . . .

"We now perceive," said Dr. Johnson as his pen flicked, "that we have to do, not with a correspondence of letter for letter, but for groups of letters. We have before us, in short, Mr. Boswell, the famous bi-literal cypher of the learned Francis Bacon; as set forth, I make no doubt, in Thrale's missing book of cyphers."

Mrs. Thrale clapped her hands.

[152]

"Now we shall understand it. Mark me, 'tis a plot of the French against us."

"Alas," said Dr. Johnson, "I do not carry the key in my head; but I shall make shift to reconstruct it. 'Tis many years since I was a corrector of the press; but the printer's case still remains in my mind to set me right on the frequencies of the letters in English."

"Depend upon it," muttered Mrs. Thrale stubbornly, "'tis in French."

"You will find," he went on calmly, "*e* occurs the oftenest; next *o,* then *a* and *i*. To find out one consonant from another, remember also their frequency, first *d, h, n, r, s, t;* then the others, in what order I forget; but with these we may make shift."

By this calculation the learned philosopher determined the combination *aabaa* to represent *e;* when a strange fact transpired. Of the sixteen groups, representing perhaps the sixteen words of the message, nine ended with that combination! Dr. Johnson considered this in conjuction with the little marks like apostrophes, and glowered at Mrs. Thrale.

"Can it be French after all?"

In fine, it was; for proceeding partly by trial and errour, and partly by his memory of the cypher's system, the learned philosopher made shift to reconstruct the key, and soon the message began to emerge:

"Fort mort n'otes te—"

"'Tis poetick!" screeched Mrs. Thrale. "*Strong death snatch thee not away!* Alack, this is a *billet doux* after all, a *lettre d'amour* to some enamoured fair!"

"Oh, ay?" commented the philosopher drily, penning the message:

"Fort mort n'otes te halle l'eau oui l'aune ire te garde haine aille firent salle lit."

"'Tis little enough poetick," I muttered, translating the strange hodgepodge:

"Strong death snatch thee not away—market—the water, yes—the alder—anger—keep thee hatred—let him go—they made room—bed."

"O lud, here's a waspish message," cried Fanny.

"Yet what's this of a market, water, and an alder tree?"

"There's an alder tree," cried Ralph with a toothy inspiration, "by the kitchen pump!"

Infected by his excitement, we all ran thither. There was the water, sure enough, in the old pump by the kitchen garden, and drooping its branches over it, not an alder, but a hoary old willow, whose hollow trunk knew the domesticities of generations of owls. There was nothing of any note in the vicinity.

This strange adventure made us none the easier; the less, as we encountered, at his ease on the bench by the kitchen door, the one-legged sailorman. He pulled his forelock surlily, but did not stir. His very particular wooden leg was strapped in its place, and the iron-shod stump was sunk deep in the mud of the door-yard. Belle snapped at it, and had a kick in the ribs for her pains.

The adventure of the cypher much disquieted the Alderman, who incontinently decreed that Miss Fanny's brilliant must be made secure in Thrale's strong-box. Now was repeated the contest of pouts against Papa; Miss Fanny moped, and would not be pleased. At last by treaty the difficulty was accommodated. Let the Alderman make the gem secure today, and Miss Fanny might wear it in honour of the twelve days of Christmas, to begin at dusk on Christmas Eve precisely.

Christmas Eve came all too slowly, but it came at last. We were all in holiday guise, I in my bloom-coloured breeches, Dr. Thomas in a large new grizzle wig, Ralph in peach-colour brocade with silk stockings on his skinny shanks. Even Dr. Sam: Johnson honoured the occasion in his attire, with his snuff-colour coat and brass buttons, and a freshly powdered wig provided by the care of Mr. Thrale.

The ladies coruscated. Mrs. Alderman Plumbe billowed in flame-colour sattin. Mrs. Thrale had a handsome gown in the classick stile, with great sleeves, and gems in her hair. Miss Fanny wore a silken gown, of the tender shade appropriately called maiden's blush; 'twas cut low and, and her brooch gleamed at her bosom. Even Belle the spaniel was adorned with a great riband tied on with care by the white hand of Miss Fanny.

'Twas Thrale's care to uphold the old customs, and play the 'squire; while at the same time he had a maccaroni's contempt for the lower orders. 'Twas decreed, therefore, that we should have our Christmas games in the library on the lower floor, while the servants might have their merrymaking in the servant's hall, and the strolling rusticks had perforce to receive their Christmas gratuities withoutside.

We supped upon Christmas furmety, a dish of wheat cakes seethed in milk with rich spices. I relished it well, and did equal justice to the noble minced pyes served up with it.

Supper done, we trooped to the library. Impeded by an armful of green stuff, Dr. Johnson came last, edging his way to the door. On the threshold, as he sought to manœuvre the unmanageable branches through, the crookedest one fairly lifted his fresh-powdered Christmas wig from his head, and as he clutched at it with a start, precipitated it in a cloud of white onto the floor. I relieved him of his awkward burden, and good-humouredly he recovered his head-covering and clapped it back in its place, all awry.

In the library all was bustle. It was my part to wreathe the mantel with green. Pretty Miss Fanny lighted the Christmas candles, looking the pret-

[154]

tier in their glow, her sparkling eyes rivalling the brilliant at her breast. Thrale ignited the mighty "Yule clog."

Dr. Johnson was in great expansion of soul, saluting his hostess gallantly under the mistletoe bough, and expatiating on the old Christmas games of his boyhood.

"Do but be patient, Dr. Johnson, we'll shew you them all," cried Thrale with unwonted vivacity. He was busied over a huge bowl. In it heated wine mingled its fumes with orange peel and spices, while whole roasted apples by the fire were ready to be set abob in it. 'Twas the old-time *wassail bowl;* though Dr. Johnson persisted in referring to its contents, in his Lichfield accent, as *poonch.*

"Here we come a-wassailing among the leaves so green,
  Here we come a-wandering, so fair to be seen . . ."

The notes of the song crept up on us gradually, coming from the direction of the common, till by the time the second verse began, the singers stood in the gravel path before the library windows; which we within threw up, the better to hear their song:

"We are not daily beggars, that beg from door to door,
  But we are your neighbours' children, whom you have seen before . . ."

Past all doubt, so they were. The servants had crowded to the door-step in the mild night, and merry greetings were interchanged as they found friends among the waits. A light snow was drifting down. The rusticks were fancifully adorned with ribands, and wore greens stuck in their hats; they carried lanthorns on poles, and sang to the somewhat dubious accompaniment of an ancient serpent and a small kit fiddle. In the ring of listening faces I spied the surly visage of the one-legged sailor. Belle the spaniel spied her enemy too. She escaped from the arms of Miss Fanny, eluded the groom at the house-door, and dashed out into the mud to snap at his heel. She came back with a satisfied swagger, the more as she had succeeded in untying her riband and befouling it in the mud. Miss Fanny admonished her, and restored the adornment.

"Now here's to the maid in the lily-white smock
  Who slipped to the door and pulled back the lock,
  Who slipped to the door and pulled back the pin
  For to let these merry wassailers walk in."

There was no suiting the action to the word. Thrale passed the cup out at window, keeping the lower orders still withoutside. The waits wiped their mouths on their sleeves, and sang themselves off:

"Wassail, wassail all over the town,
Our bread it is white and our ale it is brown,
Our bowl it is made of the green maple tree—
In our wassailing bowl we'll drink unto thee!"

Next the mummers came marching. Like the waits, they had been recruited from the lads about Streatham. Though every man was disguised in fantastick habiliments, among them the canine instinct of Belle unerringly found out her friends. His own mother would not have known the *Doctor*, he presenting to the world but a high-bridged nose and a forest of whiskers; but Belle licked his hand, the while he acknowledged the attention by scratching her ear and making her riband straight. She fawned upon *St. George* (by which, " 'Tis the butcher's boy!'' discovered Mrs. Thrale) and put muddy foot-marks on the breeches of the *Old Man,* before her attentions were repelled. She came back with her tongue out and her riband, once again, a-trail. Miss Fanny, defeated, neglected to restore it. She crowded with the rest of the company in the window as the link-boys lifted their torches, and upon the snowy sward the rusticks of Streatham played the famous mumming play of *St. George and the Dragon.*

"Pray, sir, take notice," said the pleased Dr. Johnson, "is not this a relique of great antiquity, the hieratic proceedings of yonder sorcerous *Doctor* with his magick pill? Pray, my man—" out at window to the *Doctor,* "how do you understand these doings?"

"Nor I don't, sir," replied the player huskily, and carried on his part to a chorus of laughter from within.

"And God bless this good company," concluded *St. George* piously. He caught the heavy purse that Thrale threw him, weighed it, and added in his own voice, "God bless ye, sir."

The guests added their largesse. Plumbe hurled a piece of gold; Dr. Johnson and I scattered silver; even withered little Dr. Thomas must needs add his half crown. 'Twas scarce worth the trouble he went to, first to fumble in his capacious pocket for the destined coin, then to wrap it in a leaf from his pocket book, finally to aim it precisely into the hands of *St. George.* His heart was better than his marksmanship; his shot went wide, and a scramble ensued.

"God bless all here," chorused the rusticks, and made off with their torches as we within closed windows and clustered about the fire. Then the bowl was set ablaze, and we adventured our fingers at snapdragon, catching at the burning raisins with merry cries.

"Fan, my love," said the Alderman suddenly, "where is thy Christmas box?"

Everybody looked at the flushed girl, standing with a burned finger-tip between her pink lips like a baby.

"The man," she half-whispered, "the man, Papa, he looked at it so, while the mummers played, I was affrighted and slipped it into a place of safety."

She indicated an exquisite little French enamel vase.

" 'Tis here, Papa."

The Alderman snatched the vase and turned it up. 'Twas empty. Miss Fanny's Christmas box was gone.

The Alderman turned purple.

"The servants—" he roared.

"Pray, Mr. Plumbe, calm yourself," said Dr. Johnson, "we must look for Miss Fanny's diamond within this room.".

He pointed, first to the snow now lightly veiling the ground beneath the window, then to the splotch of powder on the threshold. In neither was there any mark of boot or shoe.

But, though the cholerick Alderman turned out the chamber, and though every one present submitted to the most thorough of searches, though Plumbe even sifted out the ashes of the Yule clog, little Fanny's Christmas box was not to be found.

"This is worse than Jack Rice a thousand times," sniggered her brother in my ear.

It was so. Poor pretty Fanny was in disgrace.

" 'Tis a mean thief," cried Dr. Johnson in noble indignation, "that robs a child, and be sure I'll find him out."

Poor Fanny could only sob.

'Twas enough to mar the merriment of Christmas Day. Little Fanny kept her chamber, being there admonished by good Dr. Thomas. The lout Ralph wandered about idly, teasing Belle until the indignant spaniel nipped him soundly; upon which he retired into the sulks. The Alderman and his lady were not to be seen. The master and mistress of the house were busied doing honour to the day. I was by when they dispensed their Christmas beef upon the door-step; pretty Sally handed the trenchers about, and there in the crowd of rusticks, stolidly champing brawn, I saw the one-legged sailor. He seemed quite at home.

Dr. Johnson roamed restlessly from room to room.

BOSWELL: "Pray, sir, what do you seek so earnestly?"

JOHNSON: "Sir, a French dictionary."

BOSWELL: "To what end?"

JOHNSON: "To read yonder cypher aright; for sure 'tis the key to tell us, whither Fanny's brilliant has flown."

BOSWELL: "Why, sir, the words are plain; 'tis but the interpretation that eludes us."

JOHNSON: No, sir, the words are *not* plain; the words are somehow to be transposed. Now, sir, could I but find a French dictionary printed in *two*

[157]

columns, 'twould go hard but we should find, in the *second* column, the words we seek, jig-by-jole with the meaningless words we now have.''

Upon this I joined the search; but in twenty-four hours we advanced no further in reading the cypher.

After dinner the next day I came upon Dr. Johnson conning it over by the fire, muttering the words to himself:

"Te halle l'eau oui l'aune ire te garde haine . . .''

I was scarce attending. An idea had occurred to me.

"Yonder hollow willow near the garden—" I began.

"How?" cried Dr. Johnson, starting up.

"The hollow willow near the garden—"

"You have it, Bozzy!" cried my companion in excitement. "Te hollow willown ear te gard en.''

So strange was the accent and inflection with which my revered friend repeated my words, that I could only stare.

"Read it!" he cried. "Read it aloud!"

He thrust the decyphered message under my nose. I read it off with my best French accent, acquired in my elegant grand tour.

"Can't you see," cried Dr. Johnson, "when you speak it, the words are English—the hollow willow near the garden! 'Twill be the miscreants' post-office, 'tis clear to me now. See, they had cause to distrust the maid who was go-between.''

He pointed to the last words: *aille firent salle lit,* I fear Sally.

"How did you do it, Bozzy?"

"I, sir? Trust me, 'twas the furthest thing from my mind. It had come into my head, perhaps by the alder was meant yonder hollow willow—"

"No, sir," returned Dr. Johnson, "there came into your mind, a *picture* of the hollow willow, because you heard, without knowing that you heard, the words I uttered; and when *you* spoke the words, *I* recognized that you were repeating mine. But come, sir; let us investigate this thieves' post-office.''

He fairly ran out at the door.

Coming suddenly about the corner of the house, we surprised the sailorman standing under the wall of the kitchen garden; and I could have sworn that I caught the swirl of a skirt where the wall turned. As we came up, the one-legged man finished knotting something into his neckerchief, and made off with astonishing speed. He stumped his way across the common in the direction of the ale-house on the other side.

"Shall we not catch him up?" I cried.

"In good time," replied my friend. "First we must call for the post.''

Accordingly we lingered to sound the hollow tree. Save for some grubs and beetles, and a quantity of feathers, it was empty.

Our fortune was better when we passed under the wall where the one-legged man had stood. There we picked up the second of the strange messages that came under our eyes at Streatham.

'Twas a strip of paper, scarce an inch wide and some twelve inches long. Along both its edges someone had made chicken-tracks with a pen. One end was roughly torn away. Search as we might, the missing fragment was not to be found. At last we repaired to the house.

In the library we encountered Mrs. Thrale, in philosophical discourse with Dr. Thomas. She looked at the strange piece of paper, and gave a screech.

" 'Tis Ogam!"

"Ogam?"

"I know it well, 'tis the antique writing of the Irish," said Dr. Thomas, scanning the page with interest. "You must understand, sir, that the untutored savages of Ireland, knowing nothing of pen and paper, had perforce to contrive some way of incising letters upon wood, stone, horn, and the like. They hit upon a system of scratching lines on the edges of these objects, as perpendicular or oblique, and grouped to represent the various letters. Thus it was said of many a deceased Irish hero, 'They dug the grave and they raised the stone and they carved his name in Ogam.' "

"Why, this is a learned jewel-thief. Pray, Dr. Thomas, translate these triangles and dashes."

"Alack, sir, I cannot do it extempore. I must first have my books."

"*You,* ma'am," says Dr. Johnson to the volatile matron, "*you* are

[159]

mighty familiar with Ogam, pray read it off for us."

"O Lud, sir, not I, I am none of your antiquarians."

"Why, so. Then I must extract the meaning for myself. 'Twill be no harder than the bi-literal cypher."

But try as he would, the strange marks on the edges of the paper would not yield to the theory of the printer's case. At last he leaned back.

"Let us begin afresh."

"No, sir," I begged, "let us have our tea. I am no Spartan boy, to labour while a fox is gnawing my vitals."

"Spartan!" cried my companion. "You have earned your tea, Mr. Boswell. Do but answer me one question first, we may begin afresh and I think proceed in the right direction. Pray, what shape is this paper?"

"Sir, long and flat."

Dr. Johnson dangled it by one end.

"No, sir, 'tis helical."

Indeed as it dangled it coiled itself into a helix.

"Let us restore it to its proper shape," said Dr. Johnson. "Pray, Mr. Boswell, fetch me the besom."

I looked a question, but my sagacious friend said nothing further, and I went in search of the pretty housemaid and her besoms. After an interlude of knight-errantry, which taught me somewhat about women, but naught at all about our puzzle, I returned with such brooms as the house afforded.

I found my learned friend surrounded by stocks and staves, thick and thin, long and short. Around them, one after one, he was coiling the strange paper as a friseur curls hair about his finger. The results left him but ill satisfied.

"Could I but recall it to mind," he muttered, "there is a thing missing, that is germane to this puzzle; but now 'tis gone from my memory."

"Why, sir," said I, "we are to question the one-legged sailorman."

"Well remembered, Mr. Boswell." He stuffed the coiled paper into his capacious pocket. "Come, let us be off."

I bade farewell to my tea as I followed him. We found the publick room of the Three Crowns nigh empty, its only occupants being the idling tapster, and two men drinking in the ingle; but one of them was the man we sought. His companion was a likely-looking youth with a high-bridged nose, who pledged him in nappy ale.

"Good day, friend," Dr. Johnson accosted the maimed sailor.

The fresh-faced youth rose quietly, pulled a respectful forelock, and made off. Dr. Johnson looked at the sailorman's tankard, now empty, and signed to the tapster.

Not that the sailorman's tongue wanted loosening. Previous potations had already done the business. He was all too ready to spin his yarn.

"Nine sea fights I come through," he cried, "and lost my peg in the end, *mort dieu,* in Quiberon Bay."

He dealt his wooden member a mighty thump with the again emptied tankard. My worthy friend, ever ready to relieve the lot of the unfortunate, once more signed to the tapster. As the can was filling, he animadverted upon the wretchedness of a sea-life.

"I marvel, that any man will be a sailor, who has contrivance enough to get himself into a gaol; for being in a ship is being in gaol with the chance of being drowned."

"Ah," said the peg-legged sailor mournfully, and buried his nose in his pot.

My friend pressed upon him a gratuity in recognition of his perils passed. The sailorman accepted of it with protestations of gratitude.

"'Tis nothing, sir," replied my kindly friend. "Do you but gratify my whim, I'll call myself overpaid."

"How, whim?" says the sailorman.

"I've a whim," says Johnson, "to borrow your wooden leg for a matter of half an hour."

I stared with open mouth, but the sailorman shewed no flicker of sur-prize. He unstrapped the contrivance immediately and put it in my friend's hand.

"Pray, Bozzy," said Dr. Johnson, "see that our worthy friend here lacks for nothing until I come again."

Before I could put a question he had withdrawn, the unstrapped peg in his hand. I was left to the company of the tapster and the loquacious sailor-man. He insisted upon telling me how he had made his peg himself, and how it had often been admired for its artistry.

"Here's this young fellow now," he rattled on, gesturing vaguely across the common, "he thinks it a rarity, and but this morning he had it of me for an hour at a time."

This statement but doubled my puzzlement. What in the world could a two-legged man want with a peg-leg? Surely my learned friend was not in-tending to personate the one-legged sailorman? Had the high-nosed youth done so? I tried to recall the glimpse I had had of the one-legged beggar by the kitchen garden.

When Dr. Johnson returned, he returned in his own guise. We left the sailorman, by this time snorting with vinous stertorousness in the corner of the ingle, and walked across the common back to the house.

"Pray, sir, what success? Did you find the diamond?"

"Find the diamond? No, sir, I did not find the diamond; but I know where it is, and I know how to lay the thief by the heels.''

He dug from his pocket the strange strip of paper. Between the lines of Ogam he had penned the message:

"£140 tonight 12 a clock ye oak nighest ye 3 crowns"

"What shall this signify?"

"Nay, Bozzy, 'tis plain. But here comes our friend Dr. Thomas. Pray, not a word more.''

I was seething with curiosity as we supped at the Thrales' sumptuous table. The talk turned, willy-nilly, to the strange way in which the Christmas gem had been spirited from the library. Dr. Johnson admitted himself baffled. He was in a depression from which he could not be wooed even by the blandishments of the spaniel Belle, who, spurred by hunger, begged eagerly for scraps; until a new larceny, committed against himself, restored him to good humour.

It must be said that Dr. Sam Johnson is scarce a dainty feeder. He is a valiant trencherman, and stows away vast quantities of his favourite comestables.

"Ma'am," says he on this occasion, unbuttoning the middle button of his capacious vest and picking a capon wing in his fingers, "ma'am, where the dinner is ill gotten, the family is somehow grossly wrong; there is poverty, ma'am, or there is stupidity; for a man seldom thinks more earnestly of anything than of his dinner, and if he cannot get that well done, he should be suspected of inaccuracy in other things.''

"Oh," says Mrs. Thrale, not knowing how to take this, but willing to turn it against him, "did you never, then, sir, huff your wife about your meat?"

"Why, yes," replied he, taking a second wing in his fingers, "but then she huffed me worse, for she said one day as I was going to say grace: 'Nay, hold,' says she, 'and do not make a farce of thanking GOD for a dinner which you will presently protest to be uneatable.' ''

At this there was a general laugh; under cover of which Belle the spaniel, tempted beyond endurance, reared boldly up, snatched the capon wing from the philosopher's fingers, and ran out of door with it.

"Fie, Belle," cried out Mrs. Thrale, "you used to be upon honour!"

"Ay," replied the Doctor with his great Olympian laugh, "but here has been a *bad influence* lately!"

Not another word would he say, but devoted himself to a mighty veal pye with plums and sugar.

Yet when we rose from the table, he sought out the guilty Belle and plied her with dainties.

" 'Tis a worthy canine, Bozzy," cried he to me, "for she has told me, not only *how* Miss Fanny's diamond was spirited from the library, but by *whose* contrivance. Between the good Belle, and yonder strange paper of

Ogam, I now know *where* the conspirators shall meet, and *when,* and *who* they are, and *what* their object is; to prevent which, I shall make one at the rendezvous. Do you but join me, you shall see all made plain.''

I was eager to do so. Muffled in greatcoats, we crossed the common and took up our station under the great oak a stone's cast from the Three Crowns. As the wind rattled the dry branches over our heads, I was minded of other vigils we had shared and other miscreants we had laid by the heels.

The darkness was profound. Across the common we saw window after window darken in the Thrale house as the occupants blew out their candles. Then I became aware of motion in the darkness, and towards us, stealing along the path, came a muffled shape, utterly without noise, flitting along like a creature of the night. For a moment we stood rigid, not breathing; then Dr. Johnson stepped forward and collared the advancing figure. It gave a startled squeak, and was silent. Dr. Johnson pulled the hat from the brow. In the starlight I stared at the face thus revealed.

'Twas Dr. Thomas! I beheld with horror his awful confusion at being detected.

"Alas, Dr. Johnson, 'tis I alone am guilty! But pray, how have you smoaked me?''

"Ogam,'' says Dr. Johnson, looking sourly upon the clergyman. "Trust me, you knew that was no Ogam. Ogam is incised on *both* edges of a right angle, not scribbled on paper.''

"That is so, sir. You have been too sharp for me. I will confess all. 'Tis my fatal passion for Welsh antiquities. I have pawned the very vestments of my office to procure them. I took Miss Fanny's gem, I confess it, and flung it from the window wrapped in a leaf from my pocket book.''

"I see it!'' I exclaimed. "'Twas thrown at hazard, and the one-legged sailor carried it thence hid in the hollow of his wooden leg.''

"Nothing of the kind,'' said Dr. Johnson. "The role of the sailor and his wooden leg was quite other. But say, how much had you for the gem?''

"Two hundred pounds,'' replied the fallen clergyman. "Two hundred pounds! The price of my honour! Alas,'' he cried in a transport of remorse, falling on his knees and holding up his hands to Heaven, "had I, when I stood at those crossroads, gone another way, had I but heeded the voice within me which cried, *Turn aside, turn aside, lest thou fall into the hands of thine enemy,* had I but gone swiftly upon the strait way, then in truth we might at the grave's end have met together in the hereafter . . .''

Dr. Johnson heard this piteous avowal unmoved, but not so I. 'Twas a solemn sight to see the unfortunate man wring his hands and cry out with anguish, turning up his eyes to Heaven. Suddenly, however, his gaze fixed eagerly upon the darkened inn. In the same instant Dr. Johnson whirled, and ran, swiftly for all his bulk, to where a light coach was just getting in motion. I heard the harness jingle, and then the startled snort of a horse as my fearless friend seized the near animal by the bit and forced it to a halt.

"So," he cried angrily, "you'll meet them hereafter at *Gravesend!* Never a whit. Come down, sir! Come down, miss!"

For a moment there was only the jingle of harness as the nervous horses pranced. Then a figure stepped to earth, a tall young man muffled to his high-bridged nose in a heavy cape, and lifted down after him the cloaked figure of—

Miss Fanny Plumbe!

"Pray, Dr. Johnson," she said statelily, "why do you hinder us? What have we done?"

"You have diddled your father, and all of us," replied my companion sternly, "sending Bacon's cypher to Jack Rice here with those letters you gave up so meekly—once you had the diamond that you might turn into journey-money."

The chit's composure was wonderful.

"Why, sir," she owned with a smile, "you gave me a turn when you de-cyphered my last message by the hand of Sally; whom indeed, Mr. Bos-well—" turning to me—"I no longer dared trust when she became so great with you. But confess, Dr. Johnson, my French held you off, after all, until I was able to convey a new cypher to Jack by the hand of the sailorman."

"And Dr. Thomas was your accomplice in making away with the gem?" I cried in uncontrollable curiosity.

"Be not so gullible, Bozzy," cried my companion impatiently, "trust me, Dr. Thomas knew never a word of the matter until Miss here opened her mind to him in their close conference on Christmas Day. 'Twas the hussy herself that conveyed her diamond to her lover, that he might turn it into money for their elopement."

"Nay, how? For she never left the room."

"But *Belle* did—and carried with her the diamond, affixed to her riband by the hand of Miss Fanny. Out flies the dog to greet her friend the neigh-bour lad in his mummer's disguise; who apprised of the scheam, caresses his canine friend and removes the brilliant in the same operation."

"That is so, sir," said Jack Rice.

"Surely," said Miss Fanny, "surely I did no wrong, to convey my jewel to the man I mean to wed."

"That's as may be," said my friend, unrelenting, "but now, miss, do you accompany us back to the house, for there'll be no elopement this night."

"Pray, sir," said Dr. Thomas earnestly, "be mollified. The lad is a good lad, and will have a competence when once he turns twenty-one; and I have engaged to make one in their flight and bless their union, which the surly Alderman opposes out of mere ill nature."

"To this I cannot be a party," began my authoritarian friend. The little clergyman was fumbling in his pocket. He brought forth, not a weapon, but a prayer-book.

"Do you, John, take this woman . . ." he began suddenly.

"Hold, hold!" cried Johnson.

"I do," cried the lad in a ringing voice.

"And do you, Fanny . . ."

Jack Rice pulled a seal-ring from his finger.

"I do."

"Then I pronounce you man and wife."

The ring hung loose on the girl's slim finger, but it stayed on.

"You are witnesses, Dr. Johnson, Mr. Boswell," cried the little clergyman. "Will not you salute the bride?"

Dr. Johnson lifted his great shoulders in concession.

"I wish you joy, my dear."

As the coach with its strangely-assorted trio of honeymooners receded in the distance:

"Pray, Dr. Johnson," said I, "resolve me one thing. If the strange message was not Ogam, what was it?"

JOHNSON: "Simple English."

BOSWELL: "How can this be?"

JOHNSON: "The triangles and scratches along the edges of yonder paper were halved lines of writing, and had only to be laid together to be read off."

BOSWELL: "Yet how are the top and bottom of a single strip of paper to be laid together?"

JOHNSON: "The Spartans, of whom you yourself reminded me, did it by means of a staff or *scytale,* around which the strip is wound, edge to edge, both for writing and for reading."

BOSWELL: "Hence your search for a staff or broomstick."

JOHNSON: "Yes, sir. Now it went in my mind, yonder one-legged man had a strange wooden leg, which did not taper as they usually do, but was straight up and down like a post. Was he perhaps both the emissary and the key? At the cost of a half-crown I had it of him—carried it out of his sight that he might not babble of my proceedings—and read the communication with ease."

BOSWELL: "This is most notable, sir. I will make sure to record it this very night."

JOHNSON: "Pray, Mr. Boswell, spare me that; for though the play-acting clergyman with his two hundred pounds and his Welsh antiquities failed to deceive me, yet'tis cold truth that under my nose a green boy has conspired with a school-girl to steal first a diamond and then the lass herself; so let's hear no more on't."

[165]

"Then Mrs. Cratchit entered, smiling proudly, with the pudding. Oh. a wonderful pudding! Shaped like a cannonball, blazing in half-a-quartern of ignited brandy bedight with Christmas holly stuck into the top, and stuffed full with plums and sweetmeats and sodium diacetate and monoglyceride and potassium bromate and aluminum phosphate and calcium phosphate monobasic and chloromine T and aluminum potassium sulfate and calcium propionate and sodium alginate and butylated hydroxyanisole and..."

★

A Chaparral Christmas Gift

by O. Henry

THE ORIGINAL CAUSE of the trouble was about twenty years in growing. At the end of that time it was worth it.

Had you lived anywhere within fifty miles of Sundown Ranch you would have heard of it. It possessed a quantity of jet-black hair, a pair of extremely frank, deep-brown eyes and a laugh that rippled across the prairie like the sound of a hidden brook. The name of it was Rosita McMullen; and she was the daughter of old man McMullen of the Sundown Sheep Ranch.

There came riding on red roan steeds—or, to be more explicit, on a paint and a flea-bitten sorrel—two wooers. One was Madison Lane, and the other was the Frio Kid. But at that time they did not call him the Frio Kid, for he had not earned the honours of special nomenclature. His name was simply Johnny McRoy.

It must not be supposed that these two were the sum of the agreeable Rosita's admirers. The bronchos of a dozen others champed their bits at the long hitching rack of the Sundown Ranch. Many were the sheeps'-eyes that were cast in those savannas that did not belong to the flocks of Dan McMullen. But of all the cavaliers, Madison Lane and Johnny McRoy galloped far ahead, wherefore they are to be chronicled.

Madison Lane, a young cattleman from the Nueces country, won the race. He and Rosita were married one Christmas day. Armed, hilarious, vociferous, magnanimous, the cowmen and the sheepmen, laying aside their hereditary hatred, joined forces to celebrate the occasion.

Sundown Ranch was sonorous with the cracking of jokes and six-shooters, the shine of buckles and bright eyes, the outspoken congratulations of the herders of kine.

But while the wedding feast was at its liveliest there descended upon it Johnny McRoy, bitten by jealousy, like one possessed.

"I'll give you a Christmas present," he yelled, shrilly, at the door, with his .45 in his hand. Even then he had some reputation as an offhand shot.

His first bullet cut a neat underbit in Madison Lane's right ear. The bar-

[167]

rel of his gun moved an inch. The next shot would have been the bride's had not Carson, a sheepman, possessed a mind with triggers somewhat well oiled and in repair. The guns of the wedding party had been hung, in their belts, upon nails in the wall when they sat at table, as a concession to good taste. But Carson, with great promptness, hurled his plate of roast venison and frijoles at McRoy, spoiling his aim. The second bullet, then, only shattered the white petals of a Spanish dagger flower suspended two feet above Rosita's head.

The guests spurned their chairs and jumped for their weapons. It was considered an improper act to shoot the bride and groom at a wedding. In about six seconds there were twenty or so bullets due to be whizzing in the direction of Mr. McRoy.

"I'll shoot better next time," yelled Johnny; "and there'll be a next time." He backed rapidly out the door.

Carson, the sheepman, spurred on to attempt further exploits by the success of his plate-throwing, was first to reach the door. McRoy's bullet from the darkness laid him low.

The cattlemen then swept out upon him, calling for vengeance, for, while the slaughter of a sheepman has not always lacked condonement, it was a decided misdemeanour in this instance. Carson was innocent; he was no accomplice at the matrimonial proceedings; nor had any one heard him quote the line "Christmas comes but once a year" to the guests.

But the sortie failed in its vengeance. McRoy was on his horse and away, shouting back curses and threats as he galloped into the concealing chaparral.

That night was the birthnight of the Frio Kid. He became the "bad man" of that portion of the State. The rejection of his suit by Miss McMullen turned him to a dangerous man. When officers went after him for the shooting of Carson, he killed two of them, and entered upon the life of an outlaw. He became a marvellous shot with either hand. He would turn up in towns and settlements, raise a quarrel at the slightest opportunity, pick off his man and laugh at the officers of the law. He was so cool, so deadly, so rapid, so inhumanly blood-thirsty that none but faint attempts were ever made to capture him. When he was at last shot and killed by a little one-armed Mexican who was nearly dead himself from fright, the Frio Kid had the deaths of eighteen men on his head. About half of these were killed in fair duels depending upon the quickness of the draw. The other half were men whom he assassinated from absolute wantonness and cruelty.

Many tales are told along the border of his impudent courage and daring. But he was not one of the breed of desperadoes who have seasons of generosity and even of softness. They say he never had mercy on the object of his anger. Yet at this and every Christmastide it is well to give each one credit, if it can be done, for whatever speck of good he may have possessed. If the Frio Kid ever did a kindly act or felt a throb of generosity in his heart it was once at such a time and season, and this is the way it happened.

One who has been crossed in love should never breathe the odour from the blossoms of the ratama tree. It stirs the memory to a dangerous degree.

One December in the Frio country there was a ratama tree in full bloom, for the winter had been as warm as springtime. That way rode the Frio Kid and his satellite and co-murderer, Mexican Frank. The kid reined in his mustang, and sat in his saddle, thoughtful and grim, with dangerously narrowing eyes. The rich, sweet scent touched him somewhere beneath his ice and iron.

"I don't know what I've been thinking about, Mex," he remarked in his usual mild drawl, "to have forgot all about a Christmas present I got to give. I'm going to ride over to-morrow night and shoot Madison Lane in his own house. He got my girl—Rosita would have had me if he hadn't cut into the game. I wonder why I happened to overlook it up to now?"

"Ah, shucks, Kid," said Mexican, "don't talk foolishness. You know you can't get within a mile of Mad Lane's house to-morrow night. I see old man Allen day before yesterday, and he says Mad is going to have Christmas doings at his house. You remember how you shot up the festivities when Mad was married, and about the threats you made? Don't you suppose Mad Lane'll kind of keep his eye open for a certain Mr. Kid? You plumb make me tired, Kid, with such remarks."

"I'm going," repeated the Frio Kid, without heat, "to go to Madison Lane's Christmas doings, and kill him. I ought to have done it a long time ago. Why, Mex, just two weeks ago I dreamed me and Rosita was married instead of her and him; and we was living in a house, and I could see her smiling at me, and—oh! h——l, Mex, he got her; and I'll get him—yes, sir, on Christmas Eve he got her, and then's when I'll get him."

"There's other ways of committing suicide," advised Mexican. "Why don't you go and surrender to the sheriff?"

"I'll get him," said the Kid.

Christmas Eve fell as balmy as April. Perhaps there was a hint of far-away frostiness in the air, but it tingled like seltzer, perfumed faintly with late prairie blossoms and the mesquite grass.

When night came the five or six rooms of the ranch-house were brightly lit. In one room was a Christmas tree, for the Lanes had a boy of three, and a dozen or more guests were expected from the nearer ranches.

At nightfall Madison Lane called aside Jim Belcher and three other cowboys employed on his ranch.

"Now, boys," said Lane, "keep your eyes open. Walk around the house and watch the road well. All of you know the 'Frio Kid,' as they call him now, and if you see him, open fire on him without asking any questions. I'm not afraid of his coming around, but Rosita is. She's been afraid he'd come in on us every Christmas since we were married."

The guests had arrived in buckboards and on horseback, and were making themselves comfortable inside.

The evening went along pleasantly. The guests enjoyed and praised Rosita's excellent supper, and afterward the men scattered in groups about the rooms or on the broad "gallery," smoking and chatting.

The Christmas tree, or course, delighted the youngsters, and above all were they pleased when Santa Claus himself in magnificent white beard and furs appeared and began to distribute the toys.

"It's my papa," announced Billy Sampson, aged six. "I've seen him wear 'em before."

Berkly, a sheepman, an old friend of Lane, stopped Rosita as she was passing by him on the gallery, where he was sitting smoking.

"Well, Mrs. Lane," said he, "I suppose by this Christmas you've gotten over being afraid of that fellow McRoy, haven't you? Madison and I have talked about it, you know."

"Very nearly," said Rosita, smiling, "but I am still nervous sometimes. I shall never forget that awful time when he came so near to killing us."

"He's the most cold-hearted villain in the world," said Berkly. "The citizens all along the border ought to turn out and hunt him down like a wolf."

"He has committed awful crimes," said Rosita, "but—I—don't—know. I think there is a spot of good somewhere in everybody. He was not always bad—that I know."

Rosita turned into the hallway between the rooms. Santa Claus, in muffling whiskers and furs, was just coming through.

"I heard what you said through the window, Mrs. Lane," he said. "I was just going down in my pocket for a Christmas present for your husband. But I've left one for you, instead. It's in the room to your right."

"Oh, thank you, kind Santa Claus," said Rosita, brightly.

Rosita went into the room, while Santa Claus stepped into the cooler air of the yard.

She found no one in the room but Madison.

"Where is my present that Santa said he left for me in here?" she asked.

"Haven't seen anything in the way of a present," said her husband, laughing, "unless he could have meant me."

The next day Gabriel Radd, the foreman of the X O Ranch, dropped into the post-office at Loma Alta.

"Well, the Frio Kid's got his dose of lead at last," he remarked to the postmaster.

"That so? How'd it happen?"

"One of old Sanchez's Mexican sheep herders did it!—think of it! the Frio Kid killed by a sheep herder! The Greaser saw him riding along past his camp about twelve o'clock last night, and was so skeered that he up with a Winchester and let him have it. Funniest part of it was that the Kid was dressed all up with white Angora-skin whiskers and a regular Santy Claus rig-out from head to foot. Think of the Frio Kid playing Santy!"

"Now exactly at what hour of the evening of December the twenty-fourth did Professor Pohlman query you as to the best method of killing Miss Burkhardt?"

★

Death on the Air
by Ngaio Marsh

O N THE 25th of December at 7:30 a.m. Mr. Septimus Tonks was found dead beside his wireless set.

It was Emily Parks, an under-housemaid, who discovered him. She butted open the door and entered, carrying mop, duster, and carpet-sweeper. At that precise moment she was greatly startled by a voice that spoke out of the darkness.

"Good morning, everybody," said the voice in superbly inflected syllables, "and a Merry Christmas!"

Emily yelped, but not loudly, as she immediately realized what had happened. Mr. Tonks had omitted to turn off his wireless before going to bed. She drew back the curtains, revealing a kind of pale murk which was a London Christmas dawn, switched on the light, and saw Septimus.

He was seated in front of the radio. It was a small but expensive set, specially built for him. Septimus sat in an armchair, his back to Emily, his body tilted towards the radio.

His hands, the fingers curiously bunched, were on the ledge of the cabinet under the tuning and volume knobs. His chest rested against the shelf below and his head leaned on the front panel.

He looked rather as though he was listening intently to the interior secrets of the wireless. His head was bent so that Emily could see his bald top with its trail of oiled hairs. He did not move.

"Beg pardon, sir," gasped Emily. She was again greatly startled. Mr. Tonks' enthusiasm for radio had never before induced him to tune in at seven-thirty in the morning.

"Special Christmas service," the cultured voice was saying. Mr. Tonks sat very still. Emily, in common with the other servants, was terrified of her master. She did not know whether to go or to stay. She gazed wildly at Septimus and realized that he wore a dinner-jacket. The room was now filled with the clamor of pealing bells.

Emily opened her mouth as wide as it would go and screamed and screamed and screamed. . . .

Chase, the butler, was the first to arrive. He was a pale, flabby man but authoritative. He said: "What's the meaning of this outrage?" and then saw Septimus. He went to the arm-chair, bent down, and looked into his master's face.

He did not lose his head, but said in a loud voice: "My Gawd!" And then to Emily: "Shut your face." By this vulgarism he betrayed his agitation. He seized Emily by the shoulders and thrust her towards the door, where they were met by Mr. Hislop, the secretary, in his dressing-gown. Mr. Hislop said: "Good heavens, Chase, what is the meaning—" and then his voice too was drowned in the clamor of bells and renewed screams.

Chase put his fat white hand over Emily's mouth.

"In the study if you please, sir. An accident. Go to your room, will you, and stop that noise or I'll give you something to make you." This to Emily, who bolted down the hall, where she was received by the rest of the staff who had congregated there.

Chase returned to the study with Mr. Hislop and locked the door. They both looked down at the body of Septimus Tonks. The secretary was the first to speak.

"But—but—he's dead," said little Mr. Hislop.

"I suppose there can't be any doubt," whispered Chase.

"Look at the face. Any doubt! My God!"

Mr. Hislop put out a delicate hand towards the bent head and then drew it back. Chase, less fastidious, touched one of the hard wrists, gripped, and then lifted it. The body at once tipped backwards as if it was made of wood. One of the hands knocked against the butler's face. He sprang back with an oath.

There lay Septimus, his knees and his hands in the air, his terrible face turned up to the light. Chase pointed to the right hand. Two fingers and the thumb were slightly blackened.

Ding, dong, dang, ding.

"For God's sake stop those bells," cried Mr. Hislop. Chase turned off the wall switch. Into the sudden silence came the sound of the door-handle being rattled and Guy Tonks' voice on the other side.

"Hislop! Mr. Hislop! Chase! What's the matter?"

"Just a moment, Mr. Guy." Chase looked at the secretary. "You go, sir."

So it was left to Mr. Hislop to break the news to the family. They listened to his stammering revelation in stupefied silence. It was not until Guy, the eldest of the three children, stood in the study that any practical suggestion was made.

"What has killed him?" asked Guy.

"It's extraordinary," burbled Hislop. "Extraordinary. He looks as if he'd been—"

"Galvanized," said Guy.

[174]

"We ought to send for a doctor," suggested Hislop timidly.

"Of course. Will you, Mr. Hislop? Dr. Meadows."

Hislop went to the telephone and Guy returned to his family. Dr. Meadows lived on the other side of the square and arrived in five minutes. He examined the body without moving it. He questioned Chase and Hislop. Chase was very voluble about the burns on the hand. He uttered the word "electrocution" over and over again.

"I had a cousin, sir, that was struck by lightning. As soon as I saw the hand—"

"Yes, yes," said Dr. Meadows. "So you said. I can see the burns for myself."

"Electrocution," repeated Chase. "There'll have to be an inquest."

Dr. Meadows snapped at him, summoned Emily, and then saw the rest of the family—Guy, Arthur, Phillipa, and their mother. They were clustered round a cold grate in the drawing-room. Phillipa was on her knees, trying to light the fire.

"What was it?" asked Arthur as soon as the doctor came in.

"Looks like electric shock. Guy, I'll have a word with you if you please. Phillipa, look after your mother, there's a good child. Coffee with a dash of brandy. Where are those damn maids? Come on, Guy."

Alone with Guy, he said they'd have to send for the police.

"The police!" Guy's dark face turned very pale. "Why? What's it got to do with them?"

"Nothing, as like as not, but they'll have to be notified. I can't give a certificate as things are. If it's electrocution, how did it happen?"

"But the police!" said Guy. "That's simply ghastly. Dr. Meadows, for God's sake couldn't you—?"

"No," said Dr. Meadows, "I couldn't. Sorry, Guy, but there it is."

"But can't we wait a moment? Look at him again. You haven't examined him properly."

"I don't want to move him, that's why. Pull yourself together, boy. Look here. I've got a pal in the C.I.D.—Alleyn. He's a gentleman and all that. He'll curse me like a fury, but he'll come if he's in London, and he'll make things easier for you. Go back to your mother. I'll ring Alleyn up."

That was how it came about that Chief Detective-Inspector Roderick Alleyn spent his Christmas Day in harness. As a matter of fact he was on duty, and as he pointed out to Dr. Meadows, would have had to turn out and visit his miserable Tonkses in any case. When he did arrive it was with his usual air of remote courtesy. He was accompanied by a tall, thick-set officer—Inspector Fox—and by the divisional police-surgeon. Dr. Meadows took them into the study. Alleyn, in his turn, looked at the horror that had been Septimus.

"Was he like this when he was found?"

"No. I understand he was leaning forward with his hands on the ledge of the cabinet. He must have slumped forward and been propped up by the chair arms and the cabinet."

"Who moved him?"

"Chase, the butler. He said he only meant to raise the arm. *Rigor* is well established."

Alleyn put his hand behind the rigid neck and pushed. The body fell forward into its original position.

"There you are, Curtis," said Alleyn to the divisional surgeon. He turned to Fox. "Get the camera man, will you, Fox?"

The photographer took four shots and departed. Alleyn marked the position of the hands and feet with chalk, made a careful plan of the room and turned to the doctors.

"Is it electrocution, do you think?"

"Looks like it," said Curtis. "Have to be a p.m. of course."

"Of course. Still, look at the hands. Burns. Thumb and two fingers bunched together and exactly the distance between the two knobs apart. He'd been tuning his hurdy-gurdy."

"By gum," said Inspector Fox, speaking for the first time.

"D'you mean he got a lethal shock from his radio?" asked Dr. Meadows.

"I don't know. I merely conclude he had his hands on the knobs when he died."

"It was still going when the house-maid found him. Chase turned it off and got no shock."

"Yours, partner," said Alleyn, turning to Fox. Fox stooped down to the wall switch.

"Careful," said Alleyn.

"I've got rubber soles," said Fox, and switched it on. The radio hummed, gathered volume, and found itself.

"No-oel, No-o-el," it roared. Fox cut it off and pulled out the wall plug.

"I'd like to have a look inside this set," he said.

"So you shall, old boy, so you shall," rejoined Alleyn. "Before you begin, I think we'd better move the body. Will you see to that, Meadows? Fox, get Bailey, will you? He's out in the car."

Curtis, Hislop, and Meadows carried Septimus Tonks into a spare downstairs room. It was a difficult and horrible business with that contorted body. Dr. Meadows came back alone, mopping his brow, to find Detective-Sergeant Bailey, a fingerprint expert, at work on the wireless cabinet.

"What's all this?" asked Dr. Meadows. "Do you want to find out if he'd been fooling round with the innards?"

[176]

"He," said Alleyn, "or—somebody else."

"Umph!" Dr. Meadows looked at the Inspector. "You agree with me, it seems. Do you suspect—?"

"Suspect? I'm the least suspicious man alive. I'm merely being tidy. Well, Bailey?"

"I've got a good one off the chair arm. That'll be the deceased's, won't it, sir?"

"No doubt. We'll check up later. What about the wireless?"

Fox, wearing a glove, pulled off the knob of the volume control.

"Seems to be O.K." said Bailey. "It's a sweet bit of work. Not too bat at all, sir." He turned his torch into the back of the radio, undid a couple of screws underneath the set, lifted out the works.

"What's the little hole for?" asked Alleyn.

"What's that, sir?" said Fox.

"There's a hole-bored through the panel above the knob. About an eighth of an inch in diameter. The rim of the knob hides it. One might easily miss it. Move your torch, Bailey. Yes. There, do you see?"

Fox bent down and uttered a bass growl. A fine needle of light came through the front of the radio.

"That's peculiar, sir," said Bailey from the other side. "I don't get the idea at all."

Alleyn pulled out the tuning knob.

"There's another one there," he murmured. "Yes. Nice clean little holes. Newly bored. Unusual, I take it?"

"Unusual's the word, sir," said Fox.

"Run away, Meadows," said Alleyn.

"Why the devil?" asked Dr. Meadows indignantly. "What are you driving at? Why shouldn't I be here?"

"You ought to be with the sorrowing relatives. Where's your corpseside manner?"

"I've settled them. What are you up to?"

"Who's being suspicious now?" asked Alleyn mildly. "You may stay for a moment. Tell me about the Tonkses. Who are they? What are they? What sort of a man was Septimus?"

"If you must know, he was a damned unpleasant sort of a man."

"Tell me about him."

Dr. Meadows sat down and lit a cigarette.

"He was a self-made bloke," he said, "as hard as nails and—well, coarse rather than vulgar."

"Like Dr. Johnson perhaps?"

"Not in the least. Don't interrupt. I've known him for twenty-five years. His wife was a neighbor of ours in Dorset. Isabel Foreston. I brought the children into this vale of tears and, by jove, in many ways it's been one for

[177]

them. It's an extraordinary household. For the last ten years Isabel's condition has been the sort that sends these psycho-jokers dizzy with rapture. I'm only an out-of-date G.P., and I'd just say she is in an advanced stage of hysterical neurosis. Frightened into fits of her husband.''

''I can't understand these holes,'' grumbled Fox to Bailey.

''Go on, Meadows,'' said Alleyn.

''I tackled Sep about her eighteen months ago. Told him the trouble was in her mind. He eyed me with a sort of grin on his face and said: 'I'm surprised to learn that my wife has enough mentality to—' But look here, Alleyn, I can't talk about my patients like this. What the devil am I thinking about.''

''You know perfectly well it'll go no further unless—''

''Unless what?''

''Unless it has to. Do go on.''

But Dr. Meadows hurriedly withdrew behind his professional rectitude. All he would say was that Mr. Tonks had suffered from high blood pressure and a weak heart, that Guy was in his father's city office, that Arthur had wanted to study art and had been told to read for law, and that Phillipa wanted to go on the stage and had been told to do nothing of the sort.

''Bullied his children,'' commented Alleyn.

''Find out for yourself. I'm off.'' Dr. Meadows got as far as the door and came back.

''Look here,'' he said, ''I'll tell you one thing. There was a row here last night. I'd asked Hislop, who's a sensible little beggar, to let me know if anything happened to upset Mrs. Sep. Upset her badly, you know. To be indiscreet again, I said he'd better let me know if Sep cut up rough because Isabel and the young had had about as much of that as they could stand. He was drinking pretty heavily. Hislop rang me up at ten-twenty last night to say there'd been a hell of a row; Sep bullying Phips—Phillipa, you know; always call her Phips—in her room. He said Isabel—Mrs. Sep—had gone to bed. I'd had a big day and I didn't want to turn out. I told him to ring again in half an hour if things hadn't quieted down. I told him to keep out of Sep's way and stay in his own room, which is next to Phips' and see if she was all right when Sep cleared out. Hislop was involved. I won't tell you how. The servants were all out. I said that if I didn't hear from him in half an hour I'd ring again and if there was no answer I'd know they were all in bed and quiet. I did ring, got no answer, and went to bed myself. That's all. I'm off. Curtis knows where to find me. You'll want me for the inquest, I suppose. Goodbye.''

When he had gone Alleyn embarked on a systematic prowl round the room. Fox and Bailey were still deeply engrossed with the wireless.

''I don't see how the gentleman could have got a bump-off from the instrument," grumbled Fox. "These control knobs are quite in order. Everything's as it should be. Look here, sir."

He turned on the wall switch and tuned in. There was a prolonged humming.

". . . concludes the program of Christmas carols," said the radio.

"A very nice tone," said Fox approvingly.

"Here's something, sir," announced Bailey suddenly.

"Found the sawdust, have you?" said Alleyn.

"Got it in one," said the startled Bailey.

Alleyn peered into the instrument, using the torch. He scooped up two tiny traces of sawdust from under the holes.

"'Vantage number one," said Alleyn. He bent down to the wall plug. "Hullo! A two-way adapter. Serves the radio and the radiator. Thought they were illegal. This is a rum business. Let's have another look at those knobs."

He had his look. They were the usual wireless fitments, bake-lite knobs fitting snugly to the steel shafts that projected from the front panel.

"As you say," he murmured, "quite in order. Wait a bit." He produced a pocket lens and squinted at one of the shafts. "Ye-es. Do they ever wrap blotting-paper round these objects, Fox?"

"Blotting-paper!" ejaculated Fox. "They do not."

Alleyn scraped at both the shafts with his penknife, holding an envelope underneath. He rose, groaning, and crossed to the desk. "A corner torn off the bottom bit of blotch," he said presently. "No prints on the wireless, I think you said, Bailey?"

"That's right," agreed Bailey morosely.

"There'll be none, or too many, on the blotter, but try, Bailey, try," said Alleyn. He wandered about the room, his eyes on the floor; got as far as the window and stopped.

"Fox!" he said. "A clue. A very palpable clue."

"What is it?" asked Fox.

"The odd wisp of blotting-paper, no less." Alleyn's gaze traveled up the side of the window curtain. "Can I believe my eyes?"

He got a chair, stood on the seat, and with his gloved hand pulled the buttons from the ends of the curtain rod.

"Look at this." He turned to the radio, detached the control knobs, and laid them beside the ones he had removed from the curtain rod.

Ten minutes later Inspector Fox knocked on the drawing-room door and was admitted by Guy Tonks. Phillipa had got the fire going and the family was gathered round it. They looked as though they had not moved or spoken to one another for a long time.

[179]

It was Phillipa who spoke first to Fox. "Do you want one of us?"

"If you please, miss," said Fox. "Inspector Alleyn would like to see Mr. Guy Tonks for a moment, if convenient."

"I'll come," said Guy, and led the way to the study. At the door he paused. "Is he—my father—still—?"

"No, no, sir," said Fox comfortably. "It's all ship-shape in there again."

With a lift of his chin Guy opened the door and went in, followed by Fox. Alleyn was alone, seated at the desk. He rose to his feet.

"You want to speak to me?" asked Guy.

"Yes, if I may. This has all been a great shock to you, of course. Won't you sit down?"

Guy sat in the chair farthest away from the radio.

"What killed my father? Was it a stroke?"

"The doctors are not quite certain. There will have to be a *post-mortem*."

"Good God! And an inquest?"

"I'm afraid so."

"Horrible!" said Guy violently. "What do you think was the matter? Why the devil do these quacks have to be so mysterious? What killed him?"

"They think an electric shock."

"How did it happen?"

"We don't know. It looks as if he got it from the wireless."

"Surely that's impossible. I thought they were fool-proof."

"I believe they are, if left to themselves."

For a second undoubtedly Guy was startled. Then a look of relief came into his eyes. He seemed to relax all over.

"Of course," he said, "he was always monkeying about with it. What had he done?"

"Nothing."

"But you said—if it killed him he must have done something to it."

"If anyone interfered with the set it was put right afterwards."

Guy's lips parted but he did not speak. He had gone very white.

"So you see," said Alleyn, "your father could not have done anything."

"Then it was not the radio that killed him."

"That we hope will be determined by the *post-mortem*."

"I don't know anything about wireless," said Guy suddenly. "I don't understand. This doesn't seem to make sense. Nobody ever touched the thing except my father. He was most particular about it. Nobody went near the wireless."

"I see. He was an enthusiast?"

"Yes, it was his only enthusiasm except—except his business."

"One of my men is a bit of an expert," Alleyn said. "He says this is a remarkably good set. You are not an expert you say. Is there anyone in the house who is?''

''My young brother was interested at one time. He's given it up. My father wouldn't allow another radio in the house.''

''Perhaps he may be able to suggest something.''

''But if the thing's all right now—''

''We've got to explore every possibility.''

''You speak as if—as—if—''

''I speak as I am bound to speak before there has been an inquest,'' said Alleyn. ''Had anyone a grudge against your father, Mr. Tonks?''

Up went Guy's chin again. He looked Alleyn squarely in the eyes.

''Almost everyone who knew him,'' said Guy.

''Is that an exaggeration?''

''No. You think he was murdered, don't you?''

Alleyn suddenly pointed to the desk beside him.

''Have you ever seen those before?'' he asked abruptly. Guy stared at two black knobs that lay side by side on an ashtray.

''Those?'' he said. ''No. What are they?''

''I believe they are the agents of your father's death.''

The study door opened and Arthur Tonks came in.

''Guy,'' he said, ''what's happening? We can't stay cooped up together all day. I can't stand it. For God's sake what happened to him?''

''They think those things killed him,'' said Guy.

''Those?'' For a split second Arthur's glance slewed to the curtainrods. Then, with a characteristic flicker of his eyelids, he looked away again.

''What do you mean?'' he asked Alleyn.

''Will you try one of those knobs on the shaft of the volume control?''

''But,'' said Arthur, ''they're metal.''

''It's disconnected,'' said Alleyn.

Arthur picked one of the knobs from the tray, turned to the radio, and fitted the knob over one of the exposed shafts.

''It's too loose,'' he said quickly, ''it would fall off.''

''Not if it was packed—with blotting-paper, for instance.''

''Where did you find these things?'' demanded Arthur.

''I think you recognized them, didn't you? I saw you glance at the curtain-rod.''

''Of course I recognized them. I did a portrait of Phillipa against those curtains when—he—was away last year. I've painted the damn things.''

''Look here,'' interrupted Guy, ''exactly what are you driving at, Mr. Alleyn? If you mean to suggest that my brother—''

''I!'' cried Arthur. ''What's it got to do with me? Why should you suppose—''

[181]

"I found traces of blotting-paper on the shafts and inside the metal knobs," said Alleyn. "It suggested a substitution of the metal knobs for the bakelite ones. It is remarkable, don't you think, that they should so closely resemble one another? If you examine them, of course, you find they are not identical. Still, the difference is scarcely perceptible."

Arthur did not answer this. He was still looking at the wireless.

"I've always wanted to have a look at this set," he said surprisingly.

"You are free to do so now," said Alleyn politely. "We have finished with it for the time being."

"Look here," said Arthur suddenly, "suppose metal knobs were substituted for bakelite ones, it couldn't kill him. He wouldn't get a shock at all. Both the controls are grounded."

"Have you noticed those very small holes drilled through the panel?" asked Alleyn. "Should they be there, do you think?"

Arthur peered at the little steel shafts. "By God, he's right, Guy," he said. "That's how it was done."

"Inspector Fox," said Alleyn, "tells me those holes could be used for conducting wires and that a lead could be taken from the—the transformer, is it?—to one of the knobs."

"And the other connected to earth," said Fox. "It's a job for an expert. He could get three hundred volts or so that way."

"That's not good enough," said Arthur quickly; "there wouldn't be enough current to do any damage—only a few hundredths of an amp."

"I'm not an expert," said Alleyn, "but I'm sure you're right. Why were the holes drilled then? Do you imagine someone wanted to play a practical joke on your father?"

"A practical joke? On *him?*" Arthur gave an unpleasant screech of laughter. "Do you hear that, Guy?"

"Shut up," said Guy. "After all, he is dead."

"It seems almost too good to be true, doesn't it?"

"Don't be a bloody fool, Arthur. Pull yourself together. Can't you see what this means? They think he's been murdered."

"Murdered! They're wrong. None of us had the nerve for that, Mr. Inspector. Look at me. My hands are so shaky they told me I'd never be able to paint. That dates from when I was a kid and he shut me up in the cellars for a night. Look at me. Look at Guy. He's not so vulnerable, but he caved in like the rest of us. We were conditioned to surrender. Do you know—"

"Wait a moment," said Alleyn quietly. "Your brother is quite right, you know. You'd better think before you speak. This may be a case of homicide."

"Thank you, sir," said Guy quickly. "That's extraordinarily decent of you. Arthur's a bit above himself. It's a shock."

"The relief, you mean," said Arthur. "Don't be such an ass. I didn't

[182]

kill him and they'll find it out soon enough. Nobody killed him. There must be some explanation.''

"I suggest that you listen to me," said Alleyn. "I'm going to put several questions to both of you. You need not answer them, but it will be more sensible to do so. I understand no one but your father touched this radio. Did any of you ever come into this room while it was in use?''

"Not unless he wanted to vary the program with a little bullying," said Arthur.

Alleyn turned to Guy, who was glaring at his brother.

"I want to know exactly what happened in this house last night. As far as the doctors can tell us, your father died not less than three and not more than eight hours before he was found. We must try to fix the time as accurately as possible.''

"I saw him at about a quarter to nine," began Guy slowly. "I was going out to a supper-party at the Savoy and had come downstairs. He was crossing the hall from the drawing-room to his room.''

"Did you see him after a quarter to nine, Mr. Arthur?''

"No. I heard him, though. He was working in here with Hislop. Hislop had asked to go away for Christmas. Quite enough. My father discovered some urgent correspondence. Really, Guy, you know, he was pathological. I'm sure Dr. Meadows thinks so.''

"When did you hear him?" asked Alleyn.

"Some time after Guy had gone. I was working on a drawing in my room upstairs. It's above his. I heard him bawling at little Hislop. It must have been before ten o'clock, because I went out to a studio party at ten. I heard him bawling as I crossed the hall.''

"And when," said Alleyn, "did you both return?''

"I came home at about twenty past twelve," said Guy immediately. "I can fix the time because we had gone on to Chez Carlo, and they had a midnight stunt there. We left immediately afterwards. I came home in a taxi. The radio was on full blast.''

"You heard no voices?''

"None. Just the wireless.''

"And you, Mr. Arthur?''

"Lord knows when I got in. After one. The house was in darkness. Not a sound.''

"You had your own key?''

"Yes," said Guy. "Each of us has one. They're always left on a hook in the lobby. When I came in I noticed Arthur's was gone.''

"What about the others? How did you know it was his?''

"Mother hasn't got one and Phips lost hers weeks ago. Anyway, I knew they were staying in and that it must be Arthur who was out.''

"Thank you," said Arthur ironically.

[183]

"You didn't look in the study when you came in," Alleyn asked him.

"Good Lord, no," said Arthur as if the suggestion was fantastic. "I say," he said suddenly, "I suppose he was sitting here—dead. That's a queer thought." He laughed nervously. "Just sitting here, behind the door in the dark."

"How do you know it was in the dark?"

"What d'you mean? Of course it was. There was no light under the door."

"I see. Now do you two mind joining your mother again? Perhaps your sister will be kind enough to come in here for a moment. Fox, ask her, will you?"

Fox returned to the drawing-room with Guy and Arthur and remained there, blandly unconscious of any embarrassment his presence might cause the Tonkses. Bailey was already there, ostensibly examining the electric points.

Phillipa went to the study at once. Her first remark was characteristic. "Can I be of any help?" asked Phillipa.

"It's extremely nice of you to put it like that," said Alleyn. "I don't want to worry you for long. I'm sure this discovery has been a shock to you."

"Probably," said Phillipa. Alleyn glanced quickly at her. "I mean," she explained, "that I suppose I must be shocked but I can't feel anything much. I just want to get it all over as soon as possible. And then think. Please tell me what has happened."

Alleyn told her they believed her father had been electrocuted and that the circumstances were unusual and puzzling. He said nothing to suggest that the police suspected murder.

"I don't think I'll be much help," said Phillipa, "but go ahead."

"I want to try to discover who was the last person to see your father or speak to him."

"I should think very likely I was," said Phillipa composedly. "I had a row with him before I went to bed."

"What about?"

"I don't see that it matters."

Alleyn considered this. When he spoke again it was with deliberation.

"Look here," he said, "I think there is very little doubt that your father was killed by an electric shock from his wireless set. As far as I know the circumstances are unique. Radios are normally incapable of giving a lethal shock to anyone. We have examined the cabinet and are inclined to think that its internal arrangements were distrubed last night. Very radically disturbed. Your father may have experimented with it. If anything happened to interrupt or upset him, it is possible that in the excitement of the moment he made some dangerous readjustment."

"You don't believe that, do you?" asked Phillipa calmly.

"Since you ask me," said Alleyn, "no."

"I see," said Phillipa; "you think he was murdered, but you're not sure." She had gone very white, but she spoke crisply. "Naturally you want to find out about my row."

"About everything that happened last evening," amended Alleyn.

"What happened was this," said Phillipa; "I came into the hall some time after ten. I'd heard Arthur go out and had looked at the clock at five past. I ran into my father's secretary, Richard Hislop. He turned aside, but not before I saw . . . not quickly enough. I blurted out: 'You're crying.' We looked at each other. I asked him why he stood it. None of the other secretaries could. He said he had to. He's a widower with two children. There have been doctor's bills and things. I needn't tell you about his . . . about his damnable servitude to my father nor about the refinements of cruelty he'd had to put with. I think my father was mad, really mad, I mean. Richard gabbled it all out to me higgledy-piggledy in a sort of horrified whisper. He's been here two years, but I'd never realized until that moment that we . . . that . . ." A faint flush came into her cheeks. "He's such a funny little man. Not at all the sort I've always thought . . . not good-looking or exciting or anything."

She stopped, looking bewildered.

"Yes?" said Alleyn.

"Well, you see—I suddenly realized I was in love with him. He realized it too. He said: 'Of course, it's quite hopeless, you know. Us, I mean. Laughable, almost.' Then I put my arms round his neck and kissed him. It was very odd, but it seemed quite natural. The point is my father came out of his room into the hall and saw us."

"That was bad luck," said Alleyn.

"Yes, it was. My father really seemed delighted. He almost licked his lips. Richard's efficiency had irritated my father for a long time. It was difficult to find excuses for being beastly to him. Now, of course . . . He ordered Richard to the study and me to my room. He followed me upstairs. Richard tried to come too, but I asked him not to. My father . . . I needn't tell you what he said. He put the worst possible construction on what he'd seen. He was absolutely foul, screaming at me like a madman. He was insane. Perhaps it was D. Ts. He drank terribly, you know. I dare say it's silly of me to tell you all this."

"No," said Alleyn.

"I can't feel anything at all. Not even relief. The boys are frankly relieved. I can't feel afraid either." She stared meditatively at Alleyn. "Innocent people needn't feel afraid, need they?"

"It's an axiom of police investigation," said Alleyn and wondered if indeed she was innocent.

"It just *can't* be murder," said Phillipa. "We were all too much afraid to kill him. I believe he'd win even if you murdered him. He'd hit back somehow." She put her hands to her eyes. "I'm all muddled."

"I think you are more upset than you realize. I'll be as quick as I can. your father made this scene in your room. You say he screamed. Did any one hear him?"

"Yes. Mummy did. She came in."

"What happened?"

"I said: 'Go away, darling, it's all right.' I didn't want her to be involved. He nearly killed her with the things he did. Sometimes he'd . . . we never knew what happened between them. It was all secret, like a door shutting quietly as you walk along a passage."

"Did she go away?"

"Not at once. He told her he'd found out that Richard and I were lovers. He said . . . it doesn't matter. I don't want to tell you. She was terrified. He was stabbing at her in some way I couldn't understand. Then, quite suddenly, he told her to go to her own room. She went at once and he followed her. He locked me in. That's the last I saw of him, but I heard him go downstairs later."

"Were you locked in all night?"

"No. Richard Hislop's room is next to mine. He came up and spoke through the wall to me. He wanted to unlock the door, but I said better not in case—he—came back. Then, much later, Guy came home. As he passed my door I tapped on it. The key was in the lock and he turned it."

"Did you tell him what had happened?"

"Just that there'd been a row. He only stayed a moment."

"Can you hear the radio from your room?"

She seemed surprised.

"The wireless? Why, yes. Faintly."

"Did you hear it after your father returned to the study?"

"I don't remember."

"Think. While you lay awake all that long time until your brother came home?"

"I'll try. When he came out and found Richard and me, it was not going. They had been working, you see. No, I can't remember hearing it at all unless—wait a moment. Yes. After he had gone back to the study from mother's room I remember there was a loud crash of static. Very loud. Then I think it was quiet for some time. I fancy I heard it again later. Oh, I've remembered something else. After the static my bedside radiator went out. I suppose there was something wrong with the electric supply. That would account for both, wouldn't it? The heater went on again about ten minutes later."

"And did the radio begin again then, do you think?"

[186]

"I don't know. I'm very vague about that. It started again sometime before I went to sleep."

"Thank you very much indeed. I won't bother you any longer now."

"All right," said Phillipa calmly, and went away.

Alleyn sent for Chase and questioned him about the rest of the staff and about the discovery of the body. Emily was summoned and dealt with. When she departed, awestruck but complacent, Alleyn turned to the butler.

"Chase," he said, "had your master any peculiar habits?"

"Yes, sir."

"In regard to the wireless?"

"I beg pardon, sir. I thought you meant generally speaking."

"Well, then, generally speaking."

"If I may so, sir, he was a mass of them."

"How long have you been with him?"

"Two months, sir, and due to leave at the end of this week."

"Oh. Why are you leaving?"

Chase produced the classic remark of his kind.

"There are some things," he said, "that flesh and blood will not stand, sir. One of them's being spoke to like Mr. Tonks spoke to his staff."

"Ah. His peculiar habits, in fact?"

"It's my opinion, sir, he was mad. Stark, staring."

"With regard to the radio. Did he tinker with it?"

"I can't say I've ever noticed, sir. I believe he knew quite a lot about wireless."

"When he tuned the thing, had he any particular method? Any characteristic attitude or gesture?"

"I don't think so, sir. I never noticed, and yet I've often come into the room when he was at it. I can seem to see him now, sir."

"Yes, yes," said Alleyn swiftly. "That's what we want. A clear mental picture. How was it now? Like this?"

In a moment he was across the room and seated in Septimus's chair. He swung round to the cabinet and raised his right hand to the tuning control.

"Like this?"

"No, sir," said Chase promptly, "that's not him at all. Both hands it should be."

"Ah." Up went Alleyn's left hand to the volume control. "More like this?"

"Yes, sir," said Chase slowly. "But there's something else and I can't recollect what it was. Something he was always doing. It's in the back of my head. You know, sir. Just on the edge of my memory, as you might say."

"I know."

"It's a kind—something—to do with irritation," said Chase slowly.

"Irritation? His?"

[187]

"No. It's no good, sir. I can't get it."

"Perhaps later. Now look here, Chase, what happened to all of you last night? All the servants, I mean."

"We were all out, sir. It being Christmas Eve. The mistress sent for me yesterday morning. She said we could take the evening off as soon as I had taken in Mr. Tonks's grog-tray at nine o'clock. So we went," ended Chase simply.

"When?"

"The rest of the staff got away about nine. I left at ten past, sir, and returned about eleven-twenty. The others were back then, and all in bed. I went straight to bed myself, sir."

"You came in by a back door, I suppose?"

"Yes, sir. We've been talking it over. None of us noticed anything unusual."

"Can you hear the wireless in your part of the house?"

"No, sir."

"Well," said Alleyn, looking up from his notes, "that'll do, thank you." Before Chase reached the door Fox came in.

"Beg pardon, sir," said Fox, "I just want to take a look at the *Radio Times* on the desk."

He bent over the paper, wetted a gigantic thumb, and turned a page.

"That's it, sir," shouted Chase suddenly. "That's what I tried to think of. That's what he was always doing."

"But what?"

"Licking his fingers, sir. It was a habit," said Chase. "That's what he always did when he sat down to the radio. I heard Mr. Hislop tell the doctor it nearly drove him demented, the way the master couldn't touch a thing without first licking his fingers."

"Quite so," said Alleyn. "In about ten minutes, ask Mr. Hislop if he will be good enough to come in for a moment. That will be all, thank you, Chase."

"Well, sir," remarked Fox when Chase had gone, "if that's the case and what I think's right, it'd certainly make matters worse."

"Good heavens, Fox, what an elaborate remark. What does it mean?"

"If metal knobs were substituted for bakelite ones and fine wires brought through those holes to make contact, then he'd get a bigger bump if he tuned in with *damp* fingers."

"Yes. And he always used both hands. Fox!"

"Sir."

"Approach the Tonkses again. You haven't left them alone, of course?"

"Bailey's in there making out he's interested in the light switches. He's found the main switchboard under the stairs. There's signs of a blown fuse

[188]

having been fixed recently. In a cupboard underneath there are odd lengths of flex and so on. Same brand as this on the wireless and the heater.''

"Ah, yes. Could the cord from the adapter to the radiator be brought into play?''

"By gum,'' said Fox, "you're right! That's how it was done, Chief. The heavier flex was cut away from the radiator and shoved through. There was a fire, so he wouldn't want the radiator and wouldn't notice.''

"It might have been done that way, certainly, but there's little to prove it. Return to the bereaved Tonkses, my Fox, and ask prettily if any of them remember Septimus's peculiarities when tuning his wireless.''

Fox met little Mr. Hislop at the door and left him alone with Alleyn. Phillipa had been right, reflected the Inspector, when she said Richard Hislop was not a noticeable man. He was nondescript. Grey eyes, drab hair; rather pale, rather short, rather insignificant; and yet last night there had flashed up between those two the realization of love. Romantic but rum, thought Alleyn.

"Do sit down,'' he said. "I want you, if you will, to tell me what happened between you and Mr. Tonks last evening.''

"What happened?''

"Yes. You all dined at eight, I understand. Then you and Mr. Tonks came in here?''

"Yes.''

"What did you do?''

"He dictated several letters.''

"Anything unusual take place?''

"Oh, no.''

"Why did you quarrel?''

"Quarrel!'' The quiet voice jumped a tone. "We did not quarrel, Mr. Alleyn.''

"Perhaps that was the wrong word. What upset you?''

"Phillipa has told you?''

"Yes. She was wise to do so. What was the matter, Mr. Hislop?''

"Apart from the . . . what she told you . . . Mr. Tonks was a difficult man to please. I often irritated him. I did so last night.''

"In what way?''

"In almost every way. He shouted at me. I was startled and nervous, clumsy with papers, and making mistakes. I wasn't well. I blundered and then . . . I . . . I broke down. I have always irritated him. My very mannerisms—''

"Had he no irritating mannerisms, himself?''

"He! My God!''

"What were they?''

"I can't think of anything in particular. It doesn't matter does it?"

"Anything to do with the wireless, for instance?"

There was a short silence.

"No," said Hislop.

"Was the radio on in here last night, after dinner?"

"For a little while. Not after—after the incident in the hall. At least, I don't think so. I don't remember."

"What did you do after Miss Phillipa and her father had gone upstairs?"

"I followed and listened outside the door for a moment." He had gone very white and had backed away from the desk.

"And then?"

"I heard someone coming. I remembered Dr. Meadows had told me to ring him up if there was one of the scenes. I returned here and rang him up. He told me to go to my room and listen. If things got any worse I was to telephone again. Otherwise I was to stay in my room. It is next to hers."

"And you did this?" He nodded. "Could you hear what Mr. Tonks said to her?"

"A—a good deal of it."

"What did you hear?"

"He insulted her. Mrs. Tonks was there. I was just thinking of ringing Dr. Meadows up again when she and Mr. Tonks came out and went along the passage. I stayed in my room."

"You did not try to speak to Miss Phillipa?"

"We spoke through the wall. She asked me not to ring Dr. Meadows, but to stay in my room. In a little while, perhaps it was as much as twenty minutes—I really don't know— I heard him come back and go downstairs. I again spoke to Phillipa. She implored me not to do anything and said that she herself would speak to Dr. Meadows in the morning. So I waited a little longer and then went to bed."

"And to sleep?"

"My God, no!"

"Did you hear the wireless again?"

"Yes. At least I heard static."

"Are you an expert on wireless?"

"No. I know the ordinary things. Nothing much."

"How did you come to take this job, Mr. Hislop?"

"I answered an advertisement."

"You are sure you don't remember any particular mannerism of Mr. Tonks's in connection with the radio?"

"No."

"And you can tell me no more about your interview in the study that led to the scene in the hall?"

"No."

"Will you please ask Mrs. Tonks if she will be kind enough to speak to me for a moment?"

"Certainly," said Hislop, and went away.

Septimus's wife came in looking like death. Alleyn got her to sit down and asked her about her movements on the preceding evening. She said she was feeling unwell and dined in her room. She went to bed immediately afterwards. She heard Septimus yelling at Phillipa and went to Phillipa's room. Septimus accused Mr. Hislop and her daughter of "terrible things." She got as far as this and then broke down quietly. Alleyn was very gentle with her. After a little while he learned that Septimus had gone to her room with her and had continued to speak of "terrible things."

"What sort of things?" asked Alleyn.

"He was not responsible," said Isabel. "He did not know what he was saying. I think he had been drinking."

She thought he had remained with her for perhaps a quarter of an hour. Possibly longer. He left her abruptly and she heard him go along the passage, past Phillipa's door, and presumably downstairs. She had stayed awake for a long time. The wireless could not be heard from her room. Alleyn showed her the curtain knobs, but she seemed quite unable to take in their significance. He let her go, summoned Fox, and went over the whole case.

"What's your idea on the show?" he asked when he had finished.

"Well, sir," said Fox, in his stolid way, "on the face of it the young gentlemen have got alibis. We'll have to check them up, of course, and I don't see we can go much further until we have done so."

"For the moment," said Alleyn, "let us suppose Masters Guy and Arthur to be safely established behind cast-iron alibis. What then?"

"Then we've got the young lady, the old lady, the secretary, and the servants."

"Let us parade them. But first let us go over the wireless game. You'll have to watch me here. I gather that the only way in which the radio could be fixed to give Mr. Tonks his quietus is like this: Control knobs removed. Holes bored in front panel with fine drill. Metal knobs substituted and packed with blotting paper to insulate them from metal shafts and make them stay put. Heavier flex from adapter to radiator cut and the ends of the wires pushed through the drilled holes to make contact with the new knobs. Thus we have a positive and negative pole. Mr. Tonks bridges the gap, gets a mighty wallop as the current passes through him to the earth. The switchboard fuse is blown almost immediately. All this is rigged by murderer while Sep was upstairs bullying wife and daughter. Sep revisited study some time after ten-twenty. Whole thing was made ready between ten,

[191]

when Arthur went out, and the time Sep returned—say, about ten-forty-five. The murderer reappeared, connected radiator with flex, removed wires, changed back knobs, and left the thing tuned in. Now I take it that the burst of static described by Phillipa and Hislop would be caused by the short-circuit that killed our Septimus?''

"That's right."

"It also affected all the heaters in the house. *Vide* Miss Tonks's radiator."

"Yes. He put all that right again. It would be a simple enough matter for anyone who knew how. He'd just have to fix the fuse on the main switchboard. How long do you say it would take to—what's the horrible word?—to recondition the whole show?"

"M'm," said Fox deeply. "At a guess, sir, fifteen minutes. He'd have to be nippy."

"Yes," agreed Alleyn. "He or she."

"I don't see a female making a success of it," grunted Fox. "Look here, Chief, you know what I'm thinking. Why did Mr. Hislop lie about deceased's habit of licking his thumbs? You say Hislop told you he remembered nothing and Chase says he overheard him saying the trick nearly drove him dippy."

"Exactly," said Alleyn. He was silent for so long that Fox felt moved to utter a discreet cough.

"Eh?" said Alleyn. "Yes, Fox, yes. It'll have to be done." He consulted the telephone directory and dialed a number.

"May I speak to Dr. Meadows? Oh, it's you, is it? Do you remember Mr. Hislop telling you that Septimus Tonks's trick of wetting his fingers nearly drove Hislop demented. Are you there? You don't? Sure? All right. All right. Hislop rang up at ten-twenty, you said? And you telephoned him? At eleven. Sure of the times? I see. I'd be glad if you'd come round. Can you? Well, do if you can."

He hung up the receiver.

"Get Chase again, will you, Fox?"

Chase, recalled, was most insistent that Mr. Hislop had spoken about it to Dr. Meadows.

"It was when Mr. Hislop had flu, sir. I went up with the doctor. Mr. Hislop had a high temperature and was talking very excited. He kept on and on, saying the master had guessed his ways had driven him crazy and that the master kept on purposely to aggravate. He said if it went on much longer he'd . . . he didn't know what he was talking about, sir, really."

"What did he say he'd do?"

"Well, sir, he said he'd—he'd do something desperate to the master. But

[192]

it was only his rambling, sir. I daresay he wouldn't remember anything about it.''

"No," said Alleyn, "I daresay he wouldn't." When Chase had gone he said to Fox: "Go and find out about those boys and their alibis. See if they can put you on to a quick means of checking up. Get Master Guy to corroborate Miss Phillipa's statement that she was locked in her room."

Fox had been gone for some time and Alleyn was still busy with his notes when the study door burst open and in came Dr. Meadows.

"Look here, my giddy sleuth-hound," he shouted, "what's all this about Hislop? Who says he disliked Sep's abominable habits?"

"Chase does. And don't bawl at me like that. I'm worried."

"So am I, blast you. What are you driving at? You can't imagine that . . . that poor little broken-down hack is capable of electrocuting anybody, let alone Sep?"

"I have no imagination," said Alleyn wearily.

"I wish to God I hadn't called you in. If the wireless killed Sep, it was because he'd monkeyed with it."

"And put it right after it had killed him?"

Dr. Meadows stared at Alleyn in silence.

"Now," said Alleyn, "you've got to give me a straight answer, Meadows. Did Hislop, while he was semi-delirious, say that this habit of Tonks's made him feel like murdering him?"

"I'd forgotten Chase was there," said Dr. Meadows.

"Yes, you'd forgotten that."

"But even if he did talk wildly, Alleyn, what of it? Damn it, you can't arrest a man on the strength of a remark made in delirium."

"I don't propose to do so. Another motive has come to light."

"You mean—Phips—last night?"

"Did he tell you about that?"

"She whispered something to me this morning. I'm very fond of Phips. My God, are you sure of your grounds?"

"Yes," said Alleyn. "I'm sorry. I think you'd better go, Meadows."

"Are you going to arrest him?"

"I have to do my job."

There was a long silence.

"Yes," said Dr. Meadows at last. "You have to do your job. Goodbye, Alleyn."

Fox returned to say that Guy and Arthur had never left their parties. He had got hold of two of their friends. Guy and Mrs. Tonks confirmed the story of the locked door.

"It's a process of elimination," said Fox. "It must be the secretary. He fixed the radio while deceased was upstairs. He must have dodged back to whisper through the door to Miss Tonks. I suppose he waited somewhere down here until he heard deceased blow himself to blazes and then put everything straight again, leaving the radio turned on.''

Alleyn was silent.

"What do we do now, sir?'' asked Fox.

"I want to see the hook inside the front-door where they hang their keys.''

Fox, looking dazed, followed his superior to the little entrance hall.

"Yes, there they are,'' said Alleyn. He pointed to a hook with two latch-keys hanging from it. "You could scarcely miss them. Come on, Fox.''

Back in the study they found Hislop with Bailey in attendance.

Hislop looked from one Yard man to another.

"I want to know if it's murder.''

"We think so,'' said Alleyn.

"I want you to realize that Phillipa—Miss Tonks—was locked in her room all last night.''

"Until her brother came home and unlocked the door,'' said Alleyn.

"That was too late. He was dead by then.''

"How do you know when he died?''

"It must have been when there was that crash of static.''

"Mr. Hislop,'' said Alleyn, "why would you not tell me how much that trick of licking his fingers exasperated you?''

"But—how do you know! I never told anyone.''

"You told Dr. Meadows when you were ill.''

"I don't remember.'' He stopped short. His lips trembled. Then, suddenly he began to speak.

"Very well. It's true. For two years he's tortured me. You see, he knew something about me. Two years ago when my wife was dying, I took money from the cash-box in that desk. I paid it back and thought he hadn't noticed. He knew all the time. From then on he had me where he wanted me. He used to sit there like a spider. I'd hand him a paper. He'd wet his thumbs with a clicking noise and a sort of complacent grimace. Click, click. Then he'd thumb the papers. He knew it drove me crazy. He'd look at me and then . . . click, click. And then he'd say something about the cash. He'd never quite accused me, just hinted. And I was impotent. You think I'm insane. I'm not. I could have murdered him. Often and often I've thought how I'd do it. Now you think I've done it. I haven't. There's the joke of it. I hadn't the pluck. And last night when Phillipa showed me she cared, it was like Heaven—unbelievable. For the first time since I've been here I *didn't* feel like killing him. And last night someone else *did!*''

He stood there trembling and vehement. Fox and Bailey, who had

[194]

watched him with bewildered concern, turned to Alleyn. He was about to speak when Chase came in. "A note for you, sir," he said to Alleyn. "It came by hand."

Alleyn opened it and glanced at the first few words. He looked up.

"You may go, Mr. Hislop. Now I've got what I expected—what I fished for."

When Hislop had gone they read the letter.

Dear Alleyn,

Don't arrest Hislop. I did it. Let him go at once if you've arrested him and don't tell Phips you ever suspected him. I was in love with Isabel before she met Sep. I've tried to get her to divorce him, but she wouldn't because of the kids. Damned nonsense, but there's no time to discuss it now. I've got to be quick. He suspected us. He reduced her to a nervous wreck. I was afraid she'd go under altogether. I thought it all out. Some weeks ago I took Phips's key from the hood inside the front door. I had the tools and the flex and wire all ready. I knew where the main switchboard was and the cupboard. I meant to wait until they all went away at the New Year, but last night when Hislop rang me I made up my mind at once. He said the boys and servants were out and Phips locked in her room. I told him to stay in his room and to ring me up in half an hour if things hadn't quieted down. He didn't ring up. I did. No answer, so I knew Sep wasn't in his study.

I came round, let myself in, and listened. All quiet upstairs but the lamp still on in the study, so I knew he would come down again. He'd said he wanted to get the midnight broadcast from somewhere.

I locked myself in and got to work. When Sep was away last year, Arthur did one of his modern monstrosities of painting in the study. He talked about the knobs making good pattern. I noticed then that they were very like the ones on the radio and later on I tried one and saw that it would fit if I packed it up a bit. Well, I did the job just as you worked it out, and it only took twelve minutes. Then I went into the drawing-room and waited.

He came down from Isabel's room and evidently went straight to the radio. I hadn't thought it would make such a row, and half expected someone would come down. No one came. I went back, switched off the wireless, mended the fuse in the main switchboard, using my torch. Then I put everything right in the study.

There was no particular hurry. No one would come in while he was there and I got the radio going as soon as possible to suggest he was at it. I knew I'd be called in when they found him. My idea was to tell them he had died of a stroke. I'd been warning Isabel it might happen at any time. As soon as I saw the burned hand I knew that cat wouldn't jump. I'd have tried to get away with it if Chase hadn't gone round bleating about electrocution and burned fingers. Hislop saw the hand. I daren't do anything but report the case to the police, but I thought you'd never twig the knobs. One up to you.

I might have bluffed through if you hadn't suspected Hislop. Can't let you hang the blighter. I'm enclosing a note to Isabel, who won't forgive me, and an official one for you to use. You'll find me in my bedroom upstairs. I'm using cyanide. It's quick.

I'm sorry, Alleyn. I think you knew, didn't you? I've bungled the whole game, but if you will be a supersleuth . . . Good-bye.

Henry Meadows

★

Inspector Ghote and the Miracle Baby

by H. R. F. Keating

WHAT HAS SANTA CLAUS got in store for me, Inspector Ghote said to himself, bleakly echoing the current cheerful Bombay newspaper advertisements, as he waited to enter the office of Assistant Commissioner Naik that morning of December 25th.

Whatever the A.C. had lined up for him, Ghote knew it was going to be nasty. Ever since he had recently declined to turn up for "voluntary" hockey, A.C. Naik had viewed him with sad-eyed disapproval. But what exact form would his displeasure take?

Almost certainly it would have something to do with the big Navy Week parade that afternoon, the chief preoccupation at the moment of most of the ever-excitable and drama-loving Bombayites. Probably he would be ordered out into the crowds watching the Fire Power demonstration in the bay, ordered to come back with a beltful of pickpocketing arrests.

"Come," the A.C.'s voice barked out.

Ghote went in and stood squaring his bony shoulders in front of the papers-strewn desk.

"Ah, Ghote, yes. Tulsi Pipe Road for you. Up at the north end. Going to be big trouble there. Rioting. Intercommunity outrages even."

Ghote's heart sank even deeper than he had expected. Tulsi Pipe Road was a two-kilometers-long thoroughfare that shot straight up from the Racecourse into the heart of a densely crowded mill district where badly paid Hindus, Muslims in hundreds and Goans by the thousand, all lived in prickling closeness, either in great areas of tumbledown hutments or in high tottering chawls, floor upon floor of massed humanity. Trouble between the religious communities there meant hell, no less.

"Yes, A.C.?" he said, striving not to sound appalled.

"We are having a virgin birth business, Inspector."

"Virgin birth, A.C. sahib?"

"Come, man, you must have come across such cases."

"I am sorry, A.C.," Ghote said, feeling obliged to be true to hard-won scientific principles. "I am unable to believe in virgin birth."

The A.C.'s round face suffused with instant wrath.

"Of course I am not asking you to believe in virgin birth, man! It is not you who are to believe: it is all those Christians in the Goan community who are believing it about a baby born two days ago. It is the time of year, of course. These affairs are always coming at Christmas. I have dealt with half a dozen in my day."

"Yes, A.C.," Ghote said, contriving to hit on the right note of awe.

"Yes. And there is only one way to deal with it. Get hold of the girl and find out the name of the man. Do that pretty damn quick and the whole affair drops away to nothing, like monsoon water down a drain."

"Yes, A.C."

"Well, what are you waiting for, man? Hop it!"

"Name and address of the girl in question, A.C. sahib."

The A.C.'s face darkened once more. He padded furiously over the jumble of papers on his desk top. And at last he found the chit he wanted.

"There you are, man. And also you will find there the name of the Head Constable who first reported the matter. See him straightaway. You have got a good man there, active, quick on his feet, sharp. If he could not make that girl talk, you will be having a first-class damn job, Inspector."

Ghote located Head Constable Mudholkar one hour later at the local chowkey where he was stationed. The Head Constable confirmed at once the blossoming dislike for a sharp bully that Ghote had been harboring ever since A.C. Naik had praised the fellow. And, what was worse, the chap turned out to be very like the A.C. in looks as well. He had the same round type of face, the same puffy-looking lips, even a similar soft blur of mustache. But the Head Constable's appearance was nevertheless a travesty of the A.C.'s. His face was, simply, slewed.

To Ghote's prejudiced eyes, at the first moment of their encounter, the man's features seemed grotesquely distorted, as if in some distant time some god had taken one of the Head Constable's ancestors and had wrenched his whole head sideways between two omnipotent god-hands.

But, as the fellow supplied him with the details of the affair, Ghote forced himself to regard him with an open mind, and he then had to admit that the facial twist which had seemed so pronounced was in fact no more than a drooping corner of the mouth and of one ear being oddly longer than the other.

Ghote had to admit, too, that the chap was efficient. He had all the circumstances of the affair at his fingertips. The girl, named D'Mello, now in a hospital for her own safety, had been rigorously questioned both before and after the birth, but she had steadfastly denied that she had ever been with any man. She was indeed not the sort, the sole daughter of a Goan railway waiter on the Madras Express, a quiet girl, well brought up though her

[198]

parents were poor enough; she attended Mass regularly with her mother, and the whole family kept themselves to themselves.

"But with those Christians you can never tell," Head Constable Mudholkar concluded.

Ghote felt inwardly inclined to agree. Fervid religion had always made him shrink inwardly, whether it was a Hindu holy man spending 20 years silent and standing upright or whether it was the Catholics, always caressing lifeless statues in their churches till glass protection had to be installed, and even then they still stroked the thick panes. Either manifestation rendered him uneasy.

That was the real reason, he now acknowledged to himself, why he did not want to go and see Miss D'Mello in the hospital where she would be surrounded by nuns amid all the trappings of an alien religion, surrounded with all the panoply of a newly found goddess.

Yet go and see the girl he must.

But first he permitted himself to do every other thing that might possibly be necessary to the case. He visited Mrs. D'Mello, and by dint of patient wheedling, and a little forced toughness, confirmed from her the names of the only two men that Head Constable Mudholkar—who certainly proved to know inside-out the particular chawl where the D'Mellos lived—had suggested as possible fathers. They were both young men—a Goan, Charlie Lobo, and a Sikh, Kuldip Singh.

The Lobo family lived one floor below the D'Mellos. But that one flight of dirt-spattered stairs, bringing them just that much nearer the courtyard tap that served the whole crazily leaning chawl, represented a whole layer higher in social status. And Mrs. Lobo, a huge, tightly fat woman in a brightly flowered Western-style dress, had decided views about the unexpected fame that had come to the people upstairs.

"Has my Charlie been going with that girl?" she repeated after Ghote had managed to put the question, suitably wrapped up, to the boy. "No, he has not. Charlie, tell the man you hate and despise trash like that."

"Oh, Mum," said Charlie, a teen-age wisp of a figure suffocating in a necktie beside his balloon-hard mother.

"Tell the man, Charlie."

And obediently Charlie muttered something that satisfied his passion-filled parent. Ghote put a few more questions for form's sake, but he realized that only by getting hold of the boy on his own was he going to get any worthwhile answers. Yet it turned out that he did not have to employ any cunning. Charlie proved to have a strain of sharp slyness of his own, and hardly had Ghote climbed the stairs to the floor above the D'Mellos where Kuldip Singh lived when he heard a whispered call from the shadow-filled darkness below.

"Mum's got her head over the stove," Charlie said. "She don't know I slipped out."

"There is something you have to tell me?" Ghote said, acting the indulgent uncle. "You are in trouble—that's it, isn't it?"

"My only trouble is Mum," the boy replied. "Listen, mister, I had to tell you. I love Miss D'Mello—yes, I love her. She's the most wonderful girl ever was."

"And you want to marry her, and because you went too far before—"

"No, no, no. She's far and away too good for me. Mister, I've never even said 'Good morning' to her in the two years we've lived here. But I love her, mister, and I'm not going to have Mum make me say different."

Watching him slip cunningly back home, Ghote made his mental notes and then turned to tackle Kuldip Singh, his last comparatively easy task before the looming interview at the nun-ridden hospital he knew he must have.

Kuldip Singh, as Ghote had heard from Head Constable Mudholkar, was different from his neighbors. He lived in this teeming area from choice not necessity. Officially a student, he spent all his time in a series of antisocial activities—protesting, writing manifestoes, drinking. He seemed an ideal candidate for the unknown and elusive father.

Ghote's suspicions were at once heightened when the young Sikh opened his door. The boy, though old enough to have a beard, lacked this status symbol. Equally he had discarded the obligatory turban of his religion. But all the Sikh bounce was there, as Ghote discovered when he identified himself.

"Policewallah, is it? Then I want nothing at all to do with you. Me and the police are enemies, bhai. Natural enemies."

"Irrespective of such considerations," Ghote said stiffly, "it is my duty to put to you certain questions concerning one Miss D'Mello."

The young Sikh burst into a roar of laughter.

"The miracle girl, is it?" he said. "Plenty of trouble for policemen there, I promise you. Top-level rioting coming from that business. The fellow who fathered that baby did us a lot of good."

Ghote plugged away a good while longer—the hospital nuns awaited—but for all his efforts he learned no more than he had in that first brief exchange. And in the end he still had to go and meet his doom.

Just what he had expected at the hospital he never quite formulated to himself. What he did find was certainly almost the exact opposite of his fears. A calm reigned. White-habited nuns, mostly Indian but with a few Europeans, flitted silently to and fro or talked quietly to the patients whom Ghote glimpsed lying on beds in long wards. Above them swung frail but bright paper chains in honor of the feast day, and these were all the excitement there was.

The small separate ward in which Miss D'Mello lay in a broad bed all alone was no different. Except that the girl was isolated, she seemed to be treated in just the same way as the other new mothers in the big maternity ward that Ghote had been led through on his way in. In the face of such matter-of-factness he felt hollowly cheated.

Suddenly, too, to his own utter surprise he found, looking down at the big calm-after-storm eyes of the Goan girl, that he wanted the story she was about to tell him to be true. Part of him knew that, if it were so, or if it was widely believed to be so, appalling disorders could result from the feverish religious excitement that was bound to mount day by day. But another part of him now simply wanted a miracle to have happened.

He began, quietly and almost diffidently, to put his questions. Miss D'Mello would hardly answer at all, but such syllables as she did whisper were of blank inability to name anyone as the father of her child. After a while Ghote brought himself, with a distinct effort of will, to change his tactics. He banged out the hard line. Miss D'Mello went quietly and totally mute.

Then Ghote slipped in, with adroit suddenness, the name of Charlie Lobo. He got only a small puzzled frown.

Then, in an effort to make sure that her silence was not a silence of fear, he presented, with equal suddenness, the name of Kuldip Singh. If the care-for-nothing young Sikh had forced this timid creature, this might be the way to get an admission. But instead there came something approaching a laugh.

"That Kuldip is a funny fellow," the girl said, with an out-of-place and unexpected offhandedness.

Ghote almost gave up. But at that moment a nun nurse appeared carrying in her arms a small, long, white-wrapped, minutely crying bundle—the baby.

While she handed the hungry scrap to its mother Ghote stood and watched. Perhaps holding the child she would—?

He looked down at the scene on the broad bed, awaiting his moment again. The girl fiercely held the tiny agitated thing to her breast and in a moment or two quiet came, the tiny head applied to the life-giving nipple. How human the child looked already, Ghote thought. How much a man at two days old. The round skull, almost bald, as it might become again toward the end of its span. The frown on the forehead that would last a lifetime, the tiny, perfectly formed, plainly asymmetrical ears—

And then Ghote knew that there had not been any miracle. It was as he surmised, but with different circumstances. Miss D'Mello was indeed too frightened to talk. No wonder, when the local bully, Head Constable Mudholkar with his slewed head and its one ear so characteristically longer than the other, was the man who had forced himself on her.

[201]

A deep smothering of disappointment floated down on Ghote. So it had been nothing miraculous after all. Just a sad case, to be cleared up painfully. He stared down at the bed.

The tiny boy suckled energetically. And with a topsy-turvy welling up of rose-pink pleasure, Ghote saw that there had after all been a miracle. The daily, hourly, every-minute miracle of a new life, of a new flicker of hope in the tired world.

★

Maigret's Christmas

by *Georges Simenon*

Translated by *Lawrence G. Blochman*

THE ROUTINE never varied. When Maigret went to bed he must have muttered his usual, "Tomorrow morning I shall sleep late." And Mme. Maigret, who over the years should have learned to pay no attention to such casual phrases, had taken him at his word this Christmas day.

It was not quite daylight when he heard her stirring cautiously. He forced himself to breathe regularly and deeply as though he were still asleep. It was like a game. She inched toward the edge of the bed with animal stealth, pausing after each movement to make sure she had not awakened him. He waited anxiously for the inevitable finale, the movement when the bedspring, relieved of her weight, would spring back into place with a faint sigh.

She picked up her clothing from the chair and turned the knob of the bathroom door so slowly that it seemed to take an eternity. It was not until she had reached the distant fastness of the kitchen that she resumed her normal movements.

Maigret had fallen asleep again. Not deeply, nor for long. Long enough, however, for a confused and disturbing dream. Waking, he could not remember what it was, but he knew it was disturbing because he still felt vaguely uneasy.

The crack between the window drapes which never quite closed became a strip of pale, hard daylight. He waited a while longer, lying on his back with his eyes open, savoring the fragrance of fresh coffee. Then he heard the apartment door open and close, and he knew that Mme. Maigret was hurrying downstairs to buy him hot *croissants* from the bakery at the corner of the Rue Amelot.

He never ate in the morning. His breakfast consisted of black coffee. But his wife clung to her ritual: on Sundays and holidays he was supposed to lie in bed until mid-morning while she went out for *croissants*.

He got up, stepped into his slippers, put on his dressing gown, and drew the curtains. He knew he was doing wrong. His wife would be heartbroken. But while he was willing to make almost any sacrifice to please her, he simply could not stay in bed longer than he felt like it.

It was not snowing. It was nonsense, of course, for a man past 50 to be disappointed because there was no snow on Christmas morning; but then middle-aged people never have as much sense as young folks sometimes imagine.

A dirty, turbid sky hung low over the rooftops. The Boulevard Richard-Lenoir was completely deserted. The words *Fils et Cie., Bonded Warehouses* on the sign above the porte-cochére across the street stood out as black as mourning crêpe. The *F*, for some strange reason, seemed particularly dismal.

He heard his wife moving about in the kitchen again. She came into the dining room on tiptoe, as though he were still asleep instead of looking out the window. He glanced at his watch on the night table. It was only ten past 8.

The night before the Maigrets had gone to the theatre. They would have loved dropping in for a snack at some restaurant, like everyone else on Christmas Eve, but all tables were reserved for *Réveillon* supper. So they had walked home arm in arm, getting in a few minutes before midnight. Thus they hadn't long to wait before exchanging presents.

He got a pipe, as usual. Her present was an electric coffee pot, the latest model that she had wanted so much, and, not to break with tradition, a dozen finely embroidererd handkerchiefs.

Still looking out the window, Maigret absently filled his new pipe. The shutters were still closed on some of the windows across the boulevard. Not many people were up. Here and there a light burned in a window, probably left by children who had leaped out of bed at the crack of dawn to rush for their presents under the Christmas tree.

In the quiet Maigret apartment the morning promised to be a lazy one for just the two of them. Maigret would loiter in his dressing gown until quite late. He would not even shave. He would dawdle in the kitchen, talking to his wife while she put the lunch on the stove. Just the two of them.

He wasn't sad exactly, but his dream—which he couldn't remember—had left him jumpy. Or perhaps it wasn't his dream. Perhaps it was Christmas. He had to be extra-careful on Christmas Day, careful of his words, the way Mme. Maigret had been careful of her movements in getting out of bed. Her nerves, too, were especially sensitive on Christmas.

Oh, well, why think of all that? He would just be careful to say nothing untoward. He would be careful not to look out the window when the neighborhood children began to appear on the sidewalks with their Christmas toys.

All the houses in the street had children. Or almost all. The street would soon echo to the shrill blast of toy horns, the roll of toy drums, and the crack of toy pistols. The little girls were probably already cradling their new dolls.

A few years ago he had proposed more or less at random: "Why don't we take a little trip for Christmas?"

"Where?" she had replied with her infallible common sense.

Where, indeed? Whom would they visit? They had no relatives except her sister who lived too far away. And why spend Christmas in some second-rate country inn, or at a hotel in some strange town?

Oh, well, he'd feel better after he had his coffee. He was never at his best until he'd drunk his first cup of coffee and lit his first pipe.

Just as he was reaching for the knob, the door opened noiselessly and Mme. Maigret appeared carrying a tray. She looked at the empty bed, then turned her disappointed eyes upon her husband. She was on the verge of tears.

"You got up!" She looked as though she had been up for hours herself, every hair in place, a picture of neatness in her crisp clean apron. "And I was so happy about serving your breakfast in bed."

He had tried a hundred times, as subtly as he could, to make her understand that he didn't like eating breakfast in bed. It made him uncomfortable. It made him feel like an invalid or a senile old gaffer. But for Mme. Maigret breakfast in bed was the symbol of leisure and luxury, the ideal way to start Sunday or a holiday.

"Don't you want to go back to bed?"

No, he did not. Decidedly not. He hadn't the courage.

"Then come to breakfast in the kitchen. And Merry Christmas."

"Merry Christmas! . . . You're not angry?"

They were in the dining room. He surveyed the silver tray on a corner of the table, the steaming cup of coffee, the golden-brown *croissants*. He put down his pipe and ate a *croissant* to please his wife, but he remained standing, looking out the window.

"It's snowing."

It wasn't real snow. It was a fine white dust sifting down from the sky, but it reminded Maigret that when he was a small boy he used to stick out his tongue to lick up a few of the tiny flakes.

His gaze focused on the entrance to the building across the street, next door to the warehouse. Two women had just come out, both bareheaded. One of them, a blonde of about 30, had thrown a coat over her shoulders without stopping to slip her arms into the sleeves. The other, a brunette, older and thinner, was hugging a shawl.

The blonde seemed to hesitate, ready to turn back. Her slim little companion was insistent and Maigret had the impression that she was pointing up toward his window. The appearance of the concierge in the doorway behind them seemed to tip the scales in favor of the little brunette. The blonde looked back apprehensively, then crossed the street.

[205]

"What are you looking at?"

"Nothing . . . two women. . . ."

"What are they doing?"

"I think they're coming here."

The two women had stopped in the middle of the street and were looking up in the direction of the Maigret apartment.

"I hope they're not coming here to bother you on Christmas Day. My housework's not even done." Nobody would have guessed it. There wasn't a speck of dust on any of the polished furniture. "Are you sure they're coming here?"

"We'll soon find out."

To be on the safe side, he went to comb his hair, brush his teeth, and splash a little water on his face. He was still in his room, relighting his pipe, when he heard the doorbell. Mme. Maigret was evidently putting up a strong hedgehog defense, for it was some time before she came for him.

"They insist on speaking to you," she whispered. "They claim it's very important and they need advice. I know one of them."

"Which one?"

"The skinny little one, Mlle. Doncoeur. She lives across the street on the same floor as ours. She's a very nice person and she does embroidery for a firm in the Faubourg Saint-Honoré. I sometimes wonder if she isn't in love with you."

"Why?"

"Because she works near the window, and when you leave the house in the morning she sometimes gets up to watch you go down the street."

"How old is she?"

"Forty-five to fifty. Aren't you getting dressed?"

Doesn't a man have the right to lounge in his dressing gown, even if people come to bother him at 8:30 on Christmas morning? Well, he'd compromise. He'd put his trousers on underneath the robe.

The two women were standing when he walked into the dining room.

"Excuse me, mesdames . . ."

Perhaps Mme. Maigret was right. Mlle. Doncoeur did not blush; she paled, smiled, lost her smile, smiled again. She opened her mouth to speak but said nothing.

The blonde, on the other hand, was perfectly composed. She said with a touch of humor: "Coming here wasn't my idea."

"Would you sit down, please?"

Maigret noticed that the blonde was wearing a house dress under her coat and that her legs were bare. Mlle. Doncoeur was dressed as though for church.

"You perhaps wonder at our boldness in coming to you like this," Mlle.

[206]

Doncoeur said finally, choosing her words carefully. "Like everyone in the neighborhood, we are honored to have such a distinguished neighbor. . . ." She paused, blushed, and stared at the tray. "We're keeping you from your breakfast."

"I've finished. I'm at your service."

"Something happened in our building last night, or rather this morning, which was so unusual that I felt it was our duty to speak to you about it immediately. Madame Martin did not want to disturb you, but I told her—"

"You also live across the street, Madame Martin?"

"Yes, Monsieur." Madame Martin was obviously unhappy at being forced to take this step. Mlle. Doncoeur, however, was now fully wound up.

"We live on the same floor, just across from your windows." She blushed again, as if she were making a confession. "Monsieur Martin is often out of town, which is natural enough since he is a traveling salesman. For the past two months their little girl has been in bed, as a result of a silly accident. . . ."

Maigret turned politely to the blonde. "You have a daughter?"

"Well, not a daughter exactly. She's our niece. Her mother died two years ago and she's been living with us ever since. The girl broke her leg on the stairs. She should have been up and about after six weeks, but there were complications."

"Your husband is on the road at present?"

"He should be in Bergerac."

"I'm listening, Mlle. Doncoeur."

Mme. Maigret had detoured through the bathroom to regain the kitchen. The clatter of pots and pans had resumed. Maigret stared through the window at the leaden sky.

"I got up early this morning as usual," said Mlle. Doncoeur, "to go to first mass."

"And you did go to church?"

"Yes. I stayed for three masses. I got home about 7:30 and prepared my breakfast. You may have seen the light in my window."

Maigret's gesture indicated he had not been watching.

"I was in a hurry to take a few goodies to Colette. It's very sad for a child to spend Christmas in bed. Colette is Madame Martin's niece."

"How old is she?"

"Seven. Isn't that right, Madame Martin?"

"She'll be seven in January."

"So at 8 o'clock I knocked at the door of their apartment—"

"I wasn't up," the blonde interrupted. "I sometimes sleep rather late."

"As I was saying, I knocked. Madame Martin kept me waiting for a mo-

[207]

ment while she slipped on her négligée. I had my arms full, and I asked if I could take my presents in to Colette.''

Maigret noted that the blonde was making a mental inventory of the apartment, stopping occasionally to dart a sharp, suspicious glance in his direction.

''We opened the door to her room together. . . .''

''The child has a room of her own?''

''Yes. There are two bedrooms in the apartment, a dressing room, a kitchen, and a dining room. But I must tell you—No, I'm getting ahead of myself. We had just opened the door and since the room was dark, Madame Martin had switched on the light . . .''

''Colette was awake?''

''Yes. It was easy to see she'd been awake for some time, waiting. You know how children are on Christmas morning. If she could use her legs, she would certainly have got up long since to see what Father Christmas had brought her. Perhaps another child would have called out. But Colette is already a little lady. She's much older than her age. She thinks a lot.''

Now Madame Martin was looking out the window. Maigret tried to guess which apartment was hers. It must be the last one to the right, the one with the two lighted windows.

''I wished her a Merry Christmas,'' Mlle. Doncoeur continued. ''I said to her, and these were my exact words, 'Darling, look what Father Christmas left in my apartment for you.' ''

Madame Martin was clasping and unclasping her fingers.

''And do you know what she answered me, without even looking to see what I'd brought? They were only trifles, anyhow. She said, 'I saw him.' ''

'' 'Whom did you see?'

'' 'Father Christmas.'

'' 'When did you see him?' I asked. 'Where?'

'' 'Right here, last night. He came to my room.'

''That's exactly what she said, isn't it, Madame Martin? With any other child, we would have smiled. But as I told you, Colette is already a little lady. She doesn't joke. I said, 'How could you see him, since it was dark?''

'' 'He had a light.'

'' 'You mean he turned on the electricity?'

'' 'No. He had a flashlight. Look, Mama Loraine.'

''I must tell you that the little girl calls Madame Martin 'Mama,' which is natural enough, since her own mother is dead and Madame Martin has been taking her place.''

The monologue had become a confused buzzing in Maigret's ears. He had not drunk his second cup of coffee and his pipe had gone out. He asked without conviction: ''Did she really see someone?''

''Yes, Monsieur l'Inspecteur. And that's why I insisted that Madame

Martin come to speak to you. Colette did see someone and she proved it to us. With a sly little smile she threw back the bedsheet and showed us a magnificent doll . . . a beautiful big doll she was cuddling and which I swear was not in the house yesterday.''

"You didn't give your niece a doll, Madame Martin?"

"I was going to give her one, but mine was not nearly as nice. I got it yesterday afternoon at the Galeries, and I was holding it behind me this morning when we came into her room.''

"In other words, someone *did* come into your apartment last night.''

"That's not all," said Mlle. Doncoeur quickly; she was not to be stopped. "Colette never tells lies. She's not a child who imagines things. And when we questioned her, she said the man was certainly Father Christmas because he wore a white beard and a bright red coat.''

"At what time did she wake up?"

"She doesn't know—sometime during the night. She opened her eyes because she thought she saw a light. And there was a light, shining on the floor near the fireplace.''

"I can't understand it," sighed Madame Martin. "Unless my husband has some explanation . . .''

But Mlle. Doncoeur was not to be diverted from her story. It was obvious that she was the one who had questioned the child, just as she was the one who had thought of Maigret. She resumed:

"Colette said, 'Father Christmas was squatting on the floor, and he was bending over, as though he were working at something.'"

"She wasn't frightened?"

"No. She just watched him. This morning she told us he was busy making a hole in the floor. She thought he wanted to go through the floor to visit the people downstairs—that's the Delormes who have a little boy of three—because the chimney was too narrow. The man must have sensed she was watching him, because he got up, came over to the bed, and gave Colette the big doll. Then he put his finger to his lips.''

"Did she see him leave?"

"Yes."

"Through the floor?"

"No, by the door."

"Into what room does this door open?"

"Directly into the outside hall. There is another door that opens into the apartment, but the hall door is like a private entrance because the room used to be rented separately.''

"Wasn't the door locked?"

"Of course," Madame Martin intervened. "I wouldn't let the child sleep in a room that wasn't locked from the outside.''

"Then the door was forced?"

"Probably. I don't know. Mlle. Doncoeur immediately suggested we come to see you."

"Did you find a hole in the floor?"

Madame Martin shrugged wearily, but Mlle. Doncoeur answered for her.

"Not a hole exactly, but you could see that the floor boards had been moved."

"Tell me, Madame Martin, have you any idea what might have been hidden under the flooring?"

"No, Monsieur."

"How long have you lived in this apartment?"

"Since my marriage, five years ago."

"And this room was part of the apartment then?"

"Yes."

"You know who lived there before you?"

"My husband. He's 38. He was 33 when we were married, and he had his own furniture then. He liked to have his own home to come back to when he returned to Paris from the road."

"Do you think he might have wanted to surprise Colette?"

"He is six or seven hundred kilometers from here."

"Where did you say?"

"In Bergerac. His itinerary is planned in advance and he rarely deviates from his schedule."

"For what firm does he travel?"

"He covers the central and southwest territory for Zenith watches. It's an important line, as you probably know. He has a very good job."

"There isn't a finer man on earth!" exclaimed Mlle. Doncoeur. She blushed, then added, "Except you, Monsieur l'Inspecteur."

"As I understand it then, someone got into your apartment last night disguised as Father Christmas."

"According to the little girl."

"Didn't you hear anything? Is your room far from the little girl's?"

"There's the dining room between us."

"Don't you leave the connecting doors open at night?"

"It isn't necessary. Colette is not afraid, and as a rule she never wakes up. If she wants anything, she has a little bell on her night table."

"Did you go out last night?"

"I did not, Monsieur l'Inspecteur." Madame Martin was annoyed.

"Did you receive visitors?"

"I do not receive visitors while my husband is away."

Maigret glanced at Mlle. Doncoeur whose expression did not change. So Madame Martin was telling the truth.

"Did you go to bed late?"

"I read until midnight. As soon as the radio played *Minuit, Chrétiens,* I went to bed."

"And you heard nothing unusual?"

"Nothing."

"Have you asked the concierge if she clicked the latch to let in any strangers last night?"

"I asked her," Mlle. Doncoeur volunteered. "She says she didn't."

"And you found nothing missing from your apartment this morning, Madame Martin? Nothing disturbed in the dining room?"

"No."

"Who is with the little girl now?"

"No one. She's used to staying alone. I can't be at home all day. I have marketing to do, errands to run. . . ."

"I understand. You told me Colette is an orphan?"

"Her mother is dead."

"So her father is living. Where is he?"

"Her father's name is Paul Martin. He's my husband's brother. As to telling you where he is—" Madame Martin sketched a vague gesture.

"When did you see him last?"

"About a month ago. A little longer. It was around All Saint's Day. He was finishing a novena."

"I beg your pardon?"

"I may as well tell you everything at once," said Madame Martin with a faint smile, "since we seem to be washing our family linen." She glanced reproachfully at Mlle. Doncoeur. "My brother-in-law, especially since he lost his wife, is not quite respectable."

"What do you mean exactly?"

"He drinks. He always drank a little, but he never used to get into trouble. He had a good job with a furniture store in the Faubourg Saint-Antoine. But since the accident..."

"The accident to his daughter?"

"No, to his wife. He borrowed a car from a friend one Sunday about three years ago and took his wife and little girl to the country. They had lunch at a roadside inn near Mantes-la-Jolie and he drank too much white wine. He sang most of the way back to Paris—until he ran into something near the Bougival bridge. His wife was killed instantly. He cracked his own skull and it's a miracle he's still alive. Colette escaped without a scratch. Paul hasn't been a man since then. We've practically adopted the little girl. He comes to see her occasionally when he's sober. Then he starts over again. . . ."

"Do you know where he lives?"

Another vague gesture. "Everywhere. We've seen him loitering around the Bastille like a beggar. Sometimes he sells papers in the street. I can speak freely in front of Mlle. Doncoeur because unfortunately the whole house knows about him."

"Don't you think he might have dressed up as Father Christmas to call on his daughter?"

"That's what I told Mlle. Doncoeur, but she insisted on coming to see you anyhow."

"Because I see no reason for him to take up the flooring," said Mlle. Doncoeur acidly.

"Or perhaps your husband returned to Paris unexpectedly. . . ."

"It's certainly something of the sort. I'm not at all disturbed. But Mlle. Doncoeur—"

Decidedly Madame Martin had not crossed the boulevard light-heartedly.

"Do you know where your husband might be staying in Bergerac?"

"Yes. At the Hotel de Bordeaux."

"You hadn't thought of telephoning him?"

"We have no phone. There's only one in the house—the people on the second floor, and·they hate to be disturbed."

"Would you object to my calling the Hotel de Bordeaux?"

Madame Martin started to nod, then hesitated. "He'll think something terrible has happened."

"You can speak to him yourself."

"He's not used to my phoning him on the road."

"You'd rather he not know what's happening?"

"That's not so. I'll talk to him if you like."

Maigret picked up the phone and placed the call. Ten minutes later he was connected with the Hotel de Bordeaux in Bergerac. He passed the instrument to Madame Martin.

"Hello. . . . Monsieur Martin, please. . . . Yes, Monsieur Jean Martin. . . . No matter. Wake him up."

She put her hand over the mouthpiece. "He's still asleep. They've gone to call him."

Then she retreated into silence, evidently rehearsing the words she was to speak to her husband.

"Hello? . . . Hello darling. . . . What? . . . Yes, Merry Christmas! . . . Yes, everything's all right. . . . Colette is fine. . . . No, that's not why I phoned. . . . No, no, no! Nothing's wrong. Please don't worry!" She repeated each word separately. "Please . . . don't . . . worry! I just want to tell you about a strange thing that happened last night. Somebody dressed up like Father Christmas and came into Colette's room. . . . No, no! He didn't hurt her. He gave her a big doll. . . . Yes, *doll!* . . . And he did queer

[212]

things to the floor. He removed two boards which he put back in a hurry.... Mille. Doncoeur thought I should report it to the police inspector who lives across the street. I'm there now. . . . You don't understand? Neither do I. . . .You want me to put him on?" She passed the instrument to Maigret. "He wants to speak to you."

A warm masculine voice came over the wire, the voice of an anxious, puzzled man.

"Are you sure my wife and the little girl are all right? . . . It's all so incredible! If it were just the doll, I might suspect my brother. Loraine will tell you about him. Loraine is my wife. Ask her. . . . But he wouldn't have removed the flooring. . . . Do you think I'd better come home? I can get a train for Paris at three this afternoon. . . . What? . . . Thank you so much. It's good to know you'll look out for them."

Loraine Martin took back the phone.

"See, darling? The inspector says there's no danger. It would be foolish to break your trip now. It might spoil your chances of being transferred permanently to Paris...."

Mlle. Doncoeur was watching her closely and there was little tenderness in the spinster's eyes.

". . . I promise to wire you or phone you if there's anything new. . . . She's playing quietly with her new doll. . . . No, I haven't had time yet to give her your present. I'll go right home and do it now."

Madame Martin hung up and declared: "You see." Then, after a pause, "Forgive me for bothering you. It's really not my fault. I'm sure this is all the work of some practical joker . . . unless it's my brother-in-law. When he's been drinking there's no telling what he might do."

"Do you expect to see him today? Don't you think he might want to see his daughter?"

"That depends. If he's been drinking, no. He's very careful never to come around in that condition."

"May I have your permission to come over and talk with Colette a little later?"

"I see no reason why you shouldn't—if you think it worthwhile. . . ."

"Thank you, Monsieur Maigret!" exclaimed Mlle. Doncoeur. Her expression was half grateful, half conspiratorial. "She's such an interesting child! You'll see!"

She backed toward the door.

A few minutes later Maigret watched the two women cross the boulevard. Mlle. Doncoeur, close on the heels of Madame Martin, turned to look up at the windows of the Maigret apartment.

Mme. Maigret opened the kitchen door, flooding the dining room with the aroma of browning onions. She asked gently:

"Are you happy?"

He pretended not to understand. Luckily he had been too busy to think much about the middle-aged couple who had nobody to make a fuss over this Christmas morning.

It was time for him to shave and call on Colette.

He was just about to lather his face when he decided to make a phone call. He didn't bother with his dressing gown. Clad only in pajamas, he dropped into the easy chair by the window—*his* chair—and watched the smoke curling up from all the chimney pots while his call went through.

The ringing at the other end—in headquarters at the Quai des Orfèvres —had a different sound from all other rings. It evoked for him the long empty corridors, the vacant offices, the operator stuck with holiday duty at the switchboard. . . . Then he heard the operator call Lucas with the words: "The boss wants you."

He felt a little like one of his wife's friends who could imagine no greater joy—which she experienced daily—than lying in bed all morning, with her windows closed and curtains drawn, and telephoning all her friends, one af- ter the other. By the soft glow of her night-light she managed to maintain a constant state of just having awakened. "What? Ten o'clock already? How's the weather? Is it raining? Have you been out yet? Have you done all your marketing?" And as she established telephonic connection with the hurly-burly of the workaday world, she would sink more and more volup- tuously into the warm softness of her bed.

"That you, Chief?"

Maigret, too, felt a need for contact with the working world. He wanted to ask Lucas who was on duty with him, what they were doing, how the shop looked on this Christmas morning.

"Nothing new? Not too busy?"

"Nothing to speak of. Routine. . . ."

"I'd like you to get me some information. You can probably do this by phone. First of all, I want a list of all convicts released from prison the last two or three months."

"Which prison?"

"All prisons. But don't bother with any who haven't served at least five years. Then check and see if any of them has ever lived on Boulevard Richard-Lenoir. Got that?"

"I'm making notes."

Lucas was probably somewhat bewildered but he would never admit it.

"Another thing. I want you to locate a man named Paul Martin, a drunk, no fixed address, who frequently hangs out around the Place de la Bastille. I don't want him arrested. I don't want him molested. I just want

[214]

to know where he spent Christmas Eve. The commissariats should help you on this one.''

No use trying. Maigret simply could not reproduce the idle mood of his wife's friend. On the contrary, it embarrassed him to be lolling at home in his pajamas, unshaven, phoning from his favorite easy chair, looking out at a scene of complete peace and quiet in which there was no movement except the smoke curling from the chimney pots, while at the other end of the wire good old Lucas had been on duty since six in the morning and was probably already unwrapping his sandwiches.

"That's not quite all, old man. I want you to call Bergerac long distance. There's a traveling salesman by the name of Jean Martin staying at the Hotel de Bordeaux there. No, Jean. It's his brother. I want to know if Jean Martin got a telegram or a phone call from Paris last night or any time yesterday. And while you're about it, find out where he spent Christmas Eve. I think that's all.''

"Shall I call you back?''

"Not right away. I've got to go out for a while. I'll call you when I get home.''

"Something happen in your neighborhood?''

"I don't know yet. Maybe.''

Mme. Maigret came into the bathroom to talk to him while he finished dressing. He did not put on his overcoat. The smoke curled slowly upward from so many chimney pots blended with the gray of the sky and conjured up the image of just as many overheated apartments, cramped rooms in which he would not be invited to make himself at home. He refused to be uncomfortable. He would put on his hat to cross the boulevard, and that was all.

The building across the way was very much like the one he lived in—old but clean, a little dreary, particularly on a drab December morning. He avoided stopping at the concierge's lodge, but noted she watched him with some annoyance. Doors opened silently as he climbed the stairs. He heard whispering, the padding of slippered feet.

Mlle. Doncoeur, who had doubtless been watching for him, was waiting on the fourth floor landing. She was both shy and excited, as if keeping a secret tryst with a lover.

"This way, Monsieur Maigret. She went out a little while ago.''

He frowned, and she noted the fact.

"I told her that you were coming and that she had better wait for you but she said she had not done her marketing yesterday and that there was nothing in the house. She said all the stores would be closed if she waited too long. Come in.''

[215]

She had opened the door into Madame Martin's dining room, a small, rather dark room which was clean and tidy.

"I'm looking after the little girl until she comes back. I told Colette that you were coming to see her, and she is delighted. I've spoken to her about you. She's only afraid you might take back her doll."

"When did Madame Martin decide to go out?"

"As soon as we came back across the street, she started dressing."

"Did she dress completely?"

"I don't understand."

"I mean, I suppose she dresses differently when she goes downtown than when she merely goes shopping in the neighborhood."

"She was quite dressed up. She put on her hat and gloves. And she carried her shopping bag."

Before going to see Colette, Maigret stepped into the kitchen and glanced at the breakfast dishes.

"Did she eat before you came to see me?"

"No. I didn't give her a chance."

"And when she came back?"

"She just made herself a cup of black coffee. I fixed breakfast for Colette while Madame Martin got dressed."

There was a larder on the ledge of the window looking out on the courtyard. Maigret carefully examined its contents: butter, eggs, vegetables, some cold meat. He found two uncut loaves of fresh bread in the kitchen cupboard. Colette had eaten *croissants* with her hot chocolate.

"How well do you know Madame Martin?"

"We're neighbors, aren't we? And I've seen more of her since Colette has been in bed. She often asks me to keep an eye on the little girl when she goes out."

"Does she go out much?"

"Not very often. Just for her marketing."

Maigret tried to analyze the curious impression he had had on entering the apartment. There was something in the atmosphere that disturbed him, something about the arrangement of the furniture, the special kind of neatness that prevailed, even the smell of the place. As he followed Mlle. Doncoeur into the dining room, he thought he knew what it was.

Madame Martin had told him that her husband had lived in this apartment before their marriage. And even though Madame Martin had lived there for five years, it had remained a bachelor's apartment. He pointed to the two enlarged photographs standing on opposite ends of the mantelpiece.

"Who are they?"

"Monsieur Martin's father and mother."

"Doesn't Madame Martin have photos of her own parents about?"

"I've never heard her speak of them. I suppose she's an orphan."

Even the bedroom was without the feminine touch. He opened a closet. Next to the neat rows of masculine clothing, the woman's clothes were hanging, mostly severely tailored suits and conservative dresses. He did not open the bureau drawers but he was sure they did not contain the usual trinkets and knickknacks that women collect.

"Mademoiselle Doncoeur!" called a calm little voice.

"Let's talk to Colette," said Maigret.

The child's room was as austere and cold as the others. The little girl lay in a bed too large for her, her face solemn, her eyes questioning but trusting.

"Are you the inspector, Monsieur?"

"I'm the inspector, my girl. Don't be afraid."

"I'm not afraid. Hasn't Mama Loraine come home yet?"

Maigret pursed his lips. The Martins had practically adopted their niece, yet the child said "Mama Loraine," not just "Mama."

"Do you believe it was Father Christmas who came to see me last night?" Colette asked Maigret.

"I'm sure it was."

"Mama Loraine doesn't believe it. She never believes me."

The girl had a dainty, attractive little face, with very bright eyes that stared at Maigret with level persistence. The plaster cast which sheathed one leg all the way to the hip made a thick bulge under the blankets.

Mlle. Doncoeur hovered in the doorway, evidently anxious to leave the inspector alone with the girl. She said: "I must run home for a moment to make sure my lunch isn't burning."

Maigret sat down beside the bed, wondering how to go about questioning the girl.

"Do you love Mama Loraine very much?" he began.

"Yes, Monsieur." She replied without hesitation and without enthusiasm.

"And your papa?"

"Which one? Because I have two papas, you know—Papa Paul and Papa Jean."

"Has it been a long time since you saw Papa Paul?"

"I don't remember. Perhaps several weeks. He promised to bring me a toy for Christmas, but he hasn't come yet. He must be sick."

"Is he often sick?"

"Yes, often. When he's sick he doesn't come to see me."

"And your Papa Jean?"

"He's away on a trip, but he'll be back for New Year's. Maybe then

[217]

he'll be appointed to the Paris office and won't have to go away any more. That would make him very happy and me, too.''

"Do many of your friends come to see you since you've been in bed?''

"What friends? The girls in school don't know where I live. Or maybe they know but their parents don't let them come alone.''

"What about Mama Loraine's friends? Or your papa's?''

"Nobody comes, ever.''

"Ever? Are you sure?''

"Only the man to read the gas meter, or for the electricity. I can hear them, because the door is almost always open. I recognize their voices. Once a man came and I didn't recognize his voice. Or twice.''

"How long ago was that?''

"The first time was the day after my accident. I remember because the doctor just left.''

"Who was it?''

"I didn't see him. He knocked at the other door. I heard him talking and then Mama Loraine came and closed my door. They talked for quite a while but I couldn't hear very well. Afterward Mama Loraine said it was a man who wanted to sell her some insurance. I don't know what that is.''

"And he came back?''

"Five or six days ago. It was night and I'd already turned off my light. I wasn't asleep, though. I heard someone knock, and then they talked in low voices like the first time. Mademoiselle Doncoeur sometimes comes over in the evening, but I could tell it wasn't she. I thought they were quarreling and I was frightened. I called out, and Mama Loraine came in and said it was the man about the insurance again and I should go to sleep.''

"Did he stay long?''

"I don't know. I think I fell asleep.''

"And you didn't see him either time?''

"No, but I'd recognize his voice.''

"Even though he speaks in low tones?''

"Yes, that's why. When he speaks low it sounds just like a big bumble-bee. I can keep the doll can't I? Mama Loraine bought me two boxes of candy and a little sewing kit. She bought me a doll, too, but it wasn't nearly as big as the doll Father Christmas gave me, because she's not rich. She showed it to me this morning before she left, and then she put it back in the box. I have the big one now, so I won't need the little one and Mama Loraine can take it back to the store.''

The apartment was overheated, yet Maigret felt suddenly cold. The building was very much like the one across the street, yet not only did the rooms seem smaller and stuffier, but the whole world seemed smaller and meaner over here.

He bent over the floor near the fireplace. He lifted the loose floor boards, but saw nothing but an empty, dusty cavity smelling of dampness. There were scratches on the planks which indicated they had been forced up with a chisel or some similar instrument.

He examined the outside door and found indications that it had been forced. It was obviously an amateur's work, and luckily for him, the job had been an easy one.

"Father Christmas wasn't angry when he saw you watching him?"

"No, Monsieur. He was busy making a hole in the floor so he could go and see the little boy downstairs."

"Did he speak to you?"

"I think he smiled at me. I'm not sure, though, because of his whiskers. It wasn't very light. But I'm sure he put his finger to his lips so I wouldn't call anybody, because grown-ups aren't supposed to see Father Christmas. Did you ever see him?"

"A very long time ago."

"When you were little?"

Maigret heard footsteps in the hallway. The door opened and Madame Martin came in. She was wearing a gray tailored suit and a small beige hat and carried a brown shopping bag. She was visibly cold, for her skin was taut and very white, yet she must have hurried up the stairs, since there were two pink spots on her cheeks and she was out of breath. Unsmiling, she asked Maigret:

"Has she been a good girl?" Then, as she took off her jacket, "I apologize for making you wait. I had so many things to buy, and I was afraid the stores would all be closed later on."

"Did you meet anyone?"

"What do you mean?"

"Nothing. I was wondering if anyone tried to speak to you."

She had had plenty of time to go much further than the Rue Amelot or the Rue du Chemin-Vert where most of the neighborhood shops were located. She had even had time to go across Paris and back by taxi or the Metro.

Mlle. Doncoeur returned to ask if there was anything she could do. Madame Martin was about to say no when Maigret intervened: "I'd like you to stay with Colette while I step into the next room."

Mlle. Doncoeur understood that he wanted her to keep the child busy while he questioned the foster-mother. Madame Martin must have understood, too, but she gave no indication.

"Please come in. Do you mind if I take off my things?"

Madame Martin put her packages in the kitchen. She took off her hat and fluffed out her pale blonde hair. When she had closed the bedroom

[219]

door, she said: "Mlle. Doncoeur is all excited. This is quite an event, isn't it, for an old maid—particularly an old maid who cuts out every newspaper article about a certain police inspector, and who finally has the inspector in her own house. . . . Do you mind?"

She had taken a cigarette from a silver case, tapped the end, and snapped a lighter. The gesture somehow prompted Maigret's next question:

"You're not working, Madame Martin?"

"It would be difficult to hold a job and take care of the house and the little girl, too, even when the child is in school. Besides, my husband won't allow me to work."

"But you did work before you met him?"

"Naturally. I had to earn a living. Won't you sit down?"

He lowered himself into a rude raffia-bottomed chair. She rested one thigh against the edge of a table.

"You were a typist?"

"I have been a typist."

"For long?"

"Quite a while."

"You were still a typist when you met Martin? You must forgive me for asking these personal questions."

"It's your job."

"You were married five years ago. Were you working then? Just a moment. May I ask your age?"

"I'm thirty-three. I was twenty-eight then, and I was working for a Monsieur Lorilleux in the Palais-Royal arcades."

"As his secretary?"

"Monsieur Lorilleux had a jewelry shop. Or more exactly, he sold souvenirs and old coins. You know those old shops in the Palais-Royal. I was salesgirl, bookkeeper, *and* secretary. I took care of the shop when he was away."

"He was married?"

"And father of three children."

"You left him to marry Martin?"

"Not exactly. Jean didn't want me to go on working, but he wasn't making very much money then and I had quite a good job. So I kept it for the first few months."

"And then?"

"Then a strange thing happened. One morning I came to work at 9 o'clock as usual, and I found the door locked. I thought Monsieur Lorilleux had overslept, so I waited. . . ."

"Where did he live?"

"Rue Mazarine with his family. At half-past 9 I began to worry."

"Was he dead?"

[220]

"No. I phoned his wife, who said he had left the house at 8 o'clock as usual."

"Where did you telephone from?"

"From the glove shop next door. I waited all morning. His wife came down and we went to the commissariat together to report him missing, but the police didn't take it very seriously. They just asked his wife if he'd ever had heart trouble, if he had a mistress—things like that. But he was never seen again, and nobody ever heard from him. Then some Polish people bought out the store and my husband made me stop working."

"How long was this after your marriage?"

"Four months."

"Your husband was already traveling in the southwest?"

"He had the same territory he has now."

"Was he in Paris when your employer disappeared?"

"No, I don't think so."

"Didn't the police examine the premises?"

"Nothing had been touched since the night before. Nothing was missing."

"Do you know what became of Madame Lorilleux?"

"She lived for a while on the money from the sale of the store. Then she bought a little dry-goods shop not far from here, in the Rue du Pas-de-la-Mule. Her children must be grown up now, probably married."

"Do you still see her?"

"I go into her shop once in a while. That's how I know she's in business in the neighborhood. The first time I saw her there I didn't recognize her."

"How long ago was that?"

"I don't know. Six months or so."

"Does she have a telephone?"

"I don't know. Why?"

"What kind of man was Lorilleux?"

"You mean physically?"

"Let's start with the physical."

"He was a big man, taller than you, and broader. He was fat, but flabby, if you know what I mean. And rather sloppy-looking."

"How old?"

"Around fifty. I can't say exactly. He had a little salt-and-pepper mustache, and his clothes were always too big for him."

"You were familiar with his habits?"

"He walked to work every morning. He got down fifteen minutes ahead of me and cleared up the mail before I arrived. He didn't talk much. He was a rather gloomy person. He spent most of the day in the little office behind the shop."

"No romantic adventures?"

[221]

"Not that I know of."

"Didn't he try to make love to you?"

"No!" The monosyllable was tartly emphatic.

"But he thought highly of you?"

"I think I was a great help to him."

"Did your husband ever meet him?"

"They never spoke. Jean sometimes came to wait for me outside the shop, but he never came in." A note of impatience, tinged with anger, crept into her voice. "Is that all you want to know?"

"May I point out, Madame Martin, that you are the one who came to get me?"

"Only because a crazy old maid practically dragged me there so she could get a close-up look at you."

"You don't like Mlle. Doncoeur?"

"I don't like people who can't mind their own business."

"People like Mlle. Doncoeur?"

"You know that we've taken in my brother-in-law's child. Believe me or not, I've done everything I can for her. I treat her the way I'd treat my own child. . . ." She paused to light a fresh cigarette, and Maigret tried unsuccessfully to picture her as a doting mother. "...And now that old maid is always over here, offering to help me with the child. Every time I start to go out, I find her in the hallway, smiling sweetly, and saying, 'You mustn't leave Colette all alone, Madame Martin. Let me go in and keep her company.' I sometimes wonder if she doesn't go through my drawers when I'm out."

"You put up with her, nevertheless."

"How can I help it? Colette asks for her, especially since she's been in bed. And my husband is fond of her because when he was a bachelor, she took care of him when he was sick with pleurisy."

"Have you already returned the doll you bought for Colette's Christmas?"

She frowned and glanced at the door to the child's bedroom. "I see you've been questioning the little girl. No, I haven't taken it back for the very good reason that all the big department stores are closed today. Would you like to see it?"

She spoke defiantly, expecting him to refuse, but he said nothing. He examined the cardboard box, noting the price tag. It was a very cheap doll.

"May I ask where you went this morning?"

"I did my marketing."

"Rue Amelot or Rue du Chemin-Vert?"

"Both."

"If I may be indiscreet, what did you buy?"

Furious, she stormed into the kitchen, snatched up her shopping bag, and dumped it on the dining room table. "Look for yourself!"

There were three tins of sardines, butter, potatoes, some ham, and a head of lettuce.

She fixed him with a hard, unwavering stare. She was not in the least nervous. Spiteful, rather.

"Any more questions?"

"Yes. The name of your insurance agent."

"My insurance. . . ." She was obviously puzzled.

"Insurance agent. The one who came to see you."

"I'm sorry. I was at a loss for a moment because you spoke of *my* agent as though he were really handling a policy for me. So Colette told you that, too? Actually, a man did come to see me twice, trying to sell me a policy. He was one of those door-to-door salesmen, and I thought at first he was selling vacuum cleaners, not life insurance. I had a terrible time getting rid of him."

"Did he stay long?"

"Long enough for me to convince him that I had no desire to take out a policy."

"What company did he represent?"

"He told me but I've forgotten. Something with 'Mutual' in it."

"And he came back later?"

"Yes."

"What time does Colette usually go to sleep?"

"I put out her light at 7:30, but sometimes she talks to herself in the dark until much later."

"So the second time the insurance man called, it was later than 7:30?"

"Possibly." She saw the trap. "I remember now I was washing the dishes."

"And you let him in?"

"He had his foot in the door."

"Did he call on other tenants in the building?"

"I haven't the slightest idea, but I'm sure you will inquire. Must you cross-examine me like a criminal, just because a little girl imagines she saw Santa Claus? If my husband were here—"

"By the way, does your husband carry life insurance?"

"I think so. In fact, I'm sure he does."

Maigret picked up his hat from a chair and started for the door. Madame Martin seemed surprised.

"Is that all?"

"That's all. It seems your brother-in-law promised to come and see his daughter today. If he should come, I would be grateful if you let me know. And now I'd like a few words with Mlle. Doncoeur."

There was a convent smell about Mlle.Doncoeur's apartment, but there was no dog or cat in sight, no antimacassars on the chairs, no bricbrac on the mantelpiece.

"Have you lived in this house long, Mlle. Concoeur?"

"Twenty-five years, Monsieur l'Inspecteur. I'm one of the oldest tenants. I remember when I first moved in you were already living across the street, and you wore long mustaches."

"Who lived in the next apartment before Martin moved in?"

"A public works engineer. I don't remember his name, but I could look it up for you. He had a wife and daughter. The girl was a deaf-mute. It was very sad. They went to live somewhere in the country."

"Have you been bothered by a door-to-door insurance agent recently?"

"No recently. There was one who came around two or three years ago."

"You don't like Madame Martin, do you?"

"Why?"

"I asked if you liked Madame Martin?"

"Well, if I had a son . . ."

"Go on."

"If I had a son I don't think I would like Madame Martin for a daughter-in-law. Especially as Monsieur Martin is such a nice man, so kind."

"You think he is unhappy with his wife?"

"I wouldn't say that. I have nothing against her, really. She can't help being the kind of woman she is."

"What kind of woman is she?"

"I couldn't say, exactly. You've seen her. You're a better judge of those things than I am. In a way, she's not like a woman at all. I'll wager she never shed a tear in her life. True, she is bringing up the child properly, decently, but she never says a kind word to her. She acts exasperated when I tell Colette a fairy tale. I'm sure she's told the girl there is no Santa Claus. Luckily Colette doesn't believe her."

"The child doesn't like her either, does she?"

"Colette is always obedient. She tries to do what's expected of her. I think she's just as happy to be left alone."

"Is she alone much?"

"Not much. I'm not reproaching Madame Martin. It's hard to explain. She wants to live her own life. She's not interested in others. She doesn't even talk much about herself."

"Have you ever met her brother-in-law—Colette's father?"

"I've seen him on the landing, but I've never spoken to him. He walks with his head down, as if he were ashamed of something. He always looks as if he slept in his clothes. No, I don't think it was he last night, Monsieur Maigret. He's not the type. Unless he was terribly drunk."

On his way out Maigret looked in at the concierge's lodge, a dark cubicle where the light burned all day.

It was noon when he started back across the boulevard. Curtains stirred at the windows of the house behind him. Curtains stirred at his own window, too. Mme. Maigret was watching for him so she would know when to put the chicken in the oven. He waved to her. He wanted very much to stick out his tongue and lick up a few of the tiny snow flakes that were drifting down. He could still remember their taste.

"I wonder if that little tike is happy over there," sighed Mme. Maigret as she got up from the table to bring the coffee from the kitchen.

She could see he wasn't listening. He had pushed back his chair and was stuffing his pipe while staring at the purring stove. For her own satisfaction she added: "I don't see how she could be happy with that woman."

He smiled vaguely, as he always did when he hadn't heard what she said, and continued to stare at the tiny flames licking evenly at the mica windows of the salamander. There were at least ten similar stoves in the house, all purring alike in ten similar dining rooms with wine and cakes on the table, a carafe of cordial waiting on the sideboard, and all the windows pale with the same hard, gray light of a sunless day.

It was perhaps this very familiarity which had been confusing his subconscious since morning. Nine times out of ten his investigations plunged him abruptly into new surroundings, set him at grips with people of a world he barely knew, people of a social level whose habits and manners he had to study from scratch. But in this case, which was not really a case since he had no official assignment, the whole approach was unfamiliar because the background was too familiar. For the first time in his career something professional was happening in his own world, in a building which might just as well be his building.

The Martins could easily have been living on his floor, instead of across the street, and it would probably have been Mme. Maigret who would look after Colette when her aunt was away. There was an elderly maiden lady living just under him who was a plumper, paler replica of Mlle. Doncoeur. The frames of the photographs of Martin's father and mother were exactly the same as those which framed Maigret's father and mother, and the enlargements had probably been made by the same studio.

Was that what was bothering him? He seemed to lack perspective. He was unable to look at people and things from a fresh, new viewpoint.

He had detailed his morning activities during dinner—a pleasant little

Christmas dinner which had left him with an overstuffed feeling—and his wife had listened while looking at the windows across the street with an air of embarrassment.

"Is the concierge sure that nobody could have come in from outside?"

"She's not so sure any more. She was entertaining friends until after midnight. And after she had gone to bed, there were considerable comings and goings, which is natural for Christmas Eve."

"Do you think something more is going to happen?"

That was a question that had been plaguing Maigret all morning. First of all, he had to consider that Madame Martin had not come to see him spontaneously, but only on the insistence of Mlle. Doncoeur. If she had got up earlier, if she had been the first to see the doll and hear the story of Father Christmas, wouldn't she have kept the secret and ordered the little girl to say nothing?

And later she had taken the first opportunity to go out, even though there was plenty to eat in the house for the day. And she had been so absent-minded that she had bought butter, although there was still a pound in the cooler.

Maigret got up from the table and resettled himself in his chair by the window. He picked up the phone and called Quai des Orfèvres.

"Lucas?"

"I got what you wanted, Chief. I have a list of all prisoners released for the last four months. There aren't as many as I thought. And none of them has lived in the Boulevard Richard-Lenoir at any time."

That didn't matter any more now. At first Maigret had thought that a tenant across the street might have hidden money or stolen goods under the floor before he was arrested. His first thought on getting out of jail would be to recover his booty. With the little girl bedridden, however, the room was occupied day and night. Impersonating Father Christmas would not have been a bad idea to get into the room. Had this been the case, however, Madame Martin would not have been so reluctant to call in Maigret. Nor would she have been in so great a hurry to get out of the house afterwards on such a flimsy pretext. So Maigret had abandoned that theory.

"You want me to check each prisoner further?"

"Never mind. Any news about Paul Martin?"

"That was easy. He's known in every station house between the Bastille and the Hotel de Ville, and even on the Boulevard Saint-Michel."

"What did he do last night?"

"First he went aboard the Salvation Army barge to eat. He's a regular there one day a week and yesterday was his day. They had a special feast for Christmas Eve and he had to stand in line quite a while."

"After that?"

"About 11 o'clock he went to the Latin Quarter and opened doors for motorists in front of a night club. He must have collected enough money in tips to get himself a sinkful, because he was picked up dead drunk near the Place Maubert at 4 in the morning. He was taken to the station house to sleep it off, and was there until 11 this morning. They'd just turned him loose when I phoned, and they promised to bring him to me when they find him again. He still had a few francs in his pocket."

"What about Bergerac?"

"Jean Martin is taking the afternoon train for Paris. He was quite upset by a phone call he got this morning."

"He got only one call?"

"Only one this morning. He got a call last night while he was eating dinner."

"You know who called him?"

"The desk clerk says it was a man's voice, asking for Monsieur Jean Martin. He sent somebody into the dining room for Martin but when Martin got to the phone, the caller had hung up. Seems it spoiled his whole evening. He went out with a bunch of traveling salesmen to some local hotspot where there were pretty girls and whatnot, but after drinking a few glasses of champagne, he couldn't talk about anything except his wife and daughter. The niece he calls his daughter, it seems. He had such a dismal evening that he went home early. Three A.M. That's all you wanted to know, Chief?"

When Maigret didn't reply, Lucas had to satisfy his curiosity. "You still phoning from home, Chief? What's happening up your way? Somebody get killed?"

"I still can't say. Right now all I know is that the principals are a seven-year-old girl, a doll, and Father Christmas."

"Ah?"

"One more thing. Try to get me the home address of the manager of Zenith Watches, Avenue de l'Opera. You ought to be able to raise somebody there, even on Christmas Day. Call me back."

"Soon as I have something."

Mme. Maigret had just served him a glass of Alsatian plum brandy which her sister had sent them. He smacked his lips. For a moment he was tempted to forget all about the business of the doll and Father Christmas. It would be much simpler just to take his wife to the movies. . . .

"What color eyes has she?"

It took him a moment to realize that the only person in the case who interested Mme. Maigret was the little girl.

"Why, I'm not quite sure. They can't be dark. She has blonde hair."

"So they're blue."

"Maybe they're blue. Very light, in any case. And they are very serious."

"Because she doesn't look at things like a child. Does she laugh?"

"She hasn't much to laugh about."

"A child can always laugh if she feels herself surrounded by people she can trust, people who let her act her age. I don't like that woman."

"You prefer Mlle. Doncoeur?"

"She may be an old maid but I'm sure she knows more about children than that Madame Martin. I've seen *her* in the shops. Madame Martin is one of those women who watch the scales, and take their money out of their pocketbooks, coin by coin. She always looks around suspiciously, as though everybody was out to cheat her."

The telephone rang as Mme. Maigret was repeating, "I don't like that woman."

It was Lucas calling, with the address of Monsieur Arthur Godefroy, general manager in France for Zenith Watches. He lived in a sumptuous villa at Saint-Cloud, and Lucas had discovered that he was at home. He added:

"Paul Martin is here, Chief. When they brought him in, he started crying. He thought something had happened to his daughter. But he's all right now—except for an awful hangover. What do I do with him?"

"Anyone around who can come up here with him?"

"Torrence just came on duty. I think he could use a little fresh air. He looks as if he had a hard night, too. Anything more from me, Chief?"

"Yes. Call Palais-Royal station. About five years ago a man named Lorilleux disappeared without a trace. He sold jewelry and old coins in the Palais-Royal arcades. Get me all the details you can on his disappearance."

Maigret smiled as he noted that his wife was sitting opposite him with her knitting. He had never before worked on a case in such domestic surroundings.

"Do I call you back?" asked Lucas.

"I don't expect to move an inch from my chair."

A moment later Maigret was talking to Monsieur Godefroy, who had a decided Swiss accent. The Zenith manager thought that something must have happened to Jean Martin for anyone to be making inquiries about him on Christmas Day.

"Most able . . . most devoted . . . I'm bringing him into Paris to be assistant manager next year. . . .Next week, that is . . . Why do you ask? Has anything—? Be still, you!" He paused to quiet the juvenile hubbub in the background. "You must excuse me. All my family is with me today and—"

"Tell me, Monsieur Godefroy, has anyone called your office these last few days to inquire about Monsieur Martin's current address?"

"Yesterday morning, as a matter of fact. I was very busy with the holiday rush, but he asked to speak to me personally. I forget what name he gave. He said he had an extremely important message for Jean Martin, so I told him how to get in touch with Martin in Bergerac."

"He asked you nothing else?"

"No. He hung up at once. Is anything wrong?"

"I hope not. Thank you very much, Monsieur."

The screams of children began again in the background and Maigret said goodbye.

"Were you listening?"

"I heard what you said. I didn't hear his answers."

"A man called the office yesterday morning to get Martin's address. The same man undoubtedly called Bergerac that evening to make sure Martin was still there, and therefore would not be at his Boulevard Richard-Lenoir address for Christmas Eve."

"The same man who appeared last night as Father Christmas?"

"More than likely. That seems to clear Paul Martin. He would not have to make two phone calls to find out where his brother was. Madame Martin would have told him."

"You're really getting excited about this case. You're delighted that it came up, aren't you? Confess!" And while Maigret was racking his brain for excuses, she added: "It's quite natural. I'm fascinated, too. How much longer do you think the child will have to keep her leg in a cast?"

"I didn't ask."

"I wonder what sort of complications she could have had?"

Maigret looked at her curiously. Unconsciously she had switched his mind onto a new track.

"That's not such a stupid remark you just made."

"What did I say?"

"After all, since she's been in bed for two months, she should be up and around soon, barring really serious complications."

"She'll probably have to walk on crutches at first."

"That's not the point. In a few days then, or a few weeks at most, she will no longer be confined to her room. She'll go for a walk with Madame Martin. And the coast will be clear for anyone to enter the apartment without dressing up like Father Christmas."

Mme. Maigret's lips were moving. While listening to her husband and watching his face, she was counting stitches.

"First of all, the presence of the child forced our man to use trickery. She's been in bed for two months—two months for him to wait. Without the complications the flooring could have been taken up several weeks ago. Our man must have had urgent reasons for acting at once, without further delay."

"Monsieur Martin will return to Paris in a few days?"

"Exactly."

"What do you suppose the man found underneath the floor?"

"Did he really find anything? If not, his problem is still as pressing as it was last night. So he will take further action."

"What action?"

"I don't know."

"Look, Maigret, isn't the child in danger? Do you think she's safe with that woman?"

"I could answer that if I knew where Madame Martin went this morning on the pretext of doing her shopping." He picked up the phone again and called Police Judiciaire.

"I'm pestering you again, Lucas. I want you to locate a taxi that picked up a passenger this morning between 9 and 10 somewhere near Boulevard Richard-Lenoir. The fare was a woman in her early thirties, blonde, slim but solidly built. She was wearing a gray suit and a beige hat. She carried a brown shopping bag. I want to know her destination. There couldn't have been so many cabs on the street at that hour."

"Is Paul Martin with you?"

"Not yet."

"He'll be there soon. About that other thing, the Lorilleux matter, the Palais-Royal boys are checking their files. You'll have the data in a few minutes."

Jean Martin must be taking his train in Bergerac at this moment. Little Colette was probably taking her nap. Mlle. Doncoeur was doubtless sitting behind her window curtain, wondering what Maigret was up to.

People were beginning to come out now, families with their children, the children with their new toys. There were certainly queues in front of the cinemas. . . .

A taxi stopped in front of the house. Footsteps sounded in the stairway. Mme. Maigret went to the door. The deep bass voice of Torrence rumbled: "You there, Chief?"

Torrence came in with an ageless man who hugged the walls and looked humbly at the floor. Maigret went to the sideboard and filled two glasses with plum brandy.

"To your health," he said.

The man looked at Maigret with surprised, anxious eyes. He raised a trembling, hesitant hand.

"To your health, Monsieur Martin. I'm sorry to make you come all the way up here, but you won't have far to go now to see your daughter."

"Nothing has happened to her?"

"No, no. When I saw her this morning she was playing with her new doll. You can go, Torrence. Lucas must need you."

[230]

Mme. Maigret had gone into the bedroom with her knitting. She was sitting on the edge of the bed, counting her stiches.

"Sit down, Monsieur Martin."

The man had touched his lips to the glass and set it down. He looked at it uneasily.

"You have nothing to worry about. Just tell yourself that I know all about you."

"I wanted to visit her this morning," the man sighed. "I swore I would go to bed early so I could wish her a Merry Christmas."

"I know that, too."

"It's always the same. I swear I'll take just one drink, just enough to pick me up. . . ."

"You have only one brother, Monsieur Martin?"

"Yes, Jean. He's six years younger than I am. He and my wife and my daughter were all I had to love in this world."

"You don't love your sister-in-law?"

He shivered. He seemed both startled and embarrassed.

"I have nothing against Loraine."

"You entrusted your child to her, didn't you?"

"Well, yes, that is to say, when my wife died and I began to slip. . . ."

"I understand. Is your daughter happy?"

"I think so, yes. She never complains."

"Have you ever tried to get back on your feet?"

"Every night I promise myself to turn over a new leaf, but next day I start all over again. I even went to see a doctor. I followed his advice for a few days. But when I went back, he was very busy. He said I ought to be in a special sanatorium."

He reached for his glass, then hesitated. Maigret picked up his own glass and took a swallow to encourage him.

"Did you ever meet a man in your sister-in-law's apartment?"

"No. I think she's above reproach on that score."

"Do you know where your brother first met her?"

"In a little restaurant in the Rue Beaujolais where he used to eat when he was in Paris. It was near the shop where Loraine was working."

"Did they have a long engagement?"

"I can't say. Jean was on the road for two months and when he came back he told me he was getting married."

"Were you his best man?"

"Yes. Loraine has no family in Paris. She's an orphan. So her landlady acted as her witness. Is there something wrong?"

"I don't know yet. A man entered Colette's room last night dressed as Father Christmas. He gave your girl a doll, and lifted two loose boards from the floor."

"Do you think I'm in fit condition to see her?"

"You can go over in a little while. If you feel like it you can shave here. Do you think your brother would be likely to hide anything under the floor?"

"Jean? Never!"

"Even if he wanted to hide something from his wife?"

"He doesn't hide things from his wife. You don't know him. He's one of those rare humans—a scrupulously honest man. When he comes home from the road, she knows exactly how much money he has left, to the last centime."

"Is she jealous?"

Paul Martin did not reply.

"I advise you to tell me what you know. Remember that your daughter is involved in this."

"I don't think that Loraine is especially jealous. Not of women, at least. Perhaps about money. At least that's what my poor wife always said. She didn't like Loraine."

"Why not?"

"She used to say that Loraine's lips were too thin, that she was too polite, too cold, always on the defensive. My wife always thought that Loraine set her cap for Jean because he had a good job with a future and owned his own furniture."

"Loraine had no money of her own?"

"She never speaks of her family. I understand her father died when she was very young and her mother did housework somewhere in the Glacière quarter. My poor wife used to say, 'Loraine knows what she wants.'"

"Do you think she was Lorilleux's mistress?"

Paul Martin did not reply. Maigret poured him another finger of plum brandy. Martin gave him a grateful look, but he did not touch the glass. Perhaps he was thinking that his daughter might notice his breath when he crossed the street later on.

"I'll get you a cup of coffee in a moment. . . . Your wife must have had her own ideas on the subject."

"How did you know? Please note that my wife never spoke disparagingly of people. But with Loraine it was almost pathological. Whenever we were to meet my sister-in-law, I used to beg my wife not to show her antipathy. It's funny that you should bring all that up now, at this time in my life. Do you think I did wrong in letting her take Colette? I sometimes think so. But what else could I have done?"

"You didn't answer my question about Loraine's former employer."

"Oh, yes. My wife always said it was very convenient for Loraine to have married a man who was away from home so much."

"You know where she lived before her marriage?"

"In a street just off Boulevard Sébastopol, on the right as you walk from the Rue de Rivoli toward the Boulevard. I remember we picked her up there the day of the wedding."

"Rue Pernelle?"

"That's it. The fourth or fifth house on the left side of the street is a quiet rooming house, quite respectable. People who work in the neighborhood live there. I remember there were several little actresses from the Châtelet."

"Would you like to shave, Monsieur Martin?"

"I'm ashamed. Still, since my daughter is just across the street. . . ."

"Come with me."

Maigret took him through the kitchen so he wouldn't have to meet Mme. Maigret in the bedroom. He set out the necessary toilet articles, not forgetting a clothes brush.

When he returned to the dining room, Mme. Maigret poked her head through the door and whispered: "What's he doing?"

"He's shaving."

Once more Maigret reached for the telephone. He was certainly giving poor Lucas a busy Christmas Day.

"Are you indispensable at the office?"

"Not if Torrence sits in for me. I've got the information you wanted."

"In just a moment. I want you to jump over to Rue Pernelle. There's a rooming house a few doors down from the Boulevard Sébastopol. If the proprietor wasn't there five years ago, try to dig up someone who lived then. I want everything you can find out on a certain Loraine. . . ."

"Loraine who?"

"Just a minute, I didn't think of that."

Through the bathroom door he asked Martin for the maiden name of his sister-in-law. A few seconds later he was on the phone again.

"Loraine Boitel," he told Lucas. "The landlady of this rooming house was witness at her marriage to Jean Martin. Loraine Boitel was working for Lorilleux at the time. Try to find out if she was more than a secretary to him, and if he ever came to see her. And work fast. This may be urgent. What have you got on Lorilleux?"

"He was quite a fellow. At home in the Rue Mazarine he was a good respectable family man. In his Palais-Royal shop he not only sold old coins and souvenirs of Paris, but he had a fine collection of pornographic books and obscene pictures."

"Not unusual for the Palais-Royal."

"I don't know what else went on there. There was a big divan covered with red silk rep in the back room, but the investigation was never pushed. Seems there were a lot of important names among his customers."

"What about Loraine Boitel?"

"The report barely mentions her, except that she waited all morning for Lorilleux the day he disappeared. I was on the phone about this when Langlois of the Financial Squad came into my office. The name Lorilleux rang a bell in the back of his mind and he went to check his files. Nothing definite on him, but he'd been making frequent trips to Switzerland and back, and there was a lot of gold smuggling going on at that time. Lorilleux was stopped and searched at the frontier several times, but they never found anything on him."

"Lucas, old man, hurry over to Rue Pernelle. I'm more than ever convinced that this is urgent."

Paul Martin appeared in the doorway, his pale cheeks close-shaven.

"I don't know how to thank you. I'm very much embarrassed."

"You'll visit your daughter now, won't you? I don't know how long you usually stay, but today I don't want you to leave until I come for you."

"I can't very well stay all night, can I?"

"Stay all night if necessary. Manage the best you can."

"Is the little girl in danger?"

"I don't know, but your place today is with your daughter."

Paul Martin drank his black coffee avidly, and started for the stairway. The door had just closed after him when Mme. Maigret rushed into the dining room.

"You can't let him go to see his daughter empty-handed on Christmas Day!"

"But—" Maigret was about to say that there just didn't happen to be a doll around the house, when his wife thrust a small shiny object into his hands. It was a gold thimble which had been in her sewing basket for years but which she never used.

"Give him that. Little girls always like thimbles. Hurry!"

He shouted from the landing: "Monsieur Martin! Just a minute, Monsieur Martin!"

He closed the man's fingers over the thimble. "Don't tell a soul where you got this."

Before re-entering the dining room he stood for a moment on the threshold, grumbling. Then he sighed: "I hope you've finished making me play Father Christmas."

"I'll bet she likes the thimble as well as a doll. It's something grownups use, you know."

They watched the man cross the boulevard. Before going into the house he turned to look up at Maigret's windows, as if seeking encouragement.

"Do you think he'll ever be cured?"

"I doubt it."

"If anything happens to that woman, to Madame Martin. . . ."

[234]

"Well?"

"Nothing. I was thinking of the little girl. I wonder what would become of her."

Ten minutes passed. Maigret had opened his newspaper and lighted his pipe. His wife had settled down again with her knitting. She was counting stitches when he exhaled a cloud of smoke and murmured: "You haven't even seen her."

Maigret was looking for an old envelope, on the back of which he had jotted down a few notes summing up the day's events. He found it in a drawer into which Mme. Maigret always stuffed any papers she found lying around the house.

This was the only investigation, he mused, which he had ever conducted practically in its entirety from his favorite armchair. It was also unusual in that no dramatic stroke of luck had come to his aid. True, luck had been on his side, in that he had been able to muster all his facts by the simplest and most direct means. How many times had he deployed scores of detectives on an all-night search for some minor detail. This might have happened, for instance, if Mother Arthur Godefroy of Zenith had gone home to Zurich for Christmas, or if he had been out of reach of a telephone. Or if Monsieur Godefroy had been unaware of the telephone inquiry regarding the whereabouts of Jean Martin.

When Lucas arrived shortly after 4 o'clock, his nose red and his face pinched with the cold, he too could report the same kind of undramatic luck.

A thick yellow fog, unusual for Paris, had settled over the city. Lights shone in all the windows, floating in the murk like ships at sea or distant beacons. Familiar details had been blotted out so completely that Maigret half-expected to hear the moan of fog horns.

For some reason, perhaps because of some boyhood memory, Maigret was pleased to see the weather thicken. He was also pleased to see Lucas walk into his apartment, take off his overcoat, sit down, and stretch out his frozen hands toward the fire.

In appearance, Lucas was a reduced-scale model of Maigret—a head shorter, half as broad in the shoulders, half as stern in expression although he tried hard. Without conscious imitation but with conscious admiration, Lucas had copied his chief's slightest gestures, postures, and changes of expression—even to the ceremony of inhaling the fragrance of the plum brandy before touching his lips to the glass.

The landlady of the rooming house in the Rue Pernelle had been killed in a subway accident two years earlier, Lucas reported. Luckily, the place had been taken over by the former night watchman, who had been in trouble with the police on morals charges.

[235]

"So it was easy enough to make him talk," said Lucas, lighting a pipe much too large for him. "I was surprised that he had the money to buy the house, but he explained that he was front man for a big investor who had money in all sorts of enterprises but didn't like to have his name used."

"What kind of dump is it?"

"Looks respectable. Clean enough. Office on the mezzanine. Rooms by the month, some by the week, and a few on the second floor by the hour."

"He remembers Loraine?"

"Very well. She lived there more than three years. I got the impression he didn't like her because she was tight-fisted."

"Did Lorilleux come to see her?"

"On my way to the Rue Pernelle I picked up a photo of Lorilleux at the Palais-Royal station. The new landlord recognized him right away."

"Lorilleux went to her room often?"

"Two or three times a month. He always had baggage with him, he always arrived around 1 o'clock in the morning, and always left before 6. I checked the timetables. There's a train from Switzerland around midnight and another at 6 in the morning. He must have told his wife he was taking the 6 o'clock train."

"Nothing else?"

"Nothing, except that Loraine was stingy with tips, and always cooked her dinner on an alcohol burner, even though the house rules said no cooking in the rooms."

"No other men?"

"No. Very respectable except for Lorilleux. The landlady was witness at her wedding."

Maigret glanced at his wife. He had insisted she remain in the room when Lucas came. She stuck to her knitting, trying to make believe she was not there.

Torrence was out in the fog, going from garage to garage, checking the trip-sheets of taxi fleets. The two men waited serenely, deep in their easy chairs, each holding a glass of plum brandy with the same pose. Maigret felt a pleasant numbness creeping over him.

His Christmas luck held out with the taxis, too. Sometimes it took days to run down a particular taxi driver, particularly when the cab in question did not belong to a fleet. Cruising drivers were the hardest to locate; they sometimes never even read the newspapers. But shortly before 5 o'clock Torrence called from Saint-Ouen.

"I found one of the taxis," he reported.

"One? Was there more than one?"

"Looks that way. This man picked up the woman at the corner of Boulevard Richard-Lenoir and Boulevard Voltaire this morning. He drove her to Rue de Maubeuge, opposite the Gare du Nord, where she paid him off.''

"Did she go into the railway station?"

"No. The chauffeur says she went into a luggage shop that keeps open on Sundays and holidays. After that he doesn't know."

"Where's the driver now?"

"Right here in the garage. He just checked in."

"Send him to me, will you? Right away. I don't care how he gets here as long as it's in a hurry. Now I want you to find me the cab that brought her home."

"Sure, Chief, as soon as I get myself coffee with a stick in it. It's damned cold out here."

Maigret glanced through the window. There was a shadow against Mlle. Doncoeur's curtains. He turned to Lucas.

"Look in the phone book for a luggage shop across from the Gare du Nord."

Lucas took only a minute to come up with a number, which Maigret dialed.

"Hello, this is the Police Judiciaire. Shortly before 10 this morning a young woman bought something in your shop, probably a valise. She was a blonde, wearing a gray suit and beige hat. She carried a brown shopping bag. Do you remember her?"

Perhaps trade was slack on Christmas Day. Or perhaps it was easier to remember customers who shopped on Christmas. In any case, the voice on the phone replied:

"Certainly, I waited on her myself. She said she had to leave suddenly for Cambrai because her sister was ill, and she didn't have time to go home for her bags. She wanted a cheap valise, and I sold her a fiber model we have on sale. She paid me and went into the bar next door. I was standing in the doorway and a little later I saw her walking toward the station, carrying the valise."

"Are you alone in your shop?"

"I have one clerk on duty."

"Can you leave him alone for half an hour? Fine! Then jump in a taxi and come to this address. I'll pay the fare, of course."

"And the return fare? Shall I have the cab wait?"

"Have him wait, yes."

According to Maigret's notes on the back of the envelope, the first taxi driver arrived at 5:50 P.M. He was somewhat surprised, since he had been summoned by the police, to find himself in a private apartment. He recognized Maigret, however, and made no effort to disguise his curious interest in how the famous inspector lived.

"I want you to climb to the fourth floor of the house just across the street. If the concierge stops you, tell her you're going to see Madame Martin."

"Madame Martin. I got it."

"Go to the door at the end of the hall and ring the bell. If a blonde opens the door and you recognize her, make some excuse— You're on the wrong floor, anything you think of. If somebody else answers, ask to speak to Madame Martin personally."

"And then?"

"Then you come back here and tell me whether or not she is the fare you drove to Rue de Maubeuge this morning."

"I'll be right back, Inspector."

As the door closed, Maigret smiled in spite of himself.

"The first call will make her worry a little. The second, if all goes well, will make her panicky. The third, if Torrence has any luck—"

Torrence, too, was having his run of Christmas luck. The phone rang and he reported:

"I think I've found him, Chief. I dug up a driver who picked up a woman answering your description at the Gare du Nord, only he didn't take her to Boulevard Richard-Lenoir. He dropped her at the corner of Boulevard Beaumarchais and the Rue du Chemin-Vert."

"Send him to me."

"He's a little squiffed."

"No matter. Where are you?"

"The Barbès garage."

"Then it won't be much out of your way to stop by the Gare du Nord. Go to the check room. Unfortunately it won't be the same man on duty, but try to find out if a small new valise was checked between 9:30 and 10 this morning. It's made of fiber and shouldn't be too heavy. Get the number of the check. They won't let you take the valise without a warrant, so try to get the name and address of the man on duty this morning."

"What next?"

"Phone me. I'll wait for your second taxi driver. If he's been drinking, better write down my address for him, so he won't get lost."

Mme. Maigret was back in the kitchen, preparing the evening meal. She hadn't dared ask whether Lucas would eat with them.

Maigret wondered if Paul Martin was still across the street with his daughter. Had Madame Martin tried to get rid of him?

The bell rang again. Two men stood at the door.

The first driver had come back from Madame Martin's and had climbed Maigret's stairs behind the luggage dealer.

"Did you recognize her?"

"Sure. She recognized me, too. She turned pale. She ran to close a door behind her, then she asked me what I wanted."

"What did you tell her?"

"That I had the wrong floor. I think maybe she wanted to buy me off, but I didn't give her a chance. But she was watching from the window when I crossed the street. She probably knows I came here."

The luggage dealer was baffled and showed it. He was a middle-aged man, completely bald and equally obsequious. When the driver had gone, Maigret explained what he wanted, and the man objected vociferously.

"One just doesn't do this sort of thing to one's customers," he repeated stubbornly. "One simply does not inform on one's customers, you know."

After a long argument he agreed to call on Madame Martin. To make sure he didn't change his mind, Maigret sent Lucas to follow him.

They returned in less than ten minutes.

"I call your attention to the fact that I have acted under your orders, that I have been compelled—"

"Did you recognize her?"

"Will I be forced to testify under oath?"

"More than likely."

"That would be very bad for my business. People who buy luggage at the last minute are very often people who dislike public mention of their comings and goings."

"You may not have to go to court. Your deposition before the examining magistrate may be sufficient."

"Very well. It was she. She's dressed differently, but I recognized her all right."

"Did she recognize you?"

"She asked immediately who had sent me."

"What did you say?"

"I . . . I don't remember. I was quite upset. I think I said I had rung the wrong bell."

"Did she offer you anything?"

"What do you mean? She didn't even offer me a chair. Luckily. It would have been most unpleasant."

Maigret smiled, somewhat incredulously. He believed that the taxi driver had actually run away from a possible bribe. He wasn't so sure about this prosperous-looking shopkeeper who obviously begrudged his loss of time.

"Thank you for your cooperation."

The luggage dealer departed hastily.

"And now for Number Three, my dear Lucas."

Mme. Maigret was beginning to grow nervous. From the kitchen door she made discreet signs to her husband, beckoning him to join her. She whispered: "Are you sure the father is still across the street?"

"Why?"

"I don't know. I can't make out exactly what you're up to, but I've been thinking about the child, and I'm a little afraid. . . ."

Night had long since fallen. The families were all home again. Few windows across the street remained dark. The silhouette of Mlle. Doncoeur was still very much in evidence.

While waiting for the second taxi driver, Maigret decided to put on his collar and tie. He shouted to Lucas:

"Pour yourself another drop. Aren't you hungry?"

"I'm full of sandwiches, Chief. Only one thing I'd like when we go out: a tall beer, right from the spigot."

The second driver arrived at 6:20. At 6:35 he had returned from across the street, a gleam in his eye.

"She looks even better in her négligée than she does in her street clothes," he said thickly. "She made me come in and asked who sent me. I didn't know what to say, so I told her I was a talent scout for the Folies Bergère. Was she furious! She's a fine hunk of woman, though, and I mean it. Did you get a look at her legs?"

He was in no hurry to leave. Maigret saw him ogling the bottle of plum brandy with envious eyes, and poured him a glass—to speed him on his way.

"What are you going to do next, Chief?" Lucas had rarely seen Maigret proceed with such caution, preparing each step with such care that he seemed to be mounting an attack on some desperate criminal. And yet the enemy was only a woman, a seemingly insignificant little housewife.

"You think she'll still fight back?"

"Fiercely. And what's more, in cold blood."

"What are you waiting for?"

"The phone call from Torrence."

As if on cue, the telephone rang. Torrence, of course.

"The valise is here all right. It feels practically empty. As you predicted, they won't give it to me without a warrant. The check-room attendant who was on duty this morning lives in the suburbs near La Varenne Saint-Hilaire." A snag at last? Or at least a delay? Maigret frowned. But Torrence continued. "We won't have to go out there, though. When he finishes his day's work here, he plays cornet in a *bal musette* in the Rue de Lappe."

"Go get him for me."

"Shall I bring him to your place?"

Maigret hesitated, thinking of Lucas's yearning for a glass of draft beer.

"No, I'll be across the street. Madame Martin's apartment, fourth floor."

He took down his heavy overcoat. He filled his pipe.

[240]

"Coming?" he said to Lucas.

Mme. Maigret ran after him to ask what time he'd be home for dinner. After a moment of hesitation, he smiled.

"The usual time," was his not very reassuring answer.

"Look out for the little girl, will you?"

At 10 o'clock that evening the investigation was still blocked. It was unlikely that anyone in the whole building had gone to sleep, except Colette. She had finally dozed off, with her father sitting in the dark by her bedside.

Torrence had arrived at 7:30 with his part-time musician and check-room attendant, who declared:

"She's the one. I remember she didn't put the check in her handbag. She slipped it into a big brown shopping bag." And when they took him into the kitchen he added, "That's the bag. Or one exactly like it."

The Martin apartment was very warm. Everyone spoke in low tones, as if they had agreed not to awaken the child. Nobody had eaten. Nobody, apparently, was even hungry. On their way over, Maigret and Lucas had each drunk two beers in a little cafe on the Boulevard Voltaire.

After the cornetist had spoken his piece, Maigret took Torrence aside and murmured fresh instructions.

Every corner of the apartment had been searched. Even the photos of Martin's parents had been taken from their frames, to make sure the baggage check had not been secreted between picture and backing. The dishes had been taken from their shelves and piled on the kitchen table. The larder had been emptied and examined closely. No baggage check.

Madame Martin was still wearing her pale blue négligée. She was chain-smoking cigarettes. What with the smoke from the two men's pipes, a thick blue haze swirled about the lamps.

"You are of course free to say nothing and answer no questions. Your husband will arive at 11:17. Perhaps you will be more talkative in his presence."

"He doesn't know any more than I do."

"Does he know as much?"

"There's nothing to know. I've told you everything."

She had sat back and denied everything, all along the line. She had conceded only one point. She admitted that Lorilleux had dropped in to see her two or three times at night when she lived in the Rue Pernelle. But she insisted there had been nothing between them, nothing personal.

"In other words he came to talk business—at 1 o'clock in the morning?"

"He used to come to town by a late train, and he didn't like to walk the streets with large sums of money on him. I already told you he might have been smuggling gold, but I had nothing to do with it. You can't arrest me for his activities.''

"Did he have large sums of money on him when he disappeared?''

"I don't know. He didn't always take me into his confidence.''

"But he did come to see you in your room at night?''

Despite the evidence, she clung to her story of the morning's marketing. She denied ever having seen the two taxi drivers, the luggage dealer, or the check-room attendant.

"If I had really left a package at the Gare du Nord, you would have found the check, wouldn't you?''

She glanced nervously at the clock on the mantel, obviously thinking of her husband's return.

"Admit that the man who came last night found nothing under the floor because you changed the hiding place.''

"I know of nothing that was hidden under the floor.''

"When you learned of his visit, you decided to move the treasure to the check room for safekeeping.''

"I haven't been near the Gare du Nord. There must be thousands of blondes in Paris who answer my description.''

"I think I know where we'll find the check.''

"You're so very clever.''

"Sit over here at this table.'' Maigret produced a fountain pen and a sheet of paper. "Write your name and address.''

She hesitated, then obeyed.

"Tonight every letter mailed in this neighborhood will be examined, and I'll wager we will find one addressed in your handwriting, probably to yourself.''

He handed the paper to Lucas with an order to get in touch with the postal authorities. Much to his surprise, the woman reacted visibly.

"You see, it's a very old trick, Little One.'' For the first time he called her "Little One,'' the way he would have done if he were questioning her in his office, Quai des Orfevres.

They were alone now. Maigret slowly paced the floor, while she remained seated.

"In case you're interested,'' Maigret said slowly, "the thing that shocks me most about you is not what you have done but the cold-blooded way you have done it. You've been dangling at the end of a slender thread since early this morning, and you still haven't blinked an eye. When your husband comes home, you'll try to play the martyr. And yet you know that sooner or later we'll discover the truth.''

"But I've done nothing wrong.''

"Then why do you lie?''

[242]

She did not reply. She was still far from the breaking point. Her nerves were calm, but her mind was obviously racing at top speed, seeking some avenue of escape.

"I'm not saying anything more," she declared. She sat down and pulled the hem of her négligée over her bare knees.

"Suit yourself." Maigret made himself comfortable in the chair opposite her.

"Are you going to stay here all night?" she asked.

"At least until your husband gets home."

"Are you going to tell him about Monsieur Lorilleux's visits to my room?"

"If necessary."

"You're a cad! Jean knows nothing about all this. He had no part in it."

"Unfortunately he is your husband."

When Lucas came back, they were staring at each other in silence.

"Janvier is taking care of the letter, Chief. I met Torrence downstairs. He says the man is in that little bar, two doors down from your house."

She sprang up. "What man?"

Maigret didn't move a muscle. "The man who came here last night. You might have expected him to come back, since he didn't find what he was looking for. And he might be in a different frame of mind this time."

She cast a dismayed glance at the clock. The train from Bergerac was due in twenty minutes. Her husband could be home in forty. She asked: "You know who this man is?"

"I can guess. I could go down and confirm my suspicion. I'd say it is Lorilleux and I'd say he is very eager to get back his property."

"It's not his property!"

"Let's say that, rightly or wrongly, he considers it his property. He must be in desperate straits, this man. He came to see you twice without getting what he wanted. He came back a third time disguised as Father Christmas. And he'll come back again. He'll be surprised to find you have company. I'm convinced that he'll be more talkative than you. Despite the general belief, men always speak more freely than women. Do you think he is armed?"

"I don't know."

"I think he is. He is tired of waiting. I don't know what story you've been telling him, but I'm sure he's fed up with it. The gentleman has a vicious face. There's nothing quite as cruel as a weakling with his back up."

"Shut up!"

"Would you like us to go so that you can be alone with him?"

The back of Maigret's envelope contained the following note: "10:38 P.M.—she decides to talk."

It was not a very connected story at first. It came out in bits and pieces, fragments of sentences interlarded with venomous asides, supplemented by Maigret's own guesses which she either confirmed or amended.

"What do you want to know?"

"Was it money that you left in the check room?"

"Bank notes. Almost a million."

"Did the money belong to Lorilleux?"

"No more to him than to me."

"To one of his customers?"

"Yes. A man named Julian Boissy."

"What became of him?"

"He died."

"How?"

"He was killed."

"By whom?"

"By Monsieur Lorilleux."

"Why?"

"Because I gave him to understand that if he could raise enough money —real money—I might run away with him."

"You were already married?"

"Yes."

"You're not in love with your husband?"

"I despise mediocrity. All my life I've been poor. All my life I've been surrounded by people who have had to scrimp and save, people who have had to sacrifice and count centimes. I've had to scrimp and sacrifice and count centimes myself." She turned savagely on Maigret, as if he had been responsible for all her troubles. "I just didn't want to be poor any more."

"Would you have gone away with Lorilleux?"

"I don't know. Perhaps for a while."

"Long enough to get your hands on his money?"

"I hate you!"

"How was Boissy murdered?"

"Monsieur Boissy was a regular customer of long standing."

"Pornographic literature?"

"He was a lascivious old goat, sure. So are all men. So is Lorilleux. So are you, probably. Boissy was a widower. He lived alone in a hotel room. He was very rich and very stingy. All rich people are stingy."

"That doesn't work both ways, does it? You, for instance, are not rich."

"I would have been rich."

"If Lorilleux had not come back. How did Boissy die?"

"The devaluation of the franc scared him out of his wits. Like everybody else at that time, he wanted gold. Monsieur Lorilleux used to shuttle gold in

[244]

from Switzerland pretty regularly. And he always demanded payment in advance. One afternoon Monsieur Boissy came to the shop with a fortune in currency. I wasn't there. I had gone out on an errand.''

"You planned it that way?"

"No."

"You had no idea what was going to happen?"

"No. Don't try to put words in my mouth. When I came back, Lorilleux was packing the body into a big box.''

"And you blackmailed him?"

"No."

"Then why did he disappear after having given you the money?"

"I frightened him."

"You threatened to go to the police?"

"No. I merely told him that our neighbors in the Palais-Royal had been looking at me suspiciously and that I thought he ought to put the money in a safe place for a while. I told him about the loose floor board in my apartment. He thought it would only be for a few days. Two days later he asked me to cross the Belgian frontier with him.''

"And you refused?"

"I told him I'd been stopped and questioned by a man who looked like a police inspector. He was terrified. I gave him some of the money and promised to join him in Brussels as soon as it was safe.''

"What did he do with the corpse?"

"He put the box in a taxi and drove to a little country house he owned on the banks of the Marne. I suppose he either buried it there or threw it into the river. Nobody ever missed Monsieur Boissy.''

"So you sent Lorilleux to Belgium without you. How did you keep him away for five years?''

"I used to write him, general delivery. I told him the police were after him, and that he would probably read nothing about it in the papers because they were setting a trap for him. I told him the police were always coming back to question me. I even sent him to South America.''

"He came back two months ago?"

"About. He was at the end of his rope."

"Didn't you send him any money?"

"Not much."

"Why not?"

She did not reply. She looked at the clock.

"Are you going to arrest me? What will be the charge? I didn't kill Boissy. I wasn't there when he was killed. I had nothing to do with disposing of his body.''

"Stop worrying about yourself. You kept the money because all your life you wanted money—not to spend, but to keep, to feel secure, to feel rich and free from want.''

''That's my business.''

''When Lorilleux came back to ask for money, or to ask you to keep your promise and run away with him, you used Colette as a pretext. You tried to scare him into leaving the country again, didn't you?''

''He stayed in Paris, hiding.'' Her upper lip curled slightly. ''What an idiot! He could have shouted his name from the housetops and nobody would have noticed.''

''The business of Father Christmas wasn't idiotic.''

''No? The money wasn't under the floorboard any longer. It was right here under his nose, in my sewing basket.''

''Your husband will be here in ten or fifteen minutes. Lorilleux across the street probably knows it. He's been in touch with Bergerac by phone, and he can read a timetable. He's surely armed. Do you want to wait here for your two men?''

''Take me away! I'll slip on a dress. . . . .''

''The check-room stub?''

''General delivery, Boulevard Beaumarchais.''

She did not close the bedroom door after her. Brazenly she dropped the négligée from her shoulders and sat on the edge of the bed to pull on her stockings. She selected a woolen dress from the closet, tossed toilet articles and lingerie into an overnight bag.

''Let's hurry!''

''Your husband?''

''That fool? Leave him for the birds.''

''Colette?''

She shrugged.

Mlle. Doncoeur's door opened a crack as they passed.

Downstairs on the sidewalk she clung fearfully to the two men, peering into the fog.

''Take her to the Quai des Orfèvres, Lucas. I'm staying here.''

She held back. There was no car in sight, and she was obviously frightened by the prospect of walking into the night with only Lucas to protect her. Lucas was not very big.

''Don't be afraid. Lorilleux is not in this vicinity.''

''You lied to me! You—you—''

Maigret went back into the house.

The conference with Jean Martin lasted two hours.

When Maigret left the house at one-thirty, the two brothers were in serious conversation. There was a crack of light under Mlle. Doncoeur's door, but she did not open the door as he passed.

When he got home, his wife was asleep in a chair in the dining room. His place at table was still set. Mme. Maigret awoke with a start.

"You're alone?" When he looked at her with amused surprise, she added, "Didn't you bring the little girl home?"

"Not tonight. She's asleep. You can go for her tomorrow morning."

"Why, then we're going to . . ."

"No, not permanently. Jean Martin may console himself with some decent girl. Or perhaps his brother will get back on his feet and find a new wife. . . ."

"In other words, she won't be ours?"

"Not in fee simple, no. Only on loan. I thought that would be better than nothing. I thought it would make you happy."

"Why, yes, of course. It will make me very happy. But . . . but . . ."

She sniffled once and fumbled for her handkerchief. When she couldn't find it, she buried her face in her apron.

"Your tomato surprise, sir."

★

To be Taken with a Grain of Salt

by Charles Dickens

I AM A Cheap Jack, and my own father's name was William Marigold. It was in his lifetime supposed by some that his name was William, but my own father always consistently said No, it was Willum. As to looking at the argument throught the medium of the Register, William Marigold came into the world before Registers came up much—and went out of it too. They wouldn't have been greatly in his line neither, if they had chanced to come up before him!

I was born on the Queen's highway, but it was the King's at that time. A doctor was fetched to my mother by my own father, when it took place on a common; and in consequence of his being a very kind gentlemen, and accepting no fee but a tea-tray, I was named Doctor, out of gratitude and compliment to him. There you have me. Doctor Marigold.

The doctor having accepted a tea-tray, you'll guess that my father was a Cheap Jack before me. You are right, he was.

My father had been a lovely one in his time at the Cheap Jack work . . . But I top him. I don't say it because it's myself but because it has been universally acknowledged by all that has had the means of comparison.

I had had a first-rate autumn of it, and on the twenty-third of December, one thousand eight hundred and sixty-four, I found myself at Axbridge, Middlesex, clean sold out. So I jogged up to London with the old horse, light and easy, to have my Christmas Eve and Christmas Day alone by the fire . . . , and then to buy a regular new stock of goods all round, to sell'em again and get the money.

I am a neat hand at cookery, and I'll tell you what I knocked up for my Christmas Eve dinner . . . I knocked up a beefsteak pudding for one, with two kidneys, a dozen oysters, and a couple of mushrooms thrown in. It's a pudding to put a man in a good humor with everything, except the two bottom buttons of his waistcoat. Having relished that pudding and cleared away, I turned the lamp low, and sat down by the light of the fire, watching it as it shone upon the backs of...books,..., before I dropped off dozing. ...

I was on the road, off the road, in all sorts of places, north and south and west and east, winds liked best and winds liked least, here and there and gone astray, over the hills and far away . . . when I awoke with a start. . . .

I had started at a real sound . . . That tread . . . I believed I was a-going to see a . . . ghost.

The touch . . . was laid upon the outer handle of the door, the handle turned, and the door opened a little. . . .

Looking full at me . . . was a languid young man, which I attribute the distance between his extremities. He had a little head . . . weak eyes and weak knees, and altogether you couldn't look at him without feeling that there was greatly too much of him for his joints. . . .

"I am very glad to see you," says the Gentlemen. "Yet I have my doubts, Sir,'', says I, "if you can be half as glad to see me as I am to see you."

The creature took off . . . a straw hat, and a quantity of dark curls fell about.

I might have been too high to fall into conversation with him, had it not been for my lonely feelings.

"Sir, . . . you are affected . . ."

This made our footing . . . easier.

"Come . . . Doctor Marigold must prescribe . . . the Best of Drinks."

He was amiable, though tired, . . . and such a languid young man, that I don't known how long it didn't take him to get this story out but it passed through his defective circulation to his top extremity in course of time.

I have always noticed a prevalent want of courage, even among persons of superior intelligence and culture, as to imparting their own psychological experiences when those have been of a strange sort. Almost all men are afraid that what they could relate in such wise would find no parallel or response in a listener's internal life, and might be suspected or laughed at. A truthful traveller, who should have seen some extraordinary creature in the likeness of a sea-serpent, would have no fear of mentioning it; but the same traveller, having had some singular presentiment, impulse, vagary of thought, vision (so called), dream, or other remarkable mental impression, would hesitate considerably before he would own to it. To this reticence I attribute much of the obscurity in which such subjects are involved. We do not habitually communicate our experiences of these subjective things as we do our experiences of objective creation. The consequence is, that the general stock of experience in this regard appears exceptional, and really is so, in respect of being miserably imperfect.

In what I am going to relate, I have no intention of setting up, opposing, or supporting, any theory whatever. I know the history of the Bookseller of Berlin, I have studied the case of the wife of a late Astronomer Royal as related by Sir David Brewster, and I have followed the minutest details of a much more remarkable case of Spectral Illusion occurring within my private circle of friends. It may be necessary to state as to this last, that the sufferer (a lady) was in no degree, however distant, related to me. A mistaken assumption on that head might suggest an explanation of a part of my own case,—but only a part,—which would be wholly without foundation. It cannot be referred to my inheritance of any developed peculiarity, nor had I ever before any at all similar experience, nor have I ever had any at all similar experience since.

It does not signify how many years ago, or how few, a certain murder was committed in England, which attracted great attention. We hear more than enough of murderers as they rise in succession to their atrocious eminence, and I would bury the memory of this particular brute, if I could, as his body was buried, in Newgate Jail. I purposely abstain from giving any direct clew to the criminal's individuality.

When the murder was first discovered, no suspicion fell—or I ought rather to say, for I cannot be too precise in my facts, it was nowhere publicly hinted that any suspicion fell—on the man who was afterwards brought to trial. As no reference was at that time made to him in the newspapers, it is obviously impossible that any description of him can at that time have been given in the newspapers. It is essential that this fact be remembered.

Unfolding at breakfast my morning paper, containing the account of that first discovery, I found it to be deeply interesting, and I read it with close attention. I read it twice, if not three times. The discovery had been made in a bedroom, and, when I laid down the paper, I was aware of a flash—rush—flow—I do not know what to call it,—no word I can find is satisfactorily descriptive,—in which I seemed to see that bedroom passing through my room, like a picture impossibly painted on a running river. Though almost instantaneous in its passing, it was perfectly clear; so clear that I distinctly, and with a sense of relief, observed the absence of the dead body from the bed.

It was in no romantic place that I had this curious sensation, but in chambers in Piccadilly, very near to the corner of St. James's-street. It was entirely new to me. I was in my easy-chair at the moment, and the sensation was accompanied with a peculiar shiver which started the chair from its position. (But it is to be noted that the chair ran easily on castors.) I went to one of the windows (there are two in the room, and the room is on the second floor) to refresh my eyes with the moving objects down in Picadilly. It was a bright autumn morning, and the street was sparkling and cheerful.

The wind was high. As I looked out, it brought down from the Park a quantity of fallen leaves, which a gust took, and whirled into a spiral pillar. As the pillar fell and the leaves dispersed, I saw two men on the opposite side of the way, going from West to East. They were one behind the other. The foremost man often looked back over his shoulder. The second man followed him, at a distance of some thirty paces, with his right hand menacingly raised. First, the singularity and steadiness of this threatening gesture in so public a throughfare attracted my attention; and next, the more remarkable circumstance that nobody heeded it. Both men threaded their way among the other passengers with a smoothness hardly consistent even with the action of walking on a pavement; and no single creature, that I could see, gave them place, touched them, or looked after them. In passing before my windows, they both stared up at me. I saw their two faces very distinctly, and I knew that I could recognise them anywhere. Not that I had consciously noticed anything very remarkable in either face, except that the man who went first had an unusually lowering appearance, and that the face of the man who followed him was of the colour of impure wax.

I am a bachelor, and my valet and his wife constitute my whole establishment. My occupation is in a certain Branch Bank, and I wish that my duties as head of a Department were as light as they are popularly supposed to be. They kept me in town that autumn, when I stood in need of change. I was not ill, but I was not well. You may make the most that can be reasonably made of my feeling jaded, having a depressing sense upon me of a monotonous life, and being "slightly dyspeptic." I am assured by my renowned doctor that my real state of health at that time justifies no stronger description, and I quote his own from his written answer to my request for it.

As the circumstances of the murder, gradually unravelling, took stronger and stronger possession of the public mind, I kept them away from mine by knowing as little about them as was possible in the midst of the universal excitement. But I knew that a verdict of Wilful Murder had been found against the suspected murderer, and that he had been committed to Newgate for trial. I also knew that his trial had been postponed over one Sessions of the Central Criminal Court, on the ground of general prejudice and want of time for the preparation of the defence. I may further have known, but I believe I did not, when, or about when, the Sessions to which his trial stood postponed would come on.

My sitting-room, bedroom, and dressing-room, are all on one floor. With the last there is no communication but through the bedroom. True, there is a door in it, once communicating with the staircase; but a part of the fitting of my bath has been—and had then been for some years—fixed across it. At the same period, and as a part of the same arrangement, the door had been nailed up and canvased over.

I was standing in my bedroom late one night, giving some directions to my servant before he went to bed. My face was towards the only available door of communication with the dressing-room, and it was closed. My servant's back was towards that door. While I was speaking to him, I saw it open, and a man look in, who very earnestly and mysteriously beckoned to me. That man was the man who had gone second of the two along Piccadilly, and whose face was the colour of impure wax.

The figure, having beckoned, drew back, and closed the door. With no longer pause than was made by my crossing the bedroom, I opened the dressing-room door, and looked in. I had a lighted candle already in my hand. I felt no inward expectation of seeing the figure in the dressing-room, and I did not see it there.

Conscious that my servant stood amazed, I turned round to him, and said: "Derrick, could you believe that in my cool senses I fancied I saw a—" As I there laid my hand upon his breast, with a sudden start he trembled violently, and said, "O Lord, yes, Sir! A dead man beckoning!"

Now I do not believe that this John Derrick, my trusty and attached servant for more than twenty years, had any impression whatever of having seen any such figure, until I touched him. The change in him was so startling, when I touched him, that I fully believe he derived his impression in some occult manner from me at that instant.

I bade John Derrick bring some brandy, and I gave him a dram, and was glad to take one myself. Of what had preceded that night's phenomenon, I told him not a single word. Reflecting on it, I was absolutely certain that I had never seen that face before, except on the one occasion in Piccadilly. Comparing its expression when beckoning at the door with its expression when it had stared up at me as I stood at my window, I came to the conclusion that on the first occasion it had sought to fasten itself upon my memory, and that on the second occasion it had made sure of being immediately remembered.

I was not very comfortable that night, though I felt a certainty, difficult to explain, that the figure would not return. At daylight I fell into a heavy sleep, from which I was awakened by John Derrick's coming to my bedside with a paper in his hand.

This paper, it appeared, had been the subject of an altercation at the door between its bearer and my servant. It was a summons to me to serve upon a Jury at the forthcoming Sessions of the Central Criminal Court at the Old Bailey. I had never before been summoned on such a Jury, as John Derrick well knew. He believed—I am not certain at this hour whether with reason or otherwise—that that class of Jurors were customarily chosen on a lower qualification than mine, and he had at first refused to accept the summons. The man who served it had taken the matter very coolly. He had said that my attendance or non-attendance was nothing to him; there the summons was; and I should deal with it at my own peril, and not at his.

For a day or two I was undecided whether to respond to this call, or to take no notice of it. I was not conscious of the slightest mysterious bias, influence, or attraction, one way or other. Of that I am as strictly sure as of every other statement that I make here. Ultimately I decided, as a break in the monotony of my life, that I would go.

The appointed morning was a raw morning in the month of November. There was a dense brown fog in Piccadilly, and it became positively black and in the last degree oppressive East of Temple Bar. I found the passages and staircases of the Court-House flaringly lighted with gas, and the Court itself similarly illuminated. I *think* that, until I was conducted by officers into the Old Court and saw its crowded state, I did not know that the Murderer was to be tried that day. I *think* that, until I was so helped into the Old Court with considerable difficulty, I did not know into which of the two Courts sitting my summons would take me. But this must not be received as a positive assertion, for I am not completely satisfied in my mind on either point.

I took my seat in the place appropriated to Jurors in waiting, and I looked about the Court as well as I could through the cloud of fog and breath that was heavy in it. I noticed the black vapour hanging like a murky curtain outside the great windows, and I noticed the stifled sound of wheels on the straw or tan that was littered in the street; also, the hum of the people gathered there, which a shrill whistle, or a louder song or hail than the rest, occasionally pierced. Soon afterwards, the Judges, two in number, entered, and took their seats. The buzz in the Court was awfully hushed. The direction was given to put the Murderer to the bar. He appeared there. And in that same instant I recognized in him the first of the two men who had gone down Piccadilly.

If my name had been called then, I doubt if I could have answered to it audibly. But it was called about sixth or eighth in the panel, and I was by that time able to say "Here!" Now, observe. As I stepped into the box, the prisoner, who had been looking on attentively, but with no sign of concern, became violently agitated, and beckoned to his attorney. The prisoner's wish to challenge me was so manifest, that it occasioned a pause, during which the attorney, with his hand upon the dock, whispered with his client, and shook his head. I afterwards had it from that gentleman, that the prisoner's first affrighted words to him were, "*At all hazards, challenge that man!*" But that, as he would give no reason for it, and admitted that he had not even known my name until he heard it called and I appeared, it was not done.

Both on the ground already explained, that I wish to avoid reviving the unwholesome memory of that Murderer, and also because a detailed account of his long trial is by no means indispensable to my narrative, I shall confine myself closely to such incidents in the ten days and nights during which we, the Jury, were kept together, as directly bear on my own curious personal experience. It is in that, and not in the Murderer, that I seek to interest my reader. It is to that, and not to a page of the Newgate Calendar, that I beg attention.

I was chosen Foreman of the Jury. On the second morning of the trial, after evidence had been taken for two hours (I heard the church clocks strike), happening to cast my eyes over my brother jurymen, I found an inexplicable difficulty in counting them. I counted them several times, yet always with the same difficulty. In short, I made them one too many.

I touched the brother juryman whose place was next me, and I whispered to him, "Oblige me by counting us." He looked surprised by the request, but turned his head and counted. "Why," says he, suddenly, "we are Thirt—; but no, it's not possible. No. We are twelve."

According to my counting that day, we were always right in detail, but in the gross we were always one too many. There was no appearance—no figure—to account for it; but I had now an inward foreshadowing of the figure that was surely coming.

The Jury were housed at the London Tavern. We all slept in one large room on separate tables, and we were constantly in the charge and under the eye of the officer sworn to hold us in safe-keeping. I see no reason for suppressing the real name of that officer. He was intelligent, highly polite, and obliging, and (I was glad to hear) much respected in the City. He had an agreeable presence, good eyes, enviable black whiskers, and a fine sonorous voice. His name was Mr. Harker.

When we turned into our twelve beds at night, Mr. Harker's bed was drawn across the door. On the night of the second day, not being disposed to lie down, and seeing Mr. Harker sitting on his bed, I went and sat beside him, and offered him a pinch of snuff. As Mr. Harker's hand touched mine in taking it from my box, a peculiar shiver crossed him, and he said, "Who is this?"

Following Mr. Harker's eyes, and looking along the room, I saw again the figure I expected,—the second of the two men who had gone down Piccadilly. I rose, and advanced a few steps; then stopped, and looked round at Mr. Harker. He was quite unconcerned, laughed, and said in a pleasant way, "I thought for a moment we had a thirteenth juryman, without a bed. But I see it is the moonlight."

Making no revelation to Mr. Harker, but inviting him to take a walk with me to the end of the room, I watched what the figure did. It stood for a few moments by the bedside of each of my eleven brother jurymen, close to the pillow. It always went to the right-hand side of the bed, and always passed out crossing the foot of the next bed. It seemed, from the action of the head, merely to look down pensively at each recumbent figure. It took no notice of me, or of my bed, which was that nearest to Mr. Harker's. It seemed to go out where the moonlight came in, through a high window, as by an aërial flight of stairs.

Next morning at breakfast, it appeared that everybody present had dreamed of the murdered man last night, except myself, and Mr. Harker.

I now felt as convinced that the second man who had gone down Piccadilly was the murdered man (so to speak), as if it had been borne into my comprehension by his immediate testimony. But even this took place, and in a manner for which I was not at all prepared.

On the fifth day of the trial, when the case for the prosecution was drawing to a close, a miniature of the murdered man, missing from his bedroom upon the discovery of the deed, and afterwards found in a hiding-place where the Murderer had been seen digging, was put in evidence. Having been identified by the witness under examination, it was handed up to the Bench, and thence handed down to be inspected by the Jury. As an officer in a black gown was making his way with it across to me, the figure of the second man who had gone down Piccadilly impetuously started from the crowd, caught the miniature from the officer, and gave it to me with his own hands, at the same time saying, in a low and hollow tone,—before I saw the miniature, which was in a locket,—"*I was younger then, and my face was not then drained of blood.*" It also came between me and the brother juryman to whom I would have given the miniature, and between him and the brother juryman to whom he would have given it, and so passed it on through the whole of our number, and back into my possession. Not one of them, however, detected this.

At table, and generally when we were shut up together in Mr. Harker's custody, we had from the first naturally discussed the day's proceedings a good deal. On that fifth day, the case for the prosecution being closed, and we having that side of the question in a completed shape before us, our discussion was more animated and serious. Among our number was a vestryman,—the densest idiot I have ever seen at large,—who met the plainest evidence with the most preposterous objections, and who was sided with by two flabby parochial parasites; all the three impanelled from a district so delivered over to Fever that they ought to have been upon their own trial for five hundred Murders. When these mischievous blockheads were at their loudest, which was towards midnight, while some of us were already pre-

[256]

paring for bed, I again saw the murdered man. He stood grimly behind them, beckoning to me. On my going towards them and striking into the conversation, he immediately retired. This was the beginning of a separate series of appearances, confined to that long room in which *we* were confined. Whenever a knot of my brother jurymen laid their heads together, I saw the head of the murdered man among theirs. Whenever their comparison of notes was going against him, he would solemnly and irresistibly beckon to me.

It will be borne in mind that down to the production of the miniature, on the fifth day of the trial, I had never seen the Appearance in Court. Three changes occurred now that we entered on the case for the defence. Two of them I will mention together, first. The figure was now in Court continually, and it never there addressed itself to me, but always to the person who was speaking at the time. For instance: the throat of the murdered man had been cut straight across. In the opening speech for the defence, it was suggested that the deceased might have cut his own throat. At that very moment, the figure, with its throat in the dreadful condition referred to (this it had concealed before), stood at the speaker's elbow, motioning across and across its windpipe, now with the right hand, now with the left, vigorously suggesting to the speaker himself the impossibility of such a wound having been self-inflicted by either hand. For another instance: a witness to character, a woman, deposed to the prisoner's being the most amiable of mankind. The figure at that instant stood on the floor before her, looking her full in the face, and pointing out the prisoner's evil countenance with an extended arm and an outstretched finger.

The third change now to be added impressed me strongly as the most marked and striking of all. I do not theorise upon it; I accurately state it, and there leave it. Although the Appearance was not itself perceived by those whom it addressed, its coming close to such persons was invariably attended by some trepidation or disturbance on their part. It seemed to me as if it were prevented, by laws to which I was not amenable, from fully revealing itself to others, and yet as if it could invisibly, dumbly, and darkly overshadow their minds. When the leading counsel for the defence suggested that hypothesis of suicide, and the figure stood at the learned gentleman's elbow, frightfully sawing at its severed throat, it is undeniable that the counsel faltered in his speech, lost for a few seconds the thread of his ingenious discourse, wiped his forehead with his handkerchief, and turned extremely pale. When the witness to character was confronted by the Appearance, her eyes most certainly did follow the direction of its pointed finger, and rest in great hesitation and trouble upon the prisoner's face. Two additional illustrations will suffice. On the eighth day of the trial, after the pause which was every day made early in the afternoon for a few minutes' rest and refreshment, I came back into court with the rest of the Jury some little time before the return of the Judges. Standing up in the box and looking about me, I thought the figure was not there, until, chancing to raise my eyes to the gallery, I saw it bending forward, and leaning over a very decent woman, as if to assure itself whether the Judges had resumed their seats or not. Immediately afterwards that woman screamed, fainted, and was carried out. So with the venerable, sagacious, and patient Judge who conducted the trial. When the case was over, and he settled himself and his papers to sum up, the murdered man, entering by the Judges' door, advanced to his Lordship's desk, and looked eagerly over his shoulder at the pages of his notes which he was turning. A change came over his Lordship's face; his hand stopped; the peculiar shiver, that I knew so well, passed over him; he faltered, "Excuse me, gentlemen, for a few moments. I am somewhat oppressed by the vitiated air"; and did not recover until he had drunk a glass of water.

Through all the monotony of six of those interminable ten days,—the same Judges and others on the bench, the same Murderer in the dock, the same lawyers at the table, the same tones of question and answer rising to the roof of the Court, the same scratching of the Judge's pen, the same ushers going in and out, the same lights kindled at the same hour when there had been any natural light of day, the same foggy curtain outside the great windows when it was foggy, the same rain pattering and dripping when it was rainy, the same footmarks of turnkeys and prisoner day after day on the same sawdust, the same keys locking and unlocking the same heavy doors,—through all the wearisome monotony which made me feel as if I had been Foreman of the Jury for a vast period of time, and Piccadilly had flourished coevally with Babylon, the murdered man never lost one trace of his distinctness in my eyes, nor was he at any moment less distinct than anybody else. I must not omit, as a matter of fact, that I never once saw the Appearance which I call by the name of the murdered man look at the Murderer. Again and again I wondered, "Why does he not?" But he never did.

Nor did he look at me, after the production of the miniatrue, until the last closing minutes of the trial arrived. We retired to consider, at seven minutes before ten at night. The idiotic vestryman and his two parochial parasites gave us so much trouble that we twice returned into Court to beg to have certain extracts from the Judges notes re-read. Nine of us had not the smallest doubt about those passages, neither, I believe, had any one in the Court; the dunderheaded triumverate, however, having no idea but obstruction, disputed them for that very reason. At length we prevailed, and finally the Jury returned into Court at ten minutes past twelve.

The murdered man at that time stood directly opposite the Jury-box, on the other side of the Court. As I took my place, his eyes rested on me with great attention; he seemed satisfied, and slowly shook a great grey veil, which he carried on his arm for the first time, over his head and whole form. As I gave in our verdict, "Guilty," the veil collapsed, all was gone, and his place was empty.

The Murderer, being asked by the Judge, according to usage, whether he had anything to say before sentence of Death should be passed upon him, indistinctly muttered something which was described in the leading newspapers of the following day as "a few rambling, incoherent, and half-audible words, in which he was understood to complain that he had not had a fair trial, because the Foreman of the Jury was prepossessed against him." The remarkable declaration that he really made was this: "*My Lord, I knew I was a doomed man, when the Foreman of my Jury came into the box. My Lord, I knew he would never let me off, because, before I was taken, he somehow got to my bedside in the night, woke me, and put a rope round my neck.*"

"Oh, yeah, and forget that idea I had about hiring girl elves."

★

The Adventure of The Dauphin's Doll

by Ellery Queen

T HERE IS A LAW among story-tellers, originally passed by Editors at the cries (they say) of their constituents, which states that stories about Christmas shall have children in them. This Christmas story is no exception; indeed, misopedists will complain that we have overdone it. And we confess in advance that this is also a story about Dolls, and that Santa Claus comes into it, and even a Thief; though as to this last, whoever he was—and that was one of the questions—he was certainly not Barabbas, even parabolically.

Another section of the statute governing Christmas stories provides that they shall incline towards Sweetness and Light. The first arises, of course, from the orphans and the never-souring savor of the annual Miracle; as for Light, it will be provided at the end, as usual, by that luminous prodigy, Ellery Queen. The reader of gloomier temper will also find a large measure of Darkness, in the person and works of one who, at least in Inspector Queen's harassed view, was surely the winged Prince of that region. His name, by the way, was not Satan, it was Comus; and this is paradox enow, since the original Comus, as everyone knows, was the god of festive joy and mirth, emotions not commonly associated with the Underworld. As Ellery struggled to embrace his phantom foe, he puzzled over this *non sequitur* in vain; in vain, that is, until Nikki Porter, no scorner of the obvious, suggested that he *might* seek the answer where any ordinary mortal would go at once. And there, to the great man's mortification, it was indeed to be found: On page 262b of Volume 6, *Coleb to Damasci*, of the 175th Anniversary edition of the *Encyclopaedia Britannica*. A French conjuror of that name —Comus—performing in London in the year 1789 caused his wife to vanish from the top of a table—the very first time, it appeared, that this feat, uxorial or otherwise, had been accomplished without the aid of mirrors. To track his dark adversary's *nom de nuit* to its historic lair gave Ellery his only glint of satisfaction until that blessed moment when light burst all around him and exorcised the darkness, Prince and all.

But this is chaos.

Our story properly begins not with our invisible character but with our dead one.

Miss Ypson had not always been dead; *au contraire*. She had lived for seventy-eight years, for most of them breathing hard. As her father used to remark, "She was a very active little verb." Miss Ypson's father was a professor of Greek at a small Midwestern university. He had conjugated his daughter with the rather bewildered assistance of one of his brawnier students, an Iowa poultry heiress.

Professor Ypson was a man of distinction. Unlike most professors of Greek, he was a Greek professor of Greek, having been born Gerasymos Aghamos Ypsilonomon in Polykhnitos, on the island of Mytilini, "where," he was fond of recalling on certain occasions, "burning Sappho loved and sung"—a quotation he found unfailingly useful in his extracurricular activities; and, the Hellenic ideal notwithstanding, Professor Ypson believed wholeheartedly in immoderation in all things. This hereditary and cultural background explains the professor's interest in fatherhood—to his wife's chagrin, for Mrs. Ypson's own breeding prowess was confined to the barnyards on which her income was based—a fact of which her husband sympathetically reminded her whenever he happened to sire another wayward chick; he held their daughter to be nothing less than a biological miracle.

The professor's mental processes also tended to confuse Mrs. Ypson. She never ceased to wonder why instead of shortening his name to Ypson, her husband had not sensibly changed it to Jones. "My dear," the professor once replied, "you are an Iowa snob." "But nobody," Mrs. Ypson cried. "can spell it or pronounce it!" "This is a cross," murmured Professor Ypson, "which we must bear with Ypsilanti." "Oh," said Mrs. Ypson.

There was invariably something Sibylline about his conversation. His favorite adjective for his wife was "ypsiliform," a term, he explained, which referred to the germinal spot at one of the fecundation stages in a ripening egg and which was, therefore, exquisitely *à propos*. Mrs. Ypson continued to look bewildered; she died at an early age.

And the professor ran off with a Kansas City variety girl of considerable talent, leaving his baptized chick to be reared by an eggish relative of her mother's, a Presbyterian named Jukes.

The only time Miss Ypson heard from her father—except when he wrote charming and erudite little notes requesting, as he termed it, *lucrum*— was in the fourth decade of his odyssey, when he sent her a handsome addition to her collection, a terra cotta play doll of Greek origin over three thousand years old which, unhappily, Miss Ypson felt duty-bound to return to the Brooklyn museum from which it had unaccountably vanished. The note ac-

[262]

companying her father's gift had said, whimsically: *"Timeo Danaos et dona ferentes."*

There was poetry behind Miss Ypson's dolls. At her birth the professor, ever harmonious, signalized his devotion to fecundity by naming her Cytherea. This proved the Olympian irony. For, it turned out, her father's philoprogenitiveness throbbed frustrate in her mother's stony womb; even though Miss Ypson interred five husbands of quite adequate vigor, she remained infertile to the end of her days. Hence it is classically tragic to find her, when all passion was spent, a sweet little old lady with a vague if eager smile who, under the name of her father, pattered about a vast and echoing New York apartment playing enthusiastically with dolls.

In the beginning they were dolls of common clay: a Billiken, a kewpie, a Kathe Kruse, a Patsy, a Foxy Grandpa, and so forth. But then, as her need increased, Miss Ypson began her fierce sack of the past.

Down into the land of Pharaoh she went for two pieces of thin desiccated board, carved and painted and with hair of strung beads, and legless—so that they might not run away—which any connoisseur will tell you are the most superb specimens of ancient Egyptian paddle doll extant, far superior to those in the British Museum, although this fact will be denied in certain quarters.

Miss Ypson unearthed a foremother of "Letitia Penn," until her discovery held to be the oldest doll in America, having been brought to Philadelphia from England in 1699 by William Penn as a gift for a playmate of his small daughter's. Miss Ypson's find was a wooden-hearted "little lady" in brocade and velvet which had been sent by Sir Walter Raleigh to the first English child born in the New World. Since Virginia Dare had been born in 1587, not even the Smithsonian dared impugn Miss Ypson's triumph.

On the old lady's racks, in her plate-glass cases, might be seen the wealth of a thousand childhoods, and some riches—for such is the genetics of dolls—possessed by children grown. Here could be found "fashion babies" from fourteenth century France, sacred dolls of the Orange Free State Fingo tribe, Satsuma paper dolls and court dolls from old Japan, beady-eyed "Kalifa" dolls of the Egyptian Sudan, Swedish birch-bark dolls, "Katcina" dolls of the Hopis, mammoth-tooth dolls of the Eskimos, feather dolls of the Chippewa, tumble dolls of the ancient Chinese, Coptic bone dolls, Roman dolls dedicated to Diana, *pantin* dolls which had been the street toys of Parisian exquisites before Madame Guillotine swept the boulevards, early Christian dolls in their *crèches* representing the Holy Family—to specify the merest handful of Miss Ypson's Briarean collection. She possessed dolls of pasteboard, dolls of animal skin, spool dolls, crab-claw dolls, eggshell dolls, cornhusk dolls, rag dolls, pine-cone dolls with moss hair, stocking dolls, dolls of *bisque,* dolls of palm leaf, dolls of *papier-*

mâché, even dolls made of seed pods. There were dolls forty inches tall, and there were dolls so little Miss Ypson could hide them in her gold thimble.

Cytherea Ypson's collection bestrode the centuries and took tribute of history. There was no greater—not the fabled playthings of Montezuma, or Victoria's, or Eugene Field's; not the collection at the Metropolitan, or the South Kensington, or the royal palace in old Bucharest, or anywhere outside the enchantment of little girls' dreams.

It was made of Iowan eggs and the Attic shore, corn-fed and myrtleclothed; and it brings us at last to Attorney John Somerset Bondling and his visit to the Queen residence one December twenty-third not so very long ago.

December the twenty-third is ordinarily not a good time to seek the Queens. Inspector Richard Queen likes his Christmas old-fashioned; his turkey stuffing, for instance, calls for twenty-two hours of over-all preparation and some of its ingredients are not readily found at the corner grocer's. And Ellery is a frustrated gift-wrapper. For a month before Christmas he turns his sleuthing genius to tracking down unusual wrapping papers, fine ribbons, and artistic stickers; and he spends the last two days creating beauty.

So it was that when Attorney John S. Bondling called, Inspector Queen was in his kitchen, swathed in a barbecue apron, up to his elbows in *fines herbes,* while Ellery, behind the locked door of his study, composed a secret symphony in glittering fuchsia metallic paper, forest-green moiré ribbon, and pine cones.

"It's almost useless," shrugged Nikki, studying Attorney Bondling's card, which was as crackly-looking as Attorney Bondling. "You say you know the Inspector, Mr. Bondling?"

"Just tell him Bondling the estate lawyer," said Bondling neurotically. "Park Row. He'll know."

"Dont blame me," said Nikki, "if you wind up in his stuffing. Goodness knows he's used everything else." And she went for Inspector Queen.

While she was gone, the study door opened noiselessly for one inch. A suspicious eye reconnoitered from the crack.

"Don't be alarmed," said the owner of the eye, slipping through the crack and locking the door hastily behind him. "Can't trust them, you know. Children, just children."

"Children!" Attorney Bondling snarled. "You're Ellery Queen, aren't you?"

"Yes?"

"Interested in youth, are you? Christmas? Orphans, dolls, that sort of thing?" Mr. Bondling went on in a remarkably nasty way.

"I suppose so."

"The more fool you. Ah, here's your father. Inspector Queen—!"

"Oh, that Bondling," said the old gentleman absently, shaking his visitor's hand. "My office called to say someone was coming up. Here, use my handkerchief; that's a bit of turkey liver. Know my son? His secretary, Miss Porter? What's on your mind, Mr. Bondling?"

"Inspector, I'm handling the Cytherea Ypson estate, and—"

"Nice meeting you, Mr. Bondling," said Ellery. "Nikki, the door is locked, so don't pretend you forgot the way to the bathroom . . ."

"Cytherea Ypson," frowned the Inspector. "Oh, yes. She died only recently."

"Leaving me with the headache," said Mr. Bondling bitterly, "of disposing of her Dollection."

"Her what?" asked Ellery, looking up from the key.

"Dolls—collection. Dollection. She coined the word."

Ellery put the key back in his pocket and strolled over to his armchair.

"Do I take this down?" sighed Nikki.

"Dollection," said Ellery.

"Spent about thirty years at it. Dolls!"

"Yes, Nikki, take it down."

"Well, well, Mr. Bondling," said Inspector Queen. "What's the problem? Christmas comes but once a year, you know."

"Will provides the Dollection be sold at auction," grated the attorney, "and the proceeds used to set up a fund for orphan children. I'm holding the public sale right after New Year's."

"Dolls and orphans, eh?" said the Inspector, thinking of Javanese black pepper and Country Gentleman Seasoning Salt.

"That's *nice,*" beamed Nikki.

"Oh, is it?" said Mr. Bondling softly. "Apparently, young woman, you've never tried to satisfy a Surrogate. I've administered estates for nine years without a whisper against me, but let an estate involve the interests of just one little ba—little fatherless child, and you'd think from the Surrogate's attitude I was Bill Sykes himself!"

"My stuffing," began the Inspector.

"I've had those dolls catalogued. The result is frightening! Did you know there's no set market for the damnable things? And aside from a few personal possessions, the Dollection constitutes the old lady's entire estate. Sank every nickel she had in it."

"But it should be worth a fortune," protested Ellery.

"To whom, Mr. Queen? Museums always want such things as free and unencumbered gifts. I tell you, except for one item, those hypothetical orphans won't realize enough from that sale to keep them in—in bubble gum for two days!"

[265]

"Which item would that be, Mr. Bondling?"

"Number Eight-seventy-four," snapped the lawyer. "This one."

"Number Eight-seventy-four," read Inspector Queen from the fat catalogue Bondling had fished out of a large greatcoat pocket. "The Dauphin's Doll. Unique. Ivory figure of a boy Prince eight inches tall, clad in court dress, genuine ermine, brocade, velvet. Court sword in gold strapped to waist. Gold circlet crown surmounted by single blue brilliant diamond of finest water, weight approximately 49 carats—"

"How many carats?" exclaimed Nikki.

"Larger than the *Hope* and the *Star of South Africa*," said Ellery, with a certain excitement.

"—appraised," continued his father, "at one hundred and ten thousand dollars."

"Expensive dollie."

"Indecent!" said Nikki.

"This indecent—I mean exquisite royal doll," the Inspector read on, "was a birthday gift from King Louis XVI of France to Louis Charles, his second son, who became dauphin at the death of his elder brother in 1789. The little dauphin was proclaimed Louis XVII by the royalists during the French Revolution while in custody of the *sans-culottes*. His fate is shrouded in mystery. Romantic, historic item."

"*Le prince perdu.* I'll say," muttered Ellery. "Mr. Bondling, is this on the level?"

"I'm an attorney, not an antiquarian," snapped their visitor. "There are documents attached, one of them a sworn statement—holograph—by Lady Charlotte Atkyns, the English actress-friend of the Capet family— she was in France during the Revolution—or purporting to be in Lady Charlotte's hand. It doesn't matter, Mr. Queen. Even if the history is bad, the diamond's good!"

"I take it this hundred-and-ten-thousand dollar dollie constitutes the bone, as it were, or that therein lies the rub?"

"You said it!" cried Mr. Bondling, cracking his knuckles in a sort of agony. "For my money the Dauphin's Doll is the only negotiable asset of that collection. And what's the old lady do? She provides by will that on the day preceding Christmas the Cytherea Ypson Dollection is to be publicly displayed . . . on the main floor of Nash's Department Store! *The day before Christmas, gentlemen!* Think of it!"

"But why?" asked Nikki, puzzled.

"Why? Who knows why? For the entertainment of New York's army of little beggars, I suppose! Have you any notion how many peasants pass through Nash's on the day before Christmas? My cook tells me—she's a very religious woman—it's like Armageddon."

"Day before Christmas," frowned Ellery. "That's tomorrow."

"It does sound chancy," said Nikki anxiously. Then she brightened. "Oh, well, maybe Nash's won't co-operate, Mr. Bondling."

"Oh, won't they!" howled Mr. Bondling. "Why, old lady Ypson had this stunt cooked up with that gang of peasant-purveyors for years! They've been snapping at my heels ever since the day she was put away!"

"It'll draw every crook in New York," said the Inspector, his gaze on the kitchen door.

"Orphans," said Nikki. "The orphans' interests *must* be protected." She looked at her employer accusingly.

"Special measures, Dad," said Ellery.

"Sure, sure," said the Inspector, rising. "Don't you worry about this, Mr. Bondling. Now if you'll be kind enough to excu—"

"Inspector Queen," hissed Mr. Bondling, leaning forward tensely, "that is not all."

"Ah." Ellery briskly lit a cigaret. "There's a specific villain in this piece, Mr. Bondling, and you know who he is."

"I do," said the lawyer hollowly, "and then again I don't. I mean, it's Comus."

"Comus!" the Inspector screamed.

"Comus?" said Ellery slowly.

"Comus?" said Nikki. "Who dat?"

"Comus," nodded Mr. Bondling. "First thing this morning. Marched right into my office, bold as day—must have followed me; I hadn't got my coat off, my secretary wasn't even in. Marched in and tossed this card on my desk."

Ellery seized it. "The usual, Dad."

"His trademark," growled the Inspector, his lips working.

"But the card just says 'Comus,'" complained Nikki. "Who—?"

"Go on, Mr. Bondling!" thundered the Inspector.

"And he calmly announced to me," said Bondling, blotting his cheeks with an exhausted handkerchief, "that he's going to steal the Dauphin's Doll tomorrow, in Nash's."

"Oh, a maniac," said Nikki.

"Mr. Bondling," said the old gentleman in a terrible voice, "just what did this fellow look like?"

"Foreigner—black beard—spoke with a thick accent of some sort. To tell you the truth, I was so thunderstruck I didn't notice details. Didn't even chase him till it was too late."

The Queens shrugged at each other, Gallically.

"The old story," said the Inspector; the corners of his nostrils were greenish. "The brass of the colonel's monkey and when he does show himself nobody remembers anything but beards and foreign accents. Well, Mr. Bondling, with Comus in the game it's serious business. Where's the collection right now?''

"In the vaults of the Life Bank & Trust, Forty-third Street branch.''

"What time are you to move it over to Nash's?''

"They wanted it this evening. I said nothing doing. I've made special arrangements with the bank, and the collection's to be moved at seven-thirty tomorrow morning.''

"Won't be much time to set up,'' said Ellery thoughtfully, ''before the store opens its doors.'' He glanced at his father.

"You leave Operation Dollie to us, Mr. Bondling,'' said the Inspector grimly. ''Better give me a buzz this afternoon.''

"I can't tell you, Inspector, how relieved I am—''

"Are you?'' said the old gentleman sourly. ''What makes you think he won't get it?''

When Attorney Bondling had left, the Queens put their heads together, Ellery doing most of the talking, as usual. Finally, the Inspector went into the bedroom for a session with his direct line to Headquarters.

"Anybody would think,'' sniffed Nikki, ''you two were planning the defense of the Bastille. Who is this Comus, anyway?''

"We don't know, Nikki,'' said Ellery slowly. ''Might be anybody. Began his criminal career about five years ago. He's in the grand tradition of Lupin—a saucy, highly intelligent rascal who's made stealing an art. He seems to take a special delight in stealing valuable things under virtually impossible conditions. Master of make-up—he's appeared in a dozen different disguises. And he's an uncanny mimic. Never been caught, photographed, or fingerprinted. Imaginative, daring—I'd say he's the most dangerous thief operating in the United States.''

"If he's never been caught,'' said Nikki skeptically, ''how do you know he commits these crimes?''

"You mean and not someone else?'' Ellery smiled pallidly. ''The techniques mark the thefts as his work. And then, like Arsène, he leaves a card —with the name 'Comus' on it—on the scene of each visit.''

"Does he usually announce in advance that he's going to swipe the crown jewels?''

"No.'' Ellery frowned. ''To my knowledge, this is the first such instance. Since he's never done anything without a reason, that visit to Bondling's office this morning must be part of his greater plan. I wonder if—''

The telephone in the living room rang clear and loud.

Nikki looked at Ellery. Ellery looked at the telephone.

"Do you suppose—?'' began Nikki. But then she said, ''Oh, it's too absurd!''

"Where Comus is involved," said Ellery wildly, "nothing is too absurd!" and he leaped for the phone. "Hello!"

"A call from an old friend," announced a deep and hollowish male voice. "Comus."

"Well," said Ellery. "Hello again."

"Did Mr. Bondling," asked the voice jovially, "persuade you to 'prevent' me from stealing the Dauphin's Doll in Nash's tomorrow?"

"So you know Bondling's been here."

"No miracle involved, Queen. I followed him. Are you taking the case?"

"See here, Comus," said Ellery. "Under ordinary circumstances I'd welcome the sporting chance to put you where you belong. But these circumstances are not ordinary. That doll represents the major asset of a future fund for orphaned children. I'd rather we didn't play catch with it. Comus, what do you say we call this one off?"

"Shall we say," asked the voice gently, "Nash's Department Store—tomorrow?"

* * *

Thus the early morning of December twenty-fourth finds Messrs. Queen and Bondling, and Nikki Porter, huddled on the iron sidewalk of Forty-third Street before the holly-decked windows of the Life Bank & Trust Company, just outside a double line of armed guards. The guards form a channel between the bank entrance and an armored truck, down which Cytherea Ypson's Dollection flows swiftly. And all about gapes New York, stamping callously on the aged, icy face of the street against the uncharitable Christmas wind.

Now is the winter of his discontent, and Mr. Queen curses.

"I don't know what you're beefing about," moans Miss Porter.

"You and Mr. Bondling are bundled up like Yukon prospectors. Look at *me*."

"It's that rat-hearted public relations tripe from Nash's," says Mr. Queen murderously. "They all swore themselves to secrecy, Brother Rat included. Honor! Spirit of Christmas!"

"It was all over the radio last night," whimpers Mr. Bondling. "And in this morning's papers."

"I'll cut his creep's heart out. Here! Velie, keep those people away!"

Sergeant Velie says good-naturedly from the doorway of the bank, "You jerks stand back." Little does the Sergeant know the fate in store for him.

"Armored trucks," says Miss Porter bluishly. "Shotguns."

"Nikki, Comus made a point of informing us in advance that he meant

[269]

to steal the Dauphin's Doll in Nash's Department Store. It would be just like him to have said that in order to make it easier to steal the doll en route.''

''Why don't they hurry?'' shivers Mr. Bondling. ''Ah!''

Inspector Queen appears suddenly in the doorway. His hands clasp treasure.

''Oh!'' cries Nikki.

New York whistles.

It is magnificence, an affront to democracy. But street mobs, like children, are royalists at heart.

New York whistles, and Sergeant Thomas Velie steps menacingly before Inspector Queen, Police Positive drawn, and Inspector Queen dashes across the sidewalk between the bristling lines of guards with the Dauphin's Doll in his embrace.

Queen the Younger vanishes, to materialize an instant later at the door of the armored truck.

''It's just immorally, hideously beautiful, Mr. Bondling,'' breathes Miss Porter, sparkly-eyed.

Mr. Bondling cranes, thinly.

ENTER *Santa Claus, with bell.*

* * *

Santa. Oyez, oyez. Peace, good will. Is that the dollie the radio's been yappin' about, folks?

Mr. B. Scram.

Miss P. Why, Mr. Bondling.

Mr. B. Well, he's got no business here. Stand back, er, Santa. Back!

Santa. What eateth you, my lean and angry friend? Have you no compassion at this season of the year?

Mr. B. Oh . . . Here! (*Clink.*) Now will you *kindly* . . .?

Santa. Mighty pretty dollie. Where they takin' it, girlie?

Miss P. Over to Nash's, Santa.

Mr. B. You asked for it. Officer!!!

Santa (hurriedly). Little present for you girlie. Compliments of Santy. Merry, merry.

Miss P. For *me?* (EXIT *Santa, rapidly, with bell.*) Really, Mr. Bondling, was it necessary to . . . ?

Mr. B. Opium for the masses! What did that flatulent faker hand you, Miss Porter? What's in that unmentionable envelope?

Miss P. I'm sure I don't know, but isn't it the most touching idea? Why it's addressed to *Ellery.* Oh! Elleryyyyyy!

[270]

Mr. B (EXIT *excitedly*). Where is he? You—! Officer! Where did that baby-deceiver disappear to? A Santa Claus . . . !

Mr. Q (*entering on the run*). Yes? Nikki, what is it? What's happened?

Miss P. A man dressed as Santa Claus just handed me this envelope. It's addressed to you.

Mr. Q. Note? (*He snatches it, withdraws a miserable slice of paper from it on which is block-lettered in pencil a message which he reads aloud with considerable expression.*) "Dear Ellery, Don't you trust me? I said I'd steal the Dauphin in Nash's emporium today and that's exactly where I'm going to do it. Yours—" Signed . . .

Miss P (*craning*). "Comus." That Santa?

Mr. Q. (*Sets his manly lips. An icy wind blows.*)

*   *   *

Even the master had to acknowledge that their defenses against Comus were ingenious.

From the Display Department of Nash's they had requisitioned four miter-jointed counters of uniform length. These they had fitted together, and in the center of the hollow square thus formed they had erected a platform six feet high. On the counters, in plastic tiers, stretched the long lines of Miss Ypson's babies. Atop the platform, dominant, stood a great chair of handcarved oak, filched from the Swedish Modern section of the Fine Furniture Department; and on this Valhalla-like throne, a huge and rosy rotundity, sat Sergeant Thomas Velie of Police Headquarters, morosely grateful for the anonymity endowed by the scarlet suit and the jolly mask and whiskers of his appointed role.

Nor was this all. At a distance of six feet outside the counters shimmered a surrounding rampart of plate glass, borrowed in its various elements from *The Glass Home of the Future* display on the sixth floor rear, and assembled to shape an eight foot wall quoined with chrome, its glistening surfaces flawless except at one point, where a thick glass door had been installed. But the edges fitted intimately and there was a formidable lock in the door, the key to which lay buried in Mr. Queen's right trouser pocket.

It was 8:54 A.M. The Queens, Nikki Porter, and Attorney Bondling stood among store officials and an army of plainclothesmen on Nash's main floor surveying the product of their labors.

"I think that about does it," muttered Inspector Queen at last. "Men! Positions around the glass partition."

Twenty-four assorted gendarmes in mufti jostled one another. They took marked places about the wall, facing it and grinning up at Sergeant Velie. Sergeant Velie, from his throne, glared back.

[271]

"Hagstrom and Piggott—the door."

Two detectives detached themselves from a group of reserves. As they marched to the glass door, Mr. Bondling plucked at the Inspector's overcoat sleeve. "Can all these men be trusted, Inspector Queen?" he whispered. "I mean, this fellow Comus—"

"Mr. Bondling," replied the old gentleman coldly, "you do your job and let me do mine."

"But—"

"Picked men, Mr. Bondling! I picked 'em myself."

"Yes, yes, Inspector. I merely thought I'd—"

"Lieutenant Farber."

A little man with watery eyes stepped forward.

"Mr. Bondling, this is Lieutenant Geronimo Farber, Headquarters jewelry expert. Ellery?"

Ellery took the Dauphin's Doll from his greatcoat pocket, but he said, "If you don't mind, Dad, I'll keep holding on to it."

Somebody said, "Wow," and then there was silence.

"Lieutenant, this doll in my son's hand is the famous Dauphin's Doll with the diamond crown that—"

"Don't touch it, Lieutenant, please," said Ellery. "I'd rather nobody touched it."

"The doll," continued the Inspector, "has just been brought here from a bank vault which it ought never to have left, and Mr. Bondling, who's handling the Ypson estate, claims it's the genuine article. Lieutenant, examine the diamond and give us your opinion."

Lieutenant Farber produced a *loupe*. Ellery held the dauphin securely, and Farber did not touch it.

Finally, the expert said: "I can't pass an opinion about the doll itself, of course, but the diamond's a beauty. Easily worth a hundred thousand dollars at the present state of the market—maybe more. Looks like a very strong setting, by the way."

"Thanks Lieutenant. Okay, son," said the Inspector. "Go into your waltz."

Clutching the dauphin, Ellery strode over to the glass gate and unlocked it.

"This fellow Farber," whispered Attorney Bondling in the Inspector's hairy ear. "Inspector, are you absolutely sure he's—?"

"He's really Lieutenant Farber?" The Inspector controlled himself. "Mr. Bondling, I've known Gerry Farber for eighteen years. Calm yourself."

Ellery was crawling perilously over the nearest counter. Then, bearing

[272]

the dauphin aloft, he hurried across the floor of the enclosure to the platform.

Sergeant Velie whined, "Maestro, how in hell am I going to sit here all
day without washin' my hands?"

But Mr. Queen merely stooped and lifted from the floor a heavy little
structure faced with black velvet consisting of a floor and a backdrop, with a
two-armed chromium support. This object he placed on the platform directly between Sergeant Velie's massive legs.

Carefully, he stood the Dauphin's Doll in the velvet niche. Then he
clambered back across the counter, went through the glass door, locked it
with the key, and turned to examine his handiwork.

Proudly the prince's plaything stood, the jewel in his little golden crown
darting "on pale electric streams" under the concentrated tide of a dozen
of the most powerful floodlights in the possession of the great store.

"Velie," said Inspector Queen, "you're not to touch that doll. Don't lay
a finger on it."

The Sergeant said, "Gaaaaa."

"You men on duty. Don't worry about the crowds. Your job is to keep
watching that doll. You're not to take your eyes off it all day. Mr. Bondling, are you satisfied?" Mr. Bondling seemed about to say something, but
then he hastily nodded. "Ellery?"

The great man smiled. "The only way he can get that bawbie," he said,
"is by well-directed mortar fire or spells and incantations. Raise the port-
cullis!"

* * *

Then began the interminable day, *dies irae,* the last shopping day before
Christmas. This is traditionally the day of the inert, the procrastinating, the
undecided, and the forgetful, sucked at last into the mercantile machine by
the perpetual pump of Time. If there is peace upon earth, it descends only
afterward; and at no time, on the part of anyone embroiled, is there good
will toward men. As Miss Porter expresses it, a cat fight in a bird cage
would be more Christian.

But on this December twenty-fourth, in Nash's, the normal bedlam was
augmented by the vast shrilling of thousands of children. It may be, as the
Psalmist insists, that happy is the man that hath his quiver full of them; but
no bowmen surrounded Miss Ypson's darlings this day, only detectives
carrying revolvers, not a few of whom forbore to use same only by the most
heroic self-discipline. In the black floods of humanity overflowing the main
floor little folks darted about like electrically charged minnows, pursued by

[273]

exasperated maternal shrieks and the imprecations of those whose shins and rumps and toes were at the mercy of hot, happy little limbs; indeed, nothing was sacred, and Attorney Bondling was seen to quail and wrap his greatcoat defensively about him against the savage innocence of childhood. But the guardians of the law, having been ordered to simulate store employees, possessed no such armor; and many a man earned his citation that day for unique cause. They stood in the millrace of the tide; it churned about them, shouting, "Dollies! *Dollies!*" until the very word lost its familiar meaning and became the insensate scream of a thousand Loreleis beckoning strong men to destruction below the eye-level of their diamond Light.

But they stood fast.

And Comus was thwarted. Oh, he tried. At 11:18 A.M. a tottering old man holding to the hand of a small boy tried to wheedle Detective Hagstrom into unlocking the glass door "so my grandson here—he's terrible nearsighted—can get a closer look at the pretty dollies." Detective Hagstrom roared, "Rube!" and the old gentleman dropped the little boy's hand violently and with remarkable agility lost himself in the crowd. A spot investigation revealed that, coming upon the boy, who had been crying for his mommy, the old gentleman had promised to find her. The little boy, whose name—he said—was Lance Morganstern, was removed to the Lost and Found Department; and everyone was satisfied that the great thief had finally launched his attack. Everyone, that is, but Ellery Queen. He seemed puzzled. When Nikki asked him why, he merely said: "Stupidity, Nikki. It's not in character."

At 1:46 P.M., Sergeant Velie sent up a distress signal. He had, it seemed, to wash his hands. Inspector Queen signaled back: "O.K. Fifteen minutes." Sergeant Santa C. Velie scrambled off his perch, clawed his way over the counter, and pounded urgently on the inner side of the glass door. Ellery let him out, relocking the door immediately, and the Sergeant's red-clad figure disappeared on the double in the general direction of the main-floor gentlemen's relief station, leaving the dauphin in solitary possession of the dais.

During the Sergeant's recess, Inspector Queen circulated among his men repeating the order of the day.

The episode of Velie's response to the summons of Nature caused a temporary crisis. For at the end of the specified fifteen minutes he had not returned. Nor was there a sign of him at the end of a half hour. An aide dispatched to the relief station reported back that the Sergeant was not there. Fears of foul play were voiced at an emergency staff conference held then and there and counter-measures were being planned even as, at 2:35 P.M., the familiar Santa-clad bulk of the Sergeant was observed battling through the lines, pawing at his mask.

"Velie," snarled Inspector Queen, "where have you been?"

"Eating my lunch," growled the Sergeant's voice, defensively. "I been taking my punishment like a good soldier all this damn day, Inspector, but I draw the line at starvin' to death even in the line of duty."

"Velie—!" choked the Inspector; but then he waved his hand feebly and said, "Ellery, let him back in there."

And that was very nearly all. The only other incident of note occurred at 4:22 P.M. A well-upholstered woman with a red face yelled, "Stop! Thief! He grabbed my pocketbook! Police!" about fifty feet from the Ypson exhibit. Ellery instantly shouted, *"It's a trick! Men, don't take your eyes off that doll!"* "It's Comus disguised as a woman," exclaimed Attorney Bondling, as Inspector Queen and Detective Hesse wrestled the female figure through the mob. She was now a wonderful shade of magenta. "What are you *doing?*" she screamed. "Don't arrest *me!*—catch that crook who stole my pocketbook! "No dice, Comus," said the Inspector. "Wipe off that make-up." "McComas?" said the woman loudly. "My name is Rafferty, and all these folks saw it. He was a fat man with a mustache." "Inspector," said Nikki Porter, making a surreptitious scientific test. "This is a female. Believe me." And so, indeed it proved. All agreed that the mustachioed fat man had been Comus, creating a diversion in the desperate hope that the resulting confusion would give him an opportunity to steal the little dauphin.

"Stupid, stupid," muttered Ellery, gnawing his fingernails.

"Sure," grinned the Inspector. "We've got him nibbling his tail, Ellery. This was his do-or-die pitch. He's through."

"Frankly," sniffed Nikki, "I'm a little disappointed."

"Worried," said Ellery, "would be the word for me."

* * *

Inspector Queen was too case-hardened a sinner's nemesis to lower his guard at his most vulnerable moment. When the 5:30 bells bonged and the crowds began struggling toward the exits, he barked: "Men, stay at your posts. Keep watching that doll!" So all hands were on the *qui vive* even as the store emptied. The reserves kept hustling people out. Ellery, standing on an Information booth, spotted bottlenecks and waved his arms.

At 5:50 P.M. the main floor was declared out of the battle zone. All stragglers had been herded out. The only persons visible were the refugees trapped by the closing bell on the upper floors, and these were pouring out of elevators and funneled by a solid line of detectives and accredited store personnel to the doors. By 6:05 they were a trickle; by 6:10 even the trickle had dried up. And the personnel itself began to disperse.

"No, men!" called Ellery sharply from his observation post. "Stay where you are till all the store employees are out!'' The counter clerks had long since disappeared.

Sergeant Velie's plaintive voice called from the other side of the glass door. "I got to get home and decorate my tree. Maestro, make with the key.''

Ellery jumped down and hurried over to release him. Detective Piggott jeered, "Going to play Santa to your kids tomorrow morning, Velie?'' at which the Sergeant managed even through his mask to project a four-letter word distinctly, forgetful of Miss Porter's presence, and stamped off toward the gentlemen's relief station.

"Where you going, Velie?'' asked the Inspector, smiling.

"I got to get out of these x-and-dash Santy clothes somewheres, don't I?'' came back the Sergeant's mask-muffled tones, and he vanished in a thunderclap of his fellow-officers' laughter.

"Still worried, Mr. Queen?'' chuckled the Inspector.

"I don't understand it.'' Ellery shook his head. "Well, Mr. Bondling, there's your dauphin, untouched by human hands.''

"Yes. Well!'' Attorney Bondling wiped his forehead happily. "I don't profess to understand it, either, Mr. Queen. Unless it's simply another case of an inflated reputation . . .'' He clutched the Inspector suddenly. "Those men!'' he whispered. *"Who are they?''*

"Relax, Mr. Bondling,'' said the Inspector good-naturedly. "It's just the men to move the dolls back to the bank. Wait a minute, you men! Perhaps, Mr. Bondling, we'd better see the dauphin back to the vaults ourselves.''

"Keep those fellows back,'' said Ellery to the Headquarters men, quietly, and he followed the Inspector and Mr. Bondling into the enclosure. They pulled two of the counters apart at one corner and strolled over to the platform. The dauphin was winking at them in a friendly way. They stood looking at him.

"Cute little devil,'' said the Inspector.

"Seems silly now,'' beamed Attorney Bondling. "Being so worried all day.''

"Comus must have had *some* plan,'' mumbled Ellery.

"Sure,'' said the Inspector. "That old man disguise. And that purse-snatching act.''

"No, no, Dad. Something clever. He's always pulled something clever.''

"Well, there's the diamond,'' said the lawyer comfortably. "He didn't.''

"Disguise . . .'' muttered Ellery. "It's always been a disguise. Santa Claus costume—he used that once—this morning in front of the bank . . . Did we see a Santa Claus around here today?''

"Just Velie," said the Inspector, grinning. "And I hardly think—"

"Wait a moment, please," said Attorney Bondling in a very odd voice.

He was staring at the Dauphin's Doll.

"Wait for what, Mr. Bondling?"

"What's the matter?" said Ellery, also in a very odd voice.

"But . . . not possible . . ." stammered Bondling. He snatched the doll from its black velvet repository. *"No!"* he howled. *"This isn't the dauphin! It's a fake—a copy!"*

Something happened in Mr. Queen's head—a little *click!* like the turn of a switch. And there was light.

"Some of you men!" he roared. *"After Santa Claus!"*

"Who, Mr. Queen?"

"What's he talkin' about?"

"After who, Ellery?" gasped Inspector Queen.

"What's the matter?"

"I dunno!"

"Don't stand here! *Get him!"* screamed Ellery, dancing up and down. "The man I just let out of here! The Santa who made for the men's room!"

Detectives started running, wildly.

"But Ellery," said a small voice, and Nikki found that it was her own, "that was Sergeant Velie."

"It was *not* Velie, Nikki! When Velie ducked out just before two o'clock to relieve himself, *Comus waylaid him!* It was Comus who came back in Velie's Santa Claus rig, wearing Velie's whiskers and mask! *Comus has been on this platform all afternoon!"* He tore the dauphin from Attorney Bondling's grasp. "Copy . . . ! Somehow he did it, he did it."

"But Mr. Queen," whispered Attorney Bondling, "his voice. He spoke to us . . . in Sergeant Velie's voice."

"Yes, Ellery," Nikki heard herself saying.

"I told you yesterday Comus is a great mimic, Nikki. Lieutenant Farber! Is Farber still here?"

The jewelry expert, who had been gaping from a distance, shook his head as if to clear it and shuffled into the enclosure.

"Lieutenant," said Ellery in a strangled voice. "Examine this diamond . . . I mean, *is* it a diamond?"

Inspector Queen removed his hands from his face and said froggily, "Well, Gerry?"

Lieutenant Farber squinted once through his *loupe*. "The hell you say. It's strass—"

"It's what?" said the Inspector piteously.

"Strass, Dick—lead glass—paste. Beautiful job of imitation—as nice as I've ever seen."

"Lead me to that Santa Claus," whispered Inspector Queen.

But Santa Claus was being led to him. Struggling in the grip of a dozen detectives, his red coat ripped off, his red pants around his ankles, but his whiskery mask still on his face, came a large shouting man.

"But I tell you," he was roaring, "I'm Sergeant Tom Velie! Just take the mask off—that's all!"

"It's a pleasure," growled Detective Hagstrom, trying to break their prisoner's arm, "we're reservin' for the Inspector."

"Hold him, boys," whispered the Inspector. He struck like a cobra. His hand came away with Santa's face.

And there, indeed, was Sergeant Velie.

"Why it's Velie," said the Inspector wonderingly.

"I only told you that a thousand times," said the Sergeant, folding his great hairy arms across his great hairy chest. "Now who's the so-and-so who tried to bust my arm?" Then he said, "My pants!" and, as Miss Porter turned delicately away, Detective Hagstrom humbly stooped and raised Sergeant Velie's pants.

"Never mind that," said a cold, remote voice.

It was the master, himself.

"Yeah?" said Sergeant Velie, hostilely.

"Velie, weren't you attacked when you went to the men's room just before two?"

"Do I look like the attackable type?"

"You did go to lunch?—in person?"

"And a lousy lunch it was."

"It was *you* up here among the dolls all afternoon?"

"Nobody else, Maestro. Now, my friends, I want action. Fast patter. What's this all about? Before," said Sergeant Velie softly, "I lose my temper."

While divers Headquarters orators delivered impromptu periods before the silent Sergeant, Inspector Richard Queen spoke.

"Ellery. Son. How in the name of the second sin did he do it?"

"Pa," replied the master, "you got me."

* * *

Deck the hall with boughs of holly, but not if your name is Queen on the evening of a certain December twenty-fourth. If your name is Queen on that lamentable evening you are seated in the living room of a New York apartment uttering no falalas but staring miserably into a somber fire. And you have company. The guest list is short, but select. It numbers two, a Miss Porter and a Sergeant Velie, and they are no comfort.

No, no ancient Yuletide carol is being trolled; only the silence sings.

Wail in your crypt, Cytherea Ypson; all was for nought; your little dau-

[278]

phin's treasure lies not in the empty coffers of the orphans but in the hot clutch of one who took his evil inspiration from a long-crumbled specialist in vanishments.

Speech was spent. Should a wise man utter vain knowledge and fill his belly with the east wind? He who talks too much commits a sin, says the Talmud. He also wastes his breath; and they had now reached the point of conservation, having exhausted the available supply.

Item: Lieutenant Geronimo Farber of Police Headquarters had examined the diamond in the genuine dauphin's crown a matter of seconds before it was conveyed to its sanctuary in the enclosure. Lieutenant Farber had pronounced the diamond a diamond, and not merely a diamond, but a diamond worth in his opinion over one hundred thousand dollars.

Question: Had Lieutenant Farber lied?

Answer: Lieutenant Farber was (a) a man of probity, tested in a thousand fires, and (b) he was incorruptible. To (a) and (b) Inspector Richard Queen attested violently, swearing by the beard of his personal Prophet.

Question: Had Lieutenant Farber been mistaken?

Answer: Lieutenant Farber was a nationally famous police expert in the field of precious stones. It must be presumed that he knew a real diamond from a piece of lapidified glass.

Question: Had it *been* Lieutenant Farber?

Answer: By the same beard of the identical Prophet, it had been Lieutenant Farber and no facsimile.

Conclusion: The diamond Lieutenant Farber had examinined immediately preceding the opening of Nash's doors that morning had been the veritable diamond of the dauphin, the doll had been the veritable Dauphin's Doll, and it was this genuine article which Ellery with his own hands had carried into the glass-enclosed fortress and depositied between the authenticated Sergeant Velie's verified feet.

Item: All day—specifically, between the moment the dauphin had been deposited in his niche until the moment he was discovered to be a fraud; that is, during the total period in which a theft-and-substitution was even theoretically possible—no person whatsoever, male or female, adult or child, had set foot within the enclosure except Sergeant Thomas Velie, alias Santa Claus.

Question: Had Sergeant Velie switched dolls, carrying the genuine dauphin concealed in his Santa Claus suit, to be cached for future retrieval or turned over to Comus or a confederate of Comus's, during one of his two departures from the enclosure?

Answer (by Sergeant Velie): *

Deleted.—Editor.

Confirmation: Some dozens of persons with police training and specific instructions, not to mention the Queens themselves, Miss Porter, and Attorney Bondling, testified unqualifiedly that Sergeant Velie had not touched the doll, at any time, all day.

Conclusion: Sergeant Velie could not have stolen, and therefore he did not steal, the Dauphin's Doll.

Item: All those deputized to watch the doll swore that they had done so without lapse or hindrance the everlasting day; moreover, that at no time had anything touched the doll—human or mechanical—either from inside or outside the enclosure.

Question: The human vessel being frail, could those so swearing have been in error? Could their attention have wandered through weariness, boredom, *et cetera?*

Answer: Yes; but not all at the same time, by the laws of probability. And during the only two diversions of the danger period, Ellery himself testified that he had kept his eyes on the dauphin and that nothing whatsoever had approached or threatened it.

Item: Despite all of the foregoing, at the end of the day they had found the real dauphin gone and a worthless copy in its place.

"It's brilliantly, unthinkably clever," said Ellery at last. "A master illusion. For, of course, it *was* an illusion . . ."

"Witchcraft," groaned the Inspector.

"Mass mesmerism," suggested Nikki Porter.

"Mass bird gravel," growled the Sergeant.

Two hours later Ellery spoke again.

"So Comus had a worthless copy of the dauphin all ready for the switch," he muttered. "It's a world-famous dollie, been illustrated countless times, minutely described, photographed . . . All ready for the switch, but how did he make it? How? How?"

"You said that," said the Sergeant, "once or forty-two times."

"The bells are tolling," sighed Nikki, "but for whom? Not for us." And indeed, while they slumped there, Time, which Seneca named father of truth, had crossed the threshold of Christmas; and Nikki looked alarmed, for as that glorious song of old came upon the midnight clear, a great light spread from Ellery's eyes and beatified the whole contorted countenance, so that peace sat there, the peace that approximateth understanding; and he threw back that noble head and laughed with the merriment of an innocent child.

"Hey," said Sergeant Velie, staring.

"Son," began Inspector Queen, half-rising from his armchair; when the telephone rang.

"Beautiful!" roared Ellery. "Oh, exquisite! How did Comus make the switch, eh? Nikki—"

"From somewhere," said Nikki, handing him the telephone receiver, "a voice is calling, and if you ask me it's saying 'Comus.' Why not ask him?"

"Comus," whispered the Inspector, shrinking.

"Comus," echoed the Sergeant, baffled.

"Comus?" said Ellery heartily. "How nice. Hello there! Congratulations."

"Why, thank you," said the familiar deep and hollow voice. "I called to express my appreciation for a wonderful day's sport and to wish you the merriest kind of Yuletide."

"You anticipate a rather merry Christmas yourself, I take it."

"*Laeti triumphantes,*" said Comus jovially.

"And the orphans?"

"They have my best wishes. But I won't detain you, Ellery. If you'll look at the doormat outside your apartment door, you'll find on it—in the spirit of the season—a little gift, with the compliments of Comus. Will you remember me to Inspector Queen and Attorney Bondling?"

Ellery hung up, smiling.

On the doormat he found the true Dauphin's Doll, intact except for a contemptible detail. The jewel in the little golden crown was missing.

* * *

"It was," said Ellery later, over pastrami sandwiches, "a fundamentally simple problem. All great illusions are. A valuable object is placed in full view in the heart of an impenetrable enclosure, it is watched hawkishly by dozens of thoroughly screened and reliable trained persons, it is never out of their view, it is not once touched by human hand or any other agency, and yet, at the expiration of the danger period, it is gone—exchanged for a worthless copy. Wonderful. Amazing. It defies the imagination. Actually, it's susceptible—like all magical hocus-pocus—to immediate solution if only one is able—as I was not—to ignore the wonder and stick to the fact. But then, the wonder is there for precisely that purpose: to stand in the way of the fact.

"What is the fact?" continued Ellery, helping himself to a dill pickle. "The fact is that between the time the doll was placed on the exhibit platform and the time the theft was discovered no one and no thing touched it. Therefore between the time the doll was placed on the platform and the time the theft was discovered *the dauphin could not have been stolen.* It follows, simply and inevitably, that the dauphin must have been stolen *outside that period.*

"Before the period began? No. I placed the authentic dauphin inside the enclosure with my own hands; at or about the beginning of the period, then, no hand but mine had touched the doll—not even, you'll recall, Lieutenant Farber's.

"Then the dauphin must have been stolen after the period closed."

Ellery brandished half the pickle. "And who," he demanded solemnly, "is the only one besides myself who handled that doll after the period closed and before Lieutenant Farber pronounced the diamond to be paste? The only one?"

The Inspector and the Sergeant exchanged puzzled glances, and Nikki looked blank.

"Why, Mr. Bondling," said Nikki, "and he doesn't count."

"He counts very much, Nikki," said Ellery, reaching for the mustard, "because the facts say Bondling stole the dauphin at that time."

"Bondling!" The Inspector paled.

"I don't get it," complained Sergeant Velie.

"Ellery, you must be wrong," said Nikki. "At the time Mr. Bondling grabbed the doll off the platform, the theft had already taken place. It was the worthless copy he picked up."

"That," said Ellery, reaching for another sandwich, "was the focal point of his illusion. How do we know it was the worthless copy he picked up? Why, he said so. Simple, eh? He said so, and like the dumb bunnies we were, we took his unsupported word as gospel."

"That's right!" mumbled his father. "We didn't actually examine the doll till quite a few seconds later."

"Exactly," said Ellery in a munchy voice. "There was a short period of beautiful confusion, as Bondling knew there would be. I yelled to the boys to follow and grab Santa Claus—I mean, the Sergeant here. The detectives were momentarily demoralized. You, Dad, were stunned. Nikki looked as if the roof had fallen in. I essayed an excited explanation. Some detectives ran; others milled around. And while all this was happening—during those few moments when nobody was watching the genuine doll in Bondling's hand because everyone thought it was a fake—Bondling calmly slipped it into one of his greatcoat pockets and from the other produced the worthless copy which he'd been carrying there all day. When I did turn back to him, it was the copy I grabbed from his hand. And his illusion was complete.

"I know," said Ellery dryly. "It's rather on the let-down side. That's why illusionists guard their professional secrets so closely; knowledge is disenchantment. No doubt the incredulous amazement aroused in his periwigged London audience by Comus the French conjuror's dematerialization of his wife from the top of a table would have suffered the same fate if he'd revealed the trap door through which she had dropped. A good trick, like a good woman, is best in the dark. Sergeant, have another pastrami."

"Seems like funny chow to be eating early Christmas morning," said the

Sergeant, reaching. Then he stopped. Then he said, "Bondling," and shook his head.

"Now that we know it was Bondling," said the Inspector, who had recovered a little, "it's a cinch to get that diamond back. He hasn't had time to dispose of it yet. I'll just give downtown a buzz—"

"Wait, Dad," said Ellery.

"Wait for what?"

"Whom are you going to sic the dogs on?"

"What?"

"You're going to call Headquarters, get a warrant, and so on. Who's your man?"

The Inspector felt his head. "Why . . . Bondling, didn't you say?"

"It might be wise," said Ellery, thoughtfully searching with his tongue for a pickle seed, "to specify his alias."

"Alias?" said Nikki. "Does he have one?"

"What alias, son?"

"Comus."

"Comus!"

"Comus?"

"Comus."

"Oh, come off it," said Nikki, pouring herself a shot of coffee, straight, for she was in training for the Inspector's Christmas dinner. "How could Bondling be Comus when Bondling was with us all day?—and Comus kept making disguised appearances all over the place . . . that Santa who gave me the note in front of the bank—the old man who kidnapped Lance Morganstern—the fat man with the mustache who snatched Mrs. Rafferty's purse."

"Yeah," said the Sergeant. "How?"

"These illusions die hard," said Ellery. "Wasn't it Comus who phoned a few minutes ago to rag me about the theft? Wasn't it Comus who said he'd left the stolen dauphin—minus the diamond—on our doormat? Therefore Comus is Bondling.

"I told you Comus never does anything without a good reason," said Ellery. "Why did 'Comus' announce to 'Bondling' that he was *going* to steal the Dauphin's Doll? Bondling told us that—putting the finger on his *alter ego*—because he wanted us to believe he and Comus were separate individuals. He wanted us to watch for *Comus* and take *Bondling* for granted. In tactical execution of this strategy, Bondling provided us with three 'Comus'-appearances during the day—obviously, confederates.

"Yes," said Ellery, "I think, Dad, you'll find on backtracking that the great thief you've been trying to catch for five years has been a respectable estate attorney on Park Row all the time, shedding his quiddities and his quillets at night in favor of the soft shoe and the dark lantern. And now he'll have to exchange them all for a number and a grilled door. Well, well, it couldn't have happened at a more appropriate season; there's an old English proverb that says the Devil makes his Christmas pie of lawyers' tongues. Nikki, pass the pastrami.''

Markheim

by Robert Louis Stevenson

Y ES," said the dealer, "our windfalls are of various kinds. Some customers are ignorant, and then I touch a dividend on my superior knowledge. Some are dishonest," and here he held up the candle, so that the
light fell strongly on his visitor, "and in that case," he continued, "I profit
by my virtue."

Markheim had but just entered from the daylight streets, and his eyes
had not yet grown familiar with the mingled shine and darkness in the
shop. At these pointed words, and before the near presence of the flame, he
blinked painfully and looked aside.

The dealer chuckled. "You come to me on Christmas Day," he resumed
"when you know that I am alone in my house, put up my shutters, and
make a point of refusing business. Well, you will have to pay for that; you
will have to pay for my loss of time, when I should be balancing my books;
you will have to pay, besides, for a kind of manner that I remark in you today very strongly. I am the essence of discretion, and ask no awkward questions; but when a customer cannot look me in the eye, he has to pay for it."

The dealer once more chuckled; and then, changing to his usual business
voice, though still with a note of irony, "You can give, as usual, a clear account of how you came into the possession of the object?" he continued.
"Still your uncle's cabinet? A remarkable collector, sir!"

And the little pale, round-shouldered dealer stood almost on tip-toe,
looking over the top of his gold spectacles, and nodding his head with every
mark of disbelief. Markheim returned his gaze with one of infinite pity, and
a touch of horror.

"This time," said he, "you are in error. I have not come to sell, but to
buy. I have no curios to dispose of; my uncle's cabinet is bare to the
wainscot; even were it still intact, I have done well on the Stock Exchange,
and should more likely add to it than otherwise, and my errand to-day is
simplicity itself. I seek a Christmas present for a lady," he continued, wax-
ing more fluent as he struck into the speech he had prepared; "and certainly
I owe you every excuse for thus disturbing you upon so small a matter. But
the thing was neglected yesterday; I must produce my little compliment at

dinner; and, as you very well know, a rich marriage is not a thing to be neglected.''

There followed a pause, during which the dealer seemed to weigh this statement incredulously. The ticking of many clocks among the curious lumber of the shop, and the faint rushing of the cabs in a near thoroughfare, filled up the interval of silence.

"Well, sir," said the dealer, "be it so. You are an old customer after all; and if, as you say, you have the chance of a good marriage, far be it from me to be an obstacle. Here is a nice thing for a lady now," he went on, "this hand glass—fifteenth century, warranted; comes from a good collection, too; but I reserve the name, in the interests of my customer, who was just like yourself, my dear sir, the nephew and sole heir of a remarkable collector.''

The dealer, while he thus ran on in his dry and biting voice, had stopped to take the object from its place; and, as he had done so, a shock had passed through Markheim, a start both of hand and foot, a sudden leap of many tumultuous passions to the face. It passed as swiftly as it came, and left no trace beyond a certain trembling of the hand that now received the glass.

"A glass," he said hoarsely, and then paused, and repeated it more clearly. "A glass? For Christmas? Surely not?''

"And why not?" cried the dealer. "Why not a glass?''

Markheim was looking upon him with an indefinable expression. "You ask me why not?" he said. "Why, look here—look in it—look at yourself! Do you like to see it? No! nor—nor any man.''

The little man had jumped back when Markheim had so suddenly confronted him with the mirror; but now, perceiving there was nothing worse on hand, he chuckled. "Your future lady, sir, must be pretty hard-favoured," said he.

"I ask you," said Markheim, "for a Christmas present, and you give me this—this damned reminder of years, and sins and follies—this hand-conscience? Did you mean it? Had you a thought in your mind? Tell me. It will be better for you if you do. Come, tell me about yourself. I hazard a guess now, that you are in secret a very charitable man?''

The dealer looked closely at his companion. It was very odd, Markheim did not appear to be laughing; there was something in his face like an eager sparkle of hope, but nothing of mirth.

"What are you driving at?" the dealer asked.

"Not charitable?" returned the other gloomily. "Not charitable; not pious; not scrupulous; unloving, unbeloved; a hand to get money, a safe to keep it. Is that all? Dear God, man, is that all?''

"I will tell you what it is," began the dealer, with some sharpness, and then broke off again into a chuckle. "But I see this is a love match of yours, and you have been drinking the lady's health.''

[286]

"Ah!" cried Markheim, with a strange curiosity. "Ah, have you been in love? Tell me about that."

"I," cried the dealer. "I in love! I never had the time, nor have I the time to-day for all this nonsense. Will you take the glass?"

"Where is the hurry?" returned Markheim. "It is very pleasant to stand here talking; and life is so short and insecure that I would not hurry away from any pleasure—no, not even from so mild a one as this. We should rather cling, cling to what little we can get, like a man at a cliff's edge. Every second is a cliff, if you think upon it—a cliff a mile high—high enough, if we fall, to dash us out of every feature of humanity. Hence it is best to talk pleasantly. Let us talk of each other: why should we wear this mask? Let us be confidential. Who knows, we might become friends?"

"I have just one word to say to you," said the dealer. "Either make your purchase, or walk out of my shop!"

"True, true," said Markheim. "Enough fooling. To business. Show me something else."

The dealer stooped once more, this time to replace the glass upon the shelf, his thin blond hair falling over his eyes as he did so. Markheim moved a little nearer, with one hand in the pocket of his greatcoat; he drew himself up and filled his lungs; at the same time many different emotions were depicted together on his face—terror, horror, and resolve, fascination and a physical repulsion; and through a haggard lift of his upper lip, his teeth looked out.

"This, perhaps, may suit," observed the dealer: and then, as he began to re-arise, Markheim bounded from behind upon his victim. The long, skewerlike dagger flashed and fell. The dealer struggled like a hen, striking his temple on the shelf, and then tumbled on the floor in a heap.

Time had some score of small voices in that shop, some stately and slow as was becoming to their great age; others garrulous and hurried. All these told out the seconds in an intricate chorus of tickings. Then the passage of a lad's feet, heavily running on the pavement, broke in upon these smaller voices and startled Markheim into the consciousness of his surroundings.

He looked about him awfully. The candle stood on the counter, its flame solemnly wagging in a draught; and by that inconsiderable movement, the whole room was filled with noiseless bustle and kept heaving like a sea: the tall shadows nodding, the gross blots of darkness swelling and dwindling as with respiration, the faces of the portraits and the china gods changing and wavering like images in water. The inner door stood ajar, and peered into that leaguer of shadows with a long slit of daylight like a pointing finger.

From these fear-stricken rovings, Markheim's eyes returned to the body of his victim, where it lay both humped and sprawling, incredibly small and strangely meaner than in life. In these poor, miserly clothes, in that ungainly attitude, the dealer lay like so much sawdust. Markheim had feared to see it, and, lo! it was nothing. And yet, as he gazed, this bundle of old clothes and pool of blood began to find eloquent voices. There it must lie; there was none to work the cunning hinges or direct the miracle of loco-motion—there it must lie till it was found. Found! ay, and then? Then would this dead flesh lift up a cry that would ring over England, and fill the world with the echoes of pursuit. Ay, dead or not, this was still the enemy.

"Time was that when the brains were out," he thought; and the first word struck into his mind. Time, now that the deed was accom-plished—time, which had closed for the victim, had become instant and momentous for the slayer.

The thought was yet in his mind, when, first one and then another, with every variety of pace and voice—one deep as the bell from a cathedral tur-ret, another ringing on its treble notes the prelude of a waltz—the clocks began to strike the hour of three in the afternoon.

The sudden outbreak of so many tongues in that dumb chamber stag-gered him. He began to bestir himself, going to and fro with the candle, beleaguered by moving shadows, and startled to the soul by chance reflec-tions. In many rich mirrors, some of home designs, some from Venice or Amsterdam, he saw his face repeated and repeated, as it were an army of spies; his own eyes met and detected him; and the sound of his own steps, lightly as they fell, vexed the surrounding quiet.

And still, as he continued to fill his pockets, his mind accused him with a sickening iteration, of the thousand faults of his design. He should have chosen a more quiet hour; he should have prepared an alibi; he should not have used a knife; he should have been more cautious, and only bound and gagged the dealer, and not killed him; he should have been more bold, and killed the servant also; he should have done all things otherwise—poignant regrets, weary, incessant toiling of the mind to change what was un-changeable, to plan what was now useless, to be the architect of the ir-revocable past.

Meanwhile, and behind all this activity, brute terrors, like the scurrying of rats in a deserted attic, filled the more remote chambers of his brain with riot; the hand of the constable would fall heavy on his shoulder, and his nerves would jerk like a hooked fish; or he beheld, in galloping defile, the dock, the prison, the gallows, and the black coffin.

Terror of the people in the street sat down before his mind like a besieg-ing army. It was impossible, he thought, but that some rumour of the struggle must have reached their ears and set on edge their curiosity; and now, in all the neighbouring houses, he divined them sitting motionless and with uplifted ear—solitary people, condemned to spend Christmas dwell-ing alone on memories of the past, and now startingly recalled from that tender exercise; happy family parties, struck into silence round the table, the mother still with raised finger: every degree and age and humour, but all, by their own hearths, prying and hearkening and weaving the rope that was to hang him.

Sometimes it seemed to him he could not move too softly; the clink of the tall Bohemian goblets rang out loudly like a bell; and alarmed by the bigness of the ticking, he was tempted to stop the clocks. And then, again, with a swift transition of his terrors, the very silence of the place appeared a source of peril, and a thing to strike and freeze the passer-by; and he would step more boldly, and bustle aloud among the contents of the shop, and imitate, with elaborate bravado, the movements of a busy man at ease in his own house.

But he was now so pulled about by different alarms that, while one portion of his mind was still alert and cunning, another trembled on the brink of lunacy. One hallucination in particular took a strong hold on his credulity. The neighbour hearkening with white face beside his window, the passer-by arrested by a horrible surmise on the pavement—these could at worst suspect, they could not know; through the brick walls and shuttered windows only sounds could penetrate.

But here, within the house, was he alone? He knew he was; he had watched the servant set forth sweet-hearting, in her poor best, "out for the day" written in every ribbon and smile. Yes, he was alone, of course; and yet, in the bulk of empty house above him, he could surely hear a stir of delicate footing—he was surely conscious, inexplicably conscious of some presence. Ay, surely; to every room and corner of the house his imagination followed it; and now it was a faceless thing, and yet had eyes to see with; and again it was a shadow of himself; and yet again behold the image of the dead dealer, reinspired with cunning and hatred.

At times, with a strong effort, he would glance at the open door which still seemed to repel his eyes. The house was tall, the skylight small and dirty, the day blind with fog; and the light that filtered down to the ground story was exceedingly faint, and showed dimly on the threshold of the shop. And yet, in that strip of doubtful brightness, did there not hang wavering a shadow?

Suddenly, from the street outside, a very jovial gentleman began to beat with a staff on the shop-door, accompanying his blows with shouts and railleries in which the dealer was continually called upon by name. Markheim, smitten into ice, glanced at the dead man. But no! he lay quite still; he was fled away far beyond earshot of these blows and shoutings; he was sunk beneath seas of silence; and his name, which would once have caught his notice above the howling of a storm, had become an empty sound. And presently the jovial gentleman desisted from his knocking and departed.

Here was a broad hint to hurry what remained to be done, to get forth from this accusing neighbourhood, to plunge into a bath of London multitudes, and to reach, on the other side of day, that haven of safety and apparent innocence—his bed. One visitor had come; at any moment another might follow and be more obstinate. To have done the deed, and yet not to reap the profit, would be too abhorrent a failure. The money, that was now Markheim's concern; and as a means to that, the keys.

He glanced over his shoulder at the open door, where the shadow was still lingering and shivering; and with no conscious repugnance of the mind, yet with a tremor of the belly, he drew near the body of his victim. The human character had quite departed. Like a suit half-stuffed with bran, the limbs lay scattered, the trunk doubled, on the floor; and yet the thing repelled him. Although so dingy and inconsiderable to the eye, he feared it might have more significance to the touch.

He took the body by the shoulders, and turned it on its back. It was strangely light and supple, and the limbs, as if they had been broken, fell into the oddest postures. The face was robbed of all expression; but it was as pale as wax, and shockingly smeared with blood about one temple. That was, for Markheim, the one displeasing circumstance. It carried him back, upon the instant, to a certain fair-day in a fishers' village: a gray day, a piping wind, a crowd upon the street, the blare of the brasses, the booming of drums, the nasal voice of a ballad singer; and a boy going to and fro, buried over head in the crowd and divided between interest and fear, until, coming out upon the chief place of concourse, he beheld a booth and a great screen with pictures, dismally designed, garishly coloured: Brownrigg with her apprentice; the Mannings with their murdered guest; Weare in the death-grip of Thurtell; and a score besides of famous crimes.

The thing was as clear as an illusion; he was once again that little boy; he was looking once again, and with the same sense of physical revolt, at these vile pictures; he was still stunned by the thumping of the drums. A bar of that day's music returned upon his memory; and at that, for the first time, a qualm came over him, a breath of nausea, a sudden weakness of the joints, which he must instantly resist and conquer.

He judged it more prudent to confront than to flee from these considerations; looking the more hardily in the dead face, bending his mind to realise the nature and greatness of his crime. So little a while ago that face had moved with every change of sentiment, that pale mouth had spoken, that body had been on fire with governable energies; and now, by his act, that piece of life had been arrested, as the horologist, with interjected finger, arrests the beating of the clock. So he reasoned in vain; he could rise to no more remorseful consciousness; the same heart which had shuddered before the painted effigies of crime, looked on its reality unmoved. At best, he felt a gleam of pity for one who had been endowed in vain with all those faculties that can make the world a garden of enchantment, one who had never lived and who was now dead. But of penitence, no, not a tremor.

With that, shaking himself clear of these considerations, he found the keys and advanced towards the open door of the shop. Outside, it had begun to rain smartly; and the sound of the shower upon the roof had banished silence. Like some dripping cavern, the chambers of the house were haunted by an incessant echoing, which filled the ear and mingled with the ticking of the clocks. And, as Markheim approached the door, he seemed to hear, in answer to his own cautious tread, the steps of another foot withdrawing up the stair. The shadow still palpitated loosely on the threshold. He threw a ton's weight of resolve upon his muscles, and drew back the door.

The faint, foggy daylight glimmered dimly on the bare floor and stairs; on the bright suit of armour posted, halberd in hand, upon the landing; and on the dark wood-carvings, and framed pictures that hung against the yellow panels of the wainscot. So loud was the beating of the rain through all the house that, in Markheim's ears, it began to be distinguished into many different sounds. Footsteps and sighs, the tread of regiments marching in the distance, the chink of money in the counting, and the creaking of doors held stealthily ajar, appeared to mingle with the patter of the drops upon the cupola and the gushing of the water in the pipes.

The sense that he was not alone grew upon him to the verge of madness. On every side he was haunted and begirt by presences. He heard them moving in the upper chambers; from the shop, he heard the dead man getting to his legs; and as he began with a great effort to mount the stairs, feet fled quietly before him and followed stealthily behind. If he were but deaf, he thought, how tranquilly he would possess his soul! And then again, and hearkening with ever fresh attention, he blessed himself for that unresting sense which held the outposts and stood a trusty sentinel upon his life. His head turned continually on his neck; his eyes, which seemed starting from their orbits, scouted on every side, and on every side were half-rewarded as with the tail of something nameless vanishing. The four-and-twenty steps to the first floor were four-and-twenty agonies.

On that first story, the doors stood ajar, three of them like three ambushes, shaking his nerves like the throats of cannon. He could never again, he felt, be sufficiently immured and fortified from men's observing eyes; he longed to be home, girt in by walls, buried among bedclothes, and invisible to all but God. And at that thought he wondered a little, recollecting tales of other murderers and the fear they were said to entertain of heavenly avengers. It was not so, at least, with him. He feared the laws of nature, lest, in their callous and immutable procedure, they should preserve some damning evidence of his crime. He feared tenfold more, with a slavish, superstitious terror, some scission in the continuity of man's experience, some wilful illegality of nature. He played a game of skill, depending on the rules, calculating consequence from cause; and what if nature, as the defeated tyrant overthrew the chessboard, should break the mould of their succession?

The like had befallen Napoleon (so writers said) when the winter changed the time of its appearance. The like might befall Markheim: the solid walls might become transparent and reveal his doings like those of bees in a glass hive; the stout planks might yield under his foot like quicksands and detain him in their clutch; ay, and there were soberer accidents that might destroy him: if, for instance, the house should fall and imprison him beside the body of his victim; or the house next door should fly on fire, and the firemen invade him from all sides. These things he feared; and, in a sense, these things might be called the hands of God reached forth against sin. But about God Himself he was at ease; his act was doubtless exceptional, but so were his excuses, which God knew; it was there, and not among men, that he felt sure of justice.

When he had got safe into the drawing-room, and shut the door behind him, he was aware of a respite from alarms. The room was quite dismantled, uncarpeted besides, and strews with packing cases and incongruous furniture; several great pier-glasses, in which he beheld himself at various angles, like an actor on a stage; many pictures, framed and unframed, standing with their faces to the wall, a fine Sheraton sideboard, a cabinet of marquetry, and a great old bed, with tapestry hangings. The windows opened to the floors; but by great good fortune the lower part of the shutters had been closed, and this concealed him from the neighbours. Here, then, Markheim drew in a packing case before the cabinet, and began to search among the keys.

It was a long business, for there were many; and it was irksome, besides; for after all there might be nothing in the cabinet, and time was on the wing. But the closeness of the occupation sobered him. With the tail of his eye he saw the door—even glanced at it from time to time directly, like a besieged commander pleased to verify the good estate of his defences. But in truth he was at peace. The rain falling in the street sounded natural and pleasant. Presently, on the other side, the notes of a piano were wakened to the music of a hymn, and the voices of many children took up the air and words. How stately, how comfortable was the melody! How fresh the youthful voices!

Markheim gave ear to it smilingly, as he sorted out the keys; and his mind was thronged with answerable ideas and images; church-going children and the pealing of the high organ; children afield, bathers by the brookside, ramblers on the brambly common, kite-flyers in the windy and cloud-navigated sky; and then, at another cadence of the hymn, back again to church, and the somnolence of summer Sundays, and the high genteel voice of the parson (which he smiled a little to recall) and the painted Jacobean tombs, and the dim lettering of the Ten Commandments in the chancel.

And as he sat thus, at once busy and absent, he was startled to his feet. A flash of ice, a flash of fire, a bursting gush of blood, went over him, and then he stood transfixxed and thrilling. A step mounted the stair slowly and steadily and presently a hand was laid upon the knob, and the lock clicked, and the door opened.

Fear held Markheim in a vice. What to expect he knew not, whether the dead man walking, or the official ministers of human justice, or some chance witness blindly stumbling in to consign him to the gallows. But when a face thrust into the aperture, glanced round the room, looked at him, nodded and smiled as if in friendly recognition, and then withdrew again, and the door closed behind it, his fear broke loose from his control in a hoarse cry. At the sound of this the visitant returned.

"Did you call me?" he asked pleasantly, and with that he entered the room and closed the door behind him.

Markheim stood and gazed at him with all his eyes. Perhaps there was a film upon his sight, but the outlines of the newcomer seemed to change and waver like those of the idols in the wavering candlelight of the shop; and at times he thought he knew him; and at times he thought he bore a likeness to himself; and always, like a lump of living terror, there lay in his bosom the conviction that this thing was not of the earth and not of God.

And yet the creature had a strange air of the commonplace, as he stood looking on Markheim with a smile; and when he added: "You are looking for the money, I believe?" it was in the tones of everyday politeness.

Markheim made no answer.

"I should warn you," resumed the other, "that the maid has left her sweetheart earlier than usual and will soon be here. If Mr. Markheim be found in this house, I need not describe to him the consequences."

"You know me?" cried the murderer.

The visitor smiled. "You have long been a favourite of mine," he said; "and I have long observed and often sought to help you."

"What are you?" cried Markheim; "the devil?"

"What I may be," returned the other, "cannot affect the service I propose to render you."

"It can," cried Markheim; "it does! Be helped by you? No, never; not by you! You do not know me yet; thank God, you do not know me!"

"I know you," replied the visitant, with a sort of kind severity or rather firmness. "I know you to the soul."

"Know me!" cried Markheim. "Who can do so? My life is but a travesty and slander on myself. I have lived to belie my nature. All men do, all men are better than this disguise that grows about and stifles them. You see each dragged away by life, like one whom bravos have seized and muffled in a cloak. If they had their own control—if you could see their faces, they would be altogether different, they would shine out for heroes and saints! I am worse than most; myself is more overlaid; my excuse is known to men and God. But, had I the time, I could disclose myself.''

"To me?'' inquired the visitant.

"To you before all,'' returned the murderer. "I supposed you were intelligent. I thought—since you exist—you could prove a reader of the heart. And yet you would propose to judge me by my acts! I was born and I have lived in a land of giants; giants have dragged me by the wrists since I was born out of my mother—the giants of circumstance. And you would judge me by my acts! But can you not look within? Can you not see within me the clear writing of conscience, never blurred by any willful sophistry, although too often disregarded? Can you not read me for a thing that surely must be common as humanity—the unwilling sinner?''

"All this is very feelingly expressed,'' was the reply, "but it regards me not. These points of consistency are beyond my province, and I care not in the least by what compulsion you may have been dragged away, so as you are but carried in the right direction. But time flies; the servant delays, looking in the faces of the crowd and at the pictures on the hoardings, but still she keeps moving nearer; and remember, it is as if the gallows itself was striding towards you through the Christmas streets! Shall I help you; I, who know all? Shall I tell you where to find the money?''

"For what price?'' asked Markheim.

"I offer you the service for a Christmas gift,'' returned the other.

Markheim could not refrain from smiling with a kind of bitter triumph. "No,'' said he, "I will take nothing at your hands; if I were dying of thirst, and it was your hand that put the pitcher to my lips, I should find the courage to refuse. It may be credulous, but I will do nothing to commit myself to evil.''

"I have no objection to a deathbed repentance,'' observed the visitant.

"Because you disbelieve their efficacy!'' Markheim cried.

"I do not say so,'' returned the other; "but I look on these things from a different side, and when the life is done my interest falls. The man has lived to serve me, to spread black looks under colour of religion, or to sow tares in the wheatfield, as you do, in a course of weak compliance with desire. Now that he draws so near to his deliverence, he can add but one act of service—to repent, to die smiling, and thus to build up in confidence and hope the more timorous of my surviving followers. I am not so hard a master. Try me. Accept my help. Please yourself in life as you have done hitherto;

[294]

please yourself more amply, spread your elbows at the board; and when the night begins to fall and the curtains to be drawn, I tell you, for your greater comfort, that you will find it even easy to compound your quarrel with your conscience, and to make a truckling peace with God. I came but now from such a deathbed, and the room was full of sincere mourners, listening to the man's last words; and when I looked into that face, which had been set as a flint against mercy, I found it smiling with hope.''

"And do you, then, suppose me such a creature?'' asked Markheim. "Do you think I have no more generous aspirations than to sin, and sin, and sin, and, at the last, sneak into heaven? My heart rises at the thought. Is this, then, your experience of mankind? Or is it because you find me with red hands that you presume such baseness? And is this crime of murder indeed so impious as to dry up the very springs of good?''

"Murder is to me no special category,'' replied the other. "All sins are murder, even as all life is war. I behold your race, like starving mariners on a raft, plucking crusts out of the hands of famine and feeding on each other's lives. I follow sins beyond the moment of their acting; I find in all that the last consequence is death; and to my eyes, the pretty maid who thwarts her mother with such taking graces on a question of a ball, drips no less visibly with human gore than such a murderer as yourself. Do I say that I follow sins? I follow virtues also; they differ not by the thickness of a nail, they are both scythes for the reaping angel of Death. Evil, for which I live, consists not in action but in character. The bad man is dear to me; not the bad act, whose fruits, if we could follow them far enough down the hurtling cataract of the ages, might yet be found more blessed than those of the rarest virtues. And it is not because you have killed a dealer, but because you are Markheim, that I offer to forward your escape.''

"I will lay my heart open to you,'' answered Markheim. "This crime on which you find me is my last. On my way to it I have learned many lessons; itself is a lesson, a momentous lesson. Hitherto I have been driven with revolt to what I would not; I was a bond-slave to poverty, driven and scourged. There are robust virtues that can stand in these temptations; mine are not so: I had a thirst of pleasure. But to-day, and out of this deed, I pluck both warning and riches—both the power and a fresh resolve to be myself. I become in all things a free actor in the world; I begin to see myself all changed, hands the agents of good, this heart at peace. Something comes over me out of the past; something of what I have dreamed on Sabbath evenings to the sound of the church organ, of what I forecast when I shed tears over noble books, or talked, an innocent child, with my mother. There lies my life; I have wandered a few years, but now I see once more my city of destination.''

"You are to use this money on the Stock Exchange, I think?'' remarked the visitor; "and there, if I mistake not, you have already lost some thousands?"

"Ah," said Markheim, "but this time I have a sure thing."

"This time, again, you will lose," replied the visitor quietly.

"Ah, but I keep back the half!" cried Markheim.

"That also you will lose," said the other.

The sweat started upon Markheim's brow. "Well, then, what matter?" he exclaimed. "Say it be lost, say I am plunged again in poverty, shall one part of me, and that the worst, continue until the end to override the better? Evil and good run strong in me, haling me both ways. I do not love the one thing, I love all. I can conceive great deeds, renunciations, martyrdoms; and though I be fallen to such a crime as murder, pity is no stranger to my thoughts. I pity the poor; who knows their trials better than myself? I pity and help them; I prize love, I love honest laughter; there is no good thing nor true thing on earth but I love it from my heart. And are my vices only to direct my life, and my virtues without effect, like some passive lumber of the mind? Not so; good, also, is a spring of acts."

But the visitant raised his finger. "For six-and-thirty years that you have been in this world," said he, "through many changes of fortune and varieties of humour, I have watched you steadily fall. Fifteen years ago you would have started at a theft. Three years back you would have blanched at the name of murder. Is there any crime, is there any cruelty or meanness, from which you still recoil?—five years from now I shall detect you in the fact! Downward, downward, lies your way; nor can anything but death avail to stop you."

"It is true," Markheim said huskily, "I have in some degree complied with evil. But it is so with all; the very saints, in the mere exercise of living, grow less dainty, and take on the tone of their surroundings."

"I will propound to you one simple question," said the other; "and as you answer, I shall read to you your moral horoscope. You have grown in many things more lax; possibly you do right to be so; and at any account, it is the same with all men. But granting that, are you in any one particular, however trifling, more difficult to please with your own conduct, or do you go in all things with a looser rein?"

"In any one?" repeated Markheim, with an anguish of consideration. "No," he added, with despair, "in none! I have gone down in all."

"Then," said the visitor, "content yourself with what you are, for you will never change; and the words of your part on this stage are irrevocably written down."

Markheim stood for a long while silent, and indeed it was the visitor who first broke the silence. "That being so," he said, "shall I show you the money?"

"And grace?" cried Markheim.

"Have you not tried it?" returned the other. "Two or three years ago did I not see you on the platform of revival meetings, and was not your voice the loudest in the hymn?"

"It is true," said Markheim; "and I see clearly what remains for me by way of duty. I thank you for these lessons from my soul; my eyes are opened, and I behold myself at last for what I am."

At this moment, the sharp note of the door-bell rang through the house; and the visitant, as though this were some concerted signal for which he had been waiting, changed at once in his demeanour.

"The maid!" he cried. "She has returned, as I forewarned you, and there is now before you one more difficult passage. Her master, you must say, is ill; you must let her in, with an assured but rather serious counte-nance—no smiles, no over-acting, and I promise you success! Once the girl within, and the door closed, the same dexterity that has already rid you of the dealer will relieve you of this last danger in your path. Thenceforward you have the whole evening—the whole night, if needful—to ransack the treasures of the house and to make good your safety. This is help that comes to you with the mask of danger. Up!" he cried; "up, friend; your life hangs trembling in the scales: up, and act!"

Markheim steadily regarded his counsellor. "If I be condemned to evil acts," he said, "there is still one door of freedom open—I can cease from action. If my life be an ill thing, I can lay it down. Though I be, as you say truly, at the beck of every small temptation, I can yet, by one decisive ges-ture, place myself beyond the reach of all. My love of good is damned to barrenness; it may, and let it be! But I have still my hatred of evil; and from that, to your galling disappointment, you shall see that I can draw both energy and courage."

The features of the visitor began to undergo a wonderful and lovely change: they brightened and softened with a tender triumph, and, even as they brightened, faded and dislimned. But Markheim did not pause to watch or understand the transformation. He opened the door and went downstairs very slowly, thinking to himself. His past went soberly before him; he beheld it as it was, ugly and strenuous like a dream, random as chance-medley—a scene of defeat. Life, as he thus reviewed it, tempted him no longer; but on the farther side he perceived a quiet haven for his bark.

He paused in the passage, and looked into the shop, where the candle still burned by the dead body. It was strangely silent. Thoughts of the dealer swarmed into his mind, as he stood gazing. And then the bell once more broke out into impatient clamour.

He confronted the maid upon the threshold with something like a smile.

"You had better go for the police," said he. "I have killed your master."

"Look, Daddy — the first robin!"

★

The Necklace of Pearls

by Dorothy L. Sayers

SIR SEPTIMUS SHALE was accustomed to assert his authority once in the year and once only. He allowed his young and fashionable wife to fill his house with diagrammatic furniture made of steel; to collect advanced artists and anti-grammatical poets; to believe in cocktails and relativity and to dress as extravagantly as she pleased; but he did insist on an old-fashioned Christmas. He was a simple-hearted man, who really liked plum-pudding and cracker mottoes, and he could not get it out of his head that other people, "at bottom," enjoyed these things also. At Christmas, there-fore, he firmly retired to his country house in Essex, called in the servants to hang holly and mistletoe upon the cubist electric fittings; loaded the steel sideboard with delicacies from Fortnum & Mason; hung up stockings at the heads of the polished walnut bedsteads; and even, on this occasion only, had the electric radiators removed from the modernist grates and installed wood fires and a Yule log. He then gathered his family and friends about him, filled them with as much Dickensian good fare as he could persuade them to swallow, and, after their Christmas dinner, set them down to play "Charades" and "Clumps" and "Animal, Vegetable, and Mineral" in the drawing-room, concluding these diversions by "Hide-and-Seek" in the dark all over the house. Because Sir Septimus was a very rich man, his guests fell in with this invariable programme, and if they were bored, they did not tell him so.

Another charming and traditional custom which he followed was that of presenting to his daughter Margharita a pearl on each successive birthday —this anniversary happening to coincide with Christmas Eve. The pearls now numbered twenty, and the collection was beginning to enjoy a certain celebrity, and had been photographed in the Society papers. Though not sensationally large—each one being about the size of a marrow-fat pea— the pearls were of very great value. They were of exquisite colour and per-fect shape and matched to a hair's-weight. On this particular Christmas Eve, the presentation of the twenty-first pearl had been the occasion of a very special ceremony. There was a dance and there were speeches. On the Christmas night, following, the more restricted family party took place, with the turkey and the Victorian games. There were eleven guests, in addition to Sir Septimus and Lady Shale and their daughter, nearly all related or connected to them in some way: John Shale, a brother, with his wife and their son and daughter Henry and Betty; Betty's fiancé, Oswald Truegood, a young man with parliamentary ambitions; George Comphrey, a cousin of Lady Shale's, aged about thirty and known as a man about town; Lavinia Prescott, asked on George's account; Joyce Trivett, asked on Henry Shale's account; Richard and Beryl Dennison, distant relations of Lady Shale, who lived a gay and expensive life in town on nobody precisely knew what resources; and Lord Peter Wimsey, asked, in a touching spirit of unreasonable hope, on Margharita's account. There were also, of course, William Norgate, secretary to Sir Septimus, and Miss Tomkins, secretary to Lady Shale, who had to be there because, without their calm efficiency, the Christmas arrangements could not have been carried through.

Dinner was over—a seemingly endless succession of soup, fish, turkey, roast beef, plum-pudding, mince-pies, crystallized fruit, nuts, and five kinds of wine, presided over by Sir Septimus, all smiles, by Lady Shale, all mocking deprecation, and by Margharita, pretty and bored, with the necklace of twenty-one pearls gleaming softly on her slender throat. Gorged and dyspeptic and longing only for the horizontal position, the company had been shepherded into the drawing-room and set to play "Musical Chairs" (Miss Tomkins at the piano), "Hunt the Slipper" (slipper provided by Miss Tomkins), and "Dumb Crambo" (costumes by Miss Tomkins and Mr. William Norgate). The back drawing-room (for Sir Septimus clung to these old-fashioned names) provided an admirable dressing-room, being screened by folding doors from the large drawing-room in which the audience sat on aluminum chairs, scrabbling uneasy toes on a floor of black glass under the tremendous illumination of electricity reflected from a brass ceiling.

It was William Norgate who, after taking the temperature of the meeting, suggested to Lady Shale that they should play at something less athletic. Lady Shale agreed and, as usual suggested bridge. Sir Septimus, as usual, blew the suggestion aside.

"Bridge? Nonsense! Nonsense! Play bridge every day of your lives. This is Christmas time. Something we can all play together. How about 'Animal, Vegetable, and Mineral'?"

This intellectual pastime was a favourite with Sir Septimus; he was rather good at putting pregnant questions. After a brief discussion, it became evident that this game was an inevitable part of the programme. The party settled down to it, Sir Septimus undertaking to "go out" first and set the thing going.

Presently they had guessed among other things Miss Tomkins's mother's photograph, a gramophone record of "I want to be happy" (much scientific research into the exact composition of records, settled by William Norgate out of the *Encyclopaedia Britannica*), the smallest stickleback in the stream at the bottom of the garden, the new planet Pluto, the scarf worn by Mrs. Dennison (very confusing, because it was not silk, which would be animal, or artificial silk, which would be vegetable, but made of spun glass—mineral, a very clever choice of subject), and had failed to guess the Prime Minister's wireless speech—which was voted not fair, since nobody could decide whether it was animal by nature or a kind of gas. It was decided that they should do one more word and then go on to "Hide-and-Seek." Oswald Truegood had retired into the back room and shut the door behind him while the party discussed the next subject of examination, when suddenly Sir Septimus broke in on the argument by calling to his daughter:

"Hullo, Margy! What have you done with your necklace?"

"I took it off, Dad, because I thought it might get broken in 'Dumb Crambo.' It's over here on this table. No, it isn't. Did you take it, mother?"

"No, I didn't. If I'd seen it, I should have. You are a careless child."

"I believe you've got it yourself, Dad. You're teasing."

Sir Septimus denied the accusation with some energy. Everybody got up and began to hunt about. There were not many places in that bare and polished room where a necklace could be hidden. After ten minutes' fruitless investigation, Richard Dennison, who had been seated next to the table where the pearls had been placed, began to look rather uncomfortable.

"Awkward, you know," he remarked to Wimsey.

At this moment, Oswald Truegood put his head through the folding-doors and asked whether they hadn't settled on something by now, because he was getting the fidgets.

This directed the attention of the searchers to the inner room. Margharita must have been mistaken. She had taken it in there, and it had got mixed up with the dressing-up clothes somehow. The room was ransacked. Everything was lifted up and shaken. The thing began to look serious. After half an hour of desperate energy it became apparent that the pearls were nowhere to be found.

"They must be somewhere in these two rooms, you know," said Wimsey. "The back drawing-room has no door and nobody could have gone out of the front drawing-room without being seen. Unless the windows—"

No. The windows were all guarded on the outside by heavy shutters which it needed two footmen to take down and replace. The pearls had not gone out that way. In fact, the mere suggestion that they had left the drawing-room at all was disagreeable. Because—because—

[301]

It was William Norgate, efficient as ever, who coldly and boldly, faced the issue.

"I think, Sir Septimus, it would be a relief to the minds of everybody present if we could all be searched."

Sir Septimus was horrified, but the guests, having found a leader, backed up Norgate. The door was locked, and the search was conducted—the ladies in the inner room and the men in the outer.

Nothing resulted from it except some very interesting information about the belongings habitually carried about by the average man and woman. It was natural that Lord Peter Wimsey should possess a pair of forceps, a pocket lens, and a small folding foot-rule—was he not a Sherlock Holmes in high life? But that Oswald Truegood should have two liver-pills in a screw of paper and Henry Shale a pocket edition of *The Odes of Horace* was unexpected. Why did John Shale distend the pockets of his dress-suit with a stump of red sealing-wax, an ugly little mascot, and a five-shilling piece? George Comphrey had a pair of folding scissors, and three wrapped lumps of sugar, of the sort served in restaurants and dining-cars—evidence of a not uncommon form of kleptomania; but that the tidy and exact Norgate should burden himself with a reel of white cotton, three separate lengths of string, and twelve safety-pins on a card seemed really remarkable till one remembered that he had superintended all the Christmas decorations. Richard Dennison, amid some confusion and laughter, was found to cherish a lady's garter, a powder-compact, and half a potato; the last named, he said, was a prophylactic against rheumatism (to which he was subject), while the other objects belonged to his wife. On the ladies' side, the more striking exhibits were a little book on palmistry, three invisible hair-pins, and a baby's photograph (Miss Tomkins); a Chinese trick cigarette-case with a secret compartment (Beryl Dennison); a *very* private letter and an outfit for mending stocking-ladders (Lavinia Prescott); and a pair of eyebrow tweezers and a small packet of white powder, said to be for headaches (Betty Shale). An agitating moment followed the production from Joyce Trivett's handbag of a small string of pearls—but it was promptly remembered that these had come out of one of the crackers at dinner-time, and they were, in fact, synthetic. In short, the search was unproductive of anything beyond a general shamefacedness and the discomfort always produced by undressing and re-dressing in a hurry at the wrong time of day.

It was then that somebody, very grudgingly and haltingly, mentioned the horrid word "Police." Sir Septimus, naturally, was appalled by the idea. It was disgusting. He would not allow it. The pearls must be somewhere. They must search the rooms again. Could not Lord Peter Wimsey, with his experience of—er—mysterious happenings, do something to assist them?

"Eh?" said his lordship. "Oh, by Jove, yes—by all means, certainly. That is to say, provided nobody supposes—eh, what? I mean to say, you don't know that I'm a not a suspicious character, do you, what?"

Lady Shale interposed with authority.

"We don't think *anybody* ought to be suspected," she said, "but, if we did, we'd know it couldn't be you. You know *far* too much about crimes to want to commit one."

"All right," said Wimsey. "But after the way the place has been gone over—" He shrugged his shoulders.

"Yes, I'm afraid you won't be able to find any footprints," said Margharita. "But we may have overlooked something."

Wimsey nodded.

"I'll try. Do you all mind sitting down on your chairs in the outer room and staying there. All except one of you—I'd better have a witness to anything I do or find. Sir Septimus—you'd be the best person, I think."

He shepherded them to their places and began a slow circuit of the two rooms, exploring every surface, gazing up to the polished brazen ceiling, and crawling on hands and knees in the approved fashion across the black and shining desert of the floors. Sir Septimus followed, staring when Wimsey stared, bending with his hands upon his knees when Wimsey crawled, and puffing at intervals with astonishment and chagrin. Their progress rather resembled that of a man taking out a very inquisitive puppy for a very leisurely constitutional. Fortunately, Lady Shale's taste in furnishing made investigation easier; there were scarcely any nooks or corners where anything could be concealed.

They reached the inner drawing-room, and here the dressing-up clothes were again minutely examined, but without result. Finally, Wimsey lay down flat on his stomach to squint under a steel cabinet which was one of the very few pieces of furniture which possessed short legs. Something about it seemed to catch his attention. He rolled up his sleeve and plunged his arm into the cavity, kicked convulsively in the effort to reach farther than was humanly possible, pulled out from his pocket and extended his folding foot-rule, fished with it under the cabinet, and eventually succeeded in extracting what he sought.

It was a very minute object—in fact, a pin. Not an ordinary pin, but one resembling those used by entomologists to impale extremely small moths on the setting-board. It was about three-quarters of an inch in length, as fine as a very fine needle, with a sharp point and a particularly small head.

"Bless my soul!" said Sir Septimus. "What's that?"

"Does anybody here happen to collect moths or beetles or anything?"' asked Wimsey, squatting on his haunches and examining the pin.

[303]

"I'm pretty sure they don't," replied Sir Septimus. "I'll ask them."

"Don't do that." Wimsey bent his head and stared at the floor, from which his own face stared meditatively back at him.

"I see," said Wimsey presently. "That's how it was done. All right, Sir Septimus. I know where the pearls are, but I don't know who took them. Perhaps it would be as well—for everybody's satisfaction—just to find out. In the meantime they are perfectly safe. Don't tell anyone that we've found this pin or that we've discovered anything. Send all these people to bed. Lock the drawing-room door and keep the key, and we'll get our man—or woman—by breakfast-time."

"God bless my soul," said Sir Septimus, very much puzzled.

* * *

Lord Peter Wimsey kept careful watch that night upon the drawing-room door. Nobody, however, came near it. Either the thief suspected a trap or he felt confident that any time would do to recover the pearls. Wimsey, however, did not feel that he was wasting his time. He was making a list of people who had been left alone in the back drawing-room during the playing of "Animal, Vegetable, and Mineral." The list ran as follows:

Sir Septimus Shale
Lavinia Prescott
William Norgate
Joyce Trivett and Henry Shale (together, because they had claimed to be incapable of guessing anything unaided)
Mrs. Dennison
Betty Shale
George Comphrey
Richard Dennison
Miss Tomkins
Oswald Truegood

He also made out a list of the persons to whom pearls might be useful or desirable. Unfortunately, this list agreed in almost all respects with the first (always excepting Sir Septimus) and so was not very helpful. The two secretaries had both come well recommended, but that was exactly what they would have done had they come with ulterior designs; the Dennisons were notorious livers from hand to mouth; Betty Shale carried mysterious white powders in her handbag, and was known to be in with a rather rapid set in town; Henry was a harmless dilettante, but Joyce Trivett could twist him round her little finger and was what Jane Austen liked to call "expensive and dissipated"; Comphrey speculated; Oswald Truegood was rather frequently present at Epsom and Newmarket—the search for motives was only too fatally easy.

When the second housemaid and the under-footman appeared in the passage with household implements, Wimsey abandoned his vigil, but he was down early to breakfast. Sir Septimus with his wife and daughter were down before him, and a certain air of tension made itself felt. Wimsey, standing on the hearth before the fire, made conversation about the weather and politics.

The party assembled gradually, but, as though by common consent, nothing was said about pearls until after breakfast, when Oswald Truegood took the bull by the horns.

"Well now!" said he. "How's the detective getting along? Got your man, Wimsey?"

"Not yet," said Wimsey easily.

Sir Septimus, looking at Wimsey as though for his cue, cleared his throat and dashed into speech.

"All very tiresome," he said, "all very unpleasant. Hr'rm. Nothing for it but the police, I'm afraid. Just at Christmas, too. Hr'rm. Spoilt the party. Can't stand seeing all this stuff about the place." He waved his hand towards the festoons of evergreens and coloured paper that adorned the walls. "Take it all down, eh, what? No heart in it. Hr'rm. Burn the lot."

"What a pity, when we worked so hard over it," said Joyce.

"Oh, leave it, Uncle," said Henry Shale. "You're bothering too much about the pearls. They're sure to turn up."

"Shall I ring for James?" suggested William Norgate.

"No," interrupted Comphrey, "let's do it ourselves. It'll give us something to do and take our minds off our troubles."

"That's right," said Sir Septimus. "Start right away. Hate the sight of it."

He savagely hauled a great branch of holly down from the mantelpiece and flung it, crackling, into the fire.

"That's the stuff," said Richard Dennison. "Make a good old blaze!" He leapt up from the table and snatched the mistletoe from the chandelier. "Here goes! One more kiss for somebody before it's too late."

"Isn't it unlucky to take it down before the New Year?" suggested Miss Tomkins.

"Unlucky be hanged. We'll have it all down. Off the stairs and out of the drawing-room too. Somebody go and collect it."

"Isn't the drawing-room locked?" asked Oswald.

"No. Lord Peter says the pearls aren't there, wherever else they are, so it's unlocked. That's right, isn't it, Wimsey?"

"Quite right. The pearls were taken out of these rooms. I can't tell yet how, but I'm positive of it. In fact, I'll pledge my reputation that wherever they are, they're not up there.''

"Oh, well," said Comphrey, "in that case, have at it! Come along, Lavinia—you and Dennison do the drawing-room and I'll do the back room. We'll save a race."

"But if the police are coming in," said Dennison, "oughtn't everything to be left just as it is?"

"Damn the police!" shouted Sir Septimus. "They don't want evergreens."

Oswald and Margharita were already pulling the holly and ivy from the staircase, amid peals of laughter. The party dispersed. Wimsey went quietly upstairs and into the drawing-room, where the work of demolition was taking place at a great rate, George having bet the other two ten shillings to a tanner that they would not finish their part of the job before he finished his.

"You mustn't help," said Lavinia, laughing to Wimsey. "It wouldn't be fair."

Wimsey said nothing, but waited till the room was clear. Then he followed them down again to the hall, spluttering, suggestive of Guy Fawkes' night. He whispered to Sir Septimus, who went forward and touched George Comphrey on the shoulder.

"Lord Peter wants to say something to you, my boy," he said.

Comphrey started and went with him a little reluctantly, as it seemed. He was not looking very well.

"Mr. Comphrey," said Wimsey, "I fancy these are some of your property." He held out the palm of his hand, in which rested twenty-two fine, small-headed pins.

*   *   *

"Ingenious," said Wimsey, "but something less ingenious would have served his turn better. It was very unlucky, Sir Septimus, that you should have mentioned the pearls when you did. Of course, he hoped that the loss wouldn't be discovered till we'd chucked guessing games and taken to "Hide-and-Seek." The pearls might have been anywhere in the house, we shouldn't have locked the drawing-room door, and he could have recovered them at his leisure. He had had this possibility in mind when he came here, obviously, and that was why he brought the pins, and Miss Shale's taking off the necklace to play "Dumb Crambo" gave him his opportunity.

"He had spent Christmas here before, and knew perfectly well that 'Animal, Vegetable, and Mineral' would form part of the entertainment. He had only to gather up the necklace from the table when it came to his

turn to retire, and he knew he could count on at least five minutes by himself while we were all arguing about the choice of a word. He had only to
snip the pearls from the string with his pocket-scissors, burn the string in
the grate, fasten the pearls to the mistletoe with the fine pins. The mistletoe
was hung on the chandelier, pretty high—it's a lofty room—but he could
easily reach it by standing on the glass table, which wouldn't show foot-
marks, and it was almost certain that nobody would think of examining the
mistletoe for extra berries. I shouldn't have thought of it myself if I hadn't
found that pin which he had dropped. That gave me the idea that the pearls
had been separated and the rest was easy. I took the pearls off the mistletoe
last night—the clasp was there, too, pinned among the holly-leaves. Here
they are. Comphrey must have got a nasty shock this morning. I knew he
was our man when he suggested that the guests should tackle the decorations themselves and that he should do the back drawing-room—but I wish
I had seen his face when he came to the mistletoe and found the pearls
gone.''

"And you worked it all out when you found the pin?'' said Sir Septimus.

"Yes; I knew then where the pearls had gone to.''

"But you never even looked at the mistletoe.''

"I saw it reflected in the black glass floor, and it struck me then how
much mistletoe berries looked like pearls.''

"Straight ahead, Bernie, dear."

Blind Man's Hood
by *Carter Dickson*

ALTHOUGH one snowflake had already sifted past the lights, the great doors of the house stood open. It seemed less a snowflake than a shadow; for a bitter wind whipped after it, and the doors creaked. Inside, Rodney and Muriel Hunter could see a dingy narrow hall paved in dull red tiles, with a Jacobean staircase at the rear. (At that time, of course, there was no dead woman lying inside.)

To find such a place in the loneliest part of the Weald of Kent—a seventeenth-century country house whose floors had grown humped and its beams scrubbed by the years—was what they had expected. Even to find electricity was not surprising. But Rodney Hunter thought he had seldom seen so many lights in one house, and Muriel had been wondering about it ever since their car turned the bend in the road. "Clearlawns" lived up to its name. It stood in the midst of a slope of flat grass, now wiry white with frost, and there was no tree or shrub within twenty yards of it. Those lights contrasted with a certain inhospitable and damp air about the house, as though the owner were compelled to keep them burning.

"But why is the front door *open?*" insisted Muriel.

In the drive-way, the engine of their car coughed and died. The house was now a secret blackness of gables, emitting light at every chink, and silhouetting the stalks of the wistaria vines which climbed it. On either side of the front door were little-paned windows whose curtains had not been drawn. Towards their left they could see into a low dining-room, with table and sideboard set for a cold supper; towards their right was a darkish library moving with the reflections of a bright fire.

The sight of the fire warmed Rodney Hunter, but it made him feel guilty. They were very late. At five o'clock, without fail, he had promised Jack Bannister, they would be at "Clearlawns" to inaugurate the Christmas party.

Engine-trouble in leaving London was one thing; idling at a country pub along the way, drinking hot ale and listening to the wireless sing carols until a sort of Dickensian jollity stole into you, was something else. But both he and Muriel were young; they were very fond of each other, and of things in general; and they had worked themselves into a glow of Christmas, which—as they stood before the creaking doors of "Clearlawns"—grew oddly cool.

There was no real reason, Rodney thought, to feel disquiet. He hoisted their luggage, including a big box of presents for Jack and Molly's children, out of the rear of the car. That his footsteps should sound loud on the gravel was only natural. He put his head into the doorway and whistled. Then he began to bang the knocker. Its sound seemed to seek out every corner of the house and then come back like a questing dog; but there was no response.

"I'll tell you something else," he said. "There's nobody in the house."

Muriel ran up the three steps to stand beside him. She had drawn her fur coat close around her, and her face was bright with cold.

"But that's impossible!" she said. "I mean, even if they're out, the servants—! Molly told me she keeps a cook and two maids. Are you sure we've got the right place?"

"Yes. The name's on the gate, and there's no other house within a mile."

With the same impulse they craned their necks to look through the windows of the dining-room on the left. Cold fowl on the sideboard, a great bowl of chestnuts; and, now they could see it, another good fire, before which stood a chair with a piece of knitting put aside on it. Rodney tried the knocker again, vigorously, but the sound was all wrong. It was as though they were even more lonely in that core of light, with the east wind rushing across the Weald, and the door creaking again.

"I suppose we'd better go in," said Rodney. He added, with a lack of Christmas spirit: "Here, this is a devil of a trick! What do you think has happened? I'll swear that fire has been made up in the last fifteen minutes."

He stepped into the hall and set down the bags. As he was turning to close the door, Muriel put her hand on his arm.

"I say, Rod. Do you think you'd better close it?"

"Why not?"

"I—I don't know."

"The place is getting chilly enough as it is," he pointed out, unwilling to admit that the same thought had occurred to him. He closed both doors and shot their bar into place; and, at the same moment, a girl came out of the door to the library on the right.

She was such a pleasant-faced girl that they both felt a sense of relief. Why she had not answered the knocking had ceased to be a question; she filled a void. She was pretty, not more than twenty-one or two, and had an air of primness which made Rodney Hunter vaguely associate her with a governess or a secretary, though Jack Bannister had never mentioned any

[310]

such person. She was plump, but with a curiously narrow waist; and she wore brown. Her brown hair was neatly parted, and her brown eyes— long eyes, which might have given a hint of secrecy or curious smiles if they had not been so placid—looked concerned. In one hand she carried what looked like a small white bag of linen or cotton. And she spoke with a dignity which did not match her years.

"I am most terribly sorry," she told them. "I *thought* I heard someone, but I was so busy that I could not be sure. Will you forgive me?"

She smiled. Hunter's private view was that his knocking had been loud enough to wake the dead; but he murmured conventional things. As though conscious of some faint incongruity about the white bag in her hand, she held it up.

"For Blind Man's Buff," she explained. "They do cheat so, I'm afraid, and not only the children. If one uses an ordinary handkerchief tied round the eyes, they always manage to get a corner loose. But if you take this, and you put it fully over a person's head, and you tie it round the neck"—a sudden gruesome image ocurred to Rodney Hunter—"then it works so much better, don't you think?" Her eyes seemed to turn inward, and to grow absent. "But I must not keep you talking here. You are—"

"My name is Hunter. This is my wife. I'm afraid we've arrived late, but I understood Mr. Bannister was expecting—"

"He did not tell you?" asked the girl in brown.

"Tell me what?"

"Everyone here, including the servants, is always out of the house at this hour on this particular date. It is the custom; I believe it has been the custom for more than sixty years. There is some sort of special church service."

Rodney Hunter's imagination had been devising all sorts of fantastic explanations: the first of them being that this demure lady had murdered the members of the household, and was engaged in disposing of the bodies. What put this nonsensical notion into his head he could not tell, unless it was his own profession of detective-story writing. But he felt relieved to hear a commonplace explanation. Then the woman spoke again.

"Of course, it is a pretext, really. The rector, that dear man, invented it all those years to save embarrassment. What happened here had nothing to do with the murder, since the dates were so different; and I suppose most people have forgotten now why the tenants *do* prefer to stay away during seven and eight o'clock on Christmas Eve. I doubt if Mrs. Bannister even knows the real reason, though I should imagine Mr. Bannister must know it. But what happens here cannot be very pleasant, and it wouldn't do to have the children see it—would it?"

Muriel spoke with such directness that her husband knew she was afraid.

[311]

"Who are you?" Muriel said. "And what on earth are you talking about?"

"I am quite sane, really," their hostess assured them, with a smile that was half-cheery and half-coy. "I daresay it must be all very confusing to you, poor dear. But I am forgetting my duties. Please come in and sit down before the fire, and let me offer you something to drink."

She took them into the library on the right, going ahead with a walk that was like a bounce, and looking over her shoulder out of those long eyes. The library was a long, low room with beams. The windows towards the road were uncurtained; but those in the side-wall, where a faded red-brick fireplace stood, were bay windows with draperies closed across them. As their hostess put them before the fire, Hunter could have sworn he saw one of the draperies move.

"You need not worry about it," she assured him, following his glance towards the bay. "Even if you looked in there, you might not see anything now. I believe some gentleman did try it once, a long time ago. He stayed in the house for a wager. But when he pulled the curtain back, he did not see anything in the bay—at least, anything quite. He felt some hair, and it moved. That is why they have so many lights nowadays."

Muriel had sat down on a sofa, and was lighting a cigarette: to the rather prim disapproval of their hostess, Hunter thought.

"May we have a hot drink?" Muriel asked crisply. "And then, if you don't mind, we might walk over and meet the Bannisters coming from church."

"Oh, please don't do that!" cried the other. She had been standing by the fireplace, her hands folded and turned outwards. Now she ran across to sit down beside Muriel; and the swifness of her movement, no less than the touch of her hand on Muriel's arm, made the latter draw back.

Hunter was now completely convinced that their hostess was out of her head. Why she held such fascination for him, though, he could not understand. In her eagerness to keep them there, the girl had come upon a new idea. On a table behind the sofa, book-ends held a row of modern novels. Conspicuously displayed—probably due to Molly Bannister's tact—were two of Rodney Hunter's detective stories. The girl put a finger on them.

"May I ask if you wrote these?"

He admitted it.

"Then," she said with sudden composure, "it would probably interest you to hear about the murder. It was a most perplexing business, you know; the police could make nothing of it, and no-one ever has been able to solve it." An arresting eye fixed on his. "It happened out in the hall there. A poor woman was killed where there was no-one to kill her, and no-one could have done it. But she was murdered."

Hunter started to get up from his chair; then he changed his mind, and sat down again. "Go on," he said.

* * *

"You must forgive me if I am a little uncertain about dates," she urged. "I think it was in the early eighteen-seventies, and I am sure it was in early February—because of the snow. It was a bad winter then; the farmers' live-stock all died. My people have been bred up in this district for years, and I know that. The house here was much as it is now, except that there was none of this lighting (only paraffin lamps, poor girl!); and you were obliged to pump up what water you wanted; and people read the newspaper quite through, and discussed it for days.

"The people were a little different to look at, too. I am sure I do not un-derstand why we think beards are so strange nowadays; they seem to think that men who had beards never had any emotions. But even young men wore them then, and looked handsome enough. There was a newly-married couple living in this house at the time: at least, they had been mar-ried only the summer before. They were named Edward and Jane Way-cross, and it was considered a good match everywhere.

"Edward Waycross did not have a beard, but he had bushy side-whiskers which he kept curled. He was not a handsome man, either, being somewhat dry and hard-favoured; but he was a religious man, and a good man, and an excellent man of business, they say; a manufacturer of agri-cultural implements at Hawkhurst. He had determined that Jane Anders (as she was) would make him a good wife, and I dare say she did. The girl had several suitors. Although Mr. Waycross was the best match, I know it surprised people a little when she accepted him, because she was thought to have been fond of another man—a more striking man, whom many of the young girls were after. This was Jeremy Wilkes: who came of a very good family, but was considered wicked. He was no younger than Mr. Way-cross, but he had a great black beard, and wore white waistcoats with gold chains, and drove a gig. Of course, there had been gossip, but that was be-cause Jane Anders was considered pretty."

Their hostess had been sitting back against the sofa, quietly folding the little white bag with one hand, and speaking in a prim voice. Now she did something which turned her hearers cold.

You have probably seen the same thing done many times. She had been touching her cheek lightly with the fingers of the other hand. In doing so, she touched the flesh at the corner under her lower eyelid, and accidentally drew down the corner of that eyelid—which should have exposed the red part of the inner lid at the corner of the eye. It was not red. It was of a sickly pale colour.

"In the course of his business dealings," she went on, "Mr. Waycross had often to go to London, and usually he was obliged to remain overnight. But Jane Waycross was not afraid to remain alone in the house. She had a good servant, a staunch old woman, and a good dog. Even so, Mr. Way-cross commended her for her courage.''

The girl smiled. ''On the night I wish to tell you of, in February, Mr. Waycross was absent. Unfortunately, too, the old servant was absent; she had been called away as a midwife to attend her cousin, and Jane Waycross had allowed her to go. This was known in the village, since all such affairs are well known, and some uneasiness was felt—this house being isolated, as you know. But she was not afraid.

''It was a very cold night, with a heavy fall of snow which had stopped about nine o'clock. You must know, beyond doubt, that poor Jane Way-cross was alive after it had stopped snowing. It must have been nearly half-past nine when a Mr. Moody—a very good and sober man who lived in Hawkhurst—was driving home along the road past this house. As you know, it stands in the middle of a great bare stretch of lawn; and you can see the house clearly from the road. Mr. Moody saw poor Jane at the window of one of the upstairs bedrooms, with a candle in her hand, closing the shutters. But he was not the only witness who saw her alive.

''On that same evening, Mr. Wilkes (the handsome gentleman I spoke to you of a moment ago) had been at a tavern in the village of Five Ashes with Dr. Sutton, the local doctor, and a racing gentleman named Pawley. At about half-past eleven they started to drive home in Mr. Wilkes's gig to Cross-in-Hand. I am afraid they had all been drinking, but they were all in their sober senses. The landlord of the tavern remembered the time because he had stood in the doorway to watch the gig, which had fine yellow wheels, go spanking away as though there were no snow; and Mr. Wilkes in one of the new round hats with a curly brim.

''There was a bright moon. 'And no danger', Dr. Sutton always said afterwards; 'shadows of trees and fences as clear as though a silhouette-cutter had made 'em for sixpence.' But when they were passing this house Mr. Wilkes pulled up sharp. There was a bright light in the window of one of the downstairs rooms—this room, in fact. They sat out there looking round the hood of the gig, and wondering.

''Mr. Wilkes spoke: 'I don't like this,' he said. 'You know, gentlemen, that Waycross is still in London; and the lady in question is in the habit of retiring early. I am going up there to find out if anything is wrong.'

''With that he jumped out of the gig, his black beard jutting out and his breath smoking. He said: 'And if it is a burglar, then by Something, gentlemen'—I will not repeat the word he used—'by Something, gentle-men, I'll settle him.' He walked through the gate and up to the house—they could follow every step he made—and looked into the win-dows of this room here. Presently he returned looking relieved (they could see him by the light of the gig lamps), but wiping the moisture off his forehead.

"'It is all right,' he said to them; 'Waycross has come home. But, by Something, gentlemen, he is growing thinner these days, or it is shadows.'

"Then he told them what he had seen. If you look through the front windows—there—you can look sideways and see out through the door-way into the main hall. He said he had seen Mrs. Waycross standing in the hall with her back to the staircase, wearing a blue dressing-wrap over her nightgown, and her hair down round her shoulders. Standing in front of her, with his back to Mr. Wilkes, was a tallish, thin man like Mr. Waycross, with a long greatcoat and a tall hat like Mr. Waycross's. *She* was carrying either a candle or a lamp; and he remembered how the tall hat seemed to wag back and forth, as though the man were talking to her or putting out his hands towards her. For he said he could not see the woman's face.

"Of course, it was not Mr. Waycross; but how were they to know that?

"At about seven o'clock next morning, Mrs. Randall, the old servant, returned. (A fine boy had been born to her cousin the night before.) Mrs. Randall came home through the white dawn and the white snow, and found the house all locked up. She could get no answer to her knocking. Being a woman of great resolution, she eventually broke a window and got in. But, when she saw what was in the front hall, she went out screaming for help.

"Poor Jane was past help. I know I should not speak of these things; but I must. She was lying on her face in the hall. From the waist down her body was much charred and—unclothed, you know, because fire had burnt away most of the nightgown and the dressing-wrap. The tiles of the hall were soaked with blood and paraffin oil, the oil having come from a broken lamp with a thick blue-silk shade which was lying a little distance away. Near it was a china candlestick with a candle. This fire had also charred a part of the panelling of the wall, and a part of the staircase. Fortunately, the floor is of brick tiles, and there had not been much paraffin left in the lamp, or the house would have been set afire.

"But she had not died from burns alone. Her throat had been cut with a deep slash from some very sharp blade. But she had been alive for a while to feel both things, for she had crawled forward on her hands while she was burning. It was a cruel death, a horrible death for a soft person like that."

There was a pause. The expression on the face of the narrator, the plump girl in the brown dress, altered slightly. So did the expression of her eyes. She was sitting beside Muriel; and moved a little closer.

"Of course, the police came. I do not understand such things, I am afraid, but they found that the house had not been robbed. They also noticed the odd thing I have mentioned, that there was both a lamp *and* a candle in a candlestick near her. The lamp came from Mr. and Mrs. Waycross's bedroom upstairs, and so did the candlestick; there were no other lamps or candles downstairs except the lamps waiting to be filled next morning in the back kitchen. But the police thought she would not have come downstairs carrying both the lamp *and* the candle as well.

"She must have brought the lamp, because that was broken. When the murderer took hold of her, they thought, she had dropped the lamp, and it went out; the paraffin spilled, but did not catch fire. Then this man in the tall hat, to finish his work after he had cut her throat, went upstairs, and got a candle, and set fire to the spilled oil. I am stupid at these things; but even I should have guessed that this must mean someone familiar with the house. Also, if she came downstairs, it must have been to let someone in at the front door; and that could not have been a burglar.

"You may be sure all the gossips were like police from the start, even when the police hem'd and haw'd, because they knew Mrs. Waycross must have opened the door to a man who was not her husband. And immediately they found an indication of this, in the mess that the fire and blood had made in the hall. Some distance away from poor Jane's body there was a medicine-bottle, such as chemists use. I think it had been broken in two pieces; and on one intact piece they found sticking some fragments of a letter that had not been quite burned. It was in a man's handwriting, not her husband's, and they made out enough of it to understand. It was full of—expressions of love, you know, and it made an appointment to meet her there on that night."

Rodney Hunter, as the girl paused, felt impelled to ask a question.

"Did they know whose handwriting it was?"

"It was Jeremy Wilkes's," replied the other simply. "Though they never proved that, never more than slightly suspected it, and the circumstances did not bear it out. In fact, a knife stained with blood was actually found in Mr. Wilkes's possession. But the police never brought it to anything, poor souls. For, you see, not Mr. Wilkes—or anyone else in the world—could possibly have done the murder."

*　*　*

"I don't understand that," said Hunter, rather sharply.

"Forgive me if I am stupid about telling things," urged their hostess in a tone of apology. She seemed to be listening to the chimney growl under a cold sky, and listening with hard, placid eyes. "But even the village gossips could tell that. When Mrs. Randall came here to the house on that morning, both the front and the back doors were locked and securely bolted on the inside. All the windows were locked on the inside. If you

[316]

wil look at the fastenings in this dear place, you will know what that means.

"But, bless you, that was the least of it! I told you about the snow. The snowfall had stopped at nine o'clock in the evening, hours and hours before Mrs. Waycross was murdered. When the police came, there were only two separate sets of footprints in the great unmarked half-acre of snow round the house. One set belonged to Mr. Wilkes, who had come up and looked in through the window the night before. The other belonged to Mrs. Randall. The police could follow and explain both sets of tracks; but there were no other tracks at all, and no-one was hiding in the house.

"Of course, it was absurd to suspect Mr. Wilkes. It was not only that he told a perfectly straight story about the man in the tall hat; but both Dr. Sutton and Mr. Pawley, who drove back with him from Five Ashes, were there to swear he could not have done it. You understand, he came no closer to the house than the windows of this room. They could watch every step he made in the moonlight, and they did. Afterwards he drove home with Dr. Sutton and slept there; or, I should say, they continued their terrible drinking until daylight. It is true that they found in his possession a knife with blood on it, but he explained that he had used the knife to gut a rabbit.

"It was the same with poor Mrs. Randall, who had been up all night about her midwife's duties, though naturally it was even more absurd to think of *her*. But there were no other footprints at all, either coming to or going from the house, in all that stretch of snow; and all the ways in or out were locked on the inside."

It was Muriel who spoke then, in a voice that tried to be crisp, but wavered in spite of her. "'Are you telling us that all this is true?" she demanded.

"I am teasing you a little, my dear," said the other. "But really and truly, it all did happen. Perhaps I will show you in a moment."

"I suppose it was really the husband who did it?" asked Muriel in a bored tone.

"Poor Mr. Waycross!" said their hostess tenderly. "He spent that night in a temperance hotel near Charing Cross Station, as he always did, and, of course, he never left it. When he learned about his wife's duplicity"—again Hunter thought she was going to pull down a corner of her eyelid—"it nearly drove him out of his mind, poor fellow. I think he gave up agricultural machinery and took to preaching, but I am not sure. I know he left the district soon afterwards, and before he left he insisted on burning the mattress of their bed. It was a dreadful scandal."

"But in that case," insisted Hunter, "who did kill her? And, if there were no footprints and all the doors were locked, how did the murderer come or go? Finally, if all this happened in February, what does it have to do with people being out of the house on Christmas Eve?''

"Ah, that is the real story. That is what I meant to tell you.''

She grew very subdued.

"It must have been very interesting to watch the people alter and grow older, or find queer paths, in the years afterwards. For, of course, nothing did happen as yet. The police presently gave it all up; for decency's sake it was allowed to rest. There was a new pump built in the market square; and the news of the Prince of Wales's going to India in '75 to talk about; and presently a new family came to live at 'Clearlawns', and began to raise their children. The trees and the rains in summer were just the same, you know. It must have been seven or eight years before anything happened, for Jane Waycross was very patient.

"Several of the people had died in the meantime. Mrs. Randall had, in a fit of qunsy; and so had Dr. Sutton, but that was a great mercy, because he fell by the way when he was going to perform an amputation with too much of the drink in him. But Mr. Pawley had prospered—and, above all, so had Mr. Wilkes. He had become an even finer figure of a man, they tell me, as he drew near middle age. When he married he gave up all his loose habits. Yes, he married; it was the Tinsley heiress, Miss Linshaw, whom he had been courting at the time of the murder; and I have heard that poor Jane Waycross, even after *she* was married to Mr. Waycross, used to bite her pillow at night, because she was so horribly jealous of Miss Linshaw.

"Mr. Wilkes had always been tall, and now he was finely stout. He always wore frock-coats. Though he had lost most of his hair, his beard was full and curly; he had twinkling black eyes, and twinkling ruddy cheeks, and a bluff voice. All the children ran to him. They say he broke as many feminine hearts as before. At any wholesome entertainment he was always the first to lead the cotillion or applaud the fiddler, and I do not know what hostesses would have done without him.

"On Christmas Eve, then—remember, I am not sure of the date—the Fentons gave a Christmas party. The Fentons were the very nice family who had taken this house afterwards, you know. There was to be no dancing, but all the old games. Naturally, Mr. Wilkes was the first of all to be invited, and the first to accept; for everything was all smoothed away by time, like the wrinkles in last year's counterpane; and what's past *is* past, or so they say. They had decorated the house with holly and mistletoe, and guests began to arrive as early as two in the afternoon.

"I had all this from Mrs. Fenton's aunt (one of the Warwickshire Abbotts), who was actually staying here at the time. In spite of such a festal season, the preparations had not been going at all well that day, though such preparations usually did. Miss Abbott complained that there was a nasty earthy smell in the house. It was a dark and raw day, and the chimneys did not seem to draw as well as they should. What is more, Mrs. Fenton cut her finger when she was carving the cold fowl, because she said one of the children had been hiding behind the window-curtains in here, and peeping out at her; she was very angry. But Mr. Fenton, who was going about the house in his carpet slippers before the arrival of the guests, called her 'Mother' and said that it was Christmas.

"It is certainly true that they forgot all about this when the fun of the games began. Such squealings you never heard!—or so I am told. Foremost of all at Bobbing for Apples or Nuts in May was Mr. Jeremy Wilkes. He stood, gravely paternal, in the midst of everything, with his ugly wife beside him, and stroked his beard. He saluted each of the ladies on the cheek under the mistletoe; there was also some scampering to salute him; and, though he *did* remain for longer than was necessary behind the window-curtains with the younger Miss Twigelow, his wife only smiled. There was only one unpleasant incident, soon forgotten. Towards dusk a great gusty wind began to come up, with the chimneys smoking worse than usual. It being nearly dark, Mr. Fenton said it was time to fetch in the Snapdragon Bowl, and watch it flame. You know the game? It is a great bowl of lighted spirit, and you must thrust in your hand and pluck out a raisin from the bottom without scorching your fingers. Mr. Fenton carried it in on a tray in the half-darkness; it was flickering with that bluish flame you have seen on Christmas puddings. Miss Abbott said that once, in carrying it, he started and turned round. She said that for a second she thought there was a face looking over his shoulder, and it wasn't a nice face.

"Later in the evening, when the children were sleepy and there was tissue-paper scattered all aver the house, the grown-ups began their games in earnest. Someone suggested Blind Man's Buff. They were mostly using the hall and this room here, as having more space than the dining-room. Various members of the party were blindfolded with men's handkerchiefs; but there was a dreadful amount of cheating. Mr. Fenton grew quite annoyed about it, because the ladies almost always caught Mr. Wilkes when they could; Mr. Wilkes was laughing and perspiring heartily, and his great cravat with the silver pin had almost come loose.

"To make it certain nobody could cheat, Mr. Fenton got a little white linen bag—like this one. It was the pillow-cover off the baby's cot, really; and he said nobody could look through that if it were tied over the head.

"I should explain that they have been having some trouble with the lamp in this room. Mr. Fenton said: 'Confound it, Mother, what is wrong with that lamp? Turn up the wick, will you?' It was really quite a good lamp from Spence and Minstead's, and should not have burned so dull as it did. In the confusion, while Mrs. Fenton was trying to make the light better, and he was looking over her shoulder at her, Mr. Fenton had been rather absently fastening the bag on the head of the last person caught. He has said since that he did not notice who it was. No-one else noticed, either, the light being so dim and there being such a large number of people. It seemed to be a girl in a broad bluish kind of dress, standing over near the door.

"Perhaps you know how people act when they have just been blindfolded in this game. First they usually stand very still, as though they were smelling or sensing in which direction to go. Sometimes they make a sudden jump, or sometimes they begin to shuffle gently forward. Everyone noticed what an air of *purpose* there seemed to be about this person whose face was covered; she went forward very slowly, and seemed to crouch down a bit.

"It began to move towards Mr. Wilkes in very short but quick little jerks, the white bag bobbing on its face. At this time Mr. Wilkes was sitting at the end of the table, laughing, with his face pink above the beard, and a glass of our Kentish cider in his hand. I want you to imagine this room as being very dim, and much more cluttered, what with all the tassels they had on the furniture then; and the high-piled hair of the ladies, too. The hooded person got to the edge of the table. It began to edge along towards Mr. Wilkes's chair; and then it jumped.

"Mr. Wilkes got up and skipped (yes, skipped) out of its way, laughing. It waited quietly, after which it went, in the same slow way, towards him again. It nearly got him again, by the edge of the potted plant. All this time it did not say anything, you understand, although everyone was applauding it and crying encouraging advice. It kept its head down. Miss Abbott says she began to notice an unpleasant faint smell of burnt cloth or something worse, which turned her half-ill. By the time the hooded person came stooping clear across the room, as certainly as though it could see him, Mr. Wilkes was not laughing any longer.

"In the corner by one bookcase, he said out loud: 'I'm tired of this silly, rotten game; go away, do you hear?' Nobody there had ever heard him speak like that, in such a loud, wild way, but they laughed and thought it must be the Kentish cider. 'Go away!' cried Mr. Wilkes again, and began to strike at it with his fist. All this time, Miss Abbott says, she had observed his face gradually changing. He dodged again, very pleasant and nimble for such a big man, but with the perspiration running down his face. Back across the room he went again, with it following him; and he cried out something that most naturally shocked them all inexpressibly.

"He screamed out: 'For God's sake, Fenton, take it off me!'

"And for the last time the thing jumped.

"They were over near the curtains of that bay window, which were drawn as they are now. Miss Twigelow, who was nearest, says that Mr.

[320]

Wilkes could not have seen anything, because the white bag was still drawn over the woman's head. The only thing she noticed was that at the lower part of the bag, where the face must have been, there was a curious kind of discoloration, a stain of some sort which had not been there before: something seemed to be seeping through. Mr. Wilkes fell back between the curtains, with the hooded person after him, and screamed again. There was a kind of thrashing noise in or behind the curtains; then they fell straight again, and everything grew quiet.

"Now, our Kentish cider is very strong, and for a moment Mr. Fenton did not know what to think. He tried to laugh at it, but the laugh did not sound well. Then he went over to the curtains, calling out gruffly to them to come out of there and not play the fool. But, after he had looked inside the curtains, he turned round very sharply and asked the rector to get the ladies out of the room. This was done, but Miss Abbott often said that she had one quick peep inside. Though the bay windows were locked on the inside, Mr. Wilkes was now alone on the window seat. She could see his beard sticking up, and the blood. He was dead, of course. But, since he had murdered Jane Waycross, I sincerely think he deserved to die.''

* * *

For several seconds, the two listeners did not move. She had all too successfully conjured up this room in the late 'seventies, whose stuffiness still seemed to pervade it now.

"But look here!" protested Hunter, when he could fight down an inclination to get out of the room quickly. "You say he killed her after all? And yet you told us he had an absolute alibi. You said he never went closer to the house than the windows . . .''

"No more he did, my dear," said the other.

"He was courting the Linshaw heiress at the time," she resumed; "and Miss Linshaw was a very proper young lady who would have been horrified if she had heard about him and Jane Waycross. She would have broken off the match, naturally. But poor Jane Waycross meant her to hear. She was much in love with Mr. Wilkes, and she was going to tell the whole matter publicly: Mr. Wilkes had been trying to persuade her not to do so.''

"But—"

"Oh, don't you see what happened?" cried the other in a pettish tone. "It is so dreadfully simple. I am not clever at these things, but I should have seen it in a moment: even if I did not already know. I told you everything so that you should be able to guess.

"When Mr. Wilkes and Dr. Sutton and Mr. Pawley drove past here in the gig that night, they saw a bright light burning in the windows of this room. I told you that. But the police never wondered, as anyone should,

[321]

what caused that light. Jane Waycross never came into this room, as you know; she was out in the hall, carrying either a lamp or a candle. But that lamp in the thick blue-silk shade, held out there in the hall, would not have caused a bright light to shine through this room and illuminate it. Neither would a tiny candle; it is absurd. And I told you there were no other lamps in the house except some empty ones waiting to be filled in the back kitchen. There is only one thing they could have seen. They saw the great blaze of the paraffin oil round Jane Waycross's body.

"Didn't I tell you it was dreadfully simple? Poor Jane was upstairs waiting for her lover. From the upstairs window she saw Mr. Wilkes's gig drive along the road in the moonlight, and she did not know there were other men in it; she thought he was alone. She came downstairs—

"It is an awful thing that the police did not think more about that broken medicine-bottle lying in the hall, the large bottle that was broken in just two long pieces. She must have had a use for it; and, of course, she had. You knew that the oil in the lamp was almost exhausted, although there was a great blaze round the body. When poor Jane came downstairs, she was carrying the unlighted lamp in one hand; in the other hand she was carrying a lighted candle, and an old medicine-bottle containing paraffin oil. When she got downstairs, she meant to fill the lamp from the medicine-bottle, and then light it with the candle.

"But she was too eager to get downstairs, I am afraid. When she was more than half-way down, hurrying, that long nightgown tripped her. She pitched forward down the stairs on her face. The medicine-bottle broke on the tiles under her, and poured a lake of paraffin round her body. Of course, the lighted candle set the paraffin blazing when it fell; but that was not all. One intact side of broken that broken bottle, long and sharp and cleaner than any blade, cut into her throat when she fell on the smashed bottle. She was not quite stunned by the fall. When she felt herself burning, and the blood almost as hot, she tried to save herself. She tried to crawl forward on her hands, forward into the hall, away from the blood and oil and fire.

"That was what Mr. Wilkes really saw when he looked in through the window.

"You see, he had been unable to get rid of the two fuddled friends, who insisted on clinging to him and drinking with him. He had been obliged to drive them home. If he could not go to 'Clearlawns' now, he wondered how at least he could leave a message; and the light in the window gave him an excuse.

"He saw pretty Jane propped up on her hands in the hall, looking out at him beseechingly while the blue flame ran up and turned yellow. You might have thought he would have pitied, for she loved him very much. Her wound was not really a deep wound. If he had broken into the house at that moment, he might have saved her life. But he preferred to let her die; because now she would make no public scandal and spoil his chances with the rich Miss Linshaw. That was why he returned to his friends and told a lie about a murderer in a tall hat. It is why, in heaven's truth, he murdered her himself. But when he returned to his friends, I do not wonder that they saw him mopping his forehead. You know now how Jane Waycross came back for him, presently.''

There was another heavy silence.

The girl got to her feet, with a sort of bouncing motion which was as suggestive as it was vaguely familiar. It was as though she were about to run. She stood there, a trifle crouched in her prim brown dress, so oddly narrow at the waist after an old-fashioned pattern; and in the play of light on her face Rodney Hunter fancied that its prettiness was only a shell.

"The same thing happened afterwards, on some Christmas Eves," she explained. "They played Blind Man's Buff over again. That is why people who live here do not care to risk it nowadays. It happens at a quarter-past seven—"

Hunter stared at the curtains. "But it was a quarter-past seven when we got here!" he said. "It must now be—"

"Oh, yes," said the girl, and her eyes brimmed over. "You see, I told you you had nothing to fear; it was all over then. But that is not why I thank you. I begged you to stay, and you did. You have listened to me, as no-one else would. And now I have told it at last, and now I think both of us can sleep."

Not a fold stirred or altered in the dark curtains that closed the window bay; yet, as though a blurred lens had come into focus, they now seemed innocent and devoid of harm. You could have put a Christmas-tree there. Rodney Hunter, with Muriel following his gaze, walked across and threw back the curtains. He saw a quiet window-seat covered with chintz, and the rising moon beyond the window. When he turned round, the girl in the old-fashioned dress was not there. But the front doors were open again, for he could feel a current of air blowing through the house.

With his arm round Muriel, who was white-faced, he went out into the hall. They did not look long at the scorched and beaded stains at the foot of the panelling, for even the scars of fire seemed gentle now. Instead, they stood in the doorway looking out, while the house threw its great blaze of light across the frosty Weald. It was a welcoming light. Over the rise of a hill, black dots trudging in the frost showed that Jack Bannister's party was returning; and they could hear the sound of voices carrying far. They heard one of the party carelessly singing a Christmas carol for glory and joy, and the laughter of children coming home.

[323]

Christmas is for Cops

by Edward D. Hoch

" "GOING TO THE Christmas party, Captain? Fletcher asked from the doorway. Captain Leopold glanced up from his eternally cluttered desk. Fletcher was now a lieutenant in the newly reorganized Violent Crimes Division, and they did not work together as closely as they once had. "I'll be there," Leopold said. "In fact, I've been invited to speak."

This news brought a grin to Fletcher's face. "Nobody speaks at the Christmas party, Captain. They just drink."

"Well, this year you're going to hear a speech, and I'm going to give it."

"Lots of luck."

"Is your wife helping with the decorations again this year?"

"I suppose she'll be around," Fletcher chuckled. "She doesn't trust me at any Christmas party without her."

The annual Detective Bureau party was, by tradition, a stag affair. But in recent years Carol Fletcher and some of the other wives had come down to Eagles Hall in the afternoon to trim the tree and hang the holly. Somehow these members of the unofficial Decorations Committee usually managed to stay on for the evening's festivities.

The party was the following evening, and Captain Leopold was looking forward to it. But he had one unpleasant task to perform first. That afternoon, feeling he could delay it no longer, he summoned Sergeant Tommy Gibson to his office and closed the door.

Gibson was a tough cop of the old school, a bleak and burly man who'd campaigned actively for the lieutenancy which had finally been given to Fletcher. Leopold had never liked Gibson, but until now he'd managed to overlook the petty graft with which Gibson's name was occasionally linked.

"What seems to be the trouble, Captain?" Gibson asked, taking a seat. "You look unhappy."

"I am unhappy, Gibson. Damned unhappy! While you were working the assault and robbery detail I had no direct command over your activities. But now that I'm in charge of a combined Violent Crimes Division, I feel I should take a greater interest in them." He reached across his desk to pick up a folder. "I have a report here from the District Attorney's office.

The report mentions you, Gibson, and makes some very grave charges.''

"What kind of charges?" the sergeant's tongue forked out to lick his dry lips.

"That you've been accepting regular payments from a man named Freese."

Gibson went pale. "I don't know what you're talking about."

"Carl Freese, the man who runs the numbers racket in every factory in this city. You know who he is, and you know what he's done. Men who've opposed him, or tried to report his operations to the police, have been beaten and nearly killed. I have a report here of a foreman at Lecko Industries. When some of his men started losing a whole week's pay in the numbers and other gambling controlled by Freese, he went to his supervisor and reported it. That night on the way home his car was forced off the road and he was badly beaten, so badly that he spent three weeks in the hospital. You should be familiar with that case, Gibson, because you investigated it just last summer."

"I guess I remember it."

"Remember your report, too? You wrote it off as a routine robbery attempt, despite the fact that no money was taken from the victim. The victim reported it to the District Attorney's office, and they've been investigating the whole matter of gambling in local industrial plants. I have their report here."

"I investigate a lot of cases, Captain. I try to do the best job I can."

"Nuts!" Leopold was on his feet, angry now. There was nothing that angered him more than a crooked cop. "Look, Gibson, the D.A.'s office has all of Freese's records. They show payments of $100 a week to you. What in hell were you doing for $100 a week, unless you were covering up for them when they beat some poor guy senseless?"

"Those records are wrong," Gibson said. "I didn't get any hundred bucks a week."

"Then how much did you get?"

Leopold towered over him in the chair, and Gibson's burly frame seemed to shrivel. "I think I want a lawyer," he mumbled.

"I'm suspending you from the force without pay, effective at once. Thank God you don't have a wife and family to suffer through this."

Tommy Gibson sat silently for a moment, staring at the floor. Then at last he looked up, seeking Leopold's eyes. "Give me a chance, Captain. I wasn't in this alone."

"What's that supposed to mean?"

"I didn't get the whole hundred myself. I had to split it with one of the other men—and he's the one who introduced me to Freese in the first place."

"There's someone else involved in this? One of the detectives?"

"Yes."

"Give me his name."

"Not yet." Gibson hesitated. "Because you wouldn't believe it. Let me give you evidence."

"What sort of evidence?"

"He and Freese came to me at my apartment and told me the type of protection they needed. That was the night we agreed on the amount of money to be paid each week. I wasn't taking any chances, Captain, so I dug out an old recording machine I'd bought after the war, and rigged up a hidden microphone behind my sofa. I got down every word they said."

"When was this?" Leopold asked.

"More than a year ago, and I've kept the recording of the conversation ever since. What's it worth to me if I bring it in?"

"I'm not in a position to make deals, Gibson."

"Would the D.A. make one?"

"I could talk to him," Leopold replied cautiously. "Let's hear what you've got first."

Gibson nodded. "I'll take the reel off my machine and bring it in to you tomorrow."

"If you're kidding me, Gibson, or stalling—"

"I'm not, Captain! I swear! I just don't want to take the whole rap myself."

"I'll give you twenty-four hours. Then the suspension goes into effect regardless."

"Thank you, Captain."

"Get the hell out of here now."

"Thank you, Captain," he said again. "And Merry Christmas."

* * *

On the day of the Christmas party, activities around the Detective Bureau slacked off very little. It was always pretty much business as usual until around four o'clock, when some of the men started drifting out, exchanging friendly seasonal comments. The party would really commence around five, when the men on the day shift arrived at Eagles Hall, and it continued until well past midnight, enabling the evening men to join in after their tours of duty.

Then there would be a buffet supper, and lots of beer, and even some group singing around the big Christmas tree. Without the family attachments of Fletcher and the other men, Leopold tended to look forward to the party. In many years it was the main event of his otherwise lonely holiday season.

By four o'clock he had heard nothing from Sergeant Tommy Gibson.

With growing irritation he called Fletcher into his office. "Gibson's under your command now, isn't he, Fletcher?"

"That's right, Captain."

"What's he working on today?"

Fletcher's face flushed unexpectedly. "Well, Captain, it seems—"

"Where is he?"

"Things were a bit slower than usual, so I told him he could go over to Eagles Hall and help put up the tree for the party."

"What!"

Fletcher shifted his feet uneasily. "I know, Captain. But usually I help Carol and the other wives get it up. Now that I'm a lieutenant I didn't feel I could take the time off, so I sent Gibson in my place."

Leopold sighed and stood up. "All right, Fletcher. Let's get over there right away."

"Why? What's up?"

"I'll tell you on the way."

* * *

Eagles Hall was a large reasonably modern building that was rented out for wedding receptions and private parties by a local fraternal group. The Detective Bureau, through its Benevolent Association, had held a Christmas party there for the past five seasons, and its central location had helped make it a popular choice. It was close enough to attract some of the uniformed force as well as the detective squad. All were invited, and most came at some time during the long evening.

Now, before five o'clock, a handful of plainclothesmen from various divisions had already arrived. Leopold waved to Sergeant Riker of the Vice Squad, who was helping Carol Fletcher light her cigarette with a balky lighter. Then he stopped to exchange a few words with Lieutenant Williams, a bony young man who headed up the Narcotics Squad. Williams had made his reputation during a single year on the force, masquerading as a hippie musician to penetrate a group selling drugs to high school students. Leopold liked him, liked his honesty and friendliness.

"I hear you're giving a little speech tonight," Williams said, pouring him a glass of beer.

"Herb Clarke roped me into it." Leopold answered with a chuckle. "I'd better do it early, before you guys get too beered up to listen." He glanced around the big hall, taking in the twenty-foot Christmas tree with its lights and tinsel. Three guy wires held it firmly in place next to an old upright piano. "See Tommy Gibson around?"

Williams stood on tiptoe to see over the heads of some newly arrived uniformed men. "I think he's helping Carol finish up the decorations."

"Thanks." Leopold took his beer and drifted over to the far end of the room. Carol had put down her cigarette long enough to tug at one of the wires holding the tree in place. Leopold helped her tighten it and then stepped back. She was a charming, intelligent woman, and this was not the first time he'd envied Fletcher. As wife and mother she'd given him a fine home life.

"I'm surprised to see you here so early, Captain."

He helped her secure another of the wires and said, "I'm always on time to help charming wives with Christmas trees."

"And thank you for Sergeant Gibson too! He was a great help with the tree."

"I'll bet. Where is he now?"

"He took the hammer and things into the kitchen. I think he's pouring beer now." She produced another cigarette and searched her purse. Finally she asked, "Do you have a light?"

He lit it for her. "You smoke too much."

"Nervous energy. Do you like our tree?"

"Fine. Just like Christmas."

"Do you know, somewhere in Chesterton there's mention of a tree that devours birds nesting in its branches, and when spring comes the tree grows feathers instead of leaves!"

"You read too much, Carol."

She smiled up at him. "The nights are lonely being a detective's wife." The smile was just a bit forced. She didn't always approve of her husband's work.

He left her by the tree and went in search of Gibson. The burly sergeant was in the kitchen, filling pitchers of beer. He looked up, surprised, as Leopold entered. "Hello, Captain."

"I thought we had an appointment for today."

"I didn't forget. Fletcher wanted me over here."

"Where's the evidence you mentioned?"

"What?"

Leopold was growing impatient. "Come on, damn it!"

Tommy Gibson glanced out at the growing crowd. "I've got it, but I had to hide it. He's here."

"Who? The man who's in this with you?"

"Yes. I'm afraid Freese might have tipped him off about the D.A.'s investigation."

Leopold had never seen this side of Gibson—a lonely, trapped man who was actually afraid. Or else was an awfully good actor. "I've given you your twenty-four hours, Gibson. Either produce this recording you've got or—"

"Captain!" a voice interrupted. "We're ready for your speech."

Leopold turned to see Sergeant Turner of Missing Persons standing in the doorway. "I'll be right there, Jim." Turner seemed to linger just a bit too long before he turned and walked away. Leopold looked back at Gibson. "That him?"

"I can't talk now, Captain."

"Where'd you hide it?"

"Over by the tree. It's safe."

"Stick around till after my talk. Then we'll get to the bottom of this thing."

Leopold left him pouring another pitcher of beer and walked out through the crowd. With the end of the afternoon shifts the place had filled rapidly. There were perhaps sixty members of the force present already, about evenly divided between detectives and uniformed patrolmen. Several shook his hand or patted him on the back as he made his way to the dais next to the tree.

Herb Clarke, president of the Detective Bureau Benevolent Association, was already on the platform, holding up his hands for silence. He shook Leopold's hand and then turned to his audience. "Gather around now, men. The beer'll still be there in five minutes. You all know we're not much for speeches at these Christmas parties, but I thought it might be well this year to hear a few words from a man we all know and admire. Leopold has been in the Detective Bureau for as long as most of us can remember—" The laughter caused him to add quickly, "Though of course he's still a young man. But this year, in addition to his duties as Captain of Homicide, he's taken on a whole new set of responsibilities. He's now head of the entire Violent Crimes Division of the Bureau, a position that places him in more direct contact with us all. I'm going to ask him to say just a few words, and then we'll have some caroling around the piano."

Leopold stepped over to the microphone, adjusting it upward from the position Herb Clarke had used. Then he looked out at the sea of familiar faces. Carol Fletcher and the other wives hovered in the rear, out of the way, while their husbands and the others crowded around. Fletcher himself stood with Sergeant Riker, an old friend, and Leopold noticed that Lieutenant Williams had moved over near Tommy Gibson. He couldn't see Jim Turner at the moment.

"Men, I'm going to make this worth listening to for all that. You hear a lot at this time of the year about Christmas being the season for kids, but I want to add something to that. Christmas is for kids, sure—but Christmas is for cops, too. Know what I mean by that? I'll tell you. Christmas is perhaps the one time of the year when the cop on the beat, or the detective on assignment, has a chance to undo some of the ill will generated during the other eleven months. This has been a bad year for cops around the country—most years are bad ones, it seems. We take a hell of a lot of abuse, some deserved, but most of it not. And this is the season to maybe right some of those wrongs. Don't be afraid to get out on a corner with the Salvation Army to ring a few bells, or help some lady through a puddle of slush. Most of all, don't be afraid to smile and talk to young people."

He paused and glanced down at Tommy Gibson. "There have always been some bad cops, and I guess there always will be. That just means the rest of us have to work a lot harder. Maybe we can just pretend the whole year is Christmas, and go about righting those wrongs. Anyway, I've talked so long already I've grown a bit thirsty. Let's get back to the beer and the singing, and make it good and loud!"

Leopold jumped off the platform and shook more hands. He'd meant to speak longer, to give them something a bit meatier to chew on, but far at the back of the crowd some of the younger cops were already growing restless. And, after all, they'd come here to enjoy themselves, not to listen to a lecture. He couldn't really blame them.

Herb Clarke was gathering everyone around the piano for songs, but Leopold noticed that Tommy Gibson had suddenly disappeared. The Captain threaded his way through the crowd, searching the familiar faces for the man he wanted. "Great talk, Captain," Fletcher said, coming up by his side.

"Did he tell you any more?"

"Only that he had to hide the tape near the Christmas tree. He said the other guy was here."

"Who do you make it, Captain?"

Leopold bit his lower lip. "I make it that Tommy Gibson is one smart cookie. I think he's playing for time, maybe waiting for Freese to get him off the hook somehow."

"You don't think there's another crooked cop in the Detective Bureau?"

"I don't know, Fletcher. I guess I don't want to think so."

The door to the Men's Room sprang open with a suddenness that surprised them both. Sergeant Riker, his usually placid face full of alarm, stood motioning to them. Leopold quickly covered the ground to his side. "What is it, Riker?"

"In there! My God, Captain—in there! It's Gibson!"

"What?"

"Tommy Gibson. He's been stabbed. I think he's dead."

*   *   *

Leopold pushed past him, into the tiled Men's Room with its scrubbed look and disinfectant odor. Tommy Gibson was there, all right, crumpled between two of the wash basins, his eyes glazed and open. A long pair of scissors protruded from his chest.

"Lock all the outside doors, Fletcher," Leopold barked. "Don't let anyone leave."

"Is he dead, Captain?"

"As dead as he'll ever be. What a mess!"

"You think one of our men did it?"

"Who else? Call in and report it, and get the squad on duty over here. Everyone else is a suspect." He stood up from examining the body and turned to Riker. "Now tell me everything you know, Sergeant."

Riker was a Vice Squad detective, a middle-aged man with a placid disposition and friendly manner. There were those who said he could even make a street-walker like him while he was arresting her. Just now he looked sick and pale. "I walked in and there he was, Captain. My God! I couldn't believe my eyes at first. I thought he was faking, playing some sort of a trick."

"Notice anyone leaving before you went in?"

"No, nobody."

"But he's only been dead a few minutes. That makes you a suspect, Sergeant."

Riker's pale complexion seemed to shade into green at Leopold's words. "You can't think I killed him! He was a friend of mine! Why in hell would I kill Tommy Gibson?"

"We'll see," Leopold said, motioning him out of the Men's Room. The other detectives and officers were clustered around, trying to see. There was a low somber hum of conversation. "All right, everyone!" the Captain ordered. "Keep down at the other end of the room, away from the tree! That's right, move away from it."

"Captain!" It was little Herb Clarke, pushing his way through. "Captain, what's happened?"

"Someone killed Tommy Gibson."

"Tommy!"

"One of us. That's why nobody leaves here."

"You can't be serious, Captain. Murder at the police Christmas party—the newspapers will crucify us."

"Probably," Leopold pushed past him. "Nobody enters the Men's Room," he bellowed. "Fletcher, Williams—come with me." They were the only two lieutenants present, and he had to trust them. Fletcher he'd trust with his life. He only hoped he could rely on Williams too.

"I can't believe it," the bony young Narcotics lieutenant said. "Why would anyone kill Tommy?"

Leopold cleared his throat. "I'll tell you why, though you may not want to believe it. Gibson was implicated in the District Attorney's investigation of Carl Freese's gambling empire. He had a tape recording of a conversation between Freese, himself, and another detective, apparently concerning bribery. The other detective had a dandy motive for killing him.''

"Did he say who it was?" Williams asked.

"No. Only that it was someone who got here fairly early today. Who was here before Fletcher and I arrived?"

Williams creased his brow in thought. "Riker was here, and Jim Turner. And a few uniformed men."

"No, just detectives."

"Well, I guess Riker and Turner were the only ones. And Herb Clarke, of course. He was here all day with the ladies, arranging for the food and the beer."

"Those three," Leopold mused. "And you, of course."

Lieutenant Williams grinned. "Yeah, and me."

Leopold turned toward the big Christmas tree. "Gibson told me he hid the tape recording near the tree. Start looking, and don't miss anything. It might even be in the branches."

The investigating officers were arriving now, and Leopold turned his attention to them. There was something decidedly bizarre in the entire situation, a fact which was emphasized as the doctor and morgue attendants and police photographers exchanged muted greetings with the milling party guests. One of the young investigating detectives who'd known Tommy Gibson turned pale at the sight of the body and had to go outside.

When the photographers had finished, one of the morgue men started to lift the body. He paused and called to Leopold. "Captain, here's something. A cigarette lighter on the floor under him."

Leopold bent close to examine it without disturbing possible prints. "Initials. C.F."

Lieutenant Williams had come in behind him, standing at the door of the Men's Room. "Carl Freese?" he suggested.

Leopold used a handkerchief to pick it up carefully by the corners. "Are we supposed to believe that Freese entered this place in the midst of sixty cops and killed Gibson without anybody seeing him?"

"There's a window in the wall over there."

Leopold walked to the frosted pane and examined it. "Locked from the inside. Gibson might have been stabbed from outside, but he couldn't have locked the window and gotten across this room without leaving a trail of blood."

Fletcher had come in while they were talking. "No dice on that, Captain. My wife just identified the scissors as a pair she was using earlier with the decorations. It's an inside job, all right."

Leopold showed the lighter. "C.F. Could be Carl Freese."

Fletcher frowned and licked his lips. "Yeah." He turned away.

"Nothing," Williams reported.

"Nothing *in* the tree? It could be a fairly small reel."

"Nothing."

Leopold sighed and motioned Fletcher and Williams to one side. He didn't want the others to hear. "Look, I think Gibson was probably lying, too. But he's dead, and that very fact indicates he might have been telling the truth. I have to figure all the angles. Now that you two have searched the tree I want you to go into the kitchen, close the door, and search each other. Carefully."

"But—" Williams began. "All right, Captain."

"Then line everybody up and do a search of them. You know what you're looking for—a reel of recording tape."

"What about the wives, Captain?"

"Get a matron down for them. I'm sorry to have to do it, but if that tape is here we have to find it."

He walked to the center of the hall and stood looking at the tree. Lights and tinsel, holiday wreaths and sprigs of mistletoe. All the trappings. He tried to imagine Tommy Gibson helping to decorate the place, helping with the tree. Where would he have hidden the tape?

Herb Clarke came over and said, "They're searching everybody."

"Yes. I'm sorry to spoil the party this way, but I guess it was spoiled for Gibson already."

"Captain, do you have to go on with this? Isn't one dishonest man in the Bureau enough?"

"One is too many, Herb. But the man we're looking for is more than a dishonest cop now. He's a murderer."

Fletcher came over to them. "We've searched all the detectives, Captain. They're clean. We're working on the uniformed men now."

Leopold grunted unhappily. He was sure they'd find nothing. "Suppose," he said slowly. "Suppose Gibson unreeled the tape. Suppose he strung it on the tree like tinsel."

"You see any brown tinsel hanging anywhere, Captain? See any tinsel of any color long enough to be a taped message?"

"No, I don't," Leopold said.

Two of the sergeants, Riker and Turner, came over to join them. "Could he have done it to himself?" Turner asked. "The word is you were going to link him with the Freese investigation."

"Stabbing youself in the chest with a pair of scissors isn't exactly common as a suicide method," Leopold pointed out. "Besides, it would be out of character for a man like Gibson."

One of the investigating officers came over with the lighter. "Only smudges on it, Captain. Nothing we could identify."

"Thanks." Leopold took it, turning it over between his fingers.

C.F. Carl Freese.

He flicked the lever a couple of times but it didn't light. Finally, on the fourth try, a flame appeared. "All right," he said quietly. Now he knew.

"Captain—" Fletcher began.

"Damn it, Fletcher, it's your wife's lighter and you know it! C.F. Not Carl Freese but Carol Fletcher!"

"Captain, I—" Fletcher stopped.

Leopold felt suddenly very tired. The colored lights of the tree seemed to blur, and he wished he was far away, in a land where all cops were honest and everyone died of old age.

Sergeant Riker moved in. "Captain, are you trying to say that Fletcher's *wife* stabbed Tommy Gibson?"

"Of course not, Riker. That would have been quite a trick for her to follow him into the Men's Room unnoticed. Besides, I had to give her a match at one point this evening, because she didn't have this lighter."

"Then who?"

"When I first arrived, you were helping Carol Fletcher with a balky lighter. Yes, you, Riker! You dropped it into your pocket, unthinking, and that's why she didn't have it later. It fell out while you were struggling with Gibson. While you were killing him, Riker."

Riker uttered a single obscenity and his hand went for the service revolver on his belt. Leopold had expected it. He moved in fast and threw two quick punches, one to the stomach and one to the jaw. Riker went down and it was over.

* * *

Carol Fletcher heard what had happened and she came over to Leopold. "Thanks for recovering my lighter," she said. "I hope you didn't suspect me."

He shook his head, eyeing Fletcher. "Of course not. But I sure as hell wish your husband had told me it was yours."

"I had to find out what it was doing there," Fletcher mumbled. "God, it's not every day your wife's lighter, that you gave her two Christmases ago, turns up as a clue in a murder."

Leopold handed it back to her. "Maybe this'll teach you to stop smoking."

"You knew it was Riker anyway?"

"I was pretty sure. With sixty men drinking beer all around here, no murderer could take a chance of walking out of that Men's Room unseen. His best bet was to pretend finding the body, which is just what he did. Besides that, of the four detectives on the scene early, Riker's Vice Squad position was the most logical for Freese's bribery.''

''Was there a tape recording?'' Fletcher asked.

Leopold was staring at the Christmas tree. ''I think Gibson was telling the truth on that one. Except that *he* never called it a tape. I did that. I jumped to a conclusion. He simply told me it was an old machine, purchased after the war. In those early days tape recorders weren't the only kind. For a while wire recorders were almost as popular.''

''Wire!''

Leopold nodded and started toward the Christmas tree. ''We know that Gibson helped you put up the tree, Carol. I'm betting that one of those wires holding it in place is none other than the recorded conversation of Carl Freese, Tommy Gibson, and Sergeant Riker.''

★

The Thieves who Couldn't Help Sneezing

by *Thomas Hardy*

MANY YEARS AGO, when oak-trees now past their prime were about as large as elderly gentlemen's walking-sticks, there lived in Wessex a yeoman's son, whose name was Hubert. He was about fourteen years of age, and was as remarkable for his candor and lightness of heart as for his physical courage, of which, indeed, he was a little vain.

One cold Christmas Eve his father, having no other help at hand, sent him on an important errand to a small town several miles from home. He travelled on horseback, and was detained by the business till a late hour the evening. At last, however, it was completed; he returned to the inn, the horse was saddled, and he started on his way. His journey homeward lay through the Vale of Blackmore, a fertile but somewhat lonely district, with heavy clay roads and crooked lanes. In those days, too, a great part of it was thickly wooded.

It must have been about nine o'clock when, riding along amid the overhanging trees upon his stout-legged cob, Jerry, and singing a Christmas carol, to be in harmony with the season, Hubert fancied that he heard a noise among the boughs. This recalled to his mind that the spot he was traversing bore an evil name. Men had been waylaid there. He looked at Jerry, and wished he had been of any other color than light gray; for on this account the docile animal's form was visible even here in the dense shade. "What do I care?" he said aloud, after a few minutes of reflection. "Jerry's legs are too nimble to allow any highwayman to come near me."

"Ha! ha! indeed," was said in a deep voice; and the next moment a man darted from the thicket on his right hand, another man from the thicket on his left hand, and another from a tree-trunk a few yards ahead. Hubert's bridle was seized, he was pulled from his horse, and although he struck out with all his might, as a brave boy would naturally do, he was overpowered. His arms were tied behind him, his legs bound tightly together, and he was thrown into the ditch. The robbers, whose faces he could now dimly perceive to be artificially blackened, at once departed, leading off the horse.

As soon as Hubert had a little recovered himself, he found that by great exertion he was able to extricate his legs from the cord; but, in spite of every endeavor, his arms remained bound as fast as before. All, therefore, that he could do was to rise to his feet and proceed on his way with his arms behind him, and trust to chance for getting them unfastened. He knew that it would be impossible to reach home on foot that night, and in such a condition; but he walked on. Owing to the confusion which this attack caused in his brain, he lost his way, and would have been inclined to lie down and rest till morning among the dead leaves had he not known the danger of sleeping without wrappers in a frost so severe. So he wandered further onwards, his arms wrung and numbed by the cord which pinioned him, and his heart aching for the loss of poor Jerry, who never had been known to kick, or bite, or show a single vicious habit. He was not a little glad when he discerned through the trees a distant light. Towards this he made his way, and presently found himself in front of a large mansion with flanking wings, gables, and towers, the battlements and chimneys showing their shapes against the stars.

All was silent; but the door stood wide open, it being from this door that the light shone which had attracted him. On entering he found himself in a vast apartment arranged as a dining-hall, and brilliantly illuminated. The walls were covered with a great deal of dark wainscoting, formed into moulded panels, carvings, closet-doors, and the usual fittings of a house of that kind. But what drew his attention most was the large table in the midst of the hall, upon which was spread a sumptuous supper, as yet untouched. Chairs were placed around, and it appeared as if something had occurred to interrupt the meal just at the time when all were ready to begin.

Even had Hubert been so inclined, he could not have eaten in his helpless state, unless by dipping his mouth into the dishes, like a pig or cow. He wished first to obtain assistance; and was about to penetrate further into the house for that purpose when he heard hasty footsteps in the porch and the words, ''Be quick!'' uttered in the deep voice which had reached him when he was dragged from the horse. There was only just time for him to dart under the table before three men entered the dining-hall. Peeping from beneath the hanging edges of the tablecloth, he perceived that their faces, too, were blackened, which at once removed any remaining doubts he may have felt that these were the same thieves.

''Now, then,'' said the first—the man with the deep voice—''let us hide ourselves. They will all be back again in a minute. That was a good trick to get them out of the house—eh?''

''Yes. You well imitated the cries of a man in distress,'' said the second.

''Excellently,'' said the third.

''But they will soon find out that it was a false alarm. Come, where shall we hide? It must be some place we can stay in for two or three hours, till all are in bed and asleep. Ah! I have it. Come this way! I have learnt that the further closet is not opened once in a twelve-month; it will serve our purpose exactly.''

The speaker advanced into a corridor which led from the hall. Creeping a little farther forward, Hubert could discern that the closet stood at the end, facing the dining-hall. The thieves entered it, and closed the door. Hardly breathing, Hubert glided forward, to learn a little more of their intention, if possible; and, coming close, he could hear the robbers whispering about the different rooms where the jewels, plate, and other valuables of the house were kept, which they plainly meant to steal.

They had not been long in hiding when a gay chattering of ladies and gentlemen was audible on the terrace without. Hubert felt that it would not do to be caught prowling about the house, unless he wished to be taken for a robber himself; and he slipped softly back to the hall, out the door, and stood in a dark corner of the porch, where he could see everything without being himself seen. In a moment or two a whole troop of personages came gliding past him into the house. There were an elderly gentleman and lady, eight or nine young ladies, as many young men, besides half-a-dozen men-servants and maids. The mansion had apparently been quite emptied of its occupants.

"Now, children and young people, we will resume our meal," said the old gentleman. "What the noise could have been I cannot understand. I never felt so certain in my life that there was a person being murdered outside my door."

Then the ladies began saying how frightened they had been, and how they had expected an adventure, and how it had ended in nothing at all.

"Wait a while," said Hubert to himself. "You'll have adventure enough by-and-by, ladies."

It appeared that the young men and women were married sons and daughters of the old couple, who had come that day to spend Christmas with their parents.

The door was then closed, Hubert being left outside in the porch. He thought this a proper moment for asking their assistance; and, since he was unable to knock with his hands, began boldly to kick the door.

"Hullo!" What disturbance are you making here?" said a footman who opened it; and, seizing Hubert by the shoulder, he pulled him into the dining-hall. "Here's a strange boy I have found making a noise in the porch, Sir Simon."

Everybody turned.

"Bring him forward," said Sir Simon, the old gentleman before mentioned. "What were you doing there, my boy?"

[339]

"Why, his arms are tied!" said one of the ladies.

"Poor fellow!" said another.

Hubert at once began to explain that he had been waylaid on his journey home, robbed of his horse, and mercilessly left in this condition by the thieves.

"Only to think of it!" exclaimed Sir Simon.

"That's a likely story," said one of the gentlemen-guests, incredulously.

"Doubtful, hey?" asked Sir Simon.

"Perhaps he's a robber himself," suggested a lady.

"There is a curiously wild, wicked look about him, certainly, now that I examine him closely," said the old mother.

Hubert blushed with shame; and, instead of continuing his story, and relating that robbers were concealed in the house, he doggedly held his tongue, and half resolved to let them find out their danger for themselves.

"Well, untie him," said Sir Simon. "Come, since it is Christmas Eve, we'll treat him well. Here, my lad; sit down in that empty seat at the bottom of the table, and make as good a meal as you can. When you have had your fill we will listen to more particulars of your story."

The feast then proceeded; and Hubert, now at liberty, was not at all sorry to join in. The more they ate and drank the merrier did the company become; the wine flowed freely, the logs flared up the chimney, the ladies laughed at the gentlemen's stories; in short, all went as noisily and as happily as a Christmas gathering in old times possibly could do.

Hubert, in spite of his hurt feelings at their doubts of his honesty, could not help being warmed both in mind and in body by the good cheer, the scene, and the example of hilarity set by his neighbors. At last he laughed as heartily at their stories and repartees as the old Baronet, Sir Simon, himself. When the meal was almost over one of the sons, who had drunk a little too much wine, after the manner of men in that century, said to Hubert, "Well, my boy, how are you? Can you take a pinch of snuff?" He held out one of the snuff-boxes which were then becoming common among young and old throughout the country.

"Thank you," said Hubert, accepting a pinch.

"Tell the ladies who you are, what you are made of, and what you can do," the young man continued, slapping Hubert upon the shoulder.

"Certainly," said our hero, drawing himself up, and thinking it best to put a bold face on the matter. "I am a traveling magician."

"Indeed!"

"What shall we hear next?"

"Can you call up spirits from the vasty deep, young wizard?"

"I can conjure up a tempest in a cupboard," Hubert replied.

"Ha-ha!" said the old Baronet, pleasantly rubbing his hands. "We must see this performance. Girls, don't go away: here's something to be seen."

"Not dangerous, I hope?" said the old lady.

Hubert rose from the table. "Hand me your snuff-box, please," he said to the young man who had made free with him. "And now," he continued, "without the least noise, follow me. If any of you speak it will break the spell."

They promised obedience. He entered the corridor, and, taking off his shoes, went on tiptoe to the closet door, the guests advancing in a silent group at a little distance behind him. Hubert next placed a stool in front of the door, and, by standing upon it, was tall enough to reach to the top. He then, just as noiselessly, poured all the snuff from the box along the upper edge of the door, and, with a few short puffs of breath, blew the snuff through the chink into the interior of the closet. He held up his finger to the assembly, that they might be silent.

"Dear me, what's that?" said the old lady, after a minute or two had elapsed.

A suppressed sneeze had come from inside the closet.

Hubert held up his finger again.

"How very singular," whispered Sir Simon. "This is most interesting."

Hubert took advantage of the moment to gently slide the bolt of the closet door into its place. "More snuff," he said, calmly.

"More snuff," said Sir Simon. Two or three gentlemen passed their boxes, and the contents were blown in at the top of the closet. Another sneeze, not quite so well suppressed as the first, was heard: then another, which seemed to say that it would not be suppressed under any circumstances whatever. At length there arose a perfect storm of sneezes.

"Excellent, excellent for one so young!" said Sir Simon. "I am much interested in this trick of throwing the voice—called, I believe, ventriloquism."

"More snuff," said Hubert.

"More snuff," said Sir Simon. Sir Simon's man brought a large jar of the best scented Scotch.

Hubert once more charged the upper chink of the closet, and blew the snuff into the interior, as before. Again he charged, and again, emptying the whole contents of the jar. The tumult of sneezes became really extraordinary to listen to—there was no cessation. It was like wind, rain, and sea battling in a hurricane.

"I believe there are men inside, and that it is no trick at all!" exclaimed Sir Simon, the truth flashing on him.

"There are," said Hubert. "They are come to rob the house; and they are the same who stole my horse."

The sneezes changed to spasmodic groans. One of the thieves, hearing Hubert's voice, cried, "Oh! mercy! mercy! let us out of this!"

"Where's my horse?" said Hubert.

"Tied to the tree in the hollow behind Short's Gibbet. Mercy! mercy! let us out, or we shall die of suffocation!"

All the Christmas guests now perceived that this was no longer sport, but serious earnest. Guns and cudgels were procured; all the men-servants were called in, and arranged in position outside the closet. At a signal Hubert withdrew the bolt, and stood on the defensive. But the three robbers, far from attacking them, were found crouching in the corner, gasping for breath. They made no resistance; and, being pinioned, were placed in an outhouse till the morning.

Hubert now gave the remainder of his story to the assembled company, and was profusely thanked for the services he had rendered. Sir Simon pressed him to stay over the night, and accept the use of the best bedroom the house afforded, which had been occupied by Queen Elizabeth and King Charles successively when on their visits to this part of the country. But Hubert declined, being anxious to find his horse Jerry, and to test the truth of the robbers' statements concerning him.

Several of the guests accompanied Hubert to the spot behind the gibbet, alluded to by the thieves as where Jerry was hidden. When they reached the knoll and looked over, behold! there the horse stood, uninjured, and quite unconcerned. At sight of Hubert he neighed joyfully; and nothing could exceed Hubert's gladness at finding him. He mounted, wished his friends "Good-night!" and cantered off in the direction they pointed out, reaching home safely about four o'clock in the morning.

The Case is Altered

by *Margery Allingham*

MR. ALBERT CAMPION, sitting in a first-class smoking compartment, was just reflecting sadly that an atmosphere of stultifying decency could make even Christmas something of a stuffed-owl occasion, when a new hogskin suitcase of distinctive design hit him on the knees. At that same moment a golf bag bruised the shins of the shy young man opposite, an armful of assorted magazines burst over the pretty girl in the far corner, and a blast of icy air swept round the carriage. There was the familiar rattle and lurch which indicates that the train has started at last, a squawk from a receding porter, and Lance Feering arrived before him apparently by rocket.

"Caught it," said the newcomer with the air of one confidently expecting congratulations, but as the train bumped jerkily he teetered back on his heels and collapsed between the two young people on the opposite seat.

"My dear chap, so we noticed," murmured Campion, and he smiled apologetically at the girl, now disentangling herself from the shellburst of newsprint. It was his own disarming my-poor-friend-is-afflicted variety of smile that he privately considered infallible, but on this occasion it let him down.

The girl, who was in the early twenties and was slim and fair, with eyes like licked brandy-balls, as Lance Feering inelegantly put it afterwards, regarded him with grave interest. She stacked the magazines into a neat bundle and placed them on the seat opposite before returning to her own book. Even Mr. Feering, who was in one of his more exuberant moods, was aware of that chilly protest. He began to apologize.

Campion had known Feering in his student days, long before he had become one of the foremost designers of stage décors in Europe, and was used to him, but now even he was impressed. Lance's apologies were easy but also abject. He collected his bag, stowed it on a clear space on the rack above the shy young man's head, thrust his golf things under the seat, positively blushed when he claimed his magazines, and regarded the girl with pathetic humility. She glanced at him when he spoke, nodded cooly with just enough graciousness not to be gauche, and turned over a page.

Campion was secretly amused. At the top of his form Lance was reputed

[343]

to be irresistible. His dark face with the long mournful nose and bright eyes were unhandsome enough to be interesting and the quick gestures of his short painter's hands made his conversation picturesque. His singular lack of success on this occasion clearly astonished him and he sat back in his corner eyeing the young woman with covert mistrust.

Campion resettled himself to the two hours' rigid silence which etiquette demands from first-class travelers who, although they are more than probably going to be asked to dance a reel together if not to share a bathroom only a few hours hence, have not yet been introduced.

There was no way of telling if the shy young man and the girl with the brandy-ball eyes knew each other, and whether they too were en route for Underhill, Sir Philip Cookham's Norfolk place. Campion was inclined to regard the coming festivities with a certain amount of lugubrious curiosity. Cookham himself was a magnificent old boy, of course, "one of the more valuable pieces in the Cabinet," as someone had once said of him, but Florence was a different kettle of fish. Born to wealth and breeding, she had grown blasé towards both of them and now took her delight in notabilities, a dangerous affectation in Campion's experience. She was some sort of remote aunt of his.

He glanced again at the young people, caught the boy unaware, and was immediately interested.

The illustrated magazine had dropped from the young man's hand and he was looking out of the window, his mouth drawn down at the corners and a narrow frown between his thick eyebrows. It was not an unattractive face, too young for strong character but decent and open enough in the ordinary way. At that particular moment, however, it wore a revealing expression. There was recklessness in the twist of the mouth and sullenness in the eyes, while the hand which lay upon the inside arm-rest was clenched.

Campion was curious. Young people do not usually go away for Christmas in this top-step-at-the-dentist's frame of mind. The girl looked up from her book.

"How far is Underhill from the station?" she inquired.

"Five miles. They'll meet us." The shy young man turned to her so easily and with such obvious affection that any romantic theory Campion might have formed was knocked on the head instantly. The youngster's troubles evidently had nothing to do with love.

Lance had raised his head with bright-eyed interest at the gratuitous information and now a faintly sardonic expression appeared upon his lips. Campion sighed for him. For a man who fell in and out of love with the abandonment of a seal round a pool, Lance Feering was an impossible optimist. Already he was regarding the girl with that shy despair which so many ladies had found too piteous to be allowed to persist. Campion wash-

[344]

ed his hands of him and turned away just in time to notice a stranger glancing in at them from the corridor. It was a dark and arrogant young face and he recognized it instantly, feeling at the same time a deep wave of sympathy for old Cookham. Florence, he gathered, had done it again.

Young Victor Preen, son of old Preen of the Preen Aero Company, was certainly notable, not to say notorious. He had obtained much publicity in his short life for his sensational flights, but a great deal more for adventures less creditable; and when angry old gentlemen in the armchairs of exclusive clubs let themselves go about the blackguardliness of the younger generation, it was very often of Victor Preen that they were thinking.

He stood now a little to the left of the compartment window, leaning idly against the wall, his chin up and his heavy lids drooping. At first sight he did not appear to be taking any interest in the occupants of the compartment, but when the shy young man looked up, Campion happened to see the swift glance of recognition, and of something else, which passed between them. Presently, still with the same elaborate casualness, the man in the corridor wandered away, leaving the other staring in front of him, the same sullen expression still in his eyes.

The incident passed so quickly that it was impossible to define the exact nature of that second glance, but Campion was never a man to go imagining things, which was why he was surprised when they arrived at Minstree station to hear Henry Boule, Florence's private secretary, introducing the two and to notice that they met as strangers.

It was pouring with rain as they came out of the station, and Boule, who, like all Florence's secretaries, appeared to be suffering from an advanced case of nerves, bundled them all into two big Daimlers, a smaller car, and a shooting-brake. Campion looked round him at Florence's Christmas bag with some dismay. She had surpassed herself. Besides Lance there were at least half a dozen celebrities: a brace of political high-lights, an angry looking lady novelist, Nadja from the ballet, a startled R.A., and Victor Preen, as well as some twelve or thirteen unfamiliar faces who looked as if they might belong to Art, Money, or even mere Relations.

Campion became separated from Lance and was looking for him anxiously when he saw him at last in one of the cars, with the novelist on one side and the girl with brandy-ball eyes on the other, Victor Preen making up the ill-assorted four.

Since Campion was an unassuming sort of person he was relegated to the brake with Boule himself, the shy young man and the whole of the luggage. Boule introduced them awkwardly and collapsed into a seat, wiping the beads from off his forehead with a relief which was a little too blatant to be tactful.

Campion, who had learned that the shy young man's name was Peter

Groome, made a tentative inquiry of him as they sat jolting shoulder to shoulder in the back of the car. He nodded.

"Yes, it's the same family," he said. "Cookham's sister married a brother of my father's. I'm some sort of relation, I suppose."

The prospect did not seem to fill him with any great enthusiasm and once again Campion's curiosity was piqued. Young Mr. Groome was certainly not in seasonable mood.

In the ordinary way Campion would have dismissed the matter from his mind, but there was something about the youngster which attracted him, something indefinable and of a despairing quality, and moreover there had been that curious intercepted glance in the train.

They talked in a desultory fashion throughout the uncomfortable journey. Campion learned that young Groome was in his father's firm of solicitors, that he was engaged to be married to the girl with the brandy-ball eyes, who was a Miss Patricia Bullard of an old north country family, and that he thought Christmas was a waste of time.

"I hate it," he said with a sudden passionate intensity which startled even his mild inquisitor. "All this sentimental good-will-to-all-men-business is false and sickening. There's no such thing as good-will. The world's rotten."

He blushed as soon as he had spoken and turned away.

"I'm sorry," he murmured, "but all this bogus Dickensian stuff makes me writhe."

Campion made no direct comment. Instead he asked with affable inconsequence, "Was that young Victor Preen I saw in the other car?"

Peter Groome turned his head and regarded him with the steady stare of the wilfully obtuse.

"I was introduced to someone with a name like that, I think," he said carefully. "He was a little baldish man, wasn't he?"

"No, that's Sir George." The secretary leaned over the luggage to give the information. "Preen is the tall young man, rather handsome, with the very curling hair. He's *the* Preen, you know." He sighed. "It seems very young to be a millionaire, doesn't it?"

"Obscenely so," said Mr. Peter Groome abruptly, and returned to his despairing contemplation of the landscape.

Underhill was *en fête* to receive them. As soon as Campion observed the preparations, his sympathy for young Mr. Groome increased, for to a jaundiced eye Lady Florence's display might well have proved as dispiriting as Preen's bank balance. Florence had "gone all Dickens," as she said herself at the top of her voice, linking her arm through Campion's, clutching the R.A. with her free hand, and capturing Lance with a bright birdlike eye.

The great Jacobean house was festooned with holly. An eighteen foot tree stood in the great hall. Yule logs blazed on iron dogs in the wide hearths and already the atmosphere was thick with that curious Christmas smell which is part cigar smoke and part roasting food.

Sir Philip Cookham stood receiving his guests with pathetic bewilderment. Every now and again his features broke into a smile of genuine welcome as he saw a face he knew. He was a distinguished-looking old man with a fine head and eyes permanently worried by his country's troubles.

"My dear boy, delighted to see you. Delighted," he said, grasping Campion's hand. "I'm afraid you've been put over in the Dower House. Did Florence tell you? She said you wouldn't mind, but I insisted that Feering went over there with you and also young Peter." He sighed and brushed away the visitor's hasty reassurances. "I don't know why the dear girl never feels she has a party unless the house is so overcrowded that our best friends have to sleep in the annex," he said sadly.

The "dear girl," looking not more than fifty-five or her sixty years, was clinging to the arm of the lady novelist at that particular moment and the two women were emitting mirthless parrot cries at each other. Cookham smiled.

"She's happy, you know," he said indulgently. "She enjoys this sort of thing. Unfortunately I have a certain amount of urgent work to do this weekend, but we'll get in a chat, Campion, some time over the holiday. I want to hear your news. You're a lucky fellow. You can tell your adventures."

The lean man grimaced. "More secret sessions, sir?" he inquired.

The Cabinet Minister threw up his hands in a comic but expressive little gesture before he turned to greet the next guest.

As he dressed for dinner in his comfortable room in the small Georgian dower house across the park, Campion was inclined to congratulate himself on his quarters. Underhill itself was a little too much of the ancient monument for strict comfort.

He had reached the tie stage when Lance appeared. He came in very elegant indeed and highly pleased with himself. Campion diagnosed the symptoms immediately and remained irritatingly incurious.

Lance sat down before the open fire and stretched his sleek legs.

"It's not even as if I were a good looking blighter, you know," he observed invitingly when the silence had become irksome to him. "In fact, Campion, when I consider myself I simply can't understand it. Did I so much as speak to the girl?"

"I don't know," said Campion, concentrating on his dressing. "Did you?"

"No." Lance was passionate in his denial. "Not a word. The hard-faced female with the inky fingers and the walrus mustache was telling me her life story all the way home in the car. This dear little poppet with the eyes was nothing more than a warm bundle at my side. I give you my dying oath on that, And yet — well, it's extraordinary, isn't it?"

Campion did not turn round. He could see the artist quite well through the mirror in front of him. Lance had a sheet of note-paper in his hand and was regarding it with that mixture of feigned amusement and secret delight which was typical of his eternally youthful spirit.

"Extraordinary," he repeated, glancing at Campion's unresponsive back. "She had nice eyes. Like licked brandy-balls."

"Exactly," agreed the lean man by the dressing table. "I thought she seemed very taken up with her fiancé, young Master Groome, though," he added tactlessly.

"Well, I noticed that, you know," Lance admitted, forgetting his professions of disinterest. "She hardly recognized my existence in the train. Still, there's absolutely no accounting for women. I've studied 'em all my life and never understood 'em yet. I mean to say, take this case in point. That kid ignored me, avoided me, looked through me. And yet look at this. I found it in my room when I came up to change just now."

Campion took the note with a certain amount of distaste. Lovely women were invariably stooping to folly, it seemed, but even so he could not accustom himself to the spectacle. The message was very brief. He read it at a glance and for the first time that day he was conscious of that old familiar flicker down the spine as his experienced nose smelled trouble. He re-read the five lines.

"There is a sundial on a stone pavement just off the drive. We saw it from the car. I'll wait ten minutes there for you half an hour after the party breaks up tonight."

There was neither signature nor initial, and the summons broke off as baldly as it had begun.

"Amazing, isn't it?" Lance had the grace to look shamefaced.

"Astounding." Campion's tone was flat. "Staggering, old boy. Er — fishy."

"Fishy?"

"Yes, don't you think so?" Campion was turning over the single sheet thoughtfully and there was no amusement in the pale eyes behind his horn-rimmed spectacles. "How did it arrive?"

"In an unaddressed envelope. I don't suppose she caught my name. After all, there must be some people who don't know it yet." Lance was grinning impudently. "She's batty, of course. Not safe out and all the rest of it. But I liked her eyes and she's very young."

Campion perched himself on the edge of the table. He was still very serious.

"It's disturbing, isn't it?" he said, "Not nice. Makes one wonder."

"Oh, I don't know." Lance retrieved his property and tucked it into his pocket. "She's young and foolish, and it's Christmas."

Campion did not appear to have heard him. "I wonder," he said. "I should keep the appointment, I think. It may be unwise to interfere, but yes, I rather think I should."

"You're telling me." Lance was laughing. "I may be wrong, of course," he added defensively, "but I think that's a cry for help. The poor girl evidently saw that I looked a dependable sort of chap and — er — having her back against the wall for some reason or other she turned instinctively to the stranger with the kind face. Isn't that how you read it?"

"Since you press me, no. Not exactly," said Campion, and as they walked over to the house together he remained thoughtful and irritatingly uncommunicative.

Florence Cookham excelled herself that evening. Her guests were exhorted "to be young again," with the inevitable result that Underhill contianed a company of irritated and exhausted people long before midnight.

One of her ladyship's more erroneous beliefs was that she was a born organizer, and that the real secret of entertaining people lay in giving everyone something to do. Thus Lance and the R.A. — now even more startled-looking than ever — found themselves superintending the decoration of the great tree, while the girl with the brandy-ball eyes conducted a small informal dance in the drawing froom, the lady novelist scowled over the bridge table, and the ballet star refused flatly to arrange amateur theatricals.

Only two people remained exempt from this tyranny. One was Sir Philip himself, who looked in every now and again, ready to plead urgent work awaiting him in his study whenever his wife pounced upon him, and the other was Mr. Campion, who had work to do on his own account and had long mastered the difficult art of self-effacement. Experience had taught him that half the secret of this maneuver was to keep discreetly on the move and he strolled from one party toanother, always ready to look as if he belonged to any one of them should his hostess's eye ever come to rest upon him inquiringly.

For once his task was comparatively simple. Florence was in her element as she rushed about surrounded by breathless assistants, and at one period the very air in her vicinity seemed to have become thick with colored paper-wrappings, yards of red ribbons and a colored snowstorm of little address tickets as she directed the packing of the presents for the Tenants' Tree, a second monster which stood in the ornamental barn beyond the kitchens.

Campion left Lance to his fate, which promised to be six or seven hours' hard labor at the most moderate estimate, and continued his purposeful meandering. His lean figure drifted among the company with an apparent aimlessness which was deceptive. There was hidden urgency in his lazy movements and his pale eyes behind his spectacles were inquiring and unhappy.

He found Patricia Bullard dancing with young Preen, and paused to watch them as they swung gracefully by him. The man was in a somewhat flamboyant mood, flashing his smile and his noisy witticisms about him after the fashion of his kind, but the girl was not so content. As Campion caught sight of her pale face over her partner's sleek shoulder his eyebrows rose. For an instant he almost believed in Lance's unlikely suggestion. The girl actually did look as though she had her back to the wall. She was watching the doorway nervously and her shiny eyes were afraid.

Campion looked about him for the other young man who should have been present, but Peter Groome was not in the ballroom, nor in the great hall, nor yet among the bridge tables in the drawing-room, and half an hour later he had still not put in an appearance.

Campion was in the hall himself when he saw Patricia slip into the anteroom which led to Sir Philip's private study, that holy of holies which even Florence treated with a wholesome awe. Campion had paused for a moment to enjoy the spectacle of Lance, wild eyed and tight lipped, wrestling with the last of the blue glass balls and tinsel streamers on the Guests' Tree, when he caught sight of the flare of her silver skirt disappearing round a familiar doorway under one branch of the huge double staircase.

It was what he had been waiting for, and yet when it came his disappointment was unexpectedly acute, for he too had liked her smile and her brandy-ball eyes. The door was ajar when he reached it, and he pushed it open an inch or so farther, pausing on the threshold to consider the scene within. Patricia was on her knees before the paneled door which led into the inner room and was trying somewhat ineffectually to peer through the keyhole.

Campion stood looking at her regretfully, and when she straightened herself and paused to listen, with every line of her young body taut with the effort of concentration, he did not move.

Sir Philip's voice amid the noisy chatter behind him startled him, however, and he swung round to see the old man talking to a group on the other side of the room. A moment later the girl brushed past him and hurried away.

Campion went quietly into the anteroom. The study door was still closed and he moved over to the enormous period fireplace which stood beside it. This particular fireplace, with its carved and painted front, its wrought iron dogs and deeply recessed inglenooks, was one of the showpieces of Underhill.

At the moment the fire had died down and the interior of the cavern was dark, warm, and inviting. Campion stepped inside and sat down on the oak settle, where the shadows swallowed him. He had no intention of being unduly officious, but his quick ears had caught a faint sound in the inner room and Sir Philip's private sanctum was no place for furtive movements when its master was out of the way. He had not long to wait.

A few moments later the study door opened very quietly and someone came out. The newcomer moved across the room with a nervous, unsteady tread,and paused abruptly, his back to the quiet figure in the inglenook.

Campion recognized Peter Groome and his thin mouth narrowed. He was sorry. He had liked the boy.

The youngster stood irresolute. He had his hands behind him, holding in one of them a flamboyant parcel wrapped in the colored paper and scarlet ribbon which littered the house. A sound from the hall seemed to fluster him. for he spun round, thrust the parcel into the inglenook which was the first hiding place to present itself, and returned to face the new arrival. It was the girl again. She came slowly across the room, her hands outstretched and her face raised to Peter's.

In view of everything, Campion thought it best to stay where he was, nor had he time to do anything else. She was speaking urgently, passionate sincerity in her low voice.

"Peter, I've been looking for you. Darling, there's something I've got to say and if I'm making an idiotic mistake then you've got to forgive me. Look here, you wouldn't go and do anything silly, would you? Would you, Peter? Look at me."

"My dear girl."He was laughing unsteadily and not very convincingly with his arms around her. "What on earth are you talking about?"

She drew back from him and peered earnestly into his face.

"You wouldn't, would you? Not even if it meant an awful lot. Not even if for some reason or other you felt you *had* to. Would you?"

He turned from her helplessly, a great weariness in the lines of his sturdy back, but she drew him round, forcing him to face her.

"Would he what, my dear?"

Florence's arch inquiry from the doorway separated them so hurriedly that she laughed delightedly and came briskly into the room, her gray curls a trifle disheveled and her draperies flowing.

"Too divinely young. I love it!" she said devastatingly. "I must kiss you both. Christmas is the time for love and youth and all the other dear charming things, isn't it? That's why I adore it. But, my dears, not here. Not in

[351]

this silly poky little room. Come along and help me, both of you, and then you can slip away and dance together later on. But don't come in this room. This is Philip's dull part of the house. Come along this minute. Have you seen my precious tree? Too incredibly distinguished, my darlings, with two great artists at work on it. You shall both tie on a candle. Come along.''

She swept them away like an avalanche. No protest was possible. Peter shot a single horrified glance towards the fireplace, but Florence was gripping his arm; he was thrust out into the hall and the door closed firmly behind him.

Campion was left in his corner with the parcel less than a dozen feet away from him on the opposite bench. He moved over and picked it up. It was a long flat package wrapped in holly-printed tissue. Moreover, it was unexpectedly heavy and the ends were unbound.

He turned it over once or twice, wrestling with a strong disinclination to interfere, but a vivid recollection of the girl with the brandy-ball eyes, in her silver dress, her small pale face alive with anxiety, made up his mind for him and, sighing, he pulled the ribbon.

The typewritten folder which fell on to his knees surprised him at first, for it was not at all what he had expected, nor was its title, "Report on Messrs. Anderson and Coleridge, Messrs. Saunders, Duval and Berry, and Messrs.Birmingham and Rose," immediately enlightening, and when he opened it at random a column of incomprehensible figures confronted him. It was a scribbled pencil note in a precise hand at the foot of one of the pages which gave him his first clue.

"These figures are estimated by us to be a reliable forecast of this firm's full working capacity,"

Two hours later it was bitterly cold in the garden and a thin white mist hung over the dark shrubbery which lined the drive when Mr. Campion, picking his way cautiously along the clipped grass verge, came quietly down to the sundial walk. Behind him the gabled roofs of Underhill were shadowy against a frosty sky. There were still a few lights in the upper windows, but below stairs the entire place was in darkness.

Campion hunched his greatcoat about him and plodded on, unwonted severity in the lines of his thin face.

He came upon the sundial walk at last and paused, straining his eyes to see through the mist. He made out the figure standing by the stone column, and heaved a sigh of relief as he recognized the jaunty shoulders of the Christmas tree decorator. Lance's incurable romanticism was going to be useful at last, he reflected with wry amusement.

He did not join his friend but withdrew into the shadows of a great clump of rhododendrons and composed himself to wait. He intensely disliked the situation in which he found himself. Apart from the extreme physical discomfort involved, he had a natural aversion towards the project on hand, but little fair-haired girls with shiny eyes can be very appealing.

It was a freezing vigil. He could hear Lance stamping about in the mist, swearing softly to himself, and even that supremely comic phenomenon had its unsatisfactory side.

They were both shivering and the mist's damp fingers seemed to have stroked their very bones when at last Campion stiffened. He had heard a rustle behind him and presently there was a movement in the wet leaves, followed by the sharp ring of feet on the stones. Lance swung round immediately, only to drop back in astonishment as a tall figure bore down.

"Where is it?"

Neither the words nor the voice came as a complete surprise to Campion, but the unfortunate Lance was taken entirely off his guard.

"Why, hello, Preen," he said involuntarily. "What the devil are you doing here?"

The newcomer had stopped in his tracks, his face a white blur in the uncertain light. For a moment he stood perfectly still and then, turning on his heel, he made off without a word.

"Ah, but I'm afraid it's not quite so simple as that, my dear chap."

Campion stepped out of his friendly shadows and as the younger man passed, slipped an arm through his and swung him round to face the startled Lance, who was coming up at the double.

"You can't clear off like this," he went on, still in the same affable, conversational tone. "You have something to give Peter Groome, haven't you? Something he rather wants?"

"Who the hell are you?" Preen jerked up his arm as he spoke and might have wrenched himself free had it not been for Lance, who had recognized Campion's voice and, although completely in the dark, was yet quick enough to grasp certain essentials.

"That's right, Preen," he said, seizing the man's other arm in a bear's hug. "Hand it over. Don't be a fool. Hand it over."

This line of attack appeared to be inspirational, since they felt the powerful youngster stiffen between them.

"Look here, how many people know about this?"

"The world—" Lance was beginning cheerfully when Campion forstalled him.

"We three and Peter Groome," he said quietly. "At the moment Sir Philip has no idea that Messrs. Preen's curiosity concerning the probably placing of Government orders for aircraft parts has overstepped the bounds of common sense. You're acting alone, I suppose?"

"Oh, lord, yes, of course." Preen was cracking dangerously, "If my old man gets to hear of this I — oh, well, I might as well go and crash."

"I thought so." Campion sounded content. "Your father has a reputation to consider. So has our young friend Groome. You'd better hand it over."

"What?"

"Since you force me to be vulgar, whatever it was you were attempting to use as blackmail, my precious young friend," he said. "Whatever it may be, in fact, that you hold over young Groome and were trying to use in your attempt to force him to let you have a look at a confidential Government report concerning the orders which certain aircraft firms were likely to receive in the next six months. In your position you could have made pretty good use of them, couldn't you? Frankly, I haven't the faintest idea what this incriminating document may be. When I was young, objectionably wealthy youths accepted I.O.U.s from their poorer companions, but now that's gone out of fashion. What's the modern equivalent? An R.D. check, I suppose?"

Preen said nothing. He put his hand in an inner pocket and drew out an envelope which he handed over without a word. Campion examined the slip of pink paper within by the light of a pencil torch.

"You kept it for quite a time before trying to cash it, didn't you?" he said. "Dear me, that's rather an old trick and it was never admired. Young men who are careless with their accounts have been caught out like that before. It simply wouldn't have looked good to his legal-minded old man, I take it? You two seem to be hampered by your respective papas' integrity. Yes, well, you can go now."

Preen hesitated, opened his mouth to protest, but thought better of it. Lance looked after his retreating figure for some little time before he returned to his friend.

"Who wrote that blinking note?" he demanded.

"He did, of course," said Campion brutally. "He wanted to see the report but was making absolutely sure that young Groome took all the risks of being found with it."

"Preen wrote the note," Lance repeated blankly.

"Well, naturally," said Campion absently. "That was obvious as soon as the report appeared in the picture. He was the only man in the place with the necessary special information to make use of it."

Lance made no comment. He pulled his coat collar more closely about his throat and stuffed his hands into his pockets.

All the same the artist was not quite satisfied, for, later still, when Campion was sitting in his dressing-gown writing a note at one of the little escritoires which Florence so thoughtfully provided in her guest bedrooms, he came padding in again and stood warming himself before the fire.

"Why?" he demanded suddenly. "Why did I get the invitation?"

"Oh, that was a question of luggage." Campion spoke over his shoulder. "That bothered me at first, but as soon as we fixed it onto Preen that little mystery became blindingly clear. Do you remember falling into the carriage this afternoon? Where did you put your elegant piece of gent's natty suitcasing? Over young Groome's head. Preen saw it from the corridor and assumed that the chap was sitting *under his own bag!* He sent his own man over here with the note, told him not to ask for Peter by name but to follow the nice new pigskin suitcase upstairs."

Lance nodded regretfully. "Very likely," he said sadly. "Funny thing. I was sure it was the girl."

After a while he came over to the desk. Campion put down his pen and indicated the written sheet.

"Dear Groome," it ran, "I enclose a little matter that I should burn forthwith. The package you left in the inglenook is still there, right at the back on the left-hand side, cunningly concealed under a pile of logs. It has not been seen by anyone who could possibly understand it. If you nipped over very early this morning you could return it to its appointed place without any trouble. If I may venture a word of advice, it is never worth it."

The author grimaced. "It's a bit avuncular," he admitted awkwardly, "but what else can I do? His light is still on, poor chap. I thought I'd stick it under his door."

Lance was grinning wickedly.

"That's fine," he murmured. "The old man does his stuff for reckless youth. There's just the signature now and that ought to be as obvious as everything else has been to you. I'll write it for you. 'Merry Christmas. Love from Santa Claus.'"

"You win," said Mr. Campion.

★

Christmas Party

by Rex Stout

" " I'M SORRY, SIR," I said. I tried to sound sorry. "But I told you two days ago, Monday, that I had a date for Friday afternoon, and you said all right. So I'll drive you to Long Island Saturday or Sunday."

Nero Wolfe shook his head. "That won't do. Mr. Thompson's ship docks Friday morning, and he will be at Mr. Hewitt's place only until Saturday noon, when he leaves for New Orleans. As you know, he is the best hybridizer in England, and I am grateful to Mr. Hewitt for inviting me to spend a few hours with him. As I remember, the drive takes about an hour and a half, so we should leave at twelve-thirty."

I decided to count ten, and swiveled my chair, facing my desk, so as to have privacy for it. As usual when we have no important case going, we had been getting on each other's nerves for a week, and I admit I was a little touchy, but his taking it for granted like that was a little too much. When I had finished the count I turned my head, to where he was perched on his throne behind his desk, and darned if he hadn't gone back to his book, making it plain that he regarded it as settled. That was much too much. I swiveled my chair to confront him.

"I really am sorry," I said, not trying to sound sorry, "but I have to keep that date Friday afternoon. It's a Christmas party at the office of Kurt Bottweill—you remember him, we did a job for him a few months ago, the stolen tapestries. You may not remember a member of his staff named Margot Dickey, but I do. I have been seeing her some, and I promised her I'd go to the party. We never have a Christmas office party here. As for going to Long Island, your idea that a car is a death trap if I'm not driving it is unsound. You can take a taxi, or hire a Baxter man, or get Saul Panzer to drive you."

Wolfe had lowered his book. "I hope to get some useful information from Mr. Thompson, and you will take notes."

"Not if I'm not there. Hewitt's secretary knows orchid terms as well as I do. So do you."

I admit those last three words were a bit strong, but he shouldn't have gone back to his book. His lips tightened. "Archie. How many times in the past year have I asked you to drive me somewhere?"

[357]

"If you call it asking, maybe eighteen or twenty."

"Not excessive, surely. If my feeling that you alone are to be trusted at the wheel of a car is an aberration, I have it. We will leave for Mr. Hewitt's place Friday at twelve-thirty."

So there we were. I took a breath, but I didn't need to count ten again. If he was to be taught a lesson, and he certainly needed one, luckily I had in my possession a document that would make it good. Reaching to my inside breast pocket, I took out a folded sheet of paper.

"I didn't intend," I told him, "to spring this on you until tomorrow, or maybe even later, but I guess it will have to be now. Just as well, I suppose."

I left my chair, unfolded the paper, and handed it to him. He put his book down to take it, gave it a look, shot a glance at me, looked at the paper again, and let it drop on his desk.

He snorted. "Pfui. What flummery is this?"

"No flummery. As you see, it's a marriage license for Archie Goodwin and Margot Dickey. It cost me two bucks. I could be mushy about it, but I won't. I will only say that if I am hooked at last, it took an expert. She intends to spread the tidings at the Christmas office party, and of course I have to be there. When you announce you have caught a fish it helps to have the fish present in person. Frankly, I would prefer to drive you to Long Island, but it can't be done."

The effect was all I could have asked. He gazed at me through narrowed eyes long enough to count eleven, then picked up the document and gazed at it. He flicked it from him to the edge of the desk as if it were crawling with germs, and focused on me again.

"You are deranged," he said evenly and distinctly. "Sit down."

I nodded. "I suppose," I agreed, remaining upright, "it's a form of madness, but so what if I've got it? Like what Margot was reading to me the other night—some poet, I think it was some Greek—'O love, resistless in thy might, thou triumphest even—'"

"Shut up and sit down!"

"Yes, sir." I didn't move. "But we're not rushing it. We haven't set the date, and there'll be plenty of time to decide on adjustments. You may not want me here any more, but that's up to you. As far as I'm concerned, I would like to stay. My long association with you has had its flaws, but I would hate to end it. The pay is okay, especially if I get a raise the first of the year, which is a week from Monday. I have grown to regard this old brownstone as my home, although you own it and although there are two creaky boards in the floor of my room. I appreciate working for the greatest private detective in the free world, no matter how eccentric he is. I appreciate being able to go up to the plant rooms whenever I feel like it and look at ten thousand orchids, especially the odontoglossums. I fully appreciate—''

''Sit down!''

''I'm too worked up to sit. I fully appreciate Fritz's cooking. I like the billiard table in the basement. I like West Thirty-fifth Street. I like the one-way glass panel in the front door. I like this rug I'm standing on. I like your favorite color, yellow. I have told Margot all this, and more, including the fact that you are allergic to women. We have discussed it, and we think it may be worth trying, say for a month, when we get back from the honeymoon. My room could be our bedroom, and the other room on that floor could be our living room. There are plenty of closets. We could eat with you, as I have been, or we could eat up there, as you prefer. If the trial works out, new furniture or redecorating would be up to us. She will keep her job with Kurt Bottweill, so she wouldn't be here during the day, and since he's an interior decorator we would get things wholesale. Of course we merely suggest this for your consideration. It's your house.''

I picked up my marriage license, folded it, and returned it to my pocket.

His eyes had stayed narrow and his lips tight. ''I don't believe it,'' he growled. ''What about Miss Rowan?''

''We won't drag Miss Rowan into this,'' I said stiffly.

''What about the thousands of others you dally with?''

''Not thousands. Not even a thousand. I'll have to look up 'dally.' They'll get theirs, as Margot has got hers. As you see, I'm deranged only up to a point. I realize—''

''Sit down.''

''No, sir. I know this will have to be discussed, but right now you're stirred up and it would be better to wait for a day or two, or maybe more. By Saturday the idea of a woman in the house may have you boiling even worse than you are now, or it may have cooled you down to a simmer. If the former, no discussion will be needed. If the latter, you may decide it's worth a try. I hope you do.''

I turned and walked out.

In the hall I hesitated. I could have gone up to my room and phoned from there, but in his present state it was quite possible he would listen in from the desk, and the call I wanted to make was personal. So I got my hat and coat from the rack, let myself out, descended the stoop steps, walked to the drugstore on Ninth Avenue, found the booth unoccupied, and dialed a number. In a moment a musical little voice—more a chirp than a voice—was in my ear.

''Kurt Bottweill's studio, good morning.''

''This is Archie Goodwin, Cherry. May I speak to Margot?''

''Why, certainly. Just a moment.''

It was a fairly long moment. Then another voice. "Archie, darling!"

"Yes, my own. I've got it."

"I knew you could!"

"Sure, I can do anything. Not only that, you said up to a hundred bucks, and I thought I would have to part with twenty at least, but it only took five. And not only that, but it's on me, because I've already had my money's worth of fun out of it, and more. I'll tell you about it when I see you. Shall I send it up by messenger?"

"No, I don't think—I'd better come and get it. Where are you?"

"In a phone booth. I'd just as soon not go back to the office right now because Mr. Wolfe wants to be alone to boil, so how about the Tulip Bar at the Churchill in twenty minutes? I feel like buying you a drink."

"I feel like buying *you* a drink!"

She should, since I was treating her to a marriage license.

II

When, at three o'clock Friday afternoon, I wriggled out of the taxi at the curb in front of the four-story building in the East Sixties, it was snowing. If it kept up, New York might have an off-white Christmas.

During the two days that had passed since I got my money's worth from the marriage license, the atmosphere around Wolfe's place had not been very seasonable. If we had had a case going, frequent and sustained communication would have been unavoidable, but without one there was nothing that absolutely had to be said, and we said it. Our handling of that trying period showed our true natures. At table, for instance, I was polite and reserved, and spoke, when speaking seemed necessary, in low and cultured tones. When Wolfe spoke he either snapped or barked. Neither of us mentioned the state of bliss I was headed for, or the adjustments that would have to be made, or my Friday date with my fiancée, or his trip to Long Island. But he arranged it somehow, for precisely at twelve-thirty on Friday a black limousine drew up in front of the house, and Wolfe, with the brim of his old black hat turned down and the collar of his new gray overcoat turned up for the snow, descended the stoop, stood massively, the mountain of him, on the bottom step until the uniformed chauffeur had opened the door, and crossed the sidewalk and climbed in. I watched it from above, from a window of my room.

I admit I was relieved and felt better. He had unquestionably needed a lesson and I didn't regret giving him one, but if he had passed up a chance for an orchid powwow with the best hybridizer in England I would never have heard the last of it. I went down to the kitchen and ate lunch with

Fritz, who was so upset by the atmosphere that he forgot to put the lemon juice in the soufflé. I wanted to console him by telling him that everything would be rosy by Christmas, only three days off, but of course that wouldn't do.

I had a notion to toss a coin to decide whether I would have a look at the new exhibit of dinosaurs at the Natural History Museum or go to the Bottweill party, but I was curious to know how Margot was making out with the license, and also how the other Bottweill personnel were making out with each other. It was surprising that they were still making out at all. Cherry Quon's position in the setup was apparently minor, since she functioned chiefly as a receptionist and phone-answerer, but I had seen her black eyes dart daggers at Margot Dickey, who should have been clear out of her reach. I had gathered that it was Margot who was mainly relied upon to wrangle prospective customers into the corral, that Bottweill himself put them under the spell, and that Alfred Kiernan's part was to make sure that before the spell wore off an order got signed on the dotted line.

Of course that wasn't all. The order had to be filled, and that was handled, under Bottweill's supervision, by Emil Hatch in the workshop. Also funds were required to buy the ingredients, and they were furnished by a specimen named Mrs. Perry Porter Jerome. Margot had told me that Mrs. Jerome would be at the party and would bring her son Leo, whom I had never met. According to Margot, Leo, who had no connection with the Bottweill business or any other business, devoted his time to two important activities: getting enough cash from his mother to keep going as a junior playboy, and stopping the flow of cash to Bottweill, or at least slowing it down.

It was quite a tangle, an interesting exhibit of bipeds alive and kicking, and, deciding it promised more entertainment than the dead dinosaurs, I took a taxi to the East Sixties.

The ground floor of the four-story building, formerly a de luxe double-width residence, was now a beauty shop. The second floor was a real-estate office. The third floor was Kurt Bottweill's workshop, and on top was his studio. From the vestibule I took the do-it-yourself elevator to the top, opened the door, and stepped out into the glossy gold-leaf elegance I had first seen some months back, when Bottweill had hired Wolfe to find out who had swiped some tapestries. On that first visit I had decided that the only big difference between chrome modern and Bottweill gold-leaf modern was the color, and I still thought so. Not even skin deep; just a two-hundred-thousandth of an inch deep. But on the panels and racks and furniture frames it gave the big skylighted studio quite a tone, and the rugs and drapes and pictures, all modern, joined in. It would have been a fine den for a blind millionaire.

"Archie!" a voice called. "Come and help us sample!"

It was Margot Dickey. In a far corner was a gold-leaf bar, some eight feet long, and she was at it on a gold-leaf stool. Cherry Quon and Alfred Kiernan were with her, also on stools, and behind the bar was Santa Claus, pouring from a champagne bottle. It was certainly a modern touch to have Santa Claus tend bar, but there was nothing modern about his costume. He was strictly traditional, cut, color, size, mask, and all, except that the hand grasping the champagne bottle wore a white glove. I assumed, crossing to them over the thick rugs, that that was a touch of Bottweill elegance, and didn't learn until later how wrong I was.

They gave me the season's greetings, and Santa Claus poured a glass of bubbles for me. No gold leaf on the glass. I was glad I had come. To drink champagne with a blonde at one elbow and a brunette at the other gives a man a sense of well-being, and those two were fine specimens—the tall, slender Margot relaxed, all curves, on the stool, and little slant-eyed black-eyed Cherry Quon, who came only up to my collar when standing, sitting with her spine as straight as a plumb line, yet not stiff. I thought Cherry worthy of notice not only as a statuette, though she was highly decorative, but as a possible source of new light on human relations. Margot had told me that her father was half Chinese and half Indian—not American Indian —and her mother was Dutch.

I said that apparently I had come too early, but Alfred Kiernan said no, the others were around and would be in shortly. He added that it was a pleasant surprise to see me, as it was just a little family gathering and he hadn't known others had been invited. Kiernan, whose title was business manager, had not liked a certain step I had taken when I was hunting the tapestries, and he still didn't, but an Irishman at a Christmas party likes everybody. My impression was that he really was pleased, so I was too. Margot said she had invited me, and Kiernan patted her on the arm and said that if she hadn't he would. About my age and fully as handsome, he was the kind who can pat the arm of a queen or a president's wife without making eyebrows go up.

He said we needed another sample and turned to the bartender. "Mr. Claus, we'll try the Veuve Clicquot." To us: "Just like Kurt to provide different brands. No monotony for Kurt." To the bartender: "May I call you by your first name, Santy?"

"Certainly, sir," Santa Claus told him from behind the mask in a thin falsetto that didn't match his size. As he stooped and came up with a bottle a door at the left opened and two men entered. One of them, Emil Hatch, I had met before. When briefing Wolfe on the tapestries and telling us about his staff, Bottweill had called Margot Dickey his contact woman, Cherry Quon his handy girl, and Emil Hatch his pet wizard, and when I met Hatch I found that he both looked the part and acted it. He wasn't much taller than Cherry Quon and skinny, and something had either pushed his left shoulder down or his right shoulder up, making him lop-sided, and he had a sour face, a sour voice, and a sour taste.

When the stranger was named to me as Leo Jerome, that placed him. I was acquainted with his mother, Mrs. Perry Porter Jerome. She was a widow and an angel—that is, Kurt Bottweill's angel. During the investigation she had talked as if the tapestries belonged to her, but that might have only been her manners, of which she had plenty. I could have made guesses about her personal relations with Bottweill, but hadn't bothered. I have enough to do to handle my own personal relations without wasting my brain power on other people's. As for her son Leo, he must have got his physique from his father—tall, bony, big-eared and long-armed. He was probably approaching thirty, below Kiernan but above Margot and Cherry.

When he shoved in between Cherry and me, giving me his back, and Emil Hatch had something to tell Kiernan, sour no doubt, I touched Margot's elbow and she slid off the stool and let herself be steered across to a divan which had been covered with designs by Euclid in six or seven colors. We stood looking down at it.

"Mighty pretty," I said, "but nothing like as pretty as you. If only that license were real! I can get a real one for two dollars. What do you say?"

"*You!*" she said scornfully. "You wouldn't marry Miss Universe if she came on her knees with a billion dollars."

"I dare her to try it. Did it work?"

"Perfect. Simply perfect."

"Then you're ditching me?"

"Yes, Archie darling. But I'll be a sister to you."

"I've got a sister. I want the license back for a souvenir, and anyway I don't want it kicking around. I could be hooked for forgery. You can mail it to me, once my own."

"No, I can't. He tore it up."

"The hell he did. Where are the pieces?"

"Gone. He put them in his wastebasket. Will you come to the wedding?"

"What wastebasket where?"

"The gold one by his desk in his office. Last evening after dinner. Will you come to the wedding?"

"I will not. My heart is bleeding. So will Mr. Wolfe's—and by the way, I'd better get out of here. I'm not going to stand around and sulk."

"You won't have to. He won't know I've told you, and anyway, you wouldn't be expected—Here he comes!"

She darted off to the bar and I headed that way. Through the door on the left appeared Mrs. Perry Porter Jerome, all of her, plump and plushy, with folds of mink trying to keep up as she breezed in. As she approached, those on stools left them and got onto their feet, but that courtesy could have been as much for her companion as for her. She was the angel, but Kurt Bottweill was the boss. He stopped five paces short of the bar, extended his arms as far as they would go, and sang out, "Merry Christmas, all my blessings! Merry merry merry!"

I still hadn't labeled him. My first impression, months ago, had been that he was one of them, but that had been wrong. He was a man all right, but the question was what kind. About average in height, round but not pudgy, maybe forty-two or -three, his fine black hair slicked back so that he looked balder than he was, he was nothing great to look at, but he had something, not only for women but for men too. Wolfe had once invited him to stay for dinner, and they had talked about the scrolls from the Dead Sea. I had seen him twice at baseball games. His label would have to wait.

As I joined them at the bar, where Santa Claus was pouring Mumms Cordon Rouge, Bottweill squinted at me a moment and then grinned. "Goodwin! You here? Good! Edith, your pet sleuth!"

Mrs. Perry Porter Jerome, reaching for a glass, stopped her hand to look at me. "Who asked you?" she demanded, then went on, with no room for a reply, "Cherry, I suppose. Cherry *is* a blessing. Leo, quit tugging at me. Very well, take it. It's warm in here." She let her son pull her coat off, then reached for a glass. By the time Leo got back from depositing the mink on the divan we all had glasses, and when he had his we raised them, and our eyes went to Bottweill.

His eyes flashed around. "There are times," he said, "when love takes over. There are times—"

"Wait a minute," Alfred Kiernan cut in. "You enjoy it too. You don't like this stuff."

"I can stand a sip, Al."

"But you won't enjoy it. Wait." Kiernan put his glass on the bar and marched to the door on the left and on out. In five seconds he was back, with a bottle in his hand, and as he rejoined us and asked Santa Claus for a glass I saw the Pernod label. He pulled the cork, which had been pulled before, filled the glass halfway, and held it out to Bottweill. "There," he said. "That will make it unanimous."

"Thanks, Al." Bottweill took it. "My secret public vice." He raised the glass. "I repeat, there are times when love takes over. (Santa Claus, where is yours? but I suppose you can't drink through that mask.) There are times when all the little demons disappear down their ratholes, and ugliness itself takes on the shape of beauty; when the darkest corner is touched by light; when the coldest heart feels the glow of warmth; when the trumpet call of

[364]

good will and good cheer drowns out all the Babel of mean little noises. This is such a time. Merry Christmas! Merry merry merry!''

I was ready to touch glasses, but both the angel and the boss steered theirs to their lips, so I and the others followed suit. I thought Bottweill's eloquence deserved more than a sip, so I took a healthy gulp, and from the corner of my eye I saw that he was doing likewise with the Pernod. As I lowered the glass my eyes went to Mrs. Jerome, as she spoke.

"That was lovely," she declared. "Simply lovely. I must write it down and have it printed. That part about the trumpet call—*Kurt!* What is it? *Kurt!*"

He had dropped the glass and was clutching his throat with both hands. As I moved he turned loose of his throat, thrust his arms out, and let out a yell. I think he yelled *"Merry!"* but I wasn't really listening. Others started for him too, but my reflexes were better trained for emergencies than any of theirs, so I got him first. As I got my arms around him he started choking and gurgling, and a spasm went over him from head to foot that nearly loosened my grip. They were making noises, but no screams, and someone was clawing at my arm. As I was telling them to get back and give me room, he was suddenly a dead weight, and I almost went down with him and might have if Kiernan hadn't grabbed his arm.

I called, "Get a doctor!" and Cherry ran to a table where there was a gold-leaf phone. Kiernan and I let Bottweill down on the rug. He was out, breathing fast and hard, but as I was straightening his head his breathing slowed down and foam showed on his lips. Mrs. Jerome was commanding us, "Do something, do something!"

There was nothing to do and I knew it. While I was holding onto him I had got a whiff of his breath, and now, kneeling, I leaned over to get my nose an inch from his, and I knew that smell, and it takes a big dose to hit that quick and hard. Kiernan was loosening Bottweill's tie and collar. Cherry Quon called to us that she had tried a doctor and couldn't get him and was trying another. Margot was squatting at Bottweill's feet, taking his shoes off, and I could have told her she might as well let him die with his boots on but didn't. I had two fingers on his wrist and my other hand inside his shirt, and could feel him going.

When I could feel nothing I abandoned the chest and wrist, took his hand, which was a fist, straightened the middle finger, and pressed its nail with my thumbtip until it was white. When I removed my thumb the nail stayed white. Dropping the hand, I yanked a little cluster of fibers from the rug, told Kiernan not to move, placed the fibers against Bottweill's nostrils, fastened my eyes on them, and held my breath for thirty seconds, The fibers didn't move.

I stood up and spoke. "His heart has stopped and he's not breathing. If a doctor came within three minutes and washed out his stomach with chemicals he wouldn't have with him, there might be one chance in a thousand. As it is—"

"Can't you *do* something?" Mrs. Jerome squawked.

"Not for him, no. I'm not an officer of the law, but I'm a licensed detective, and I'm supposed to know how to act in these circumstances, and I'll get it if I don't follow the rules. Of course—"

"*Do something!*" Mrs. Jerome squawked.

Kiernan's voice came from behind me. "He's dead."

I didn't turn to ask what test he had used. "Of course," I told them, "his drink was poisoned. Until the police come no one will touch anything, especially the bottle of Pernod, and no one will leave this room. You will—"

I stopped dead. Then I demanded, "Where is Santa Claus?"

Their heads turned to look at the bar. No bartender. On the chance that it had been too much for him, I pushed between Leo Jerome and Emil Hatch to step to the end of the bar, but he wasn't on the floor either.

I wheeled. "Did anyone see him go?"

They hadn't. Hatch said, "He didn't take the elevator. I'm sure he didn't. He must have—" He started off.

I blocked him. "You stay here. I'll take a look. Kiernan, phone the police. Spring seven-three-one-hundred."

I made for the door on the left and passed through, pulling it shut as I went, and was in Bottweill's office, which I had seen before. It was one-fourth the size of the studio, and much more subdued, but was by no means squalid. I crossed to the far end, saw through the glass panel that Bottweill's private elevator wasn't there, and pressed the button. A clank and a whirr came from inside the shaft, and it was coming. When it was up and had jolted to a stop I opened the door, and there on the floor was Santa Claus, but only the outside of him. He had molted. Jacket, breeches, mask, wig . . . I didn't check to see if it was all there, because I had another errand and not much time for it.

Propping the elevator door open with a chair, I went and circled around Bottweill's big gold-leaf desk to his gold-leaf wastebasket. It was one-third full. Bending, I started to paw, decided that was inefficient, picked it up and dumped it, and began tossing things back in one by one. Some of the items were torn pieces of paper, but none of them came from a marriage license. When I had finished I stayed down a moment, squatting, wondering if I had hurried too much and possibly missed it, and I might have gone through it again if I hadn't heard a faint noise from the studio that sounded like the elevator door opening. I went to the door to the studio and opened it, and as I crossed the sill two uniformed cops were deciding whether to give their first glance to the dead or the living.

III

Three hours later we were seated, more or less in a group, and my old friend and foe, Sergeant Purley Stebbins of Homicide, stood surveying us, his square jaw jutting and his big burly frame erect.

He spoke. "Mr. Kiernan and Mr. Hatch will be taken to the District Attorney's office for further questioning. The rest of you can go for the present, but you will keep yourselves available at the addresses you have given. Before you go I want to ask you again, here together, about the man who was here as Santa Claus. You have all claimed you know nothing about him. Do you still claim that?"

It was twenty minutes to seven. Some two dozen city employees—medical examiner, photographer, fingerprinters, meat-basket bearers, the whole kaboodle—had finished the on-the-scene routine, including private interviews with the eyewitnesses. I had made the highest score, having had sessions with Stebbins, a precinct man, and Inspector Cramer, who had departed around five o'clock to organize the hunt for Santa Claus.

"I'm not objecting," Kiernan told Stebbins, "to going to the District Attorney's office. I'm not objecting to anything. But we've told you all we can, I know I have. It seems to me your job is to find him."

"Do you mean to say," Mrs. Jerome demanded, "that no one knows anything at all about him?"

"So they say," Purley told her. "No one even knew there was going to be a Santa Claus, so they say. He was brought to this room by Bottweill, about a quarter to three, from his office. The idea is that Bottweill himself had arranged for him, and he came up in the private elevator and put on the costume in Bottweill's office. You may as well know there is some corroboration of that. We have found out where the costume came from—Burleson's on Forty-sixth Street. Bottweill phoned them yesterday afternoon and ordered it sent here, marked personal. Miss Quon admits receiving the package and taking it to Bottweill in his office."

For a cop, you never just state a fact, or report it or declare it or say it. You admit it.

"We are also," Purley admitted, "covering agencies which might have supplied a man to act Santa Claus, but that's a big order. If Bottweill got a man through an agency there's no telling what he got. If it was a man with a record, when he saw trouble coming he beat it. With everybody's attention on Bottweill, he sneaked out, got his clothes, whatever he had taken off, in Bottweill's office, and went down in the elevator he had come up in. He shed the costume on the way down and after he was down, and left it in the elevator. If that was it, if he was just a man Bottweill hired, he wouldn't have had any reason to kill him—and besides, he wouldn't have known that

Bottweill's only drink was Pernod, and he wouldn't have known where the poison was.''

"Also," Emil Hatch said, sourer than ever, "if he was just hired for the job he was a damn fool to sneak out. He might have known he'd be found. So he wasn't just hired. He was someone who knew Bottweill, and knew about the Pernod and the poison, and had some good reason for wanting to kill him. You're wasting your time on the agencies.''

Stebbins lifted his heavy broad shoulders and dropped them. "We waste most of our time, Mr. Hatch. Maybe he was too scared to think. I just want you to understand that if we find him and that's how Bottweill got him, it's going to be hard to believe that he put poison in that bottle, but somebody did. I want you to understand that so you'll understand why you are all to be available at the addresses you have given. Don't make any mistake about that.''

"Do you mean," Mrs. Jerome demanded, "that we are under suspicion? That *I* and *my son* are under suspicion?''

Purley opened his mouth and shut it again. With that kind he always had trouble with his impulses. He wanted to say, "You're goddam right you are." He did say, "I mean we're going to find that Santa Claus, and when we do we'll see. If we can't see him for it we'll have to look further, and we'll expect all of you to help us. I'm taking it for granted you'll all want to help. Don't you want to, Mrs. Jerome?''

"I would help if I could, but I know nothing about it. I only know that my very dear friend is dead, and I don't intend to be abused and threatened. What about the poison?''

"You know about it. You have been questioned about it.''

"I know I have, but what about it?''

"It must have been apparent from the questions. The medical examiner thinks it was cyanide and expects the autopsy to verify it. Emil Hatch uses potassium cyanide in his work with metals and plating, and there is a large jar of it on a cupboard shelf in the workshop one floor below, and there is a stair from Bottweill's office to the workroom. Anyone who knew that, and who also knew that Bottweill kept a case of Pernod in a cabinet in his office, and an open bottle of it in a drawer of his desk, couldn't have asked for a better setup. Four of you have admitted knowing both of those things. Three of you—Mrs. Jerome, Leo Jerome, and Archie Goodwin—admit they knew about the Pernod but deny they knew about the potassium cyanide. That will—''

"That's not true! She did know about it!''

Mrs. Perry Porter Jerome's hand shot out across her son's knees and slapped Cherry Quon's cheek or mouth or both. Her son grabbed her arm. Alfred Kiernan sprang to his feet, and for a second I thought he was going to sock Mrs. Jerome, and he did too, and possibly would have if Margot Dickey hadn't jerked at his coattail. Cherry put her hand to her face but, except for that, didn't move.

"Sit down," Stebbins told Kiernan. "Take it easy. Miss Quon, you say that Mrs. Jerome knew about the potassium cyanide?"

"Of course she did." Cherry's chirp was pitched lower than normal, but it was still a chirp. "In the workshop one day I heard Mr. Hatch telling her how he used it and how careful he had to be."

"Mr. Hatch? Do you verify—"

"Nonsense," Mrs. Jerome snapped. "What if he did? Perhaps he did. I had forgotten all about it. I told you I won't tolerate this abuse!"

Purley eyed her. "Look here, Mrs. Jerome. When we find that Santa Claus, if it was someone who knew Bottweill and had a motive, that may settle it. If not, it won't help anyone to talk about abuse, and that includes you. So far as I know now, only one of you has told us a lie. You. That's on the record. I'm telling you, and all of you, lies only make it harder for you, but sometimes they make it easier for us. I'll leave it at that for now. Mr. Kiernan and Mr. Hatch, these men"—he aimed a thumb over his shoulder at two dicks standing back of him—"will take you downtown. The rest of you can go, but remember what I said. Goodwin, I want to see you."

He had already seen me, but I wouldn't make a point of it. Kiernan, however, had a point to make, and made it: he had to leave last so he could lock up. It was so arranged. The three women, Leo Jerome, and Stebbins and I took the elevator down, leaving the two dicks with Kiernan and Hatch. Down the sidewalk, as they headed in different directions, I could see no sign of tails taking after them. It was still snowing, a fine prospect for Christmas and the street cleaners. There were two police cars at the curb, and Purley went to one and opened the door and motioned to me to get in.

I objected. "If I'm invited downtown too I'm willing to oblige, but I'm going to eat first. I damn near starved to death there once."

"You're not wanted downtown, not right now. Get in out of the snow."

I did so, and slid across under the wheel to make room for him. He needs room. He joined me and pulled the door shut.

"If we're going to sit here," I suggested, "we might as well be rolling. Don't bother to cross town, just drop me at Thirty-fifth."

He objected. "I don't like to drive and talk. Or listen. What were you doing there today?"

"I've told you. Having fun. Three kinds of champagne. Miss Dickey invited me."

"I'm giving you another chance. You were the only outsider there. Why? You're nothing special to Miss Dickey. She was going to marry Bottweill. Why?"

"Ask her."

"We have asked her. She says there was no particular reason, she knew Bottweill liked you, and they've regarded you as one of them since you found some tapestries for them. She stuttered around about it. What I say, any time I find you anywhere near a murder, I want to know. I'm giving you another chance."

So she hadn't mentioned the marriage license. Good for her. I would rather have eaten all the snow that had fallen since noon than explain that damn license to Sergeant Stebbins or Inspector Cramer. That was why I had gone through the wastebasket. "Thanks for the chance," I told him, "but I can't use it. I've told you everything I saw and heard there today." That put me in a class with Mrs. Jerome, since I had left out my little talk with Margot. "I've told you all I know about those people. Lay off and go find your murderer."

"I know you, Goodwin."

"Yeah, you've even called me Archie. I treasure that memory."

"I know you." His head was turned on his bull neck, and our eyes were meeting. "Do you expect me to believe that guy got out of that room and away without you knowing it?"

"Nuts. I was kneeling on the floor, watching a man die, and they were around us. Anyway, you're just talking to hear yourself. You don't think I was accessory to the murder or to the murderer's escape."

"I didn't say I did. Even if he was wearing gloves—and what for if not to leave no prints?—I don't say he was the murderer. But if you knew who he was and didn't want him involved in it and let him get away, and if you let us wear out our ankles looking for him, what about that?"

"That would be bad. If I asked my advice I would be against it."

"Goddam it," he barked, "do you know who he is?"

"No."

"Did you or Wolfe have anything to do with getting him there?"

"No."

"All right, pile out. They'll be wanting you downtown."

"I hope not tonight. I'm tired." I opened the door. "You have my address." I stepped out into the snow, and he started the engine and rolled off.

It should have been a good hour for an empty taxi, but in a Christmas-season snowstorm it took me ten minutes to find one. When it pulled up in front of the old brownstone on West Thirty-fifth Street it was eight minutes to eight.

As usual in my absence, the chain-bolt was on, and I had to ring for Fritz to let me in. I asked him if Wolfe was back, and he said yes, he was at dinner. As I put my hat on the shelf and my coat on a hanger I asked if there was any left for me, and he said plenty, and moved aside for me to precede him down the hall to the door of the dining room. Fritz has fine manners.

Wolfe, in his oversized chair at the end of the table, told me good evening, not snapping or barking. I returned it, got seated at my place, picked up my napkin, and apologized for being late. Fritz came, from the kitchen, with a warm plate, a platter of braised boned ducklings, and a dish of potatoes baked with mushrooms and cheese. I took enough. Wolfe asked if it was still snowing and I said yes. After a good mouthful had been disposed of, I spoke.

"As you know, I approve of your rule not to discuss business during a meal, but I've got something on my chest and it's not business. It's personal."

He grunted. "The death of Mr. Bottweill was reported on the radio at seven o'clock. You were there."

"Yeah. I was there. I was kneeling by him while he died." I replenished my mouth. Damn the radio. I hadn't intended to mention the murder until I had dealt with the main issue from my standpoint. When there was room enough for my tongue to work I went on, "I'll report on that in full if you want it, but I doubt if there's a job in it. Mrs. Perry Porter Jerome is the only suspect with enough jack to pay your fee, and she has already notified Purley Stebbins that she won't be abused. Besides, when they find Santa Claus that may settle it. What I want to report on happened before Bottweill died. That marriage license I showed you is for the birds. Miss Dickey has called it off. I am out two bucks. She told me she had decided to marry Bottweill."

He was sopping a crust in the sauce on his plate. "Indeed," he said.

"Yes, sir. It was a jolt, but I would have recovered, in time. Then ten minutes later Bottweill was dead. Where does that leave me? Sitting around up there through the routine, I considered it. Perhaps I could get her back now, but no thank you. That license has been destroyed. I get another one, another two bucks, and then she tells me she has decided to marry Joe Doakes. I'm going to forget her. I'm going to blot her out."

I resumed on the duckling. Wolfe was busy chewing. When he could he said, "For me, of course, this is satisfactory."

"I know it is. Do you want to hear about Bottweill?"

"After dinner."

"Okay. How did you make out with Thompson?"

But that didn't appeal to him as a dinner topic either. In fact, nothing did. Usually he likes table talk, about anything from refrigerators to Republicans, but apparently the trip to Long Island and back, with all its dangers, had tired him out. It suited me all right, since I had had a noisy afternoon too and could stand a little silence. When we had both done well with the duckling and potatoes and salad and baked pears and cheese and coffee, he pushed back his chair.

"There's a book," he said, "that I want to look at. It's up in your room—*Here and Now,* by Herbert Block. Will you bring it down, please?"

Though it meant climbing two flights with a full stomach, I was glad to oblige, out of appreciation for his calm acceptance of my announcement of my shattered hopes. He could have been very vocal. So I mounted the stairs cheerfully, went to my room, and crossed to the shelves where I keep a few books. There were only a couple of dozen of them, and I knew where each one was, but *Here and Now* wasn't there. Where it should have been was a gap. I looked around, saw a book on the dresser, and stepped to it. It was *Here and Now,* and lying on top of it was a pair of white cotton gloves.

I gawked.

IV

I would like to say that I caught on immediately, the second I spotted them, but I didn't. I had picked them up and looked them over, and put one of them on and taken it off again, before I fully realized that there was only one possible explanation. Having realized it, instantly there was a traffic jam inside my skull, horns blowing, brakes squealing, head-on collisions. To deal with it I went to a chair and sat. It took me maybe a minute to reach my first clear conclusion.

He had taken this method of telling me he was Santa Claus, instead of just telling me, because he wanted me to think it over on my own before we talked it over together.

Why did he want me to think it over on my own? That took a little longer, but with the traffic under control I found my way through to the only acceptable answer. He had decided to give up his trip to see Thompson, and instead to arrange with Bottweill to attend the Christmas party disguised as Santa Claus, because the idea of a woman living in his house—or of the only alternative, my leaving—had made him absolutely desperate, and he had to see for himself. He had to see Margot and me together, and to talk with her if possible. If he found out that the marriage license was a hoax he would have me by the tail; he could tell me he would be delighted to welcome my bride and watch me wriggle out. If he found that I really meant it he would know what he was up against and go on from there. The point was this, that he had shown what he really thought of me. He had shown that rather than lose me he would do something that he wouldn't have done for any fee anybody could name. He would rather have gone without beer for a week than admit it, but now he was a fugitive from justice in a murder case and needed me. So he had to let me know, but he wanted it understood that that aspect of the matter was not to be mentioned. The assumption would be that he had gone to Bottweill's instead of Long Island because he loved to dress up like Santa Claus and tend bar.

A cell in my brain tried to get the right of way for the question, considering this development, how big a raise should I get after New Year's? but I waved it to the curb.

I thought over other aspects. He had worn the gloves so I couldn't recognize his hands. Where did he get them? What time had he got to Bottweill's and who had seen him? Did Fritz know where he was going? How had he got back home? But after a little of that I realized that he hadn't sent me up to my room to ask myself questions he could answer, so I went back to considering whether there was anything else he wanted me to think over alone. Deciding there wasn't, after chewing it thoroughly, I got *Here and Now* and the gloves from the dresser, went to the stairs and descended, and entered the office.

From behind his desk, he glared at me as I crossed over.

"Here it is," I said, and handed him the book. "And much obliged for the gloves." I held them up, one in each hand, dangling them from thumb and fingertip.

"It is no occasion for clowning," he growled.

"It sure isn't." I dropped the gloves on my desk, whirled my chair, and sat. "Where do we start? Do you want to know what happened after you left?"

"The details can wait. First where we stand. Was Mr. Cramer there?"

"Yes. Certainly."

"Did he get anywhere?"

"No. He probably won't until he finds Santa Claus. Until they find Santa Claus they won't dig very hard at the others. The longer it takes to find him the surer they'll be he's it. Three things about him: nobody knows who he was, he beat it, and he wore gloves. A thousand men are looking for him. You were right to wear the gloves, I would have recognized your hands, but where did you get them?"

"At a store on Ninth Avenue. Confound it, I didn't know a man was going to be murdered!"

"I know you didn't. May I ask some questions?"

He scowled. I took it for yes. "When did you phone Bottweill to arrange it?"

"At two-thirty yesterday afternoon. You had gone to the bank."

"Have you any reason to think he told anyone about it?"

[373]

"No. He said he wouldn't."

"I know he got the costume, so that's okay. When you left here today at twelve-thirty did you go straight to Bottweill's?"

"No. I left at that hour because you and Fritz expected me to. I stopped to buy the gloves, and met him at Rusterman's, and we had lunch. From there we took a cab to his place, arriving shortly after two o'clock, and took his private elevator up to his office. Immediately upon entering his office, he got a bottle of Pernod from a drawer of his desk, said he always had a little after lunch, and invited me to join him. I declined. He poured a liberal portion in a glass, about two ounced, drank it in two gulps, and returned the bottle to the drawer."

"My God." I whistled. "The cops would like to know *that*."

"No doubt. The costume was there in a box. There is a dressing room at the rear of his office, with a bathroom—"

"I know. I've used it."

"I took the costume there and put it on. He had ordered the largest size, but it was a squeeze and it took a while. I was in there half an hour or more. When I re-entered the office it was empty, but soon Bottweill came, up the stairs from the workshop, and helped me with the mask and wig. They had barely been adjusted when Emil Hatch and Mrs. Jerome and her son appeared, also coming up the stairs from the workshop. I left, going to the studio, and found Miss Quon and Miss Dickey and Mr. Kiernan there."

"And before long I was there. Then no one saw you unmasked. When did you put the gloves on?"

"The last thing. Just before I entered the studio."

"Then you may have left prints. I know, you didn't know there was going to be a murder. You left your clothes in the dressing room? Are you sure you got everything when you left?"

"Yes. I am not a complete ass."

I let that by. "Why didn't you leave the gloves in the elevator with the costume?"

"Because they hadn't come with it, and I thought it better to take them."

"That private elevator is at the rear of the hall downstairs. Did anyone see you leaving it or passing through the hall?"

"No. The hall was empty."

"How did you get home? Taxi?"

"No. Fritz didn't expect me until six or later. I walked to the public library, spent some two hours there, and then took a cab."

I pursed my lips and shook my head to indicate sympathy. That was his longest and hardest tramp since Montenegro. Over a mile. Fighting his way through the blizzard, in terror of the law on his tail. But all the return I got for my look of sympathy was a scowl, so I let loose. I laughed. I put my head back and let it come. I had wanted to ever since I had learned he was Santa Claus, but had been too busy thinking. It was bottled up in me, and I let it out, good. I was about to taper off to a cackle when he exploded.

"Confound it," he bellowed, "marry and be damned!"

That was dangerous. That attitude could easily get us onto the aspect he had sent me up to my room to think over alone, and if we got started on that anything could happen. It called for tact.

"I beg your pardon," I said. "Something caught in my throat. Do you want to describe the situation, or do you want me to?"

"I would like to hear you try," he said grimly.

"Yes, sir. I suspect that the only thing to do is to phone Inspector Cramer right now and invite him to come and have a chat, and when he comes open the bag. That will—"

"No. I will not do that."

"Then, next best, I go to him and spill it there. Of course—"

"No." He meant every word of it.

"Okay, I'll describe it. They'll mark time on the others until they find Santa Claus. They've got to find him. If he left any prints they'll compare them with every file they've got, and sooner or later they'll get to yours. They'll cover all the stores for sales of white cotton gloves to men. They'll trace Bottweill's movements and learn that he lunched with you at Ruster-man's, and you left together, and they'll trace you to Bottweill's place. Of course your going there won't prove you were Santa Claus, you might talk your way out of that, and it will account for your prints if they find some, but what about the gloves? They'll trace that sale if you give them time, and with a description of the buyer they'll find Santa Claus. You're sunk."

I had never seen his face blacker.

"If you sit tight till they find him," I argued, "it will be quite a nuisance. Cramer has been itching for years to lock you up, and any judge would commit you as a material witness who had run out. Whereas if you call Cramer now, and I mean now, and invite him to come and have some beer, while it will still be a nuisance, it will be bearable. Of course he'll want to know why you went there and played Santa Claus, but you can tell him anything you please. Tell him you bet me a hundred bucks, or what the hell, make it a grand, that you could be in a room with me for ten minutes and I wouldn't recognize you. I'll be glad to cooperate."

I leaned forward. "Another thing. If you wait till they find you, you won't dare tell them that Bottweill took a drink from that bottle shortly after two o'clock and it didn't hurt him. If you told about that after they dug you up, they could book you for withholding evidence, and they probably would, and make it stick. If you get Cramer here now and tell him he'll ap-

[375]

preciate it, though naturally he won't say so. He's probably at his office. Shall I ring him?''

''No. I will not confess that performance to Mr. Cramer. I will not unfold the morning paper to a disclosure of that outlandish masquerade.''

''Then you're going to sit and read *Here and Now* until they come with a warrant?''

''No. That would be fatuous.'' He took in air through his mouth, as far down as it would go, and let it out through his nose. ''I'm going to find the murderer and present him to Mr. Cramer. There's nothing else.''

''Oh. You are.''

''Yes.''

''You might have said so and saved my breath, instead of letting me spout.''

''I wanted to see if your appraisal of the situation agreed with mine. It does.''

''That's fine. They you also know that we may have two weeks and we may have two minutes. At this very second some expert may be phoning Homicide to say that he has found fingerprints that match on the card of Wolfe, Nero—''

The phone rang, and I jerked around as if someone had stuck a needle in me. Maybe we wouldn't have even two minutes. My hand wasn't trembling as I lifted the receiver, I hope. Wolfe seldom lifts his until I have found out who it is, but that time he did.

''Nero Wolfe's office, Archie Goodwin speaking.''

''This is the District Attorney's office, Mr. Goodwin. Regarding the murder of Kurt Bottweill. We would like you to be here at ten o'clock tomorrow morning.''

''All right. Sure.''

''At ten o'clock sharp, please.''

''I'll be there.''

We hung up. Wolfe sighed. I sighed.

''Well,'' I said, ''I've already told them six times that I know absolutely nothing about Santa Claus, so they may not ask me again. If they do, it will be interesting to compare my voice when I'm lying with when I'm telling the truth.''

He grunted. ''Now. I want a complete report of what happened there after I left, but first I want background. In your intimate association with Miss Dickey you must have learned things about those people. What?''

''Not much.'' I cleared my throat. ''I guess I'll have to explain something. My association with Miss Dickey was not intimate.'' I stopped. It wasn't easy.

"Choose your own adjective. I meant no innuendo."

"It's not a question of adjectives. Miss Dickey is a good dancer, exceptionally good, and for the past couple of months I have been taking her here and there, some six or eight times altogether. Monday evening at the Flamingo Club she asked me to do her a favor. She said Bottweill was giving her a runaround, that he had been going to marry her for a year but kept stalling, and she wanted to do something. She said Cherry Quon was making a play for him, and she didn't intend to let Cherry take the rail. She asked me to get a marriage-license blank and fill it out for her and me and give it to her. She would show it to Bottweill and tell him now or never. It struck me as a good deed with no risk involved, and, as I say, she is a good dancer. Tuesday afternoon I got a blank, no matter how, and that evening, up in my room, I filled in, including a fancy signature."

Wolfe made a noise.

"That's all," I said, "except that I want to make it clear that I had no intention of showing it to you. I did that on the spur of the moment when you picked up your book. Your memory is as good as mine. Also, to close it up, no doubt you noticed that today just before Bottweill and Mrs. Jerome joined the party Margot and I stepped aside for a little chat. She told me the license did the trick. Her words were, 'Perfect, simply perfect.' She said that last evening, in his office, he tore the license up and put the pieces in his wastebasket. That's okay, the cops didn't find them. I looked before they came, and the pieces weren't there."

His mouth was working, but he didn't open it. He didn't dare. He would have liked to tear into me, to tell me that my insufferable flummery had got him into this awful mess, but if he did so he would be dragging in the aspect he didn't want mentioned. He saw that in time, and saw that I saw it. His mouth worked, but that was all. Finally he spoke.

"Then you are not on intimate terms with Miss Dickey."

"No, sir."

"Even so, she must have spoken of that establishment and those people."

"Some, yes."

"And one of them killed Bottweill. The poison was put in the bottle between two-ten, when I saw him take a drink, and three-thirty when Kiernan went and got the bottle. No one came up in the private elevator during the half-hour or more I was in the dressing room. I was getting into that costume and gave no heed to footsteps or other sounds in the office, but the elevator shaft adjoins the dressing room, and I would have heard it. It is a strong probability that the opportunity was even narrower, that the poison was put in the bottle while I was in the dressing room, since three of

[377]

them were in the office with Bottweill when I left. It must be assumed that one of those three, or one of the three in the studio, had grasped an earlier opportunity. What about them?''

''Not much. Mostly from Monday evening, when Margot was talking about Bottweill. So it's all hearsay, from her. Mrs. Jerome has put half a million in the business—probably you should divide that by two at least—and thinks she owns him. Or thought. She was jealous of Margot and Cherry. As for Leo, if his mother was dishing out the dough he expected to inherit to a guy who was trying to corner the world's supply of gold leaf, and possibly might also marry him, and if he knew about the jar of poison in the workshop, he might have been tempted. Kiernan, I don't know, but from a remark Margot made and from the way he looked at Cherry this afternoon, I suspect he would like to mix some Irish with her Chinese and Indian and Dutch, and if he thought Bottweill had him stymied he might have been tempted too. So much for hearsay.''

''Mr. Hatch?''

''Nothing on him from Margot, but, dealing with him during the tapestry job, I wouldn't have been surprised if he had wiped out the whole bunch on general principles. His heart pumps acid instead of blood. He's a creative artist, he told me so. He practically told me that he was responsible for the success of that enterprise but got no credit. He didn't tell me that he regarded Bottweill as a phony and a fourflusher, but he did. You may remember that I told you he had a persecution complex and you told me to stop using other people's jargon.''

''That's four of them. Miss Dickey?''

I raised my brows. ''I got her a license to marry, not to kill. If she was lying when she said it worked, she's almost as good a liar as she is a dancer. Maybe she is. If it didn't work she might have been tempted too.''

''And Miss Quon?''

''She's half Oriental. I'm not up on Orientals, but I understand they slant their eyes to keep you guessing. That's what makes them inscrutable. If I had to be poisoned by one of that bunch I would want it to be her. Except for what Margot told me—''

The doorbell rang. That was worse than the phone. If they had hit on Santa Claus's trail and it led to Nero Wolfe, Cramer was much more apt to come than to call. Wolfe and I exchanged glances. Looking at my wristwatch and seeing 10:08, I arose, went to the hall and flipped the switch for the stoop light, and took a look through the one-way glass panel of the front door. I have good eyes, but the figure was muffled in a heavy coat with a hood, so I stepped halfway to the door to make sure. Then I returned to the office and told Wolfe, ''Cherry Quon. Alone.''

He frowned. ''I wanted—'' He cut it off. ''Very well. Bring her in.''

V

As I have said, Cherry was highly decorative, and she went fine with the red leather chair at the end of Wolfe's desk. It would have held three of her. She had let me take her coat in the hall and still had on the neat little woolen number she had worn at the party. It wasn't exactly yellow, but there was yellow in it. I would have called it off-gold, and it and the red chair and the tea tint of her smooth little carved face would have made a very nice koda-chrome.

She sat on the edge, her spine straight and her hands together in her lap. "I was afraid to telephone," she said, "because you might tell me not to come. So I just came. Will you forgive me?"

Wolfe grunted. No commitment. She smiled at him, a friendly smile, or so I thought. After all, she was half Oriental.

"I must get myself together," she chirped. "I'm nervous because it's so exciting to be here." She turned her head. "There's the glove, and the bookshelves, and the safe, and the couch, and of course Archie Goodwin. And you. You behind your desk in your enormous chair! Oh, I know this place! I have read about you so much—everything there is, I think. It's exciting to be here, actually here in this chair, and see you. Of course I saw you this afternoon, but that wasn't the same thing, you could have been anybody in that silly Santa Claus costume. I wanted to pull your whiskers."

She laughed, a friendly little tinkle like a bell.

I think I looked bewildered. That was my idea, after it had got through my ears to the switchboard inside and been routed. I was too busy handling my face to look at Wolfe, but he was probably even busier, since she was looking straight at him. I moved my eyes to him when he spoke.

"If I understand you, Miss Quon, I'm at a loss. If you think you saw me this afternoon in a Santa Claus costume, you're mistaken."

"Oh, I'm sorry!" she exclaimed. "Then you haven't told them?"

"My dear madam." His voice sharpened. "If you must talk in riddles, talk to Mr. Goodwin. He enjoys them."

"But I *am* sorry, Mr. Wolfe. I should have explained first how I know. This morning at breakfast Kurt told me you had phoned him and arranged to appear at the party as Santa Claus, and this afternoon I asked him if you had come and he said you had and you were putting on the costume. That's how I know. But you haven't told the police? Then it's a good thing I haven't told them either, isn't it?"

"This is interesting," Wolfe said coldly. "What do you expect to accomplish by this fantastic folderol?"

She shook her pretty little head. "You, with so much sense. You must

[379]

see that it's no use. If I tell them, even if they don't like to believe me they will investigate. I know they can't investigate as well as you can, but surely they will find something.''

He shut his eyes, tightened his lips, and leaned back in his chair. I kept mind open, on her. She weighed about a hundred and two. I could carry her under one arm with my other hand clamped on her mouth. Putting her in the spare room upstairs wouldn't do, since she could open a window and scream, but there was a cubbyhole in the basement, next to Fritz's room, with an old couch in it. Or, as an alternative, I could get a gun from my desk drawer and shoot her. Probably no one knew she had come here.

Wolfe opened his eyes and straightened up. ''Very well. It is still fantastic, but I concede that you could create an unpleasant situation by taking that yarn to the police. I don't suppose you came here merely to tell me that you intend to. What do you intend?''

''I think we understand each other,'' she chirped.

''I understand only that you want something. What?''

''You are so direct,'' she complained. ''So very abrupt, that I must have said something wrong. But I do want something. You see, since the police think it was the man who acted Santa Claus and ran away, they may not get on the right track until it's too late. You wouldn't want that, would you?''

No reply.

''I wouldn't want it,'' she said, and her hands on her lap curled into little fists. ''I wouldn't want whoever killed Kurt to get away, no matter who it was, but you see, I know who killed him. I have told the police, but they won't listen until they find Santa Claus, or if they listen they think I'm just a jealous cat, and besides, I'm an Oriental and their ideas of Orientals are very primitive. I was going to make them listen by telling them who Santa Claus was, but I know how they feel about you from what I've read, and I was afraid they would try to prove it was you who killed Kurt, and of course it could have been you, and you did run away, and they still wouldn't listen to me when I told them who did kill him.''

She stopped for breath. Wolfe inquired, ''Who did?''

She nodded. ''I'll tell you. Margot Dickey and Kurt were having an affair. A few months ago Kurt began on me, and it was hard for me because I—I—'' she frowned for a word, and found one. ''I had a feeling for him. I had a strong feeling. But you see, I am a virgin, and I wouldn't give in to him. I don't know what I would have done if I hadn't known he was having an affair with Margot, but I did know, and I told him the first man I slept with would be my husband. He said he was willing to give up Margot, but even if he did he couldn't marry me on account of Mrs. Jerome, because she would stop backing him with her money. I don't know what he was to Mrs. Jerome, but I know what she was to him.''

Her hands opened and closed again to be fists. "That went on and on, but Kurt had a feeling for me too. Last night late, it was after midnight, he phoned me that he had broken with Margot for good and he wanted to marry me. He wanted to come and see me, but I told him I was in bed and we would see each other in the morning. He said that would be at the studio with other people there, so finally I said I would go to his apartment for breakfast, and I did, this morning. But I am still a virgin, Mr. Wolfe."

He was focused on her with half-closed eyes. "That is your privilege, madam."

"Oh," she said. "Is it a privilege? It was there, at breakfast, that he told me about you, your arranging to be Santa Claus. When I got to the studio I was surprised to see Margot there, and how friendly she was. That was part of her plan, to be friendly and cheerful with everyone. She has told the police that Kurt was going to marry her, that they decided last night to get married next week. Christmas week. I am a Christian."

Wolfe stirred in his chair. "Have we reached the point? Did Miss Dickey kill Mr. Bottweill?"

"Yes. Of course she did."

"Have you told the police that?"

"Yes. I didn't tell them all I have told you, but enough."

"With evidence?"

"No. I have no evidence."

"Then you're vulnerable to an action for slander."

She opened her fists and turned her palms up. "Does that matter? When I know I'm right? When I *know* it? But she was so clever, the way she did it, that there can't be any evidence. Everybody there today knew about the poison, and they all had a chance to put it in the bottle. They can never prove she did it. They can't even prove she is lying when she says Kurt was going to marry her, because he is dead. She acted today the way she would have acted if that had been true. But it has got to be proved somehow. There has got to be evidence to prove it."

"And you want me to get it?"

She let that pass. "What I was thinking, Mr. Wolfe, you are vulnerable too. There will always be the danger that the police will find out who Santa Claus was, and if they find it was you and you didn't tell them—"

"I haven't conceded that," Wolfe snapped.

"Then we'll just say there will always be the danger that I'll tell them what Kurt told me, and you did concede that that would be unpleasant. So it would be better if the evidence proved who killed Kurt and also proved who Santa Claus was. Wouldn't it?"

"Go on."

"So I thought how easy it would be for you to get the evidence. You have

[381]

men who do things for you, who would do anything for you, and one of them can say that you asked him to go there and be Santa Claus, and he did. Of course it couldn't be Mr. Goodwin, since he was at the party, and it would have to be a man they couldn't prove was somewhere else. He can say that while he was in the dressing room putting on the costume he heard someone in the office and peeked out to see who it was, and he saw Margot Dickey get the bottle from the desk drawer and put something in it and put the bottle back in the drawer, and go out. That must have been when she did it, because Kurt always took a drink of Pernod when he came back from lunch."

Wolfe was rubbing his lip with a fingertip. "I see," he muttered.

She wasn't through. "He can say," she went on, "that he ran away because he was frightened and wanted to tell you about it first. I don't think they would do anything to him if he went to them tomorrow morning and told them all about it, would they? Just like me. I don't think they would do anything to me if I went to them tomorrow morning and told them I had remembered that Kurt told me that you were going to be Santa Claus, and this afternoon he told me you were in the dressing room putting on the costume. That would be the same kind of thing, wouldn't it?"

Her little carved mouth thinned and widened with a smile. "That's what I want," she chirped. "Did I say it so you understand it?"

"You did indeed," Wolfe assured her. "You put it admirably."

"Would it be better, instead of him going to tell them, for you to have Inspector Cramer come here, and you tell him? You could have the man here. You see, I know how you do things, from all I have read."

"That might be better," he allowed. His tone was dry but not hostile. I could see a muscle twitching beneath his right ear, but she couldn't. "I suppose, Miss Quon, it is futile to advance the possibility that one of the others killed him, and if so it would be a pity—"

"Excuse me. I interrupt." The chirp was still a chirp, but it had hard steel in it. "I know she killed him."

"I don't. And even if I bow to your conviction, before I could undertake the stratagem you propose I would have to make sure there are no facts that would scuttle it. It won't take me long. You'll hear from me tomorrow. I'll want—"

She interrupted again. "I can't wait longer than tomorrow morning to tell them what Kurt told me."

"Pfui. You can and will. The moment you disclose that, you no longer have a whip to dangle at me. You will hear from me tomorrow. Now I want to think. Archie?"

I left my chair. She looked up at me and back at Wolfe. For some seconds she sat, considering, inscrutable of course, then stood up.

"It was very exciting to be here," she said, the steel gone, "to see you here. You must forgive me for not phoning. I hope it will be early tomorrow.'' She turned and headed for the door, and I followed.

After I had helped her on with her hooded coat, and let her out, and watched her picking her way down the seven steps, I shut the door, put the chain-bolt on, returned to the office, and told Wolfe, ''It has stopped snowing. Who do you think will be best for it, Saul or Fred or Orrie or Bill?''

''Sit down,'' he growled. ''You see through women. Well?''

''Not that one. I pass. I wouldn't bet a dime on her one way or the other. Would you?''

''No. She is probably a liar and possibly a murderer. Sit down. I must have everything that happened there today after I left. Every word and gesture.''

I sat and gave it to him. Including the question period, it took an hour and thirty-five minutes. It was after one o'clock when he pushed his chair back, levered his bulk upright, told me good night, and went up to bed.

VI

At half past two the following afternoon, Saturday, I sat in a room in a building on Leonard Street, the room where I had once swiped an assistant district attorney's lunch. There would be no need for me to repeat the performance, since I had just come back from Ost's restaurant, where I had put away a plateful of pig's knuckles and sauerkraut.

As far as I knew, there had not only been no steps to frame Margot for murder; there had been no steps at all. Since Wolfe is up in the plant rooms every morning from nine to eleven, and since he breakfasts from a tray up in his room, and since I was expected downtown at ten o'clock, I had buzzed him on the house phone a little before nine to ask for instructions and had been told that he had none. Downtown Assistant DA Farrell, after letting me wait in the anteroom for an hour, had spent two hours with me, together with a stenographer and a dick who had been on the scene Friday afternoon, going back and forth and zigzag, not only over what I had already reported, but also over my previous association with the Bottweill personnel. He only asked me once if I knew anything about Santa Claus, so I only had to lie once, if you don't count my omitting any mention of the marriage license. When he called a recess and told me to come back at two-thirty, on my way to Ost's for the pig's knuckles I phoned Wolfe to tell him I didn't know when I would be home, and again he had no instructions. I said I doubted if Cherry Quon would wait until after New Year's to spill the beans, and he said he did too and hung up.

When I was ushered back into Farrell's office at two-thirty he was alone—no stenographer and no dick. He asked me if I had had a good lunch, and even waited for me to answer, handed me some typewritten sheets, and leaned back in his chair.

"Read it over," he said, "and see if you want to sign it."

His tone seemed to imply that I might not, so I went over it carefully, five full pages. Finding no editorial revisions to object to, I pulled my chair forward to a corner of his desk, put the statement on the desk top, and got my pen from my pocket.

"Wait a minute," Farrell said. "You're not a bad guy even if you are cocky, and why not give you a break? That says specifically that you have reported everything you did there yesterday afternoon."

"Yeah, I've read it. So?"

"So who put your fingerprints on some of the pieces of paper in Bottweill's wastebasket?"

"I'll be damned," I said. "I forgot to put gloves on."

"All right, you're cocky. I already know that." His eyes were pinning me. "You must have gone through that wastebasket, every item, when you went to Bottweill's office ostensibly to look for Santa Claus, and you hadn't just forgotten it. You don't forget things. So you have deliberately left it out. I want to know why, and I want to know what you took from that wastebasket and what you did with it."

I grinned at him. "I am also damned because I thought I knew how thorough they are and apparently I didn't. I wouldn't have supposed they went so far as to dust the contents of a wastebasket when there was nothing to connect them, but I see I was wrong, and I hate to be wrong." I shrugged. "Well, we learn something new every day." I screwed the statement around to position, signed it at the bottom of the last page, slid it across to him, and folded the carbon copy and put it in my pocket.

"I'll write it in if you insist," I told him, "but I doubt if it's worth the trouble. Santa Claus had run, Kiernan was calling the police, and I guess I was a little rattled. I must have looked around for something that might give me a line on Santa Claus, and my eye lit on the wastebasket, and I went through it. I haven't mentioned it because it wasn't very bright, and I like people to think I'm bright, especially cops. There's your why. As for what I took, the answer is nothing. I dumped the wastebasket, put everything back in, and took nothing. Do you want me to write that in?"

"No. I want to discuss it. I know you *are* bright. And you weren't rattled. You don't rattle. I want to know the real reason you went through the wastebasket, what you were after, whether you got it, and what you did with it."

It cost me more than an hour, twenty minutes of which were spent in the office of the District Attorney himself, with Farrell and another assistant present. At one point it looked as if they were going to hold me as a material witness, but that takes a warrant, the Christmas weekend had started, and there was nothing to show that I had monkeyed with anything that could be evidence, so finally they shooed me out, after I had handwritten an insert in my statement. It was too bad keeping such important public servants sitting there while I copied the insert on my carbon, but I like to do things right.

By the time I got home it was ten minutes past four, and of course Wolfe wasn't in the office, since his afternoon session up in the plant rooms is from four to six. There was no note on my desk from him, so apparently there were still no instructions, but there was information on it. My desk ashtray, which is mostly for decoration since I seldom smoke—a gift, not to Wolfe but to me, from a former client—is a jade bowl six inches across. It was there in its place, and in it were stubs from Pharaoh cigarettes.

Saul Panzer smokes pharoahs, Egyptians. I suppose a few other people do too, but the chance that one of them had been sitting at my desk while I was gone was too slim to bother with. And not only had Saul been there, but Wolfe wanted me to know it, since one of the eight million things he will not tolerate in the office is ashtrays with remains. He will actually walk clear to the bathroom himself to empty one.

So steps were being taken, after all. What steps? Saul, a free lance and the best operative anywhere around, asks and gets sixty bucks a day, and is worth twice that. Wolfe had not called him in for any routine errand, and of course the idea that he had undertaken to sell him on doubling for Santa Claus never entered my head. Framing someone for murder, even a woman who might be guilty, was not in his bag of tricks. I got at the house phone and buzzed the plant rooms, and after a wait had Wolfe's voice in my ear.

"Yes, Fritz?"

"Not Fritz. Me. I'm back. Nothing urgent to report. They found my prints on stuff in the wastebasket, but I escaped without loss of blood. Is it all right for me to empty my ashtray?"

"Yes. Please do so."

"Then what do I do?"

"I'll tell you at six o'clock. Possibly earlier."

He hung up. I went to the safe and looked in the cash drawer to see if Saul had been supplied with generous funds, but the cash was as I had last seen it and there was no entry in the book. I emptied the ashtray. I went to the kitchen, where I found Fritz pouring a mixture into a bowl of pork tenderloin, and said I hoped Saul had enjoyed his lunch, and Fritz said he hadn't stayed for lunch. So steps must have been begun right after I left in the morning. I went back to the office, read over the carbon copy of my statement before filing it, and passed the time by thinking up eight different steps that Saul might have been assigned, but none of them struck me as promising. A little after five the phone rang and I answered. It was Saul. He said he was glad to know I was back home safe, and I said I was too.

"Just a message for Mr. Wolfe," he said. "Tell him everything is set, no snags."

"That's all?"

"Right. I'll be seeing you."

I cradled the receiver, sat a moment to consider whether to go up to the plant rooms or use the house phone, decided the latter would do, and pulled it to me and pushed the button. When Wolfe's voice came it was peevish; he hates to be disturbed up there.

"Yes?"

"Saul called and said to tell you everything is set, no snags. Congratulations. Am I in the way?"

"Oddly enough, no. Have chairs in place for visitors; ten should be enough. Four or five will come shortly after six o'clock; I hope not more. Others will come later."

"Refreshments?"

"Liquids, of course. Nothing else."

"Anything else for me?"

"No."

He was gone. Before going to the front room for chairs, and to the kitchen for supplies, I took time out to ask myself whether I had the slightest notion what kind of charade he was cooking up this time. I hadn't.

VII

It was four. They all arrived between six-fifteen and six-twenty—first Mrs. Perry Porter Jerome and her son Leo, then Cherry Quon, and last Emil Hatch. Mrs. Jerome copped the red leather chair, but I moved her, mink and all, to one of the yellow ones when Cherry came. I was willing to concede that Cherry might be headed for a very different kind of chair, wired for power, but even so I thought she rated that background and Mrs. Jerome didn't. By six-thirty, when I left them to cross the hall to the dining room, not a word had passed among them.

In the dining room Wolfe had just finished a bottle of beer. "Okay," I told him, "it's six-thirty-one. Only four. Kiernan and Margot Dickey haven't shown."

"Satisfactory." He arose. "Have they demanded information?"

"Two of them have, Hatch and Mrs. Jerome. I told them it will come from you, as instructed. That was easy, since I have none."

He headed for the office, and I followed. Though they didn't know, except Cherry, that he had poured champagne for them the day before, introductions weren't necessary because they had all met him during the tapestry hunt. After circling around Cherry in the red leather chair, he stood behind his desk to ask them how they did, then sat.

"I don't thank you for coming," he said, "because you came in your own interest, not mine. I sent—"

"I came," Hatch cut in, sourer than ever, "to find out what you're up to."

"You will," Wolfe assured him. "I sent each of you an identical message, saying that Mr. Goodwin has certain information which he feels he must give the police not later than tonight, but I have persuaded him to let me discuss it with you first. Before I—"

"I didn't know others would be here," Mrs. Jerome blurted, glaring at Cherry.

"Neither did I," Hatch said, glaring at Mrs. Jerome.

Wolfe ignored it. "The message I sent Miss Quon was somewhat different, but that need not concern you. Before I tell you what Mr. Goodwin's information is, I need a few facts from you. For instance, I understand that any of you—including Miss Dickey and Mr. Kiernan, who will probably join us later—could have found an opportunity to put the poison in the bottle. Do any of you challenge that?"

Cherry, Mrs. Jerome, and Leo all spoke at once. Hatch merely looked sour.

Wolfe showed them a palm. "If you please. I point no finger of accusation at any of you. I merely say that none of you, including Miss Dickey and Mr. Kiernan, can prove that you had no opportunity. Can you?"

"Nuts." Leo Jerome was disgusted. "It was that guy playing Santa Claus. Of course it was. I was with Bottweill and my mother all the time, first in the workshop and then in his office. I can prove *that*."

"But Bottweill is dead," Wolfe reminded him, "and your mother is your mother. Did you go up to the office a little before them, or did your mother go up a little before you and Bottweill did? Is there acceptable proof that you didn't? The others have the same problem. Miss Quon?"

There was no danger of Cherry's spoiling it. Wolfe had told me what he had told her on the phone: that he had made a plan which he thought she would find satisfactory, and if she came at a quarter past six she would see it work. She had kept her eyes fixed on him ever since he entered. Now she chirped, "If you mean I can't prove I wasn't in the office alone yesterday, no, I can't."

"Mr. Hatch?"

"I didn't come here to prove anything. I told you what I came for. What information has Goodwin got?"

"We'll get to that. A few more facts first. Mrs. Jerome, when did you learn that Bottweill had decided to marry Miss Quon?"

Leo shouted, "No!" but his mother was too busy staring at Wolfe to hear him. "What?" she croaked. Then she found her voice. "Kurt marry *her?* That little strumpet?"

Cherry didn't move a muscle, her eyes still on Wolfe.

"This is wonderful!" Leo said. "This is marvelous!"

"Not so damn wonderful," Emil Hatch declared. "I get the idea, Wolfe. Goodwin hasn't got any information, and neither have you. Why you wanted to get us together and start us clawing at each other, I don't see that, I don't know why you're interested, but maybe I'll find out if I give you a hand. This crowd has produced as fine a collection of venom as you could find. Maybe we all put poison in the bottle and that's why it was such a big dose. If it's true that Kurt had decided to marry Cherry, and Al Kiernan knew it, that would have done it. Al would have killed a hundred Kurts if it would get him Cherry. If Mrs. Jerome knew it, I would think she would have gone for Cherry instead of Kurt, but maybe she figured there would soon be another one and she might as well settle it for good. As for Leo, I think he rather liked Kurt, but what can you expect? Kurt was milking mamma of the pile Leo hoped to get some day, and I suspect that the pile is not all it's supposed to be. Actually—"

He stopped, and I left my chair. Leo was on his way up, obviously with the intention of plugging the creative artist. I moved to head him off, and at the same instant I gave him a shove and his mother jerked at his coattail. That not only halted him but nearly upset him, and with my other hand I steered him back onto his chair and then stood beside him.

Hatch inquired, "Shall I go on?"

"By all means," Wolfe said.

"Actually, though, Cherry would seem to be the most likely. She has the best brain of the lot and by far the strongest will. But I understand that while she says Kurt was going to marry her, Margot claims that he was going to marry *her.* Of course that complicates it, and anyway Margot would be my second choice. Margot has more than her share of the kind of pride that is only skin deep and therefore can't stand a scratch. If Kurt did decide to marry Cherry and told Margot so, he was even a bigger imbecile than I thought he was. Which brings us to me. I am in a class by myself. I despise all of them. If I had decided to take to poison I would have put it in the champagne as well as the Pernod, and I would have drunk vodka, which I prefer—and by the way, on that table is a bottle with the Korbeloff vodka label. I haven't had a taste of Korbeloff for fifteen years. Is it real?"

"It is. Archie?"

Serving liquid refreshment to a group of invited guests can be a pleasant chore, but it wasn't that time. When I asked Mrs. Jerome to name it she only glowered at me, but by the time I had filled Cherry's order for scotch and soda, and supplied Hatch with a liberal dose of Korbeloff, no dilution, and Leo had said he would take bourbon and water, his mother muttered that she would have that too. As I was pouring the bourbon I wondered where we would go from there. It looked as if the time had come for Wolfe to pass on the information which I felt I must give the police without delay, which made it difficult because I didn't have any. That had been fine for a bait to get them there, but what now? I suppose Wolfe would have held them somehow, but he didn't have to. He had rung for beer, and Fritz had brought it and was putting the tray on his desk when the doorbell rang. I handed Leo his bourbon and water and went to the hall. Out on the stoop, with his big round face nearly touching the glass, was Inspector Cramer of Homicide.

Wolfe had told me enough, before the company came, to give me a general idea of the program, so the sight of Cramer, just Cramer, was a let-down. But as I went down the hall other figures appeared, none of them strangers, and that looked better. In fact it looked fine. I swung the door wide and in they came—Cramer, then Saul Panzer, then Margot Dickey, then Alfred Kiernan, and, bringing up the rear, Sergeant Purley Stebbins. By the time I had the door closed and bolted they had their coats off, including Cramer, and it was also fine to see that he expected to stay a while. Ordinarily, once in, he marches down the hall and into the office without ceremony, but that time he waved the others ahead, including me, and he and Stebbins came last, herding us in. Crossing the sill, I stepped aside for the pleasure of seeing his face when his eyes lit on those already there and the empty chairs waiting. Undoubtedly he had expected to find Wolfe alone, reading a book. He came in two paces, glared around, fastened the glare on Wolfe, and barked, "What's all this?"

"I was expecting you," Wolfe said politely. "Miss Quon, if you don't mind moving, Mr. Cramer likes that chair. Good evening, Miss Dickey. Mr. Kiernan, Mr. Stebbins. If you will all be seated—"

"Panzer!" Cramer barked. Saul, who had started for a chair in the rear, stopped and turned.

"I'm running this," Cramer declared. "Panzer, you're under arrest and you'll stay with Stebbins and keep your mouth shut. I don't want—"

"No," Wolfe said sharply. "If he's under arrest take him out of here. You are not running this, not in my house. If you have warrants for anyone present, or have taken them by lawful police power, take them and leave these premises. Would you bulldoze me, Mr. Cramer? You should know better."

That was the point, Cramer did know him. There was the stage, all set.

There were Mrs. Jerome and Leo and Cherry and Emil Hatch, and the empty chairs, and above all, there was the fact that he had been expected. He wouldn't have taken Wolfe's word for that; he wouldn't have taken Wolfe's word for anything; but whenever he appeared on our stoop *not* expected I always left the chain-bolt on until he had stated his business and I had reported to Wolfe. And if he had been expected there was no telling what Wolfe had ready to spring. So Cramer gave up the bark and merely growled, "I want to talk with you."

"Certainly." Wolfe indicated the red leather chair, which Cherry had vacated. "Be seated."

"Not here. Alone."

Wolfe shook his head. "It would be a waste of time. This way is better and quicker. You know quite well, sir, it was a mistake to barge in here and roar at me that you are running my house. Either go, with whomever you can lawfully take, or sit down while I tell you who killed Kurt Bottweill." Wolfe wiggled a finger. "Your chair."

Cramer's round red face had been redder than normal from the outside cold, and now was redder still. He glanced around, compressed his lips until he didn't have any, and went to the red leather chair and sat.

VIII

Wolfe sent his eyes around as I circled to my desk. Saul had got to a chair in the rear after all, but Stebbins had too and was at his elbow. Margot had passed in front of the Jeromes and Emil Hatch to get to the chair at the end nearest me, and Cherry and Al Kiernan were at the other end, a little back of the others. Hatch had finished his Korbeloff and put the glass on the floor, but Cherry and the Jeromes were hanging on to their tall ones.

Wolfe's eyes came to rest on Cramer and he spoke. "I must confess that I stretched it a little. I can't tell you, at the moment, who killed Bottweill; I have only a supposition; but soon I can, and will. First some facts for you. I assume you know that for the past two months Mr. Goodwin has been seeing something of Miss Dickey. He says she dances well."

"Yeah." Cramer's voice came over sandpaper of the roughest grit. "You can save that for later. I want to know if you sent Panzer to meet—"

Wolfe cut him off. "You will. I'm headed for that. But you may prefer this firsthand. Archie, if you please. What Miss Dickey asked you to do last Monday evening, and what happened."

I cleared my throat. "We were dancing at the Flamingo Club. She said Bottweill had been telling her for a year that he would marry her next week, but next week never came, and she was going to have a showdown with him. She asked me to get a blank marriage license and fill it out for her and me and give it to her, and she would show it to Bottweill and tell him now or never. I got the blank on Tuesday, and filled it in, and Wednesday I gave it to her.''

I stopped. Wolfe prompted me. ''And yesterday afternoon?''

''She told me that the license trick had worked perfectly. That was about a minute before Bottweill entered the studio. I said in my statement to the District Attorney that she told me Bottweill was going to marry her, but I didn't mention the license. It was immaterial.''

''Did she tell you what had happened to the license?''

So we were emptying the bag. I nodded. ''She said Bottweill had torn it up and put the pieces in the wastebasket by the desk in his office. The night before. Thursday evening.''

''And what did you do when you went to the office after Bottweill had died?''

''I dumped the wastebasket and put the stuff back in it, piece by piece. No part of the license was there.''

''You made sure of that?''

''Yes.''

Wolfe left me and asked Cramer, ''Any questions?''

''No. He lied in his statement. I'll attend to that later. What I want—''

Margot Dickey blurted, ''Then Cherry took it!'' She craned her neck to see across the others. ''You took it, you slut!''

''I did not.'' The steel was in Cherry's chirp again. Her eyes didn't leave Wolfe, and she told him, ''I'm not going to wait any longer—''

''Miss Quon!'' he snapped. ''I'm doing this.'' He returned to Cramer. ''Now another fact. Yesterday I had a luncheon appointment with Mr. Bottweill at Rusterman's restaurant. He had once dined at my table and wished to reciprocate. Shortly before I left to keep the appointment he phoned to ask me to do him a favor. He said he was extremely busy and might be a few minutes late, and he needed a pair of white cotton gloves, medium size, for a man, and would I stop at some shop on the way and get them. It struck me as a peculiar request, but he was a peculiar man. Since Mr. Goodwin had chores to do, and I will not ride in taxicabs if there is any alternative, I had engaged a car at Baxter's, and the chauffeur recommended a shop on Eighth Avenue between Thirty-ninth and Fortieth Streets. We stopped there and I bought the gloves.''

Cramer's eyes were such narrow slits that none of the blue-gray showed. He wasn't buying any part of it, which was unjustified, since some of it was true.

Wolfe went on. ''At the lunch table I gave the gloves to Mr. Bottweill, and he explained, somewhat vaguely, what he wanted them for. I gathered that he had taken pity on some vagabond he had seen on a park bench, and had hired him to serve refreshments at his office party, costumed as Santa Claus, and he had decided that the only way to make his hands presentable was to have him wear gloves. You shake your head, Mr. Cramer?''

''You're damn right I do. You would have reported that. No reason on earth not to. Go ahead and finish.''

''I'll finish this first. I didn't report it because I thought you would find the murderer without it. It was practically certain that the vagabond had merely skedaddled out of fright, since he couldn't possibly have known of the jar of poison in the workshop, not to mention other considerations. And as you know, I have a strong aversion to involvement in matters where I have no concern or interest. You can of course check this—with the staff at Rusterman's, my presence there with Mr. Bottweill, and with the chauffeur, my conferring with him about the gloves and our stopping at the shop to buy them.''

''You're reporting it now.''

''I am indeed.'' Wolfe was unruffled. ''Because I understood from Mr. Goodwin that you were extending and intensifying your search for the man who was there as Santa Claus, and with your army and your resources it probably wouldn't take you long when the holiday had ended to learn where the gloves were bought and get a description of the man who bought them. My physique is not unique, but it is—uncommon, and the only question was how long it would take you to get to me, and then I would be under inquisition. Obviously I had to report the episode to you and suffer your rebuke for not reporting it earlier, but I wanted to make it as tolerable as possible. I had one big advantage: I knew that the man who acted as Santa Claus was almost certainly not the murderer, and I decided to use it. I needed first to have a talk with one of those people, and I did so, with Miss Quon, who came here last evening.''

''Why Miss Quon?''

Wolfe turned a hand over. ''When I have finished you can decide whether such details are important. With her I discussed her associates at that place and their relationships, and I became satisfied that Bottweill had in fact decided to marry her. That was all. You can also decide later whether it is worth while to ask her to corroborate that, and I have no doubt she will.''

He was looking at Cherry, of course, for any sign of danger. She had started to blurt it out once, and might again. But, meeting his gaze, she didn't move a muscle.

Wolfe returned to Cramer. ''This morning I acted. Mr. Goodwin was absent, at the District Attorney's office, so I called in Mr. Panzer. After spending an hour with me here he went to do some errands. The first one was to learn whether Bottweill's wastebasket had been emptied since his conversation with Miss Dickey in his office Thursday evening. As you know, Mr. Panzer is highly competent. Through Miss Quon he got the name and address of the cleaning woman, found her and talked with her, and was told that the wastebasket had been emptied at about six o'clock Thursday afternoon and not since then. Meanwhile I—''

"Cherry took it—the pieces," Margot said.

Wolfe ignored her. "Meanwhile I was phoning everyone concerned— Mrs. Jerome and her son, Miss Dickey, Miss Quon, Mr. Hatch, and Mr. Kiernan—and inviting them to come here for a conference at six-fifteen. I told them that Mr. Goodwin had information which he intended to give the police, which was not true, and that I thought it best to discuss it first with them.''

"I told you so," Hatch muttered.

Wolfe ignored him too. "Mr. Panzer's second errand, or series of errands, was the delivery of some messages. He had written them in longhand, at my dictation here this morning, on plain sheets of paper, and had addressed plain envelopes. They were identical and ran as follows:

"When I was there yesterday putting on my costume I saw you through a crack in the door and I saw what you did. Do you want me to tell the cops? Be at Grand Central information booth upper level at 6:30 today. I'll come up to you and say 'Saint Nick.' "

"By god," Cramer said, "you admit it."

Wolfe nodded. "I proclaim it. The messages were signed 'Santa Claus.' Mr. Panzer accompanied the messenger who took them to the persons I have named, and made sure they were delivered. They were not so much shots at random as they may appear. If one of those people had killed Bottweill it was likely that the poison had been put in the bottle while the vagabond was donning the Santa Claus costume; Miss Quon had told me, as no doubt she has told you, that Bottweill invariably took a drink of Pernod when he returned from lunch; and, since the appearance of Santa Claus at the party had been a surprise to all of them, and none of them knew who he was, it was highly probable that the murderer would believe he had been observed and would be irresistibly impelled to meet the writer of the message. So it was a reasonable assumption that one of the shots would reach its target. The question was, which one?''

Wolfe stopped to pour beer. He did pour it, but I suspected that what he really stopped for was to offer an opening for comment or protest. No one had any, not even Cramer. They all just sat and gazed at him. I was thinking that he had neatly skipped one detail: that the message from Santa Claus had not gone to Cherry Quon. She knew too much about him.

Wolfe put the bottle down and turned to go on to Cramer. "There was the possibility, of course, that more than one of them would go to you with the message, but even if you decided, because it had been sent to more than one, that it was some hoax, you would want to know who perpetrated it, and you would send one of them to the rendezvous under surveillance. Any one or more, excepting the murderer, might go to you, or none might; and surely only the murderer would go to the rendezvous without first consulting you. So if one of those six people was guilty, and if it had been possible for Santa Claus to observe him, disclosure seemed next to certain. Saul, you may now report. What happened? You were in the vicinity of the information booth shortly before six-thirty?"

Necks were twisted for a view of Saul Panzer. He nodded. "Yes, sir. At six-twenty. Within three minutes I had recognized three Homicide men scattered around in different spots. I don't know if they recognized me or not. At six twenty-eight I saw Alfred Kiernan walk up near the booth and stand there, about ten feet away from it. I was just about to go and speak to him when I saw Margot Dickey coming up from the Forty-second Street side. She approached to within thirty feet of the booth and stood looking around. Following your instructions in case more than one of them appeared and Miss Dickey was one of them, I went to her and said, 'Saint Nick.' She said, 'Who are you and what do you want?' I said, 'Excuse me, I'll be right back,' and went over to Alfred Kiernan and said to him, 'Saint Nick.' As soon as I said that he raised a hand to his ear, and then here they came, the three I had recognized and two more, and then Inspector Cramer and Sergeant Stebbins. I was afraid Miss Dickey would run, and she did start to, but they had seen me speak to her, and two of them stopped her and had her."

Saul halted because of an interruption. Purley Stebbins, seated next to him, got up and stepped over to Margot Dickey and stood there behind her chair. To me it seemed unnecessary, since I was sitting not much more than arm's length from her and might have been trusted to grab her if she tried to start anything, but Purley is never very considerate of other people's feelings, especially mine.

Saul resumed, "Naturally it was Miss Dickey I was interested in, since they had moved in on a signal from Kiernan. But they had her, so that was okay. They took us to a room back of the parcel room and started in on me, and I followed your instructions. I told them I would answer no questions, would say nothing whatever, except in the presence of Nero Wolfe, because I was acting under your orders. When they saw I meant it they took us out to two police cars and brought us here. Anything else?"

"No," Wolfe told him. "Satisfactory." He turned to Cramer. "I assume Mr. Panzer is correct in concluding that Mr. Kiernan gave your men a signal. So Mr. Kiernan had gone to you with the message?"

"Yes." Cramer had taken a cigar from his pocket and was squeezing it in his hand. He does that sometimes when he would like to squeeze Wolfe's throat instead. "So had three of the others—Mrs. Jerome, her son, and Hatch."

"But Miss Dickey hadn't?"

"No. Neither had Miss Quon."

"Miss Quon was probably reluctant, understandably. She told me last evening that the police's ideas of Orientals are very primitive. As for Miss Dickey, I may say that I am not surprised. For a reason that does not concern you, I am even a little gratified. I have told you that she told Mr. Goodwin that Bottweill had torn up the marriage license and put the pieces in his wastebasket, and they weren't there when Mr. Goodwin looked for them, and the wastebasket hadn't been emptied since early Thursday evening. It was difficult to conceive a reason for anyone to fish around in the wastebasket to remove those pieces, so presumably Miss Dickey lied; and if she lied about the license, the rest of what she told Mr. Goodwin was under suspicion."

Wolfe upturned a palm. "Why would she tell him that Bottweill was going to marry her if it wasn't true? Surely a stupid thing to do, since he would inevitably learn the truth. But it wasn't so stupid if she knew that Bottweill would soon die; indeed it was far from stupid if she had already put the poison in the bottle; it would purge her of motive, or at least help. It was a fair surmise that at their meeting in his office Thursday evening Bottweill had told her, not that he would marry her, but that he had decided to marry Miss Quon, and she decided to kill him and proceeded to do so. And it must be admitted that she would probably never have been exposed but for the complications injected by Santa Claus and my resulting intervention. Have you any comment, Miss Dickey?"

Cramer left his chair, commanding her, "Don't answer! I'm running this now," but she spoke.

"Cherry took those pieces from the wastebasket! She did it! She killed him!" She started up, but Purley had her arm and Cramer told her, moving for her, "She didn't go there to meet a blackmailer, and you did. Look in her bag, Purley. I'll watch her."

IX

Cherry Quon was back in red in the red leather chair. The others had gone, and she and Wolfe and I were alone. They hadn't put cuffs on Margot Dickey, but Purley had kept hold of her arm as they crossed the threshold, with Cramer right behind. Saul Panzer, no longer in custody, had gone along by request. Mrs. Jerome and Leo had been the first to leave. Kiernan had asked Cherry if he could take her home, but Wolfe had said no, he wanted to speak with her privately, and Kiernan and Hatch had left together, which showed a fine Christmas spirit, since Hatch had made no exceptions when he said he despised all of them.

Cherry was on the edge of the chair, spine straight, hands together in her lap. "You didn't do it the way I said," she chirped, without steel.

"No," Wolfe agreed, "but I did it." He was curt. "You ignored one complication, the possibility that you had killed Bottweill yourself. I didn't, I assure you. I couldn't very well send you one of the notes from Santa Claus, under the circumstances; but if those notes had flushed no prey, if none of them had gone to the rendezvous without first notifying the police, I would have assumed that you were guilty and would have proceeded to expose you. How, I don't know; I let that wait on the event; and now that Miss Dickey has taken the bait and betrayed herself it doesn't matter."

Her eyes had widened. "You really thought I might have killed Kurt?"

"Certainly. A woman capable of trying to blackmail me to manufacture evidence of murder would be capable of anything. And, speaking of evidence, while there can be no certainty about a jury's decision when a personable young woman is on trial for murder, now that Miss Dickey is manifestly guilty you may be sure that Mr. Cramer will dig up all he can get, and there should be enough. That brings me to the point I wanted to speak about. In the quest for evidence you will all be questioned, exhaustively and repeatedly. It will—"

"We wouldn't," Cherry put in, "if you had done it the way I said. That would have been proof."

"I preferred my way." Wolfe, having a point to make, was controlling himself. "It will be an ordeal for you. They will question you at length about your talk with Bottweill yesterday morning at breakfast, wanting to know all that he said about his meeting with Miss Dickey in his office Thursday evening, and under the pressure of inquisition you might inadvertently let something slip regarding what he told you about Santa Claus. If you do they will certainly follow it up. I strongly advise you to avoid making such a slip. Even if they believe you, the identity of Santa Claus is no longer important, since they have the murderer, and if they come to me with such a tale I'll have no great difficulty dealing with it."

He turned a hand over. "And in the end they probably won't believe you. They'll think you invented it for some cunning and obscure purpose— as you say, you are an Oriental—and all you would get for it would be more questions. They might even suspect that you were somehow involved in the murder itself. They are quite capable of unreasonable suspicions. So

[396]

I suggest these considerations as much on your behalf as on mine. I think you will be wise to forget about Santa Claus.''

She was eying him, straight and steady. ''I like to be wise,'' she said.

''I'm sure you do, Miss Quon.''

''I still think you should have done it my way, but it's done now. Is that all?''

He nodded. ''That's all.''

She looked at me, and it took a second for me to realize that she was smiling at me. I thought it wouldn't hurt to smile back, and did. She left the chair and came to me, extending a hand, and I arose and took it. She looked up at me.

''I would like to shake hands with Mr. Wolfe, but I know he doesn't like to shake hands. You know, Mr. Goodwin, it must be a very great pleasure to work for a man as clever as Mr. Wolfe. So extremely clever. It has been very exciting to be here. Now I say good-by.''

She turned and went.

★

The Flying Stars
by G. K. Chesterton

"THE MOST BEAUTIFUL CRIME I ever committed," Flambeau would say in his highly moral old age, "was also, by a singular coincidence, my last. It was committed at Christmas. As an artist I had always attempted to provide crimes suitable to the special season or landscapes in which I found myself, choosing this or that terrace or garden for a catastrophe, as if for a statuary group. Thus squires should be swindled in long rooms panelled with oak; while Jews, on the other hand, should rather find themselves unexpectedly penniless among the lights and screens of the Café Riche. Thus, in England, if I wished to relieve a dean of his riches (which is not so easy as you might suppose), I wished to frame him, if I make myself clear, in the green lawns and grey towers of some cathedral town. Similarly, in France, when I had got money out of a rich and wicked peasant (which is almost impossible), it gratified me to get his indignant head relieved against a grey line of clipped poplars, and those solemn plains of Gaul over which broods the mighty spirit of Millet.

"Well, my last crime was a Christmas crime, a cheery, cosy, English middle-class crime; a crime of Charles Dickens. I did it in a good old middle-class house near Putney, a house with a crescent of carriage drive, a house with a stable by the side of it, a house with the name on the two outer gates, a house with a monkey tree. Enough, you know the species. I really think my imitation of Dickens's style was dexterous and literary. It seems almost a pity I repented the same evening."

Flambeau would then proceed to tell the story from the inside; and even from the inside it was odd. Seen from the outside it was perfectly incomprehensible, and it is from the outside that the stranger must study it. From this standpoint the drama may be said to have begun when the front doors of the house with the stable opened on the garden with the monkey tree, and a young girl came out with bread to feed the birds on the afternoon of Boxing Day. She had a pretty face, with brave brown eyes; but her figure was beyond conjecture, for she was so wrapped up in brown furs that it was hard to say which was hair and which was fur. But for the attractive face she might have been a small toddling bear.

The winter afternoon was reddening towards evening, and already a

[399]

ruby light was rolled over the bloomless beds, filling them, as it were, with the ghosts of the dead roses. On one side of the house stood the stable, on the other an alley or cloister of laurels led to the larger garden behind. The young lady, having scattered bread for the birds (for the fourth or fifth time that day, because the dog ate it), passed unobtrusively down the lane of laurels and into a glimmering plantation of evergreens behind. Here she gave an exclamation of wonder, real or ritual, and looking up at the high garden wall above her, beheld it fantastically bestridden by a somewhat fantastic figure.

"Oh, don't jump, Mr. Crook," she called out in some alarm; "it's much too high."

The individual riding the party wall like an aerial horse was a tall, angular young man, with dark hair sticking up like a hair brush, intelligent and even distinguished lineaments, but a sallow and almost alien complexion. This showed the more plainly because he wore an aggressive red tie, the only part of his costume of which he seemed to take any care. Perhaps it was a symbol. He took no notice of the girl's alarmed adjuration, but leapt like a grasshopper to the ground beside her, where he might very well have broken his legs.

"I think I was meant to be a burglar," he said placidly, "and I have no doubt I should have been if I hadn't happened to be born in that nice house next door. I can't see any harm in it, anyhow."

"How can you say such things?" she remonstrated.

"Well," said the young man, "if you're born on the wrong side of the wall, I can't see that it's wrong to climb over it."

"I never know what you will say or do next," she said.

"I don't often know myself," replied Mr. Crook; "but then I am on the right side of the wall now."

"And which is the right side of the wall?" asked the young lady, smiling.

"Whichever side you are on," said the young man named Crook.

As they went together through the laurels towards the front garden a motor horn sounded thrice, coming nearer and nearer, and a car of splendid speed, great elegance, and a pale green colour swept up to the front doors like a bird and stood throbbing.

"Hullo, hullo!" said the young man with the red tie, "here's somebody born on the right side, anyhow. I didn't know, Miss Adams, that your Santa Claus was so modern as this."

"Oh, that's my godfather, Sir Leopold Fischer. He always comes on Boxing Day."

Then, after an innocent pause, which unconsciously betrayed some lack of enthusiasm, Ruby Adams added:

"He is very kind."

[400]

John Crook, journalist, had heard of that eminent City magnate; and it was not his fault if the City magnate had not heard of him; for in certain articles in *The Clarion* or *The New Age* Sir Leopold had been dealt with austerely. But he said nothing and grimly watched the unloading of the motor-car, which was rather a long process. A large, neat chauffeur in green got out from the front, and a small, neat manservant in grey got out from the back, and between them they deposited Sir Leopold on the door-step and began to unpack him, like some very carefully protected parcel. Rugs enough to stock a bazaar, furs of all the beasts of the forest, and scarves of all the colours of the rainbow were unwrapped one by one, till they revealed something resembling the human form; the form of a friend-ly, but foreign-looking old gentleman, with a grey goat-like beard and a beaming smile, who rubbed his big fur gloves together.

Long before this revelation was complete the two big doors of the porch had opened in the middle, and Colonel Adams (father of the furry young lady) had come out himself to invite his eminent guest inside. He was a tall, sunburnt, and very silent man, who wore a red smoking-cap like a fez, making him look like one of the English Sirdars or Pashas in Egypt. With him was his brother-in-law, lately come from Canada, a big and rather boisterous young gentleman-farmer, with a yellow beard, by name James Blount. With him also was the more insignificant figure of the priest from the neighbouring Roman Church; for the colonel's late wife had been a Catholic, and the children, as is common in such cases, had been trained to follow her. Everything seemed undistinguished about the priest, even down to his name, which was Brown; yet the colonel had always found something companionable about him, and frequently asked him to such family gather-ings.

In the large entrance hall of the house there was ample room even for Sir Leopold and the removal of his wraps. Porch and vestibule, indeed, were unduly large in proportion to the house, and formed, as it were, a big room with the front door at one end, and the bottom of the staircase at the other. In front of the large hall fire, over which hung the colonel's sword, the pro-cess was completed and the company, including the saturnine Crook, pre-sented to Sir Leopold Fischer. That venerable financier, however, still seemed struggling with portions of his well-lined attire, and at length pro-duced from a very interior tail-coat pocket, a black oval case which he radiantly explained to be his Christmas present for his god-daughter. With an unaffected vain-glory that had something disarming about it he held out the case before them all; it flew open at a touch and half-blinded them. It was just as if a crystal fountain had spurted in their eyes. In a nest of orange velvet lay like three eggs, three white and vivid diamonds that seemed to set the very air on fire all round them. Fischer stood beaming benevolently and drinking deep of the astonishment and ecstasy of the girl, the grim admiration and gruff thanks of the colonel, the wonder of the whole group.

"I'll put 'em back now, my dear," said Fischer, returning the case to the tails of his coat. "I had to be careful of 'em coming down. They're the three great African diamonds called 'The Flying Stars,' because they've been stolen so often. All the big criminals are on the track; but even the rough men about in the streets and hotels could hardly have kept their hands off them. I might have lost them on the road here. It was quite possible."

"Quite natural, I should say," growled the man in the red tie. "I shouldn't blame 'em if they had taken 'em. When they ask for bread, and you don't even give them a stone, I think they might take the stone for themselves."

"I won't have you talking like that," cried the girl, who was in a curious glow. "You've only talked like that since you became a horrid what's-his-name. You know what I mean. What do you call a man who wants to embrace the chimney-sweep?"

"A saint," said Father Brown.

"I think," said Sir Leopold, with a supercilious smile, "that Ruby means a Socialist."

"A radical does not mean a man who lives on radishes," remarked Crook, with some impatience; "and a Conservative does not mean a man who preserves jam. Neither, I assure you, does a Socialist mean a man who desires a social evening with the chimney-sweep. A Socialist means a man who wants all the chimneys swept and all the chimney-sweeps paid for it."

"But who won't allow you," put in the priest in a low voice, "to own your own soot."

Crook looked at him with an eye of interest and even respect. "Does one want to own soot" he asked.

"One might," answered Brown, with speculation in his eye. "I've heard that gardeners use it. And I once made six children happy at Christmas when the conjuror didn't come, entirely with soot—applied externally."

"Oh, splendid," cried Ruby. "Oh, I wish you'd do it to this company."

The boisterous Canadian, Mr. Blount, was lifting his loud voice in applause, and the astonished financier his (in some considerable deprecation), when a knock sounded at the double front doors. The priest opened them, and they showed again the front garden of evergreens, monkey-tree and all, now gathering gloom against a gorgeous violet sunset. The scene thus framed was so coloured and quaint, like a back scene in a play, that they forgot a moment the insignificant figure standing in the door. He was dusty-looking and in a frayed coat, evidently a common messenger. "Any of you gentlemen Mr. Blount?" he asked, and held forward a letter doubtfully. Mr. Blount started, and stopped in his shout of assent. Ripping up the envelope with evident astonishment he read it; his face clouded a little, and then cleared, and he turned to his brother-in-law and host.

"I'm sick at being such a nuisance, colonel," he said, with the cheery colonial conventions; "but would it upset you if an old acquaintance called on me here tonight on business? In point of fact it's Florian, that famous French acrobat and comic actor; I knew him years ago out West (he was a French-Canadian by birth), and he seems to have business for me, though I hardly guess what."

"Of course, of course," replied the colonel carelessly. "My dear chap, any friend of yours. No doubt he will prove an acquisition."

"He'll black his face, if that's what you mean," cried Blount, laughing. "I don't doubt he'd black everyone else's eyes. I don't care; I'm not refined. I like the jolly old pantomime where a man sits on his top hat."

"Not on mine, please," said Sir Leopold Fischer, with dignity.

"Well, well," observed Crook, airly, "don't let's quarrel. There are lower jokes than sitting on a top hat."

Dislike of the red-tied youth, born of his predatory opinions and evident intimacy with the pretty godchild, led Fischer to say, in his most sarcastic, magisterial manner: "No doubt you have found something much lower than sitting on a top hat. What is it, pray?"

"Letting a top hat sit on you, for instance," said the Socialist.

"Now, now, now," cried the Canadian farmer with his barbarian benevolence, "don't let's spoil a jolly evening. What I say is let's do something for the company tonight. Not blacking faces or sitting on hats, if you don't like those—but something of the sort. Why couldn't we have a proper old English pantomime—clown, columbine, and so on. I saw one when I left England at twelve years old, and it's blazed in my brain like a bonfire ever since. I came back to the old country only last year, and I find the thing's extinct. Nothing but a lot of snivelling fairy plays. I want a hot poker and a policeman made into sausages, and they give me princesses moralising by moonlight, Blue Birds, or something. Blue Beard's more in my line, and him I liked best when he turned into the pantaloon."

"I'm all for making a policeman into sausages," said John Crook. "It's a better definition of Socialism than some recently given. But surely the get-up would be too big a business."

"Not a scrap," cried Blount, quite carried away. "A harlequinade's the quickest thing we can do, for two reasons. First, one can gag to any degree; and, second, all the objects are household things—tables and trowel-horses and washing baskets, and things like that."

"That's true," admitted Crook, nodding eagerly and walking about. "But I'm afraid I can't have my policeman's uniform? Haven't killed a policeman lately."

[403]

Blount frowned thoughtfully a space, and then smote his thigh. "Yes, we can!" he cried. "I've got Florian's address here, and he knows every *costumier* in London. I'll 'phone him to bring a police dress when he comes." And he went bounding away to the telephone.

"Oh, it's glorious, godfather," cried Ruby, almost dancing. "I'll be columbine and you shall be pantaloon."

The millionaire held himself stiff with a sort of heathen solemnity. "I think, my dear," he said, "you must get someone else for pantaloon."

"I will be pantaloon, if you like," said Colonel Adams, taking his cigar out of his mouth, and speaking for the first and last time.

"You ought to have a statue," cried the Canadian, as he came back, radiant, from the telephone. "There, we are all fitted. Mr. Crook shall be clown; he's a journalist and knows all the oldest jokes. I can be harlequin, that only wants long legs and jumping about. My friend Florian 'phones he's bringing the police costume; he's changing on the way. We can act it in this very hall, the audience sitting on those broad stairs opposite, one row above another. These front doors can be the back scene, either open or shut. Shut, you see an English interior. Open, a moonlit garden. It all goes by magic." And snatching a chance piece of billiard chalk from his pocket, he ran it across the hall floor, half-way between the front door and the staircase, to mark the line of the footlights.

How even such a banquet of bosh was got ready in the time remained a riddle. But they went at it with that mixture of recklessness and industry that lives when youth is in a house; and youth was in that house that night, though not all may have isolated the two faces and hearts from which it flamed. As always happens, the invention grew wilder and wilder through the very tameness of the *bourgeois* conventions from which it had to create. The columbine looked charming in an outstanding skirt that strangely resembled the large lamp-shade in the drawing-room. The clown and pantaloon made themselves white with flour from the cook, and red with rouge from some other domestic, who remained (like all true Christian benefactors) anonymous. The harlequin, already clad in silver paper out of cigar boxes, was, with difficulty, prevented from smashing the old Victorian lustre chandeliers, that he might cover himself with resplendent crystals. In fact he would certainly have done so, had not Ruby unearthed some old pantomime paste jewels she had worn at a fancy dress party as the Queen of Diamonds. Indeed, her uncle, James Blount, was getting almost out of hand in his excitement; he was like a schoolboy. He put a paper donkey's head unexpectedly on Father Brown, who bore it patiently, and even found some private manner of moving his ears. He even essayed to put the paper donkey's tail to the coat-tails of Sir Leopold Fischer. This, however, was frowned down. "Uncle is too absurd," cried Ruby to Crook, round whose

[404]

shoulders she had seriously placed a string of sausages. "Why is he so wild?"

"He is harlequin to your columbine," said Crook. "I am only the clown who makes the old jokes."

"I wish you were the harlequin," she said, and left the string of sausages swinging.

Father Brown, though he knew every detail done behind the scenes, and had even evoked applause by his transformation of a pillow into a pantomime baby, went round to the front and sat among the audience with all the solemn expectation of a child at his first matinée. The spectators were few, relations, one or two local friends, and the servants; Sir Leopold sat in the front seat, his full and still fur-collared figure largely obscuring the view of the little cleric behind him; but it has never been settled by artistic authorities whether the cleric lost much. The pantomime was utterly chaotic, yet not contemptible; there ran through it a rage of improvisation which came chiefly from Crook the clown. Commonly he was a clever man, and he was inspired tonight with a wild omniscience, a folly wiser than the world, that which comes to a young man who has seen for an instant a particular expression on a particular face. He was supposed to be the clown, but he was really almost everything else, the author (so far as there was an author), the prompter, the scene-painter, the scene-shifter, and, above all, the orchestra. At abrupt intervals in the outrageous performance he would hurl himself in full costume at the piano and bang out some popular music equally absurd and appropriate.

The climax of this, as of all else, was the moment when the two front doors at the back of the scene flew open, showing the lovely moonlit garden, but showing more prominently the famous professional guest; the great Florian, dressed up as a policeman. The clown at the piano played the constabulary chorus in the "Pirates of Penzance," but it was drowned in the deafening applause, for every gesture of the great comic actor was an admirable though restrained version of the carriage and manner of the police. The harlequin leapt upon him and hit him over the helmet; the pianist playing "Where did you get that hat?" he faced about in admirably simulated astonishment, and then the leaping harlequin hit him again (the pianist suggesting a few bars of "Then we had another one"). Then the harlequin rushed right into the arms of the policeman and fell on top of him, amid a roar of applause. Then it was that the strange actor gave that celebrated imitation of a dead man, of which the fame still lingers round Putney. It was almost impossible to believe that a living person could appear so limp.

The athletic harlequin swung him about like a sack or twisted or tossed him like an Indian club; all the time to the most maddeningly ludicrous

[405]

tunes from the piano. When the harlequin heaved the comic constable heavily off the floor the clown played "I arise from dreams of thee." When he shuffled him across his back, "With my bundle on my shoulder," and when the harlequin finally let fall the policeman with a most convincing thud, the lunatic at the instrument struck into a jingling measure with some words which are still believed to have been, "I sent a letter to my love and on the way I dropped it."

At about this limit of mental anarchy Father Brown's view was obscured altogether; for the City magnate in front of him rose to his full height and thrust his hands savagely into all his pockets. Then he sat down nervously, still fumbling, and then stood up again. For an instant it seemed seriously likely that he would stride across the footlights; then he turned a glare at the clown playing the piano; and then he burst in silence out of the room.

The priest had only watched for a few more minutes the absurd but not inelegant dance of the amateur harlequin over his splendidly unconscious foe. With real though rude art, the harlequin danced slowly backwards out of the door into the garden, which was full of moonlight and stillness. The vamped dress of silver paper and paste, which had been too glaring in the footlights, looked more and more magical and silvery as it danced away under a brilliant moon. The audience was closing in with a cataract of applause, when Brown felt his arm abruptly touched, and he was asked in a whisper to come into the colonel's study.

He followed his summoner with increasing doubt, which was not dispelled by a solemn comicality in the scene of the study. There sat Colenel Adams, still unaffectedly dressed as a pantaloon, with the knobbed whalebone nodding above his brow, but with his poor old eyes sad enough to have sobered a Saturnalia. Sir Leopold Fischer was leaning against the mantelpiece and heaving with all the importance of panic.

"This is a very painful matter, Father Brown," said Adams. "The truth is, those diamonds we all saw this afternoon seem to have vanished from my friend's tail-coat pocket. And as you—"

"As I," supplemented Father Brown, with a broad grin, "was sitting just behind him—"

"Nothing of the sort shall be suggested," said Colonel Adams, with a firm look at Fischer, which rather implied that some such thing *had* been suggested. "I only ask you to give me the assistance that any gentleman might give."

"Which is turning out his pockets," said Father Brown, and proceeded to do so, displaying seven and sixpence, a return ticket, a small silver crucifix, a small breviary, and a stick of chocolate.

The colonel looked at him long, and then said, "Do you know, I should like to see the inside of your head more than the inside of your pockets. My daughter is one of your people, I know; well, she has lately—'' and he stopped.

"She has lately," cried out old Fischer, "opened her father's house to a cut-throat Socialist, who says openly he would steal anything from a richer man. This is the end of it. Here is the richer man—and none the richer."

"If you want the inside of my head you can have it," said Brown rather wearily. "What it's worth you can say afterwards. But the first thing I find in that disused pocket is this: that men who mean to steal diamonds don't talk Socialism. They are more likely," he added demurely, "to denounce it."

Both the others shifted sharply and the priest went on:

"You see, we know these people, more or less. That Socialist would no more steal a diamond than a Pyramid. We ought to look at once to the one man we don't know. The fellow acting the policeman—Florian. Where is he exactly at this minute, I wonder."

The pantaloon sprang erect and strode out of the room. An interlude ensued, during which the millionaire stared at the priest, and the priest at his breviary; then the pantaloon returned and said, with *staccato* gravity, "The policeman is still lying on the stage. The curtain has gone up and down six times; he is still lying there."

Father Brown dropped his book and stood staring with a look of blank mental ruin. Very slowly a light began to creep in his grey eyes, and then he made the scarcely obvious answer.

"Please forgive me, colonel, but when did your wife die?"

"Wife!" replied the staring soldier, "she died this year two months. Her brother James arrived just a week too late to see her."

The little priest bounded like a rabbit shot. "Come on!" he cried in quite unusual excitement. "Come on! We've got to go and look at that policeman!"

They rushed on to the now curtained stage, breaking rudely past the columbine and clown (who seemed whispering quite contentedly), and Father Brown bent over the prostrate comic policeman.

"Chloroform," he said as he rose; "I only guessed it just now."

There was a startled stillness, and then the colonel said slowly, "Please say seriously what all this means."

Father Brown suddenly shouted with laughter, then stopped, and only struggled with it for instants during the rest of his speech. "Gentlemen," he gasped, "there's not much time to talk. I must run after the criminal. But this great French actor who played the policeman—this clever corpse the harlequin waltzed with and dandled and threw about—he was—'' His voice again failed him, and he turned his back to run.

"He was?" called Fischer inquiringly.

[407]

"A real policeman," said Father Brown, and ran away into the dark.

There were hollows and bowers at the extreme end of that leafy garden, in which the laurels and other immortal shrubs showed against sapphire sky and silver moon, even in that mid-winter, warm colours as of the south. The green gaiety of the waving laurels, the rich purple indigo of the night, the moon like a monstrous crystal, make an almost irresponsible romantic picture; and among the top branches of the garden trees a strange figure is climbing, who looks not so much romantic as impossible. He sparkles from head to heel, as if clad in ten million moons; the real moon catches him at every movement and sets a new inch of him on fire. But he swings, flashing and successful, from the short tree in this garden to the tall, rambling tree in the other, and only stops there because a shade has slid under the smaller tree and has unmistakably called up to him.

"Well, Flambeau," says the voice, "you really look like a Flying Star; but that always means a Falling Star at last."

The silver, sparkling figure above seems to lean forward in the laurels and, confident of escape, listens to the little figure below.

"You never did anything better, Flambeau. It was clever to come from Canada (with a Paris ticket, I suppose) just a week after Mrs. Adams died, when no one was in a mood to ask questions. It was cleverer to have marked down the Flying Stars and the very day of Fischer's coming. But there's no cleverness, but mere genius, in what followed. Stealing the stones, I suppose, was nothing to you. You could have done it by sleight of hand in a hundred other ways besides that pretence of putting a paper donkey's tail to Fisher's coat. But in the rest you eclipsed yourself."

The silvery figure among the green leaves seems to linger as if hypnotised, though his escape is easy behind him; he is staring at the man below.

"Oh, yes," says the man below, "I know all about it. I know you not only forced the pantomime, but put it to a double use. You were going to steal the stones quietly; news came by an accomplice that you were already suspected, and a capable police officer was coming to rout you up that very night. A common thief would have been thankful for the warning and fled; but you are a poet. You already had the clever notion of hiding the jewels in a blaze of false stage jewellery. Now, you saw that if the dress were a harlequin's the appearance of a policeman would be quite in keeping. The worthy officer started from Putney police station to find you, and walked into the queerest trap ever set in this world. When the front door opened he walked straight on to the stage of a Christmas pantomime, where he could be kicked, clubbed, stunned and drugged by the dancing harlequin, amid roars of laughter from all the most respectable people in Putney. Oh, you will never do anything better. And now, by the way, you might give me back those diamonds."

[408]

The green branch on which the glittering figure swung, rustled as if in astonishment; but the voice went on:

"I want you to give them back, Flambeau, and I want you to give up this life. There is still youth and honour and humour in you; don't fancy they will last in that trade. Men may keep a sort of level of good, but no man has ever been able to keep on one level of evil. That road goes down and down. The kind man drinks and turns cruel; the frank man kills and lies about it. Many a man I've known started like you to be an honest outlaw, a merry robber of the rich, and ended stamped into slime. Maurice Blum started out as an anarchist of principle, a father of the poor; he ended a greasy spy and tale-bearer that both sides used and despised. Harry Burke started his free money movement sincerely enough; now he's sponging on a half-starved sister for endless brandies and sodas. Lord Amber went into wild society in a sort of chivalry; now he's paying blackmail to the lowest vultures in London. Captain Barillon was the great gentleman-apache before your time; he died in a madhouse, screaming with fear of the "narks" and receivers that had betrayed him and hunted him down. I know the woods look very free behind you, Flambeau; I know that in a flash you could melt into them like a monkey. But some day you will be an old grey monkey, Flambeau. You will sit up in your free forest cold at heart and close to death, and the tree-tops will be very bare."

Everything continued still, as if the small man below held the other in the tree in some long invisible leash; and he went on:

"Your downward steps have begun. You used to boast of doing nothing mean, but you are doing something mean tonight. You are leaving suspicion on an honest boy with a good deal against him already; you are separating him from the woman he loves and who loves him. But you will do meaner things than that before you die."

Three flashing diamonds fell from the tree to the turf. The small man stooped to pick them up, and when he looked up again the green cage of the tree was emptied of its silver bird.

The restoration of the gems (accidentally picked up by Father Brown, of all people) ended the evening in uproarious triumph; and Sir Leopold, in his height of good humour, even told the priest that though he himself had broader views, he could respect those whose creed required them to be cloistered and ignorant of this world.

Boxing Day
Bonus

⁂

★

Ring Out, Wild Bells
by D. B. Wyndham Lewis

NOTHING could be more festive than the breakfast-room at Merry-weather Hall this noontide of 29th December. On the hearth a huge crackling fire bade defiance to the rain which lashed the tall french windows. The panelled walls were gay with holly and mistletoe and paper decorations of every hue. On the long sideboard were displayed eggs in conjunction with ham, bacon, and sausages, also boiled and scrambled; kedgeree, devilled kidneys, chops, grilled herrings, sole, and haddock, cold turkey, cold goose, cold grouse, cold game pie, cold ham, cold beef, brawn, potted shrimps, a huge Stilton, fruit of every kind, rolls, toast, tea, and coffee, all simmering on silver heaters or tempting the healthy appetite from huge crested salvers. Brooding over all this with an evil leer, the but-ler, Mr. Banks, looked up to see a youngish guest with drawn and yellow face, shuddering violently.

"Breakfast, sir?" asked Banks, rubbing his hands.

The guest, a Mr. Reginald Parable, nodded and held out his palm. Banks shook into it two tablets from a small bottle.

"They're all in the library," said Banks, pouring half a tumbler of water. "Cor, what they look like—well," said Banks, chuckling, "it's just too bad."

Mr. Parable finished breakfast in one swallow and went along to the library. In every arm-chair, and lying against each other on every settee, eyes closed, faces worn with misery, each wearing a paper cap from a cracker, lay Squire Merryweather's guests. The squire believed in a real old-fashioned Christmas, and for five days now his guests had tottered, stiff with eating, from table to chair, only to be roused by the jovial squire with a festive roar ten minutes later.

The countryside was under water; and as nobody could go out from morning to night, Squire Merryweather could, and did, devise every kind of merrie old-time entertainment for his raving guests.

Thunderous distant chuckles as Mr. Parable wavered into the only unoc-cupied corner of a huge leather settee announced that the squire had been consulting his secret store of books of merriment once more. And even as

[413]

Mr. Parable hastily turned to feign epilepsy in his corner, Squire Merry-weather bustled in.

"Morning," said a weak voice, that of Lord Lymph.

"Wake all these people up," said the squire.

When everybody was awake the squire said: "Colonel Rollick has five daughters, Gertrude, Mabel, Pamela, Edith, and Hilda. Mabel is half the age that Gertrude and Edith were when Hilda and Mabel were respectively twice and one-and-a-half times as old as Pamela will be on 8th May 1940. Wait a minute—that's right, 8th May. Every time the colonel takes his five daughters to town for the day it costs him three pounds fifteen and eight-pence-halfpenny in railway fares, first return. One Christmas night Colonel Rollick says to his guests: 'Let's play rectangles.' 'I don't know how it's played,' says old Mrs. Cheeryton, who happens to be present. 'why,' says the colonel, 'like this: we get the Ague-Browns to drop in, and form ourselves into four units, the square on the hypotenuse of which is equal to the sum of the squares on the—'"

At this point a lovely, lazy, deep-voiced blonde, Mrs. Wallaby-Threep, roused herself sufficiently to produce a dainty pearl-handled revolver from her corsage and fire at Squire Merryweather twice, missing him each time.

"Eh? Who spoke?" asked the squire abruptly, without raising his eyes from *Ye Merrie Christmasse Puzzle-Booke*.

"Tiny Tim," replied Mrs. Wallaby-Threep, taking one more shot. This time, however, she missed as before.

"You probably took too much of a pull on the trigger," murmured the rector with a deprecating smile. The squire was patron of the living and he felt a duty towards his guests.

"I'll get him yet," said Mrs. Wallaby-Threep.

"Charades!" shouted Squire Merryweather suddenly, waving a sprig of holly in his right hand.

"Again?" said a querulous Old Etonian voice. It was that of Mr. Egbert Frankleigh, the famous gentleman-novelist, who wanted to tell more stories. Since Christmas Eve there had been five story-telling sessions, each guest supplying some tale of romance, adventure, mystery, or plain bore-dom. After every story the squire had applauded loudly and called for was-sail, frumenty, old English dances, and merry-making—even after two very peculiar stories about obsessional neuroses told by two sombre young Oxford men, Mr. Ebbing and Mr. Crafter, both of whom took hashish with Avocado pears, wore black suède shoes, and practised Mithraism.

"Charades!" roared Squire Merryweather, tucking his book under his arm and rubbing his hands with a roar of laughter. "Hurrah! Come along, everybody. Jump to it, boys and girls! This is going to be fun! Two of you, quick!"

[414]

A choking snore from poor old Lady Emily Wainscot, who was quite worn out (she died the following week, greatly regretted), was the only reply. Fourteen pairs of lack-luster-ringed-with-blue eyes stared at him in haggard silence.

"Eh? What?" asked the squire, more bewildered than hurt.

"You said *charades,* sir?" said Mr. Ebbing. "We shall be delighted to assist!"

Booming like a happy bull, the squire flung an arm round each of the two young men and danced them out of the room.

"Me for the hay," said Mrs. Wallaby-Threep, snuggling into a cushion and closing her eyes. The rest of the company were not slow to follow suit. Very soon all were asleep, and snoring yelps and groans filled the library of Merryweather Hall.

* * *

It was bright, sunshiny daylight when the banging of the gong by the second footman roused the squire's guests from nearly twenty-four hours of deep, refreshing sleep. The sardonic Banks stood before them. He seemed angry, and addressed himself to Lord Lymph.

"I just found the squire's body in a wardrobe trunk, my lord."

"In a *trunk,* Banks?"

"That's all right," said Lady Ura Treate, yawning. "It's an old Oxford trick. Body in a trunk. All these neurotics do it. Where *are* those two sweet chaps, Banks?"

"They've hopped it, my lady."

"Well, that's all right, Banks," said Freddie Slouche. "Body in trunk. Country-house mystery. Quite normal."

As he spoke, the guests, chattering happily, were already streaming out to order the packing and see to their cars. In a few moments only Banks and Mr. Parable were left in the room. Banks seemed aggrieved.

"It's all pretty dam fine, Mr. Whoosis, but who gets it in the neck when the cops get down? Who'll be under suspicion as per usual? Who always is? The butler! Me!"

"Just an occupational risk," said Mr. Parable, politely.

"It would be if I wasn't a bit smart," said Banks.

Mr. Parable nodded and hurried out as the servants began looting the hall.

MERRY CHRISTMAS!